Se

Moments Of Madness

Alex Finch

CHAPTER 1 – BEFORE

He's bleeding heavily, to the extent that my alcohol addled mind doesn't quite understand how he's still alive, and I certainly have no fucking clue what to do or say. "Put pressure on the wound," he grunts, before shoving my hand into his open gut. Nausea rises, until he begins uttering words of a language I've never heard before. His skin slowly repairs itself, the blood disappears. He smiles, gently, and speaks once more: "I have to confess that I've just stolen one hour from your life Mr Holland. So thanks, I owe you for that."

One day earlier, and trust me, I hate films, tv shows or books that do this so I'll cut back to the chase as soon as I can, I promise, but twenty four hours beforehand and life seemed to be doing its best to destroy me. My mind and I were no longer friends, that's for sure. I was single, heartbroken, and working in a job I could barely tolerate, with a selection of people who seemed to have one purpose in life, that being my eventual mental breakdown. Jesus and Buddha could be all loved up on MDMA (from the nineties too, not the modern day crap), to the extent that they would find the universally hated television personality Piers Morgan a delightful chap, but upon meeting my colleagues I've no doubt they would've murdered them. Slowly and weirdly. Most mornings my brain would do its very best to persuade me not to move. Not to get dressed and leave the house. Once I somehow made it out of bed and into the bathroom, hell, that just pissed it off even more. I'd look at myself in the mirror and wonder when my body would give up on me, always hoping that it might be soon. I'm six foot two but a good few stone overweight, nearly all of which hovers around my stomach leading me to look about five months pregnant. With a big old fat child at that. It seems I've learnt how to hide it well, mostly by wearing black t-shirts and a smart if unbuttoned black shirt over that, as the very few women who have been kind enough to sleep with me have always confessed, they didn't realise I was potentially the first man to ever give birth on this planet.

At least I still had my hair, and dear god do I appreciate that as I'd just look extremely weird bald. It's a basic fact. I've done a mock up on Photoshop and children screamed when I showed it to them. But that doesn't make up for the fact that people thought I looked a good five years older than I am, so instead of being in my early thirties most presumed I was nearly forty. And sorry, I know this is all very vain, but I was single you know. So very, very single. I wanted to hope that someone out there might find me attractive, and maybe if I spent a year at the gym, and a year with a kind plastic surgeon, I might have been good looking to someone, maybe. But increasingly I thought about giving up hope. It had almost always been needlessly cruel, after all.

On the days I made it out of the door and traipsed to my local underground station whenever I was stood by the edge of the platform my mind would often whisper "Kill yourself. Jump. Now you shit, now. I mean, why not? Is there a single good reason for you to stick around?" Every time I crossed a road it'd plead with me to stop. Let some poor sod break my body and leave it lifeless in the street. I'd suffered from depression on and off over the years but this was a place I'd never visited before.

Life hadn't always been that bleak, I feel I should stress, it hadn't been miserable the moment I was born, at least according to my mother who said I rarely made a peep for the first two years, and oh how she wishes I'd stopped growing right then. My biological father had died before I was born but of course I wasn't aware of that, the bitterness concerning that situation only occurred much later on, and a fairly normal middle class childhood took place, we weren't well off but we got by, and then my mother married the dullest man alive and we became more affluent, and despite not being close to the man I was still relatively well-adjusted, larking about with my friends and only occasionally getting into trouble for setting something on fire. My teenage years were messier, and I'll no doubt whinge about that at some point, as this is the part where I try to persuade you that I was once fairly rational and normal, I was once okay, maybe even once sort of likeable? Eh, perhaps that's going too far but I'd like to think it was sometimes true.

Post sixteen and at college I became a little more outgoing, and I look back on my University years with real affection, as I was placed in a shared house with four other students who were laid back, funny and easy to get along with, we were the opposite of pretty much every student based sitcom, I don't really have many anecdotes which would make you burst out laughing but there'd be a lot where you might quietly smile. I met my first real girlfriend there and for two and a quarter years I was madly in love with her, perhaps too madly as by the end I'd burnt out our relationship, she'd had too much of me, felt she needed a break, a hiatus, it wouldn't be permanent, but she needed to know who she was without me constantly by her side. Unfortunately she found herself happier like that, and once we'd graduated a note was written and she disappeared.

Despite this I cherished what we'd once had, and the only real negative about my time at university was that it had given me hope. I had ambition, dreams where I'd move to London, get a well-paid job, meet someone else, fall in love, and just live a normal fucking life. The house, the kids, the heart attack in my early fifties which would come as a warning to slow down a little, retirement, death, it wasn't too much to ask for was it? Yet aged 34 it appeared it had been. I'd made it to London but it had been temp job after temp job for the first couple of years until I took an IT course in the evenings and ended up working for a living doing something I barely tolerated. I know that's the story of many people's lives too, and I should quit moaning, but my arse of a brain refused to make that a possibility. I didn't want to be depressed, I didn't want to think about the thoughts I had, and I took the medication that was prescribed, I saw a therapist who offered little but took a lot, and still spiralled into all new territory that I wasn't sure I could come back from, as my brain constantly reminded me of every single mistake I'd ever made, the shitty old bastard that he was.

All of which is cheery stuff, I know, but it goes some way to explain why on that peculiar night in 2014 I'd found myself in a cheap Soho pub hell-bent on trying to stop my mind from existing, to drown out its whiny utterances for a few hours at least, to find a place where the combination of music and alcohol would destroy all irrational thought, and I could escape myself for a while.

And of course there was the vague but persistent belief that it wasn't impossible that some charitable woman might take pity on me and invite me home with her. I tried to prevent such idiotic ideas, but it had happened before, so occasionally I stupidly believed it could again. That night there was brief optimism as well, as for a short while a woman talked to me, she was smart and funny and seemed interested, and as much as I hated it the tiniest flower of hope emerged. But then it was cut down before it had the chance to even begin to flourish, as she explained that she had to go as she had to be up early the next day. That moment was an especially upsetting one. Not unusual, but still unpleasant as I chastised myself for ever thinking life wouldn't be unkind.

Inevitably at closing time I stumbled out alone, feeling lower than before and being surprised that this was possible, and while wandering the streets considering whether or not I should find some club and drink to the point of no return, I saw them. Saw them impossibly fighting, and for a second I presumed that someone had spiked my drink, and that I had no issues with this as it appeared to have turned my life into a straight to DVD sci-fi flick. But it quickly became apparent that this was really happening, even if it was almost too much to take in, as what appeared to be electricity erupted from their fingertips, a blaze of almost blinding light, and one which was vicious and hungry. I knew what I was seeing was unfeasible, that it couldn't be real and yet the moment the old man's gut burst open I knew this was no stunt, this was no fakery. The stench of his entrails pouring over the pavement made me gag, the look of terror in his eyes was something that horrified me to the extent that for a second I thought I might faint for the first time in my life, until I dug my nails into my hands in the hope that I wouldn't feel anything and would discover it was only a lucid dream, yet it was sadly not to be as pain sprinted through my fist. As I presumed I was seeing the final seconds of his life I felt the absolute urge to run, to not look back, to leave and never speak of this event again, and perhaps any other day I would have, should have, but instead I stumbled towards him, the alcohol propelling me forward, not even caring about the other individual who had caused such anguish, barely registering that he had decided to flee, and not understanding why I hadn't either. But I went to him, fell to my knees, asked if there was anything I could do to help, a question so absurd it seems appalling now, and why I didn't reach for my phone and call an ambulance I will never know. Instead I only attempted vacuous words which were never going to be able to assist, and he reached out and grabbed my arm and a wave of darkness hit me, panic hit as I was briefly blinded but only so briefly, and then I opened my eyes and despite all of the blood circulating around us he was now unharmed. Smiling. Thanking me. I had absolutely no fucking idea what was going on at all, and yet felt strangely calm. Strangely okay, and not crazed or unbalanced or berserk.

"One hour of my life?" I asked, but he was only bemused by my confusion.
"Later," he replied, as he slowly stood up and dusted himself off. Given a chance to stop and breathe I took a good look at him and guessed that he was about seventy, and he came complete with the bushiest of white beards, one that looked like it had been through a hurricane. And while it would be impolite to say such a

description to his face, I couldn't help but think that he looked like he'd been living on the streets for a while, and not exactly in a pleasant crescent, either.

"Now, Ben, this could be quite a long story and brandy will no doubt be required, so follow me," he said, and I did. I'm not sure why, but his voice was oddly calming and charming, and hell, the prospect of more alcohol on a night where I suddenly felt sober was irresistible.

After leading me through more of Soho's grimier streets we arrived at an open doorway, with a handwritten sign reading "Model" taped to the door.

"Right, here we are," he said, before diving up the stairs with impressive gusto for a man of his age. And the fact that he'd nearly died three minutes ago. I was on autopilot but also confused as I was pretty sure that most brothels didn't sell alcohol, yet before I knew it he'd knocked on the door and a woman in her fifties answered. She hugged him and they made small talk, while a bored if unbelievably attractive woman stood by the bedroom door in her underwear. I was starting to wonder if I was going to spend the night engaging in sexual acts that would haunt me for the rest of the life when he opened a second door that I hadn't noticed before, and beckoned me to follow him. We walked down a long hallway, a damp, mouldy and oddly muggy passageway that made my skin crawl for reasons I couldn't quite explain, until we reached another door. He knocked four times and whispered a few words before it opened to reveal a rather charming Gentlemen's Club. Large regal armchairs surrounded a fireplace, several oak tables were placed near the finely decorated walls, and the bar had an enormous array of drinks, some of which looked like they would cost more than I make in a week.

As soon as he saw us the barman froze, before smiling nervously. "George, good evening. I... I hope that the misunder-" he said before he was cut off by George exclaiming "There will be repercussions. But not tonight. Now, a bottle of my usual, please."

Once seated questions poured out, like what the hell had I just seen, how was he still alive, and how did he know my name, and George just smiled at me and then said "I've been doing this for a couple of hundred years now, you'd think I'd know how to tell the story, but Christ it's a protracted one, I would start at the beginning but that would take all day, and probably the following week. But basic facts might be the best way. So. Magic exists. Magicians exist."

From what I'd seen in the short time that I'd known George I felt like I knew that. But hearing him say it out loud made it seem all the more incredible. Unbelievable. Yet truthful. I was convinced one moment and then doubted everything the next, and I wanted to trust him, and yet it surely couldn't be. Except it was. He looked at me, smiled again.

"I imagine your brain is trying to process all of this and not quite managing it. That's been the experience I've had when I've told this story before at least. But how about giving your mind some time off, and once I've finished perhaps it won't be quite so bewildered."

"Yeah. Okay, I think," I managed to reply.

"It's dying out. There are fewer and fewer of us now, and that is in no way accidental. Perhaps unsurprisingly governments really don't like the idea that people exist who can alter reality at will, at least to a certain extent. That's what you walked in on earlier, which isn't good news considering I'd managed to stay off their radar until now. So, how's this all sounding so far?"

"Still unbelievable," I replied, "But I'd really like to believe it."

"I would have thought that seeing two men fight with magical lightning bolts might have been enough. Plus the part where you helped me not die," George responded, again in a gentle manner which suggested that he understood my confusion

"I know, but, you know, the whole magic thing, it's all a bit... Impossible? Or at least I'd spent my entire life thinking that," I said, before knocking down a shot of whiskey in the hope it'd make the madness he was spouting more acceptable.

"I understand, and you're not exactly the first to have such issues. A little display might just help then. So, how's this for you?" George asked, and as he whispered a spell which caused me to slowly transform into Gillian Anderson I have to say I was somewhat surprised. I'd expected him to pull a few rabbits out of a hat or something, not that he'd been wearing one, but hey, I'm sure he could have bought one just for me. Either way, I had not expected to experience my penis being absorbed into my body, nor that I'd learn what it was like to have a vagina and breasts, and luscious, lovely long hair. Admittedly being overweight the breasts thing was nothing new, but the vagina, yeah, that was unexpected. As was the fact I was now a world famous actress. George held a mirror to my face, and I have to admit, it was a strange sensation to fancy myself for the first time ever.

"You said you wanted to believe. But I thought turning you into David Duchovny would be too obvious an affair. Plus look at your cheekbones, they're a work of fucking art."

"This is... Ha... Fucked up. Amazing. Please say you can turn me back."

"Oh, sorry, no, but it does wear off after a couple of days."

"What?" I all but screeched. He laughed.

"Just messing with you kid. Of course I can." And before I knew it I had a cock and balls again, which was a far more peculiar sensation than when they disappeared.

"Bloody hell. Jesus. I mean. This is all really happening, isn't it?" George just smiled and nodded.

"And what now? Why are you telling me all of this?"

"It's a little complicated," he replied, "Tell me, Ben, what's your life like right now?"

I told him the truth. It lasted far longer than the truth ever should. Once I'd finally finished spewing out my life story and the tears no longer tore down my face, he sat back in the chair, sighed, and said "Good lord. You poor fucking bastard." Then he laughed. Before sighing again. It was a little bewildering.

"Fuck it," George said, "Give me a few days, and I'll be back in touch. If all works out well, you won't regret this. But whatever you do, don't tell a single soul about what happened tonight. That would be all rather bloody and messy and quite the inconvenience to clean up."

The next morning I woke up in my bed, naked but for socks, a sight no one should be subjected to when suffering a hangover the size of the one I was only just enduring. Or if they were sober, to be honest. Mentally I was a mess, manic one moment, over excited and astonished by what I'd learnt, but an hour later I'd be sinking into a pit of despair, my brain deciding that I wasn't going to get out of the depression I'd been suffering from that easily. So one moment I was like the most annoying of overexcited children, lurching around the place with far too much energy, imagining all of the things I'd do if I could become a magician myself. Or even just knew someone who was. But doubt was never far away, and I even began to question if any of it had actually happened. What if it had been some weird, distressing and sadly unsexy dream? Or what if my drink had been laced with something akin to LSD and it was all a hallucination? The latter loomed large in my mind, but then, it wouldn't make sense, would it? I'd seen things, felt things that I knew had taken place. Things I couldn't rationalise. Yet even when I'd persuaded myself that George did exist I began to worry that I'd never see him again, that I'd spend every waking moment praying and hoping he'd contact me and then years later I'd finally snap and die brutally.

And blah blah blah, and so on and so forth. For three fucking days. Which should give you an idea of how irritating I was during this time, though you probably need to times it by a hundred to really understand. When at work I spent the majority of the day staring at my mobile phone hoping he would call, and in the evening every time the landline rang I threw myself at it, gasping for air as I held it to my ear, only to be enraged by some poor sod of a telemarketer, where I uttered phrases so appalling that I phoned them back ten minutes later to apologise.

Fortunately, before I lost all semblance of sanity, he phoned and gave directions as to where I should meet him, which is why I found myself standing in one of North London's grottier Laundromats. He spoke to the owner and once more I suddenly became aware of a door I previously hadn't noticed. He led me through the door and down that same unsettling corridor, knocking six times on this occasion and uttering yet another selection of words that had no meaning to me. Despite the change of location the same barman stood behind the bar, and still looked nervous, but attempted a vague smile as he greeted us, and we took a bottle of wine and two glasses back to a small table by the fireplace.

"I've spent the last few days checking you out Ben. Talking to friends, looking at your online presence, I even have to confess to spending a couple of hours watching you at work," George informed me.

"Jesus, I know I zone out but I'd have thought I'd have spotted you," I said.

"Invisibility, lad, it works a treat," George replied, "Now ultimately this is all about your doing a favour for me. Possibly life threatening, but I reckon our odds of surviving this are reasonably high. Seventy six percent, something like that. And in exchange for this favour, I will make you a magician. Now. Well, tomorrow, I've a dentist appointment at 1AM."

"That's an odd time," I said.

"He's an odd dentist. But that's a story for another day. Look, Ben, I'm offering you a new life. Your current one really doesn't seem to be agreeing with you, and while this will be dangerous, it will be an existence beyond your wildest dreams. And I know your wildest dreams, you sick puppy you, and still want you involved. Plus what I'll need your help with, it isn't immediate, it's likely to be in a year, maybe two, depending on how everything else pans out."

I didn't know quite how to respond. I mean it felt like a dream come true, but part of me was worried that everything might not be as it seemed.

"I've got to say, this sounds all kinds of complicated. Can't say I like the life-threatening bit, either, but then again you know I've been fairly suicidal of late. That gets annoying, I can tell you." George moved closer to me and took hold of my hand. "I know this will all be a lot to take in. And it's completely up to you. But let me fill you in on... Everything. Then you can choose," he said. He didn't stop talking for about five hours. Five fucking hours. I mean it was fascinating and it kind of blew me away and I suddenly realised that everything I'd ever known was absolute nonsense, that the real history of humanity, well by Christ if that wasn't a right old barmy story. At the same time I'm a child of the nineties, my attention span is all messed up and it felt like I was trapped listening to this never-ending tale, to the point that on a few occasions I pretended to need the toilet just for a brief break, at least until he began to follow me in and noticed the lack of urine. By the end my brain felt like eighteen bombs had exploded within it, and yet after a while nothing surprised me anymore. There's only so many times reality can be rewritten before you become numb to the shock I suppose.

The following is roughly what he told me, and I'll try and do this as briefly as I can, but buckle in, as it's still going to take a while. The Universe, then. Created by an alien life form who is such an advanced being that it's almost impossible to explain. But he set off the Big Bang, watched everything unfold for billions of years, and gently tinkered with things when he became bored. So if creatures on a planet weren't evolving quickly enough, or in the way he hoped, he'd give them a small nudge. Oh, and yeah, I know I keep on calling him a he, but that is just the way it is apparently. Enormous cock, tiny balls, for the record.

We're not the only planet with life forms present either, oh dear lord no, but he's kept the interesting ones separated by millions of light years so that we don't meet until we're civilised enough not to blow the crap out of each other - hopefully at least, there's no way of knowing if we'll ever get to that point. Thus thousands if not millions of planets have highly civilised life on them, some far beyond humanity's current state, some a few hundred or thousand years prior to it, and he doesn't really give a fuck about any particular one. To the extent that while he was apparently pretty fond of the super evolved but still really cute bunny rabbit populated planets, that didn't mean he stopped any of the nuclear wars on them. Or any of the other apocalyptic disasters. Jumexic 14 for instance is an insanely mental place right now, with zombie donkeys tearing each other apart while angry flying jellyfish are dashing about spitting poison into the eyes of Neolithic man with glee. Oh, and there's also a planet where it's all floating eyeballs, which the creator made just to freak out mankind when we finally land there. It's that kind of universe. It almost made me feel glad to have ended up on this planet, until I remembered, you know, having read the news my entire life, and some of those history books you get these days too.

And the point of it all? We're a sort of power source. Every life form creates both positive and negative energy depending on its behaviour, with each planet supposed to create an equal amount of both types of energy, and once a creature dies, depending on how it lived it joins one of two eternal consciousnesses. A kind of Heaven or Hell set up, and combined they both contain the souls of every creature that has ever lived, from every planet, and we all continue to exist until the universe ends, at which point we're used... Though for what purpose no one knows. Maybe we're a unique form of energy that powers his reality, or it might simply be the way he charges his phone. Or we could be just a really nice sandwich filler. We'll never discover the truth sadly, what with this pesky deity refusing to sit down and explain it all. Or so George claimed. I have to admit I was never completely sure if he was on occasion winding me up, and there were several times he couldn't help wryly smiling, or a tale was told that seemed so absurd I thought he had to be taking the piss. Yet whenever I suggested that he was being at least slightly playful with the truth he denied it, claimed he was fully aware of how "absolutely doolally" it might all sound, and promised it was all true. I thought I'd caught him out when it came to his knowledge of other planets but he had an answer for everything, explaining how after a particularly nasty break up in eighteen forty-seven he'd spent several decades travelling around the universe, that magic allowed him to visit places mankind won't for centuries. He even suggested I could do the same thing if I didn't believe him, and he'd give me the coordinates to the rabbit world saying I could visit it once we'd carried out this mysterious favour of his. As for the history of Earth, well that could take days to tell apparently, and is a messy, complicated and downright depressing tale, kind of similar to the one you might know and despise but at the same time often very different. The story was filled with contradictions that rarely made sense, though the differences often revolved around the creator's inclination to pop in on occasion and fuck about with his demented handiwork - although even then there was a fair amount George claimed to not be certain about. The big changes came around circa 600 AD due to reasons related to the whole positive / negative energies situation, as the Good Lord granted a special few the knowledge that allowed them to control reality. Knowledge of how to do magic. Supposedly because at that point the energy disparity was really out of whack and ninety per cent of people were abjectly miserable and only ten percent happy, and he hoped that by giving such information to a trusted minority it might even things out a little.

Over time more and more magicians were created however, which of course was a recipe for disaster, and in 748AD an outbreak of magic took place. And as with everything in life, though some tried to change the world for the better, others wished for it to be thoroughly stained with blood, and they were by far the more dangerous of the two. Battles lasted decades, rivers and lakes were filled with bile and blood and all of the other foul liquids we're able to create, until there was a final epic battle that was responsible for thousands of deaths, the outcome of which saw the majority of magicians departing this reality and checking into one of the two afterlives. The good guys supposedly won, or we hope that's the case, as is always the case those that survived edited history, though this lot went further than usual and destroyed all proof of the existence of magic in our world, and then disappeared behind the scenes, sometimes subtly influencing those in power but never attempting to take it for themselves. Or at least not often. Once or twice a century someone might try and take over the world, but the other magicians quickly murdered such callous individuals. Unfortunately, as George had mentioned, it's all coming to an end now. Only about ninety magicians still exist, and that's an optimistic estimation. The British Government became aware of magic during the Second World War, as did the Axis powers, and the race to capture anyone with arcane abilities became rather riotous. As you might've guessed it was Churchill who managed to recruit enough to win, but the true tale of Hitler's demise involves him being turned into a sentient toilet, which was another of George's stories I didn't believe until I met the former führer myself several months later, though that was a very drunken night that I'm rather embarrassed about so shall never mention it again. It's for the best, trust me, you really don't want to know which royal bottom often uses Adolf as he screams obscenities and begs for death, it's something that still haunts me to this day and makes me feel sorry for the bastard, and I'm half Jewish.

Moving on, after the war magicians went back into hiding, but the knowledge of their existence was passed down from British leader to British leader, and now someone had finally decided to do something about it. Well, I say someone, the disgusting shithead who was our current prime minister at the time had made that particular choice, and because of him several magicians had already been found dead in unsuspicious circumstances, with rumours suggesting that far worse was to come. Which was where George's favour came into play as he wanted me to help him stop "The genocide of the magicians" as he put it, even though that sounded like a particularly melodramatic *Doctor Who* episode title. I was the first of a few he planned to recruit apparently, and there would be at least a year before my services would be required, which I read as suggesting that I might die in an agonisingly unusual and unwholesome way quite soon. Yet weirdly I wasn't discouraged at all as George explained why he simply could not sit by and watch the Government remove magic from our world completely any longer.

When George eventually took a gasp for air, I asked him about a million or so more questions, the main one being why and how no one had destroyed the world before now, that one rogue magician hadn't decided to turn every man, woman and child into radioactive ashes, or adorable dogs that would all die before they hit twenty. But like science, it had taken a hell of a long time for magic to develop to the point we're now at. The two often went hand in hand as scientists made discoveries that led to magicians understanding how reality worked, and thus how they could fuck about with it. In the 1800s no magician knew what a nuclear explosion was, for instance, so had no ability to create one, but by the 1950s every single one could have, and the world might've ended in the blink of an eye. So why no apocalypse since then? Blind luck, it seems, currently all of the magicians alive aren't despotic or genocidal. Or if they are they're doing a damn good job of hiding it, along with the fact that there was supposedly a taskforce that existed to monitor world-threatening magical psychopaths and would extinguish the life of anyone intent on such annihilation.

To complicate matters further, magicians were supposedly also put off by how troublesome such a matter would be, as they're limited as to how much magic they can produce each day. Casting simple spells is easy enough but the convoluted ones eat up energy like nobody's business, and you need to both eat and sleep to regain your abilities. Or steal an hour, in the way George had when we first met, which led to this conversation:

"So what is the situation with this hour of my life thing then? How does it work exactly? Does it mean I'm going to have a heart attack one hour prior to the original plan? Or die of cancer an hour before? What happens if I die by getting run over by a truck, does that truck just turn up sixty minutes earlier? And what if I'm on a plane or on the toilet when that happens?"

Amazingly my ramblings didn't annoy George.

"No, no, it's nothing like the latter. It's all to do with the choices you make, and the way you treat your body and only applies if you were to die of natural causes. In which case you'll now die an hour earlier than you would have before."

"That's not so bad, I guess."

"That depends on where the individual is at the time. It's not a spell that should be cast unless there is absolutely no alternative."

"Yeah, sure, I mean, I wouldn't, an hour's still an hour. An hour holding a loved one. Or watching the *Twin Peaks* season two finale one last time."

Which led to George shaking his head, as he mocked my love for David Lynch and I lost a little respect for him.

Now there was a lot more of our conversation that I could convey, I truly could go on and on and on in the way George did, but I'm

not a cruel man, and that covers most of the important things, I
think. The big exposition bit is out of the way now, I swear. And I
apologise if I've missed out anything important, which I probably
have, but hey, I'm condensing five hours of madness as succinctly
as I can.

"So," George finally said when I'd run out of queries, "Are you up
for this?"

It turned out I was.

November 18th 2014 was the day my life changed completely.
Though what I hadn't expected was for the process to be an
utterly deranged nightmare, the kind that scars for life, the
darkest of times that are so twisted and severe and mentally
damaging that you have no doubt that you'll never be able to
forget them, or the anger you feel for having been put through
such a thing. He said it was all part of the procedure, but to this
day I'm not certain whether or not at some points George was
enjoying my misery. Yes, I was thankful at the end, don't get me
wrong, but being transformed into a magician was like having
your brain shredded with a blunt cheese grater in the hands of an
old-age pensioner who had knocked back twenty shots of vodka
despite being previously teetotal, and much hysterical laughter
occurred. Once again George said it was all part of the ceremony,
that the energy running through him caused such a reaction, that
magic needed to be burnt into my soul and it was a procedure
that was uncomfortable for the both of us. But I still wasn't
completely convinced, if only because for me it was akin to an
acid trip where everything slowed down to a tortuously sluggish
state and seconds appeared to last for years, while my

temperature skyrocketed to the extent that it felt like my skin was bubbling and boiling, which may well have been the case, and there were only a few times that I thought I might not be dying. Yet paradoxically it felt like I would never die, and that the rest of my life would be like this. There was so much screaming, for so long a time. That said, it was better than the time I watched an episode of the Charlie Sheen sitcom *Two and a Half Men*, so perhaps I shouldn't complain too much.

Afterwards I was unconscious for forty hours, but when I awoke, everything had changed. I'd never been one for praising the lord, but oh, this time he got my gratitude and then some. It was like I could feel every molecule of my being, and each pulsated with a crazed mix of pleasure and power. Without wishing to be crude, the only comparison I could make was it being like a permanently orgasmic state.

"It won't last forever," George told me, "Only a couple of days or so. But considering what you've just been through, I think it's well deserved."

"That's the understatement of the year. And just to clear things up, I'm a magician now?"

"Oh yes," George said, smiling, "I need to teach you a great deal, but hopefully that won't take too long. And then enjoy magic. I know this has all been a bit strange and peculiar up until now, but here's where it gets good. If you do it right, at least. And you won't. Not all of the time. But that's all part of the fun."

Learning magic it turned out was an odd old thing, perplexing on some fronts and easy on others, an entirely different language with its own rules that often didn't really make any sense. Luckily one of the first spells I learnt was the ability to obtain a photographic memory, but that still led to spending hours and hours poring over the oldest of books, for months on end between various escapades, gradually learning more and more. It wasn't only books of magic either but scientific texts with the most complicated of theoretical physics, and medical books where I learnt exactly how the human body functions, and how to repair it in any possible situation. It was an arduous process and if I'd been warned that I'd essentially be going back to school I might have bailed at the beginning, but then that says more about me being a lazy twat than anything else. George's tutoring helped a little thankfully, especially after a couple of weeks learning the basics when we nipped over to an island he'd created a couple of hundred miles off of the coast of Brazil.

"Right, time for a practical day," he said, "I know a lot of what I've taught you is the basic mechanics of magic, but you can bend the rules, or mix them up a bit and that's when it starts to get really quite delectable."

In the middle of the island was a jungle setting, filled with a selection of exquisite plants and trees and some rather charming animals, all of whom George had created and made affectionate. Sometimes too affectionate, and why *that* might be I decided not to think about for a single second more. We were miles away from the nearest human heartbeat but despite this a slightly paranoid George made us both invisible, with him explaining we needed to be careful just in case a lost plane flew past and noticed us doing all kinds of impossible fuckery and reported its findings to the rest of the world. That led to George going on a bit of a rant about how camera phones had spoilt his fun a little too often in the recent past and if he could uninvent anything it would be them, for the first time sounding like a grumpy old man. But then I guess that's exactly what he was, if not indeed the grumpiest old man as though he hadn't told me when he'd been born, and always dodged the question when I asked his age, I suspected from the stories that he told that there weren't any non-magical beings on this planet who were older.

Eventually he stopped moaning, and explained how on this island "We can do anything we like, anything at all, as I created everything. Take that tiger for instance, the one wearing high heels, upon his creation I removed his ability to feel pain, so feel free to experiment on him."

Never one to miss an opportunity to toy with a tiger, the first thing I did was make his legs twenty feet tall, though I suspect it wasn't the first time this had happened as he looked unimpressed and carried on wandering around aimlessly, occasionally doing a little dance as it appeared that George was seemingly fond of tap dancing animals.

"That's the stuff," George chuckled, "Now go really crazy."

So I did. It kind of came easy. Firstly I transformed the tiger's tail into a snake with three heads which hissed menacingly whenever I clicked my fingers once, and when I did so twice it attempted to eat itself. Another click sent the heads hurtling towards the sky, plucking a passing parrot out of it and then juggling it for a bit. Following that I made his stomach a big flat screen television showing episodes of *Orange Is The New Black* because visual puns are sometimes my favourite thing. It didn't really work but hey, that's just life sometimes.

"Okay. You know what crazy is. That's good to know," George

said, "Now, transform him back into his original shape."

That took longer, but soon I began to work out how to truly manipulate magic, how to make it flow, how to control every atom of a life form and wield it in any way I so chose.

"Now, have a play with yourself," George suggested. Predictably I snickered, and predictably he sighed. "You know what I meant. But remember, whatever you do, make sure you always have a mouth and vocal cords, you won't be able to change back if you don't. Too many people have made that mistake in the past." Concentrating on that was probably why I forgot to turn off my ability to feel pain, as I made my own body triple the size, which wasn't pleasant at all. Stretching the bones in my legs so that they were several feet longer really did smart and I do not recommend the experience. On the plus side it was an error I never made again, and after I stopped weeping and switched off my pain receptors I turned myself into a gigantic spider with a cheeky grin, which was followed by a quick change into a very tall lady with fifteen breasts, with George unsurprisingly shaking his head at my juvenile behaviour.

"Ah, the fifteen-breasted lady thing," George mocked, "Something pretty much all male magicians do on their first day out and about."

"Hey," I replied, "You knew from the get go that I was a sad, sad man, you can't say I didn't warn you."

He laughed, and agreed with me a little too much.

"That reminds me," I said, "I forgot to ask, but as we can create animals does that mean we can make humans? Clones?"

George sighed. Laughed. Then sighed again. "Yes. Yes you can do that, if you have absolutely no morality whatsoever. Which I'm hoping isn't the case. And even if you're the first magician to ever create them for non-perverted reasons they will drain your energy by existing. Only tend to last about a few hours on average, and even less if you were to have four or five on the go at the same time."

"Hey, I wasn't necessarily talking about sex. Maybe it would be just nice to have someone to go, um, fishing with?" I suggested, unconvincingly.

"Firstly, like all non-boring human beings you hate fishing, so don't give me that. Plus it's obviously going to be for disgusting reasons, and is normally the first question a new magician asks."

I tried to persuade him otherwise, thought about the moral aspect some more, kind of felt a bit sickened that I'd ever considered creating living, breathing sex dolls, and then changed the subject completely.

The rest of the afternoon continued with much messing about with reality. Among various slices of outlandish daftness I converted all of the trees into cotton candy and ate many a branch, and made the muddy ground into a variety of different pizzas. Probably shouldn't have let the tiger eat so much of it though, he had terrible diarrhoea by the end of the night, pleasant smelling but ghastly nonetheless.

The only time George stopped me from creating a new entity was when I attempted to cross a rabbit with a donkey. He said it was too dangerous, both animals were surly twats at the best of times and that blending them both together might lead to the downfall of humanity. Initially I presumed he was joking, but when I thought about it for a few seconds I realised he was absolutely right, and made a mental note of how dangerous magic could be when thoughtlessly used, and shuddered at how close I'd come to destroying us all.

Due to splurging magic in such a ridiculous way I was pretty exhausted by the evening, so George suggested we head back to the magician's bar in England. This time a few others were present along with the barman and they smiled and nodded at us both, but otherwise kept themselves to themselves. Once seated and with a couple of bottles of the sort of wine I imagined only incredibly snobbish millionaire's consumed, George began to explain how despite his better judgement he was going to leave me alone for a few days.

"I've a few things to attend to that really need to be dealt with, so I'm going to be leaving you to your own devices soon. So please don't do anything too stupid Ben. Remember that if anyone in authority was to learn of your existence they'd do their best to end it as quickly as they could. And I know you're going to have so many stupid ideas that you'll think you can get away with, and I'm sure they'll seem like the best ideas in the world, but before you do anything - anything at all – please sit down and work out how it might go wrong and what you might do in that situation."

"That's more than fair enough George, I get it, I truly do," I replied, though of course I was fooling myself.

"Now, ask me questions," he said, "Everything. Anything. Get it all out of your system. I drank a bottle of wine when you nipped to the toilet, so I should be tipsy enough to cope with them all," he teased. We talked for about three hours, so these are the edited highlights. Or lowlights. Both, sometimes.

"Can I travel in time?" was first up. Out of everything it was the one question I hoped and prayed that the answer would be yes. A Doctor Who fan from the moment I was four days old, at least according to my mother who rarely lies about my tv watching habits, I'd loved the show right up until Colin Baker made it painfully unwatchable shite with his pompous overacting and an inability to slap the script writers until they wrote something interesting. It wasn't just Doctor Who either, I was obsessed with pretty much every tv show, film, comic or book that featured time travel. I'd daydreamed about it so much, of all of the things that I'd do, like going back to Victorian England and becoming the only person in the world to know both Jack the Ripper's identity and penis size. Oh, and to kill him and stop him from being such a shit and all that of course. Hell, maybe I already had, and that was why he stopped when he did. There was also the urge to meet Henry VIII and perform a vasectomy upon him while he was passed out one night in his early twenties, so the history of the royal family would be completely different. Or it might not even exist, and would anyone really care? Diana Spencer would be damn thankful at the very least.

"No," was George's succinct and devastating answer, "No you cannot. Time's a complicated beast, and cannot be controlled or manipulated in any way."

"So I wouldn't even be able to freeze time? It's just that there's this eighties Twilight Zone episode wher-"

"No," George replied, stamping on my dreams once again. Which may sound petty given that I'd basically been given the keys to controlling the universe, or messing about with it in very silly ways at least, but I was still all a bit gutted.

"Sorry my boy, but while you can do incredible things, moving through time, or making every single thing in the universe stop in unison, ha, you don't have the power to do that. No one does. If every magician that had ever existed all attempted to stop time at the same moment it wouldn't have the tiniest effect. See, in a way we've been given the knowledge of how to change the programming code of reality, and we can alter it slightly and recode it a small amount, but only to a certain extent. It's why you could make a pond attack someone viciously, but only get a fairly big wave from the ocean to mildly upset others."

I guess I instantly looked rather dismayed, which led him to say "Hey, there's no need to frown Ben, and I'm sure there are some spells that you might think impossible but aren't. Some of the finest magicians have teamed up with the greatest scientists to allow you to do incredible things. Like invisibility, mind reading, and the ability to converse with dogs."

"I can talk to dogs now?"

"Yep."

"Then I know the first thing I'm doing tomorrow morning. And every morning for the rest of my life."

"I thought that, but it gets surprisingly dull, you know," George replied, to which I called him the C-word, and he didn't find it funny in the way I'd intended.

"Moving on, what else would you like to know?" George asked, while pouring himself yet another large glass of wine. I briefly wondered how his liver could take such abuse until I remembered he could grow himself a new one at will, and probably did so daily.

"What about ageing? And dying for that matter, can either be prevented?" I asked.

"Yes and no. You can be killed, quite easily, if your head gets detached from your neck it's not going to suddenly jump back on without a care in the world. Ditto your heart being torn out of your chest by a pissed off giant cat you'd forgotten not to make malevolent, or any other mortal wounding that takes place in under a second or two. But if you've enough time to utter a healing spell you should survive. Plus of course you can put up all kinds of force fields around yourself too. At least until they run out."

"What about the ageing thing?" I asked.

"That's up to you. You can manipulate every cell in your body if you so choose."

"So I'm essentially immortal?" I replied, "Bloody hell, I'm not sure I like the sound of that, I'd like to live for a while but I'm not sure if I want to be around when the world ends. And, er, I don't wish to offend, but if you can do magic and you can do nearly anything and the world's your oyster and those sort of clichés, why do you look so old?"

George sighed. It was a sound I was finding increasingly familiar. "Thank you for that, you're massaging my ego in such a lovely way. And the reason is because this is how I looked when I became a magician, some of us had to study for decades before such power was bestowed upon them you see. I could of course transform every single cell in my face and become a younger version of myself at least visually, but I've come to like how I look. It's a reminder of everything I've been through and witnessed. Plus it would seem somewhat disingenuous to change it, to pretend to be younger than I am given that I'm in fact several centuries older than I look."

Which confirmed at least some of my suspicions as to how old he was, but before I could ask anything more on that front he began to talk about his past, and it was pretty astonishing stuff, though as always with George, God knows how much of it was actually true. Take the final part of the evening for instance:

"I spent time with so many artists and writers in the 1940s, consuming many a bottle of scotch with the brightest of minds," George said, "I even wrote a novel myself once, though I couldn't of course publish it under my own name, I didn't want to risk ever being well known."

"So what happened?" I asked.

"I showed it to a friend, he liked it a lot, and said he'd publish it under his name."

"Was it a hit?"

"Ever hear of a little book called *Animal Farm*?"

"No fucking way. You're saying one of the greatest writers of this century is a fraud?"

"Not a fraud exactly. Just happy to do me a favour. And earn a little money. Or rather lots and lots of money."

"Whoa... This is one of those mind exploding things. I mean, one of the most famous books ever written and-"

At this moment George burst out laughing.

"Sorry, sorry, I can't continue this charade. Of course I didn't fucking write the thing. Ha. My apologies again lad, but you are incredibly gullible."

"It appears so. Jesus, I really shouldn't believe everything you say, should I?"

"All the important stuff is true," he replied, "But I can't help taking the piss on occasion."

"It's alright. Just don't expect me to completely trust you anymore."

"Good," he said, with a wry smile dancing upon his lips, "That's exactly how it should be with all magicians."

CHAPTER 2 - A BEGINNING

Those first few months, then, before George and his bastard of a favour became prevalent in my life, yeah, they were kinda joyous. I feel like I should apologise for having such a time of it, it's the British way after all, but I can't be self-deprecating about this. It was just frickin' amazing. The perfect anti-depressant, I'd gone from dejected and suicidal to happier than I ever thought possible. I was rich beyond my wildest dreams within seconds, after buying one reasonably expensive diamond ring and then replicating it a couple of thousand times. And then a couple of thousand more. Pretty soon I was living in an eight bedroom house near Regent's Park with a walk-in wardrobe the size of my former bedsit, a cinema the size of the BFI Imax in the basement, and a swimming pool populated with doting puffer fish that took up the entire second floor. I know boasting in this way is odious and obnoxious too but the room I'd lived in previously was smaller than a prison cell, and far mouldier, so I couldn't believe my luck. It felt like I'd won the lottery every week for the past twenty years and then placed that money on a three legged horse, who despite being given odds of a thousand to one had somehow won the race.

Never let it be said that I am not a very petty man though, of that there can be no doubt. I had abilities that could change the world, and what was among the very first things I chose to do? Revenge. That's what. And an extremely childish revenge at that. Not that it played out as I first intended, which is soon to be a painfully common theme in this tale, but before embarking on many a ridiculous adventure I felt it only fair I hand my notice in at my place of employment, and while I was there make the life of one specific individual rather miserable. Which may sound needlessly cruel and pathetic, but I swear it's a rare case where the man in question truly deserved it. Or maybe not so rare thinking about it, as humanity does seem all a bit shit in the twenty first century. The company I'd worked for was one of those places where every department had twenty managers of various incompetency, no one really knew what was going on around them, and all carried knives at all times on the off chance some gleeful back stabbing might take place. The worst wasn't even my direct manager, even though he'd committed many a crime against humanity, but a vice president who saw us as petty worker ants, insects that he hated and had specifically bought an enormous magnifying glass to burn us all with in the midday sun, or at least he would have if he'd been legally allowed. It was a rare day that he didn't take pleasure in belittling those who mistakenly crossed his path, which given how much he stomped around the building looking for random victims was probably about one hundred and fourteen times in those eight sodding hours we were forced to spend there. The words "Alexander Martin-Miller makes me want to kill myself" had been carved into one of the toilet cubicle doors and underneath it "Go on then" had been written in felt tip pen in what looked suspiciously like his handwriting. Rumour had it that he was a corrupt little shit as well, that his lifestyle could not be maintained by a man on double his wages, all of which is why one afternoon I waited until the CEO - one Edward Clifton, a surprisingly debonair man in his late fifties of the type who looked like he hadn't really worked in years - had left for the day and I transformed into him. With a nod to Clifton's secretary I entered his office, set up some invisible cameras to record the meeting, and then phoned Martin-Miller's office and demanded he come in at once. I uttered "I know everything Alexander. Everything," before hanging up on him in a preposterously melodramatic manner, I'd meant it to be threatening but it quickly became apparent that my GCSE drama teacher had not done a good job when teaching me.

Miller-Martin arrived within sixty seconds, out of breath, and I'd never seen a man with so much fake tan look so pale.

"Please close the door and then sit down," I quietly uttered, attempting to tone it down a little, "There is a rather serious matter we need to discuss." It was at this point I wish I could read minds, but alas it was a spell I'd yet to learn, but Miller-Martin's reaction suggested there was more than one concern running through his.

"Now, I think we both know why you're here Alexander. Please, explain your choices to me. I really want to understand why you did what you did. I'd like to make this go away Alexander, but I'm not sure that I can. Everything's gotten out of hand, hasn't it?" Alexander smiled. Rather unexpectedly.

"Yes. Yes it has. But do you know something? It's a relief that you finally know. And I don't regret a thing. I enjoyed every second of it. Laughed every time I pissed in their jars of coffee. Took enormous pleasure in breaking the air conditioning last summer so that they sweated like the fetid pigs they are. And I was the one who defecated inside Martin Collins' shoe that time at the office Christmas party. But what are you going to do Edward? I'll deny it all. You can't fire me, knowing what I know about this company."

I hadn't been expecting this. Admittedly It had been a half arsed plan that had always had the potential to go wrong, but I'd kind of hoped he'd confess to something more serious, maybe an illegal financial matter that I could have used to blackmail him into being a better human being. Instead he was rabbiting on about shitting in a shoe. I mean, who hasn't done that after a particularly frustrating day at work?

"Cat got your tongue, old man?" Martin-Miller said, "Didn't think I knew about all of your fraudulent practices? All of those payments to a supposedly secret account in the Cayman Islands?"

My original plan clearly wasn't working, and it was tempting to panic, and though I had a Plan B it was an even more terrible idea. Devised when half asleep I'd dismissed it the next morning as being far too hare-brained and dangerous a scheme, but what choice did I have now? Actually don't answer that, I know I had plenty of others, but that would rely on me not being a lazy idiot after all.

"I was hoping I wouldn't have to do this Alexander," I said, "I truly was. I hoped the matter of your extreme pettiness could have been dealt with without threats or violence. But that no longer seems to be the case."

Still far too smug, Alexander asked "What the hell are you talking about Edward?"

"Oh please do be quiet, and listen. For I am not Edward Clifton. He left the building over an hour ago," I replied.

"Have you gone barking mad? Of course you're Edward Clifton."

"No Alexander, I am not. I am in fact Beelzebub jr, the son of the devil."

He looked like I was presumably about to be diagnosed with a very unusual mental disorder at that point, and quite understandably too. Until I burst into flames. He leapt out of his chair and was almost out of the door before I was able to cast a spell to make him sit down. Then another to stop the screaming.

"You see Alexander, you're such an unbearably horrible turd, such a putrid and poor example of a human being, that you're creating rather a lot of problems for me and my dear old papa. Statistically you're actually worse than Jeremy Clarkson, and he was recently voted the person the citizens of Hell would least like to spend an eternity with, and that was from a list of truly hideous, loathsome people on it including Charles Manson and the members of the unpopular indie band Shed Seven."

He looked a little confused at this point, presumably not sharing my dislike of those Britpop bastards, but hey, I stand by it, and you would too if you'd witnessed their beyond crappy attempt at headlining the Brighton Essential Festival in 1997. But before he had the chance to query my nonsense I continued to annoy him.

"Now you see, the reason you're such an issue for me is because Hell is becoming overcrowded, and it's down to people like you. People who are monstrously pointless yet induce misery every second of every day of their lives. Nearly all of the people who work for this company, nearly all of the people who know you in everyday life, Christ, even some of the people who encountered you for just a couple of minutes, they despise you with such a passion that they eventually lose faith in God. They can't believe He would create someone who fills their lives with such abject anguish, and if they don't believe in God that means they go straight to Hell. Now fifty years ago we'd have loved that. Bloody loved it. But not now. We just don't have the space, not even after we introduced bunk beds to the afterlife, and that cost a pretty penny I can tell you, even though we got them from IKEA."

Alexander was in shock and looking gloriously disturbed, a sight I found myself briefly wishing I could have watched for hours, but I didn't want to damage him for good. Or that's what I tried to tell myself.

"There is however a solution, one I've been tasked with by my father somewhat annoyingly, as I'm tracking down all of the world's worst life forms and making them change. Which you're going to have to do, and radically at that. You're going to need to become a better, more decent, kinder human being. You're going to have to smile, and be charming and nice. And if you don't, I'll give you erectile dysfunction for the rest of your life. No more sex, ever. Not even with yourself, however hard you'd try. And I know you Alexander. I know how crazy that would make you, it's why I chose such a specific punishment."

Predictably he replied with a mixture of confusion and fear. So I cast a few spells and eventually he stopped squealing, and he sat there looking dumbfounded instead.

"Right, now I'm going to stop being on fire," I said, because you rarely get the chance to say such things, "And it is time for me to leave you. But before I go you must confirm that you are going to do what I demand?"

Sweating profusely he nodded repeatedly and swore that he'd become a better man. I wasn't sure I believed him but I didn't really have much choice in the matter. So I bid him farewell with a final warning of what his betrayal would mean, and then turned myself invisible and buggered off.

Initially rather smug, it didn't take me long to start thinking that what I had done was ridiculously moronic, as pretending to be the son of Satan wasn't an exactly fool proof way to change a person, and he may well think that he'd had some kind of hallucination or psychotic break and that none of it was real. I wouldn't have blamed him either, but I checked back in a couple of weeks later and was surprised to see how different he was. When alone the bitterness and anger returned, but when in public he attempted to smile and say pleasant things, and I could more than live with that.

Those who have been paying attention, and hey, I so don't blame if you haven't, might have noticed that I'd already completely ignored George's advice about thinking very carefully before doing something involving magic, and the only explanation that I've come up with, after thinking about it for a very long time, is that I'm an dumbass idiot. But the above at least gave me cause for concern and the realisation that he might have been right, so I thought it was time to calm down a little. Not mutate into fictional creations in the hope of terrifying others, that sort of thing, at least for a day or two. Which is why if you'd ever popped over to my house on the fridge door you'd have seen a Post-it note reading "Remember, power corrupts even the best of people. And you're definitely not one of them, so please don't get carried away again. Love ya. Xxx."

It was actually quite easy not to mess with people for a while too, for I had a whole bucket list of magical experiments I wanted to try out, and had no difficulties choosing what came first either. Mastering flying was actually a little more complicated than I'd first imagined however, and it's possible I would have died at least three times if it were not for a handy force field spell. But after a few hours I was bursting through the sky, flying from one city to the next within a couple of minutes. And drunk, hell, that was stupidly crazy fun. Sure, I misjudged my landings a couple of times, there is one cow who I owe an apology too after I accidentally obliterated his wife, but ninety eight percent of the time flying was the stuff that dreams are made of. If your dreams included flying over to Buckingham Palace, in through an open window of one of the bedrooms, and then planting copies of Razzle from 1988 on top of Prince Philip's bedside cabinet. The fireworks flew that night, and the Queen's response was so grotty that even a jaded bastard like myself ended up feeling sickened. Next up was greed. Pure, ugly, disgusting, glorious greed. Not that I'd exactly held back in the past, but now I could eat whatever I wanted, mainly because there was a spell where everything which slithered down my throat was transformed into vegetables and lean meat high in vitamins and all that healthy crap I'd stupidly not taken any notice of before. Whoever created that spell deserved a Nobel prize, or a big kiss on the cheek at the very least, though I think I should get one too as I spent a fair time creating the perfect dessert, one so sublime that I dived naked into a vat of it on a regular basis. Sure that was a sight so sordid and odious that it could be used to torture many, but it was bloody fun. If I ever lose my magical powers I'm going to open a restaurant selling that and that alone, and I have no doubt I'd become a millionaire. Sure, the downside would be that a lot of my customers would have heart attacks and die, and the rest would instantly become diabetic even if they'd been perfectly healthy before, but them's the breaks, and trust me, it would have been worth it given how it tasted.

What followed, I don't hear you ask? Ah, that was a bout of transformation, turning myself into a number of different animals. Hence one sunny day I found myself with four legs and a wagging tail and the ability to lick my own balls. But I didn't, I mean I'd already done that as a human and not enjoyed the experience so why would I try it again? But as for spending the day as a dog, I've got to say, there were no real negatives. I was a big, bouncy Labrador, wandering around Hampstead Heath on a gloriously beautiful afternoon, dashing around, chasing my own tail, pissing and shitting wherever I wanted which I know I shouldn't have found as liberating as I did, but it is what it is. When hungry I'd gently shuffle towards families having picnics and stand on my hind legs and say "I love you!" in my best Scooby Doo voice. Yes, some screamed, but most were charmed which led to free food, which as everyone knows is always the best kind of food. Afterwards I'd roll around on the grass and get them to stroke my belly, and it's genuinely not a sexual thing, at least for me, it just feels really lovely, I want to have a stomach that hairy for life now. Being called a "good boy" over and over again is the best too, because I was. Back then at least.

The day spent as a cat was unfortunately rubbish. I like cats as well, at least the non-sociopathic kind, but there's so little to do. Chasing flies and spiders and randomly hissing at human beings who have done nothing to deserve such behaviour soon became dull, I'm fond of mice and birds and so had no urge to slay any, and while being petted and affectionately stroked passed the time well enough even that became boring after a while. By midafternoon I decided I'd had enough and instead spent a quick hour as a mouse, just to see the world in a completely different light. It was intriguing initially but people kept on running away from me while squealing and such rejection soon became depressing, bringing back memories of every time I've been in a nightclub. As did the assassination attempts from various cats, thanks to a force field I was unharmed but climbing out of a cat's stomach is an unpleasant enterprise, the part where one vomited me out on to a pavement especially. It was such a tepid experience that I was almost tempted to leave some of my old antidepressants out for the mice on the streets as I'm sure they desperately needed them, but I feared it might kill them so I didn't. See, I do try to be thoughtful sometimes.

As for other animals, it's a mixed bag really, especially as the transformations looked a little strange as I insisted on keeping my vocal chords, tongue and teeth so that I'd have no problem returning to my human form. But if you ever get the chance, I'd recommend changing into a snake, bull, eagle, horse, or frog as they were easily the most enjoyable, though a lot of animals were surprisingly disappointing. There's no fun to be had being a giraffe for instance, as for some reason you're massively racist towards horses. And turning yourself into a fish is immensely mundane, my local swimming pool with all the inflatables and water slides is so much more fun than the rivers I splashed about in.

It just happened to work out in this order, I swear, but after the animal incidents I realised that bar the brief stint as Gillian Anderson and the fifteen breasted woman idiocy on George's island, I'd not spent any time as a member of the fairer sex, not witnessed what that was like. Predictably once I'd changed sex the first thing was masturbation related, because I believe we established the fact that I'm a tedious male type a long time back, and yeah, it's all kinds of fucking amazing. Women do have better orgasms than men, it's now a fact. Sorry men. But going outside, ah, I was so stupid and naïve. Put it down to pure folly and thoughtlessness, but I'd never realised just how deplorable so many men were. I should have known to be honest, I'd read too many articles on the subject, heard too many stories from close friends, but I didn't realise how much of an epidemic it was until that day. Walking around London at night led to my being wolf whistled at and chatted up by random strangers, and on the tube wandering hands frustrated at a disturbing frequency. Anyone who did touch me got a quick dose of public lice as repayment, and I wish I could have done more but a lot of the time they were lost in a crowd before I got the chance to utter a second spell. Subsequently I spent several nights putting up posters on billboards around the city, with a picture of my female self and the words "Touch a woman that you don't know and I will stab you to death." It became a bit of a story on the BBC London news, but only for a day or two before everyone forgot about it. It's also why I curtailed the activity far sooner than planned, as even after I avoided public transport it still proved to be deeply distressing. Perhaps due to that, my mind started being pesky and annoying, and I couldn't help but think I should stop being a daft idiot and do something positive. Something good. Having the ability to heal people seemed to be the obvious road to travel down, but the question loomed, where should I start? I didn't have the ability to cure the most serious of diseases like cancer, but I could remove them from an individual. Hit a kind of reset button so that their body was like it was before the disease existed in them. Whether or not it'd return I didn't know, I asked George but magicians aren't great at keeping in depth medical records unfortunately, but he figured it'd buy them another year or so at the very least. Yet he also reminded me that if a boat load of cancer patients suddenly recovered, or if paralysed kiddies began jumping out of bed and running marathons, it would undoubtedly draw someone's attention, the kind of attention we really didn't need. So for a while I really didn't know what to do, and in the end I did less than I should have. Every week I'd visit a few different hospitals, and try to help those who seemed greatest in need. Still had to let some children die though, and that's a fucker you really don't want to have to live with.

I was in a particularly low mood after one such hospital visit when I went out to a local pub and met up with a few friends. We had an okay if fairly predictable night, one where alcohol flowed and gossip was exchanged, and I pretended to be interested in the fact that Arsenal weren't having that great a season while my friends nodded and smiled when I rambled away about how I'd not been around as I'd won a couple of grand on the lottery and so had been travelling a little. Which was partially true, though of course I left out all of the magic elements of my life. If I'd told them about pretty much anything that I'd seen and done they'd have had me sectioned instantly, I'd had a feeling that they'd been looking for an excuse for a while as it is. But they did seem glad that I was happier, commenting upon how worried they'd been about me of late, how morose I'd seemed, and how much of a relief it was that I was now okay. The more I drank the greater the temptation to show them what I was capable of grew, but even if I avoided incarceration, I knew they wouldn't be able to keep it a secret. All would want much bigger penises as well and if I did that for one person I kind of felt like I'd have to do it for everyone, and then what would happen to women who like small penises? Eh? What? Ah, right, fine, I'll get round to it sooner rather than later then.

Thanks to having had at least two pints of lager too many by the time I was stumbling home I found myself reacquainted with loneliness, a feeling I'd had on and off throughout this time. Even though my magical hijinks had been fun I missed that crazy old feeling called love. It would be disingenuous to not mention that from the very first day I became a magician I'd experimented with sex and magic, which had essentially involved my building a few sex robots. To make sure it was morally okay they had no artificial intelligence or anything approaching sentience, and they didn't look like anyone I'd ever met. Even then I had a sneaking suspicion that it was still a bit creepy, mainly because it definitely was still a bit creepy.

Yet what surprised me, and I never thought this would be the case - was that I got bored of it. My fifteen year old self would not have been able to comprehend such a situation, and would probably want to slap me several hundred times, but it started to make me feel lonelier than before. It wasn't real. It wasn't love. Or even like.

So fuelled with alcohol from the evening out I decided it was time to dip my toe back into the dating world, and there was a person I was rather enamoured with, a friend of a friend called Amy. We'd flirted occasionally at various parties but despite always gravitating towards each other and spending a lot of time talking, nothing had ever quite happened. There was also a downside as she had a son called Ted, and though I don't mind most children, Ted was a right dirty little shit. That might seem harsh as well, but I first met him four years ago when he was nine years old, when I'd been asked to dress up as Santa Claus for my Godchildren's Christmas party. I thought such a thing would be a fun affair, a chance to be frivolous and playful, and I definitely did not expect it to be a situation where I'd end up on the floor of the living room clutching my balls and trying not to cry. That's exactly what happened though, as the aforementioned child had mocked my attempts at being Father Christmas from the beginning, shouting "You're not Santa, Santa doesn't exist," and though other children present started to cry and he was admonished by miscellaneous parents, that didn't stop him from saying "If you're the real Santa this wouldn't hurt you." Thereupon I ended up with bruised testicles. Ted wasn't to blame however, at least according to Amy, who told me he was simply free spirited and must be allowed to do whatever he chooses. Still, despite this I'd hoped things might one day work out between Amy and I, and after more than a bit of online flirting that night, and over the course of the next couple of days, she suggested I come over for dinner.

All was going well initially, our chat had remained flirty, never crossing lines into indecency, but there was minor teasing which suggested that perhaps she really did like me. Hearing more about her life, and the things she loved or hates, I became more and more attracted to her. But a now thirteen year old Ted had decided against his mother being happy, or he held a grudge against me, or maybe he was just an awful human being. I'll never find out, as after Amy nipped out to the kitchen to get the main course, Ted wandered over with a devious smile on his face and held up a stink bomb. I knew what was coming next but before I had the chance to say or do anything he'd smashed it on the ground, Amy re-entered, and gasped in horror, commenting "Jesus, I could never share a house with a man capable of making a smell like that."

Despite my protestations that I was not responsible for the odour, Ted decided to make my life worse by faking outrage and saying that I'd farted on his head, and Amy believed him because he was already worthy of an Oscar at that age. And that was the end of that. Our romance was crushed, out of politeness I stayed for the rest of the meal, drank a sod load of wine, and left without bursting into tears, so that was a minor win I suppose. As was what happened after I left the house, as I turned myself invisible and waited for both of them to go to bed, and once they were definitely asleep I nipped back in and cast a spell to give Ted a rather nasty case of accelerated male pattern baldness. I heard from friends that his bald spot grew at an alarming rate over a period of a couple of weeks until he was completely bald, and he was then mercilessly bullied at school, which caused him much distress. I'm not a complete bastard of course, and did return and cure him. Eventually.

My failed attempts at wooing Amy made me feel rather low alas, but at the same time it sadly hadn't diminished my libido. Yet despite the whole magic situation I still struggled with having the confidence to approach women in pubs or clubs. It all felt so fake to me, that I was wishing to get to know someone based on their appearance alone. Face to face rejection being somewhat agonising might also have come into it too, I'd experienced enough of that for a lifetime.

So on to the internet it was, and surprisingly it went okay. I'm not going to lie, I had to send out about twenty messages to get one response, but most of those replies at least led to a first date, and no one was horrified when they met me. Despite that the first three dates ended with a kiss on the cheek and false promises of a possible future date, one day, maybe, but then the fourth date took place, and I knew there never needed to be a fifth.

Oddly enough when we met I wasn't in the best of moods, as George had only an hour ago given me a right bollocking for an incident that wasn't my fault at all. Someone had uploaded a poor quality video of two unicorns fornicating on the Yorkshire Moors, and he presumed I was behind such inanity. I swore to him that I'd had nothing to do with it, that at the time I'd once again been over the local park partaking in a game of fetch, but I couldn't get him to believe me. All of which is why I arrived at the pub early and subsequently lost touch of time, and when she approached me I still looked a tad downbeat.

"Hi, Ben, yeah?" she asked. I smiled and nodded.

"I don't mean to be rude, but is life really so bad? You look like your dog's committed suicide because he couldn't stand being around you, even though before meeting you he was the happiest dog alive," she said.

"Ha. But no, sorry, I was just having a bit of a bad day. Was. Not anymore," I burbled, as my attempts at flirting really are that embarrassing.

"Life's good in general too," I continued, "Sort of amazing, recently."

This made her smile.

"If you've won the lottery I think we should get married," she said.

"I kind of have."

"Let's do it then. Let's drive to Gretna Green, we can be there by the morning, as long as you don't mind me divorcing you in the afternoon."

"You're on."

"Cool. But before that, let's get a drink first and at least briefly get to know each other, yeah?"

Karoline, then. Karoline Haugen. A Norwegian brunette, funny, incredibly smart, and like me she was also someone who enjoyed her food way too much, but that only made me like her more, I could finally go to an all you can eat Chinese buffet with someone and risk putting the restaurant out of business and not feel shame. I was taken aback by just how amazing her English was as well, though perhaps it shouldn't have been a surprise since she'd been in the country since she'd studied history at Leicester University, and I later learnt she'd spent much of her childhood watching American sitcoms thanks to her parents being narcissistic and shit.

That night we drank and talked until they threw us out at closing time, and then we walked around London through to the early hours, heading to Trafalgar Square to do impersonations of the lions, then on to Marble Arch in the hope that mockery of city types might take place, but as we didn't earn several million pounds a year they ignored us. Later we ended up in the all night McDonalds in Leicester Square, as it turned out Karoline had a fondness for horrible tasting throwaway food as well, and the combination of all of the above made me realise that I was already beginning to fall in love with her.

Due to that I wanted to take things slowly, and the fact that I didn't try to sleep with her that night apparently impressed, as she was tired of men who only wanted sex. Indeed we didn't become intimate until we'd known each other for three weeks, largely as I hoped by then that she'd like me enough to stay with me even if the sex was disappointing. Which it was, or I was, at least, but hey premature ejaculation's sort of a compliment, isn't it? Maybe?

The day after we first slept together I knew it was time to tell her about the magic side of my life, I couldn't delay it any further, that I needed to be honest. And I was terrified. I didn't know what to expect, how she'd react, and if she'd spend the rest of her life questioning whether I'd cast a spell on her in an all too literal manner. But I had to tell her. So I invited her over to my place, and asked her to sit down.

"Oh God, you're pregnant, aren't you?" She asked, grinning.

"No, it's nothing like that. I mean, I was, yeah, but I gave birth a while back and it didn't work out so I threw it away."

"So what is it?" she asked, "You do look a little pale."

"Look," I said, "This is going to freak you out a bit, but it's a good thing I promise."

"Okay," she replied, a little wearily.

"Firstly you're going to think I'm a lunatic. Full blown oh God I'm dating someone with severe psychological issues. But you're not.

And as soon as you give me the chance, well I hope you'll be amazed. And then you're going to have a million questions. And then, well, fuck it, I don't know. That's why I haven't told you before. But only because I was scared of what might happen. But just... Trust me. I'm still me. And this is a good thing, I swear."

"You're starting to freak me out a little," she said, the smile now gone.

"Sorry. And well, just let me blurt everything out. Wait until I've stopped before saying anything, which I know sounds shitty, but try to give me a chance to explain all of this."

"Okay," she replied, possibly while considering what she could do to knock me unconscious if need be.

"Right, well, I found out a few months ago that magic exists. I can cast spells, and, um, stuff happens," I rambled, because I was nothing if not ineloquent. "And before you call the insane asylum, er, you see that vase of flowers by the window, well now I'll turn it into an antelope."

And so I did. Before turning the antelope into a large chocolate fountain, and then a bowl of apples and oranges, before I realised neither of us liked such healthy monstrosities and reverted it back into its chocolate state.

"Fuck," she said, "Fuck, fuck, fuck. I mean... Fuck."

"That was pretty much my initial response too. And it's all such a crazy and insane and long and complicated story, but I will tell you all of it if you want me to?"

That led to a sleepless night, during which a lot of hard questions were asked, and I had to spend a lot of time reassuring her that I was the person I'd always appeared to be. That she was in this relationship by choice, with bleak horrible conversations taking place with regard to that. As were the explanations concerning our place in this universe, and God, or what passes for a creator of this place, and the situation with the governments of the world and the status of other magicians and all of that madness. There were times I'm sure she thought I was making it up, or that I was more deranged than I claimed, but as dawn reared its sexy head it seemed she believed me. Especially as I chucked in a few spectacular spells throughout to keep reminding her that my words weren't the fanciful ramblings of a mad man.

Eventually sleep beckoned, and it wasn't until the middle of the afternoon that I woke up. Karoline was already dressed, and full of worry I was about to speak, when I saw that she was smiling.

"Okay. Have slept on this. It's all insane. But I need more insanity in my life, and I really want to see what you can do. So how about on Friday you organise a night that I'll never forget?"

"No, I can't," I replied, "I've always sworn not to use magic on my genitals. Just in case it goes wrong and I end up with an angry cock that never lets me sleep. I mean, that was what my teenage years were like and I do not want to experience anything like that ever again."

She laughed, sarcastically.

"You know that's not what I meant."

"I know. Sorry. And Friday, yes. Definitely. One hundred percent, definitely."

CHAPTER 3 - A WEEKEND AWAY

Four days later we were on a small island in the middle of the Pacific Ocean, far, far away from even the nearest hint of civilisation. Just twelve miles in diameter but hopefully big enough to get lost in for a few days, I'd put an invisibility spell around the entire isle along with a force field so that ships would gently bounce off of it, though I'd done my research before creating the place and none were due to travel in the area this weekend. Which may not be exciting to hear, but it's a rare case of my being diligent and not a thoughtless idiot so I wanted it on the record.

When we arrived the sandy beaches were drenched in moonlight and the waves gently slipped across them. We sat by the shore where I'd laid down a blanket and provided us with miscellaneous bottles of champagne and trays of the most exotic of foods. Admittedly bought from Marks & Spencer because I had no idea what I was doing on that front, but hey, I was giving it my best. After getting slightly drunk, I guided Karoline away from the beach to a large wooden fence that was hidden among the palm trees, along with two ominous looking doors.

"Welcome to Ben Park," I said, and she laughed at my terrible impersonation of Richard Attenborough.

"Oh God, please tell me this is going to be like Jurassic Park," Karoline said, "Except it's hundreds of you trying to gnaw us to pieces."

"Ah, no, and now I really wish I'd thought of that," I replied, "But this is just a big old theme park, designed in a way that you'll hopefully like."

"Okay, what's first then?"

Being aware of her fondness for the big Marvel and DC movies I thought an ultimate battle between superheroes might turn out to be fun, so I guided her into a huge carnival tent that contained a ridiculously large boxing ring. Standing by it were a whole bunch of well-known characters growling in a surly manner, and I wish I could name names but parody law doesn't cover it apparently.

It was far over in three rounds, I'd bet on the Big Angry Grass Coloured Man to win as I'd given him such sharp teeth, but Captain Very Proud Of His Country But Is Jingoism Really That Good A Thing? had knocked him out early by shoving his shield down his throat, and though Sexy Bastard In A Big Robot Suit held his own for a long old while, and got up to some frisky stuff with Another Sexy Bastard In A Big Robot Suit, Albeit One Who Gets Paid A Great Deal Less Money, unfortunately for both of them their erotic endeavours were interrupted by Cool Female Character Who Should Have Been In A Lot More Movies By Now, who I'd accidentally made a bit too angry and who decimated all with way too much lung removal. Still, Karoline seemed amused by it all, and that was of course the point.

Following this I wanted to share with her the best weekend of my life, so upon leaving the back entrance of the tent Karoline discovered I'd recreated 1995's Reading music festival in its entirety. It might seem odd to take a woman I'd fallen for into a field full of sweaty teenagers and adults in Berkshire considering I could have recreated any place in any country in the entire world (or created entirely brand new ones for that matter), but those three days were some of the happiest of my life and I wanted her to experience it. Gloriously sunny, and thus almost the anti-Glastonbury, there were so many bands playing that there was never a dull moment, or if there was it could be quickly quashed by moving on to another stage. Which is why I've only ever seen fifteen minutes of Neil Young play, he might be an iconic figure but Carter USM were on in one of the smaller tents and were much more palatable.

My line up stayed pretty faithful to the original and so included The Smashing Pumpkins, Bjork and Soundgarden, but I transferred a few acts from the smaller stages on to the main one, bright and shiny and lovable indie pop like My Life Story and David Devant and His Spirit Wife, and other bands that should have been huge but sadly never found the fame they deserved.

It wasn't just the bands that made it so memorable for me either, but the people in general. I couldn't recreate all of them, even with George's considerable assistance in constructing this island the vast majority were paper cut outs as I'd have run out of magic shockingly quickly if I'd tried to create fifty odd thousand life forms, but the people who had been the strangest and funniest and kindest were in attendance, and chatted to us at various points in between acts.

I also made a few additions to the festival site including a huge water slide that went straight from the festival gates right down to the main stage, with it ending in a small ball pit next to the bands, because that really should have been a feature of the original festival. Alcohol and kissing ensued, and I'll spare you more details so you don't hate how sickly the two of us were.

The next day the festival was still ongoing so we hung around the main stage listening to a robotic version of Ash while working off our hangovers, eating the greasiest of burgers until it felt like the world was no longer our enemy.

"So this has been cool, and I want to come back here later for sure if you can quickly clone Kate Bush," Karoline said, "But what's next?"

"I'm going to take you into the woods," I said, "Which, er, wasn't meant to sound saucy. Honest."

"I doubt that. But okay, what do you have planned?"

"Hopefully a pleasant surprise," was all I could utter as I started to wonder if what I had devised might have been a bit too crazy, even for me.

We left the festival via the backstage area, briefly giving Morrissey the finger because he was being racist again, and into a large wood, filled with ancient oak trees, ferocious looking thorny shrubs, and a couple of horny shrubs, because something's deeply wrong with me. It grew steadily darker as we made our way through the woods, but there was a muddy path that was just about identifiable, and for about fifteen minutes we aimlessly wandered along it, swapping stories and daft memories, until a wolf howled and Karoline burst out laughing.

"Oh great, we're in a horror movie."

"Well you do love them, plus I hope there's aspects that you'll never have seen before," I tried to explain.

"Yes. I love watching them, that's true" she said, "But I'm pretty sure I told you on our first date that it was my plan in life to never be stabbed to death by a blood thirsty psychopath."

"Hey, trust me, I said you wouldn't die this weekend and I'm really going to do my best to keep that particular promise," I replied, "Unless I get distracted by a cute puppy when we're attacked by vampires or something. Then we're probably both screwed."

It grew darker and darker as the trees blocked out the sun, though we were still just about able to follow the path thanks to a few shards of sunlight that broke through the branches and leaves from time to time. Sometimes we'd hear things nearby, something shuffling through the woodland, with the occasional quiet yet unsettling growl, and I sensed Karoline was beginning to start becoming bored when the ground suddenly gave away beneath us and we plummeted into a darkened pit, where one solid steel stake pierced my stomach something terrible. Karoline chuckled at the sight of my intestines for a bit until a wolf leapt down and joined us in the hole. Then two. And three. All circling us, saliva dripping from their open mouths.

"Oh shit, they weren't supposed to turn up until later," I screamed, and attempted to move, but it's pretty hard when your body has been pierced by a large metal object, and I made a mental note to avoid them in the future. The wolves then ignored me, the rude bastards that they'd turned out to be, and slowly moved towards Karoline, growling louder than was normally possible. Yet this was a mistake they wouldn't live down, as Karoline had grabbed a steel stake and started waving it in the air.

"Come on then you little buggers, come at me," she cried out. The wolves were predictable, but Karoline wasn't. Twenty seconds later all of them were whimpering on the ground, bleeding heavily.

"Fucking hell," I said, looking clearly quite disturbed.

"Oh," she replied, "You're not dead then?"

"No. Sorry. But Jesus, you dealt with them... Effectively."

"I grew up in Norway, remember? I killed my first wolf when I was four and a half."

"Ah, that makes sense," I replied, perhaps a little too earnestly, to which she burst out laughing.

"Bloody hell, you British have such a backwards view of Norway. Or maybe it's just you. But if I have to tell the truth, I knew they were fake and wouldn't hurt me Ben, so it's not like I exactly had anything to lose."

"Well quite, and I'd hoped you'd guessed that as well," I claimed, as I briefly changed into something less blood stained, and we climbed out of the pit and walked further down the path.

A few minutes later we reached a small clearing, in the middle of which was a stone well. Arcane symbols had been etched into the stone, and as we moved closer something could be heard in the water below.

"Oh Christ, there's going to be some kind of giant snake fish thing down there isn't there?" Caroline asked, "Or a weird Japanese girl who moves like Bjork having an epileptic fit?"

But for once she hadn't guessed correctly, as it was actually the popular tv presenters Ant and Dec.

For those outside of the United Kingdom, Ant and Dec are two guys who started out as actors in a teen soap in the nineties, and as their star began to rise they released an amusingly daft album, made a long forgotten and really rather bad sketch show, before morphing into presenters of countless reality tv and game shows. Amazingly they'd stayed best friends throughout, and everyone kind of liked them, even people like me who can be a bit snotty when it comes to mainstream tv, universal popularity is largely unheard of in these isles but they pretty much had it.

They weren't having the best of times on this particular day however, given that they'd clearly been murdered, taken a trip to the mortuary, with scarring suggesting they'd been sliced and diced before being put back together, complete with extra teeth. Sharp ones at that.

"Flesh!" Dec screamed, his voice filled with desire, "New scrumptious flesh!"

But Ant hissed at him before he had a chance to attack. "One stinks of magic, kill him, kill him before he can destroy us," he said, which they attempted to do with Ant raising his fist in the air and plunging it into my chest, removing my heart and then raising into the air while screaming triumphantly. Karoline screamed at the bloodshed, as the duo happily consumed large chunks of my body, before smashing my skull against the wall of the well, grabbing my brain and sinking their teeth into it. Once they'd finished eating, briefly complimenting my deceased body by saying what a tasty mind I'd had, both Ant and Dec turned towards Karoline.

"Okay, Ben, let's just end this bit now, yeah?" she said a little nervously. What was left of my corpse didn't move. They did however. Closer and closer, snarling loudly, as droplets of my blood fell from their broken, open mouths. Yet before they had a chance to snack on my beloved I sped out of the woods at fifty miles per hour, knocked them unconscious by slamming their heads together, and dunked the duo back into the well. Then I vomited about twenty litres of unset concrete into it so that they wouldn't return.

"Jesus, Ben, that was… I don't even know how to describe it. Bar that it was fucking horrible."

"Sorry," I mumbled, "It's just that I thought you liked horror films?"

"I do," she said, "But enjoying something on the big screen is very different to experiencing it in real life. It was one thing to see your body being pierced by a stake, that was distasteful for sure, but I knew you could magic your way out of that. Yet the way they just mauled you to pieces, and I was covered in your blood and your limbs and your organs… Christ, you went too far Ben, too far."

"Um, yeah, I suppose, I mean, you're right, of course you're right. It was supposed to be amusing though, like the over the top gore you get in Japanese horror films," I managed to say, albeit in a very flustered way.

"Yeah, you misjudged that one. Not by a small amount either," she replied.

"Okay, notes taken, and I am really, really sorry. And will beg for forgiveness for as long as you need me to?" I said.

"Nah, I think that's enough. For now. And how did you survive all of that, anyhow?" Karoline asked.

"Ah, it was the whole switcheroo in the dark woods thing, as I left you wandering about with a clone of myself for a bit."

"Hmmmm. Right. Well if you ever do that again, for whatever reason you may have, do at the very least let me know in advance?" she suggested, and of course I agreed, as apologies began anew.

After a trip back to Reading Festival and the previously promised performance from Kate Bush and about ten other musicians we loved, we ended the night lying on top of a recreation of the Eiffel Tower. Which was less painful than you'd think, especially if you're in the world's most expensive bed, the Baldacchino Supreme designed by Stuart Hughes and Fratelli Basile. Previously I'd no idea who they were, but a quick search online had led me to it and all I can say is that it's great and all but not worth six million dollars, indeed I'm pretty certain I wouldn't pay a penny over five. On a very small, floating stage at the end of the bed we also had a robotic version of Leonard Cohen, serenading us with a few of his gorgeously bittersweet ballads.

"I feel a bit weird being semi-naked in front of Leonard," Karoline said.

"Ah, don't worry about it," I replied, "I mean, it's not like he really exists."

"Still, every time you caress me I'm sure he gets an erection."

"That's true, but I wanted the robot to be as close as possible to the original," I replied.

"Okay, but if we do stuff... He can fuck off to the bottom of the tower then, yeah?"

"It's a deal. He can go right now if you want?"

"Nah," Karoline said, "Not right now."

"So how did I do?" I asked, "As random displays of magic go, was it okay?"

"Well," Karoline said, making the word last a worryingly long time, "It was alright I suppose. Fine, fine, you're fishing for compliments and I'll give you one. You mostly did good Ben Holland. I mean you know my feelings about the way Ant and

Dec murdered you, but otherwise it was fun, and the festival was amazing, and I guess this is okay too. Six out of ten then. A decent enough start."

"Got it, I'll definitely make it a lot more enjoyable and slightly less traumatic next time," I replied. Glasses of champagne were then drunk, and ridiculously expensive food consumed, and I was just about to suggest that Leonard Cohen buggered off when Karoline looked at me in a serious manner.

"There's one thing I wanted to talk about though," Karoline said, in a manner which gave me cause for concern.

"We've done the crazy magic thing and that's been amazing, and we've chatted about pop culture to death, and it's been enjoyable, but I'd really like to get to know you better. I know bits about your life but only tiny snippets, whereas I could list every one of your favourite films and tv shows. So maybe you could tell me about the things you want to tell me, but haven't had the courage to bring up yet."

"Ah. Yeah. There are a few of those I guess. Nothing too shocking, I hope, but there's been the odd murky time. And you know I'm kind of slightly crazy about you, so yeah, you can ask me anything and I'll answer it."

"Anything?" Karoline asked.

"I could even cast a spell on myself so that I only speak the truth?" I suggested.

"Eh, I'd prefer it to be by choice,"

"That's fair enough. So where shall we start?"

"Okay," Karoline replied, "Here's a tester for you. Have you ever committed a crime?"

"Um, well, little ones, sure. Nothing major, a bit of petty

shoplifting when I was eleven and couldn't afford a Toblerone. Oh, and minor dalliances with drugs. And not so minor dalliances when it came to marijuana when I was a student, but hey, I've never claimed I'm not a clichéd stereotype. But apart from that I don't think I've... Oh, bollocks. I forgot, when I was drunk one time I did steal a kitten for three days."

"What?" Karoline spluttered.

"She just followed me home one night from the pub. It was snowing and viciously cold and I tried to dissuade her, but she wouldn't leave my side. Then the next day I was too hungover to return her to her home, I let her out and everything, kept the door open for half an hour but she just wouldn't leave. So I thought she might be homeless or something, until the next day I saw signs for a lost cat. And a reward. Which I sort of claimed."

"Ha. I mean, you twat. But I guess you weren't actually setting out to defraud someone?"

"No, no, god no. It was just... Circumstances."

"Well hey, it turns out I'm a much worse person than you," Karoline said, "They're honestly the only crimes you've committed?"

"Uh, I guess there's one other thing. I mean, it wasn't a crime. Ish. I just got fired from a job once, though it's one of those stories that takes a while to tell."

"We've got time."

"Okay. Er, it was about three and a half years ago I guess, I was working as a live subtitler for one of the 24 Hour News channels, where I had to write up what the presenter was saying as it happened so that those without hearing could stay in touch with the world. At first I found it interesting, and hoped I was kind of making a difference to people's lives, but it soon became bleak. If only because it becomes impossible to escape just how unhinged the world is, and there was no escape from hearing the worst of it over and over again."

"I can understand how that might make a man a little crazy," Karoline said with a gentle smile.

"I'd been there a year when I started to really struggle, if it had been only the inanity of the work I might have coped, but my superior treated everyone so harshly, if we made any kind of error, spelt anything wrong, or if grammatically it wasn't always perfect, Jesus, the tantrums he'd have. And it's impossible not to screw up doing that sort of thing on occasion, especially if it's a live interview with a twatty politician who's nonsensically rambling away at a hundred words a minute. By that point I was already hoping to leave, was applying for jobs left, right and centre and not getting anywhere, until one day when I was given a bollocking for a mistake someone else had made I kind of decided I didn't want to stick around anymore. Kind of snapped a little. I didn't do it immediately, and I didn't really have a plan, but I just knew I wanted out, and when it became quite late and there weren't many people around I knew I could do something which wouldn't initially be noticed. Now a lot of the time not that much happens late in the day, there's the ten o'clock news and normally after that repeats of previously aired reports, but that night we had a breaking story on Terrence Fallow, that Conservative MP who'd had an affair with a UKIP member and had leaked supposedly valuable information about the party. So I thought it was the perfect opportunity really, what with the responses from a whole host of well-known political figures."

Karoline placed her head in her palms. "I think I can see where this is going," she said.

"I like to think I'm nothing if predictable."

"Details would be interesting though."

"At first I started off gently-ish, just the odd rude word or phrase here and there, like having David Cameron call Fallow 'A longstanding and once honourable member of the party whose face I'd now like to curl out a turd upon', but once I'd started I couldn't stop. They'd managed to get Boris Johnson in for a quote, and instead of putting on screen what he really said I had him quoting all of the lyrics to Leonard Cohen's The Future."

"Isn't that the one where he politely requests crack and anal sex?"

"Yep, that's the one," I replied. At this point the Leonard Cohen robot on the end of the bed was halfway through Famous Blue Raincoat, but I interrupted him and asked him to sing The Future instead so Karoline would know exactly what I'd done, and if you don't know the song you can check it out on YouTube here: https://www.youtube.com/watch?v=3VAxwimExno

"So that's how you got fired, yeah?" Karoline asked.

"That would have done it, by this point I'd already broken seven rules of the ITC code, but then Nick Clegg appeared on screen."

"Oh god, that bloke who was the leader of the Liberal Democrats?" Karoline said, "The one who went into the coalition government with the Tories?"

"Yep, that's the one. And because of the broken promises, and the outright lies, he wasn't exactly my favourite person."

"Oh dear," Karoline sighed, "What did you do to the poor bastard?"

"I made it seem like he'd learnt that the new Antichrist had recently been born, and that all children under the age of two must be taken away and murdered. That he was taking an absolute and definite pro death stance when it came to any devilish deities arriving on the planet."

"It's a good policy if you think about it," Karoline said, laughing.

"I would have gone on to make it an even more outrageous speech, but someone had noticed at that point, security were called and I was removed from the premises. The following day I was summoned by HR and very quickly dismissed, along with a warning that there was an investigation going on into my, er, hijinks, and if anyone pressed charges for libel or defamation of character they'd hang me out to dry. Which admittedly was fair enough. Fortunately no one did."

"Oh Ben."

"I Know. It was stupid. I was stupid. But I hope I've learnt not to be since then. Or at least not that stupid."

"Okay, so we've shoplifting, drug abuse, kitten theft, and defamation of character, anything else you want to share? Ever killed a herd of horses, or something?" Karoline asked.

"No, no, I like horses. And besides, my parents instilled this pesky moral code in me that I've never been able to shrug the majority of the time, damn them. Though I am trying, I promise." Karoline just smiled and shook her head at that.

"So what about you, have you ever broken the law?" I asked.

"Oh, all the time," She said, "But nothing major. I stole some sweets as a kid, set fire to a small mattress I found in the woods when I was nine, that sort of thing, but it never led to anyone getting hurt. The worst thing I ever did was steal five bottles of tequila from a nightclub I worked at as a student. But in my defence, I was on minimum wage working until three in the morning, being perved at by nearly all of the male customers and most of the other staff, so on my final night I stuffed everything I could fit into my bag and did a runner."

"That sounds fair enough to me."

"Why thank you kind sir," She replied, before becoming more serious once again.

"So, I appreciate everything you've told me Ben, I do, and it's fun and everything, but is there anything really major you haven't told me? Like a big life changing event and all that? Something which you'd like to share, but are worried about scaring me off? Because you won't, you know, and I want you to know you can tell me anything. Unless it's actual murder. Then I'll ditch you in a second."

I'd kind of been dreading this question. It was worse than explaining magic. I mean, it shouldn't have been, but it was something terribly messy and unpleasant, and while telling some people had gone well, and had been met with empathy and sympathy, others had reacted less well. Been freaked out about it.

"Just the one thing. And it's not as bad as it sounds. I hope. But when I was fifteen I did spend six months in a psychiatric institution," I said, still terrified despite her assurances.

"You poor, poor thing," she replied, her face beyond sympathetic, "If it helps, I've friends who have had to have a stay in one, and I get it. Christ, there's been times I'd have loved to check myself in for a year and take the time out to get my head in order."

"That's kind of what happened to me. I just needed time out, and a fuck load of help on the mental side of things, admittedly. For a long time I was so ashamed though. I was only fifteen and thought if anyone knew about my issues they'd freak out. And it was back in the early nineties where there was still a pretty huge stigma about mental health. And my step-father Brian didn't believe in psychiatric illnesses, despite his own father being batshit crazy. Sorry, rambling. I guess the point is that it was a fucking horrible time, but it all worked out well in the end thankfully."

"You can tell me more," she said, "You won't frighten me off, I promise."

"The short version is that I had a bloody annoying OCD, and became agoraphobic due to it. Started missing school, struggled to leave the house for any reason at all, until a social worker finally asked me if I needed help."

"That sounds all kinds of shitty."

"You don't know the half of it."

"What was your OCD?" She asked.

"It's embarrassing. I hate it. I look back and I can't even really understand it, either, but that's the nature of mental illness I guess. But it was cleanliness related. And toilet related. Like I knew I had to spend ages in there before I could even begin to cope with the idea of leaving the house."

"I'm so sorry you had to go through that."

"Me too," I replied, "At least sort of. Definitely the two years before I was institutionalised, they were fucking bleak and no one should ever get as close to killing themselves as I did at that age. I just thought I'd never be normal, that I was an utter freak, that if anyone ever knew about the problems I had they'd judge me and torment me and destroy me... If anyone at school found out I'd never be able to return. I'd have to leave the town I lived in. The country. The world. Which might sound a bit over dramatic, but like I said I was young at the time."

"It's okay, it really is," Karoline said, "Trust me, I know how your own mind can be a bastard to you sometimes."

"Ain't that the truth. But in the end I got the help I needed, after one day when I decided I couldn't cope anymore, I locked myself in the bathroom and refused to come out. My Mum called the police, I guess she just didn't know what to do, but I refused to speak to them, and then the social worker I mentioned before was contacted. The next day I was driven to a psychiatric hospital, one with a special adolescent ward for those between twelve and sixteen"

Even though it was a tale I'd told many times, the sudden appearance of tears surprised me.

"Hey, it's alright," Caroline said, "I promise you, all I want to do is hug you right now."

"It's just, Christ, I can still remember exactly how I felt when my parents left and I was alone. And hysterical. Reality had suddenly hit me and I couldn't believe where I was and what was happening and I wanted to be anywhere else than where I was. It was so so fucked up. And I wish I could describe it more eloquently, but all I can remember is the emotion of it all, the fear, the feeling that my life had been torn apart and I'd never recover," I continued, "Yet the funny thing is, once there, well, the next six months, they kind of were some of the best times of my life. Everyone was suffering there, and it helped to be surrounded by people who were as damaged as I was, that I fitted in just swell. And some of the darker times, it's weird, I've kind of blanked them out I guess, there's some bits I don't remember at all, like according to my Mum in one therapy session where my parents were in attendance I screamed 'I fucking hate you' at my step-father with such intent, such anger, that it shook him to his core. He was a pretty emotionless man, and terrible around children, a real Victorian father type, but he was genuinely upset. We kind of got on well after that, but then of course he died three years later. Timing never was his forte."

"And what about your actual Dad?"

"He died two months before I was born. Cancer, again. If my Mum wasn't still alive I'd worry I was somehow radioactive."

"Aw Ben. I'm so, so sorry."

"Nah, I mean it sucks, and there have been times where I've been bitter that I never got the chance to meet him, that I was never brought up by a man who cared about me. But without a doubt it could have been worse. At least I had a mum and dad, even if my step-father was shockingly rubbish."

"Mine too, for the record," Karoline replied, "And my mum as well. I've no idea why or how but Jesus they've malfunctioned."

I uttered an attempt at sympathy, a trite but well-meaning one.

"Ah, it is what it is, and I'll tell you more later," Karoline responded, "But first, if it's okay, I'd like to hear more about you, about the hospital, what it was like there. Though only if you want to."

"I do. And it was mostly a pretty calm and serene place. The fucking enormous pills they had me attempt to swallow each morning might have been responsible for that though. I mean there were incidents, being smashed around the head with a pool cue on my first evening wasn't a highlight, or a particularly great way to meet new people. And I'll never forget the night a friend and I helped this guy, Henry, secretly go through severe heroin withdrawal as he begged us not to tell anyone that he'd relapsed, and was terrified that he'd be thrown out for doing so. Not that we knew what to do other than hold him and hope he'd eventually become lucid. And with hindsight we should have sought out help, but we thought we were doing the right thing at the time."

"Of course," Karoline said, "And was he okay?"

"In the end, yeah. It was the longest night but eventually he fell asleep, and we never mentioned it again. It's so strange looking back, I was surrounded by anorexics, manic depressives and people whose arms were scarred by a horrendous number of failed suicide attempts, but outside of group therapy sessions we just tried to find some elements of fun in life. Which again was probably due to the tablets we were on, but the nurses were also incredibly kind, and I even met my first girlfriend there. Not that we exactly set the world on fire with our lust, it was the early nineties and in Surrey after all, so we only held hands and occasionally kissed on the lips, and the most exciting date we went on was a trip to the cinema to see The Mighty Ducks."

"That Emilio Estevez movie? Christ, you poor, poor thing," Karoline said, with a sympathetic smile.

"Ha, quite. But hey, I was still all kinds of over the moon to have a girlfriend. My geek friends considered me some kind of miracle worker. But then they didn't know I'd been in the hospital, at least not a mental one, I'd told them I'd had glandular fever and everyone bought it, thankfully. But like I said, it was often surprisingly a positive experience, and talking to the nurses and friends there more than anything else got me through my problems, and helped me come to terms with my OCD and agoraphobia and got me back to normal. At least as normal as I ever get. And I know I'm kind of casual about talking about all of this now, but for a long time afterwards I was still deeply ashamed at having been in such a place, and fucked up as to what had happened."

"Have you ever had any relapses? Or other mental health issues?" Karoline asked.

"I've suffered from depression a couple of times over the years. But I'm used to that happening now and head off to my GP whenever I'm low. Take anti-depressants for a time, curse the fact that it destroys my sex drive, and have some therapy if I've needed it. I have to admit that this last year wasn't the greatest either, until the whole magic thing came and saved the day."

"I can imagine. And I know where you're coming from on the depression front Ben, I've been there myself. Once I was terrifying close to suicide until a good friend all but moved in with me and forced me to get the help I needed."

"Ah, Life, it really is a bastard sometimes," I replied.

"It is. But hey, this way it means we're depression buddies. Or recovery buddies. Or something. And I've got to say, and this might be a completely unfair thing to think, but I don't really completely trust anyone who hasn't had a bit of a shit time of it during life. Not that I want anyone to have horrible things happen, but people who have been through darker days, I just connect with them more. Think they've got a more realistic take on existence."

"Thinking about it, most of my friends have been through the wringer more than once. Maybe we're drawn to each other somehow."

Silence fell briefly, as we found ourselves both staring in to the distance.

"Is there anything you'd like to talk about?" I eventually asked.

She told me everything. All the hidden away secrets that she feared I might be appalled by, but which only made me love her more. But I can't repeat them, I promised I wouldn't without her permission, they're her story and only she has the right to reveal them after all. So we'll skip to:

"Fuck. I'm so sorry you had to go through that," I replied.

"It's okay. I mean, it's not okay. So not okay. You know, one time a therapist actually said to me 'Well at least you're not a starving child in Africa,' and I was so fucked off with him, because I know that, I do, trust me, but that makes it worse, that I'm a spoilt first world idiot, but I'm sorry, things happened to me that I need help with, and why aren't you at least trying to help? I should have walked out that very minute and reported him, but I didn't have the energy."

"I understand that. I'd have been infuriated by the idiot as well. And hey, if you ever want me to turn that therapist into, I don't know, a cat or a rubbish fish or something, just say the word."

"Don't tempt me," Karoline said. "Or do tempt me, but later. Right now I just want to hold you. Without Leonard being present."

CHAPTER 4 - A WASTAGE OF TIME

Then she was gone.

Thankfully not permanently, but long enough that it hurt. On holiday with friends in Italy for a couple of weeks, I'd hinted that I'd like to join her but she said she'd all but abandoned her friends since she'd met me, and really should spend some time with them without my being by her side. Which I understood, but still, I missed her like hell, every day felt like a year, and one of the really shit ones like two thousand and seven. I tried to distract myself as much as I could, and over the course of the first few days I spent a couple of hours in Africa making lions as cuddly as kittens and annoying them with a laser pointer, before nipping to America to disturb a few folk by impersonating Bigfoot, though the version from the eighties movie *Harry and the Hendersons* of course, because he's the cutest. When back in London I made all of the bus timetable displays honest for an hour, so that they read things like "God knows, stuck in traffic, maybe in the next ten minutes? Can't promise anything to be honest" and "Will arrive in four minutes but not stop because I'm one of those bastard drivers."

Meanwhile on a particularly drunken night at Piccadilly Station I made all the mice jump on to the end of the platform and do a little song, it was only a verse and a half however as some idiot got his camera phone out and I had to end it abruptly. The poor things didn't even get the chance to sing the chorus to the terrible eighties atrocity "*Shaddap You Face.*" Though thinking about it, as they might have been cancelled for their dodgy accents maybe it wasn't such a bad thing.

But despite such stupid larks I couldn't stop thinking about her, and found myself missing her beyond words. These love related emotions were something I hadn't experienced in a painfully long time and I was all over the place, one minute I could lie back, wallowing in the happiness she'd brought me, but the next I'd be pacing frantically, unable to stop thinking about how much I wanted to be with her that very second. Hell, there was even the occasional flare of jealousy as I worried she might be seduced by some handsome Italian sex god, I'd seen photos, the country had at least seven of them. Most of the time I could persuade myself I was being irrational, but only most of the time, and I was all too aware of how annoying I was being as well and that I needed to dull my mind.

A few spells later and I had a new hybrid of marijuana that quietened my brain and made even the worst tv shows tolerable, I hadn't smoked since I was a student as I'd ended up becoming rather paranoid and oh so lazy, but it was fun at first. But only at first, as when I found myself laughing at something that Peter Andre had said on a panel show that he was guesting on I knew I'd gone too far, that I was risking damaging my brain in a permanent manner. Hence I found myself fidgety and anxious yet again, at least until I had one of those terrible idea type things I'd been warned about. Which led to this:

"I'm not Batman," I exclaimed in the deepest, roughest voice I could muster, having smoked forty cigarettes prior to leaving the house in the hope of achieving such an effect, "Batman and all related characters and elements are trademarks of and copyright

DC Comics and its parent company Warner Bros. Discovery and may not be copied or reproduced in any way."

And before you say it, yes, I've already made a variation on that joke a while back, but he didn't know that.

"What are you talking about?" said a guy with a knife and a jittery look in his eyes, "You look just like him."

"Perhaps, but I've made just enough modifications to the outfit, and to the Bat, er, I mean, my CarMobile not to get sued. Trust me. I don't screw around with multinational corporations. Anyway, that's not the point. The point is, put that knife down now."

"Give me one good reason. In fact, shut the fuck up, and get the fuck out of here."

"I'm afraid I can't do that," I replied, "Indeed quite the opposite. I'm here to make a difference. I'm here to clean scum like you off of the streets of London."

Understandably he didn't appreciate that, and hurtled towards me with the knife. Also understandably, he was quite surprised when the knife suddenly turned out to be made of jelly.

"What the hell?"

I punched him in the face, twice, and then kicked him hard in the shins. He cried out loud, and I cried out loud, as it turns out it bloody hurts hitting and kicking people. A quick spell to remedy that helped at least.

"Listen to me. Listen to me good," I said, "This is your one chance. If I ever see you out here on the streets again armed and ready to commit crime, that will be the last thing you ever do. I'm guessing you're desperate. I'm guessing your life is screwed up and a mess and you don't want to be doing these things. At least I hope that's the case. Either way, seek help. Turn to charities, hell turn to the Church, I don't care, just stop hurting others. And tell anyone you meet the same thing. Tell everyone. This is my city now, and I'm going to change it forever."

As you may have noticed, I hadn't quite got the dialogue down to a tee at that point, I'd read too many bad superhero comics in the past and was making it up on the spot, but hey, my intentions were good, I swear. George may have told me I couldn't use magic on a large scale, but he'd never said that I couldn't try to help others in tiny other ways, ways that people would assume were being carried out by a normal person at that. This way I could then look back at my life and think, I made a difference, if only to a few people, at least this life wasn't completely wasted. I wasn't always a bit of a useless twat, as one Grandfather who I hate to this day once said.

What I hadn't expected was how hard it was to actually be in the right place at the right time when it came to stopping crime, the first couple of nights I'd patrolled the streets, invisible and leaping from one roof to the next often in the hope I'd come across a robbery or some sort of violence, but didn't see or hear even a hint of wrongdoing. A little online research helped, and during weekends when lurking around some of the shittier nightclubs I managed to stop a few fights, but it was all pretty minor stuff, as London didn't have any super villains. At least of the non-political variety, because oh yeah, I know how to do satire baby, albeit not in a very subtle manner.

Despite this word began to get around that some idiot was dressing up as a costumed vigilante, but no one knew if it was true or if it was just another urban myth. When Karoline returned from her holiday we picked up where we left off, all of my idiocy assuaged as she hadn't fallen madly in love with anyone else on holiday and for some reason still seemed to really like me, and initially I stopped going out late at night in the aforementioned garb, indeed I considered at one point stopping completely. Yet two weeks after her return I found myself craving the excitement, it had become addictive, and soon even on the nights that she stayed over I found myself heading out once I was sure she was fast asleep.

Most of the time very little happened when patrolling the streets, a few muggings were prevented, the odd fight was interrupted, but I still felt like it was worthwhile, that at least due to my existence a few people's lives would be improved for the better, and I hadn't exactly been able to say that previously.

Nothing vaguely interesting lasts forever however, as the old saying goes, and late one Sunday morning everything changed. The previous night had at first been like most of the others as I'd been randomly wandering around some of the murkier parts of South London and not come across anything illegal for all too long, when I finally saw two men outside of a pub lay into a seemingly innocent passer-by, who was at this point bleeding in ways which sickened. I swooped down upon them and shoved the first man into the side of the van, knocking him out cold. The second turned around just in time to see my fist crush his nose. He stumbled back a bit, then regained his composure, and attempted to assault me. I'm sure it would have hurt like a bastard if I hadn't previously cast a force field spell, and so I just stood there dramatically, as if all he had done was an attempt at a tickle.

"That the best you can muster?" I asked him, before punching him again, twice. Unfortunately he was something of a hard bastard, and seemingly used to being hurt, and it didn't faze him that much. He attempted to rugby tackle me to the floor, but bounced off, and at this point I realised I'd have to use far more force than I'd ever previously had to. So I cast a spell to make the impact of my blows twice as powerful, and knocked him to the ground, and now he was kind enough to be out like a light. With two unconscious men on the floor next to me I wasn't quite sure what to do, but decided the best option was to handcuff them together, tie them up with rope and strap them to a nearby lamp post, leaving a note for the police stating that both had tried to kill someone. I'd no idea if it would be taken seriously, or if it would legally stand up in court, but I hoped the victim of the attack would cooperate at least. Unfortunately when I bent down and gently shook him he only groaned, and it became apparent as to just how hurt he was. Hence I cast a spell that healed the worst of his wounds, took out his mobile phone and called for an ambulance and the police, and left, thinking I'd done as much as I could and that was that.

Sometimes I think *Now That's What I Call Naive 19* should be the soundtrack to my life, as it wasn't over in the slightest. Someone from a building opposite the pub had filmed the whole thing and within half an hour it was posted on you tube, and spread like the wildest of furious fire. I didn't know that until the next morning of course, having returned home in the early hours, crept back into bed and fallen to sleep within seconds, and it wasn't until around ten o'clock the next day when Karoline gently tapped me on my arm that I woke up, and noticed she looked concerned.

"Did you know you're famous?" she asked, but in my bleary eyed state I had no idea what she was going on about.

"I found your costume. The one which looks awfully like something a caped crusader might wear."

"Oh. I... I was going to tell you... But you'd been away and-" I replied, trailing off at the end.

"It's okay," she said, "Though I wish you'd said something, and I don't quite understand why you didn't."

"I thought... I thought you'd laugh. I thought you'd think it was ridiculous."

"Well, it is," Karoline replied, "But it's kind of fantastic too. I'd been kind of hoping, at least, I don't know, I mean, fuck it Ben, you're a magician. You've got crazily cool powers. And I'd hoped you might use them for good at some point or another, and not just on yet another spell which breaks the world record for the most amount of calories in a cake."

"That was kind of my thinking too," I told her, "But, er, what do you mean I'm famous?"

"You've gone viral," she replied, "The assault that took place last night, and your involvement in stopping it, someone filmed it. It's on all the news channels, they're loving it."

"So could you tell it was me?" I asked.

"No," she replied, "Don't worry, no one knows it's you. I wasn't in any way sure initially either, but I just had a nagging feeling you might have been involved. Then while casually digging about in your wardrobe my suspicions were confirmed. But the media just think some crazy bloke's dressing up as Batman and doing the whole vigilante thing."

"It's not Batman though. It's, um, just a bit like him. ManMan or something."

"Whatever, the net's gone crazy. Twitter's insane right now, and 99% of it is positive. Which I don't think has ever happened before."

After that, everything became a lot more complicated, and ended way too soon. And somewhat depressingly violent crime suddenly increased as various all round shitty characters hoped I'd attempt to stop them in the middle of committing an offence, and have the chance to face off against me. Soon there were another three videos online, and I even featured in a five minute snippet on the ITN London news where the Mayor Of London pleaded with me to stop due to the harm I was causing.

"I bet Batman never had to put up with this shit," Karoline said, but soon regretted doing so when I explained it had been an often repeated plot point in the films and the comics, rambling away for ages as it was a storyline I'd always hated.

"My Dad told me never to date a nerd," she replied, laughing, "Then again he was a bit of one himself. Hmmm. Really don't want to think too much about that."

"The thing is," I said, "I know this has to stop, that I'm already in danger of exposing myself." This made her laugh even more.

"Sigh, not like that. Unless you want me to. But no, I mean, well you know what I mean. I don't want people to get hurt just so that someone has a chance to take a swing at me. But I feel I should go out with a bang, not just disappear."

Karoline smiled. "That seems fair enough to me," she said, "So how about this one last time you head out with a sidekick?"

The first outfit I designed for her gained me a slap on the cheek, albeit a soft one. Her words stung more. "Christ you're a sad fuck sometimes, though I suppose it was my fault for letting one of your fantasies come true. But please redesign this without it revealing 98% of my cleavage, thank you very much." On the fifth go I eventually came up with something she tolerated.

"So what's the plan Bat- Sorry, Man-Man" she asked, meaning I didn't have to repeat that annoying copyright nonsense once again.

"I figure we need to track down some real bastard and prevent him from making money from misery," I replied.

"Ah, so you need to find our own personal Joker," Karoline said, "A Lex Luthor, a, I don't know, who does Aquaman hate?"

"Black Manta."

"It's so sad that you know that."

"Hey, he kidnapped Aquaman's two year old son and that eventually led to his marriage falling apart."

"You need to stop now."

"I know," I admitted.

"Anyhow, you need a nemesis, an arch villain to take down," Karoline said, "Think about it, who do you hate most in the world?"

I paused, for a short while, and then said "Peter Stringfellow."

"Ha. Okay. Not quite what I was expecting. But okay, how come? I mean I know he owns a lot of strip clubs but surely that just makes him bleakly exploitative rather than demonically evil?"

"Oh, you don't know the real Stringfellow," I uttered in the most melodramatic way that I could.

"Go on," Karoline replied.

"You see, a couple of years ago I was minding my own business, queuing up to buy a magazine in WH Smith at Victoria Station, when, outrageously, he pushed in front of me in the queue."

"That bastard!" Karoline teased.

"Oh, if only it were that alone. Because a few weeks ago when I mentioned this story online, I found out from an old friend that he'd done the same thing to him at WH Smith in Heathrow!"

"Truly the worst of all crimes," Karoline replied.

"I know, right? He treats it like his own personal playground, or, er, his own personal newsagent at least, without a care in the world for anyone else. Plus, you know, the whole strip club thing, and sure, sure I know there are some women who feel empowered by it and enjoy the money and avoid the downsides, but I'm guessing they're in the minority. Even if it's sixty forty it's a pretty bad outcome."

"I'm so with you, except, he's not technically a criminal, is he? Just, in your view, someone who is a bit scuzzy?"

"Can't we bend the rules a little?"

Karoline just smiled at me.

"Okay, fine, I guess it's true that he never has done anything illegal, and I'm not just stressing this for legal reasons in case anyone is recording our conversation and printed it somewhere, or if I later recount it all in an overlong and annoying way."

"So someone else then," Karoline said "There must be someone you really despise. That you know is a dirty fuckbird who makes money out of other people's misery. And no, before you suggest it, not David Cameron."

"Yeah, as much as I'd like to, he's a bit too high profile. Hmmm.

This is harder than I thought it'd be. I've kind of got nothing. I mean, sure, there are plenty of heads of corporations and members of the Royal Family and all those pieces of excrement, but that would not only put us on the radar, but on the front page of every newspaper tomorrow. And I'm simply just not as up on the shadowy crime bosses of old London town as I used to be," I said.

"But you could be," Karoline said. Looking at me like I was an absolute idiot. Which I was.

"I guess a mixture of spells would make interrogating people pretty easy."

"No, I meant Google. Just do some flipping googling. It'll give us somewhere to start at the very least."

Alas Karoline had overestimated how easy something like this might be, as it took quite a few days and several false starts until we found a suitable target. Beforehand much of our searching online lead us down a number of garden paths which didn't even have pretty flowers to keep us entertained, as perhaps unsurprisingly it became apparent that people talked absolute nonsense ninety seven point two percent of the time, and boasted and exaggerated and point blank lied about their exploits. But eventually we discovered the existence of Andrew Fisher, a man who was apparently quite the turd in human form. Drugs, human trafficking, prostitution, if there was a human atrocity taking place in the city he was likely to be involved, and on one particular forum there were tales of his exploits that deeply appalled, that suggested he really should be avoided at all costs, but if, and only if, you were stupid enough to want to contact him then there were ways.

The easiest of which seemed to be by speaking to an intermediary, most of whom hung out in a strip pub called The Honeypot in Camberwell, which we'd soon find out was one of the bleakest places on Earth. It really was the kind of place you'd hope wouldn't exist anymore in these supposedly enlightened times, but oh Jesus so it does. Outside it appeared to be a slightly run down but mostly normal pub, but inside the decor looked like it was fifty odd years old, and posters adorned the back wall of racist comedians who are thankfully now dead. At the bar there were only three beers on tap, and the selection of spirits behind it all had brand names which suggested a trip to Eastern Europe had occurred, I'd certainly never seen them on sale anywhere else in this country. A quick transformation spell meant that Karoline and I both looked like seedy old men in our fifties, and the certain change in genitals was something Karoline did not find appealing at all, but she realised the need to not look out of place in such an establishment, and we were both pretty sure that apart from those who were employed to work there no female had entered it on purpose in years.

After walking in and our eyes had become accustomed to the gloom I noticed that there were only four customers present, while at the back of the badly lit room was a small stage and a woman in her thirties was taking off her clothes. No one was watching her, presumably having seen such nudity countless times before, and she looked on the verge of tears, broken, trapped and quite possibly unable to escape.

The barman was a brick shithouse of a man, except a brick shithouse that giants defecated in, and normally I'd have run a mile upon seeing him, if not a couple of hundred. The four patrons currently in residence turned and looked at us as we entered, not saying a word, but expressing a very obvious "Yeah, you can fuck off right now" vibe, which they'd clearly practiced many times before, they'd got it down to a tee. Ignoring them I headed to the bar, and the barman said nothing as I ordered two pints of lager, but reluctantly served us and more silence ensued. It appeared it was up to me to break the ice.

"Sorry, Gentlemen, I don't wish to bother you in any way but I'm trying to track down Andrew Fisher. I, er, went to school with him." Inevitably Karoline laughed, yet the four men declined to follow suit. One of them stood up, introducing himself as Graham Candle. He was wearing a suit that must have been bought decades ago, and it looked like that was the last time he'd bathed or showered too.

"Fuck off son, if you know what's good for you."

"I don't!" I replied, truthfully.

"John, Dave, Simon, looks like this idiot here-" Graham began to say, and perhaps it would have been entertaining to let this pathetic man speak and threaten and express his violent desires, but I'd been in this pub for far too long as it was, too long of course being more than two seconds, so I cast a couple of spells including one which forced them to tell the truth, and soon all four were spilling the beans. Indeed way too many beans, cans of the bloody stuff, and no one needed to know about Graham's sexual preferences and lust for sploshing, that's for sure, but that's the problem with magic, the spells tended to be rather broad in nature and you can't just get someone to tell you exactly what you wanted and nothing more. At least in the end we learnt that we needed to go to Angelic Dreams, a strip club in Soho that Fisher covertly ran, but before leaving I cast a spell to make them forget we'd ever existed. Along with one where they'd be violently sick if they ever said anything sexist or racist, which probably was a little stupid of me as there was a good chance they'd be vomiting for the rest of their lives. Heading out of the door Karoline sighed.

"Great. First that, now a West End strip club. Tonight's like your greatest fantasy ever coming true, isn't it?"

"Half and half," I replied, "I promise you that I find strip pubs and clubs truly depressing, but on the flip side, I'm out and about doing the vigilante thing with a woman I'm falling madly in love with, and together we're going to beat the shite out of a criminal monster, so life could be worse."

"Oh you," she replied, smiling now, but notably not saying that she was falling in love with me too, something I'd obsess about later that night for far too long a time.

One quick flight across London and there we were in the centre of the capital. Soho had changed an enormous amount in the fifteen odd years I'd lived in the city, and though there were fewer strip clubs in the area there were still more than anyone could ever really need. I'd genuinely never been into one prior to this evening, which no girlfriend had ever believed me about, but I couldn't think of anything more bleak and depressing. On a purely selfish note, when I'm single I don't want to be near incredibly attractive naked women of the type I will never carnally know, it seems a ridiculously masochistic thing to do. Plus, you know, the objectification of women bothered greatly as well. All of which meant that I'd not heard of Angelic Dreams, but

I don't think Karoline could have been more delighted when it turned out to be an all male gay strip club. Ah, so much mocking took place then. After about ten minutes of it, she decided we should carry on with the plan.

"We can go about this two different ways," I said, "One, we can go in as paying customers and just sneak about, or two, we can put on our costumes, enter via the back door and see what we can find out via the use of shouting and punching."

"I prefer the latter idea," Karoline replied, "It's about time we started doing something illegal quite frankly." One quick transformation spell later we were in our vigilante outfits, and we approached the back entrance to the venue. A couple of the men were smoking outside of it.

"Um, hi," I said.

"Afraid you've got the wrong night," the shorter of the men replied, "Fantasy night is Sunday."

"It's okay," Karoline said, "We're a treat for the boss. Paid for by one his most appreciative associates. Trust me, the things he can do with his tongue will amaze, and my arse is all kinds of cute too."

"If you say so," The taller of the men chuckled, "Who paid for all this then?" he asked. That was an unexpected roadblock.

"Um, Jimmy," I replied. I mean, chances are, right?

"Never heard of him," he responded, and gave the other guy a quizzical look, "Jimmy who?"

"Jimmy... Jamima?" I all but muttered, realising I really should have thought this through beforehand.

"Yeah, right," He replied, "Look, I've no idea what you two think you're doing, but I'll very politely suggest you should leave now, please? And if you don't I can also be very impolite. Positively uncouth, in fact."

"Yeah, yeah," said Karoline before turning to me, "Can we just cut to the chase now?"

So I did, transforming my right hand into a giant teapot, and knocking both men out with a single spin of my spout, before changing it back into its previously disappointing meaty appendage.

"I take it you turned off the CCTV before doing that?" Karoline asked, "So you're not once again going to be a YouTube star?"

Being an idiot I of course hadn't, but a brief invisibility spell and a bit of mooching around the building led to it being switched off, and the digital recording wiped. Despite being invisible it was still a pain in the arse a lot of the time when trying to dash around too, you mostly have to fly next to the ceiling so that you don't bump into people, and in this venue that meant also avoiding the tackiest of chandeliers. But once I'd dealt with everything we found Fisher's office on the third floor of the building, though frustratingly it was empty.

At least that gave us a chance to look around, and immediately I noticed it had one of those expensive see through mirrors so that he could watch the club without being seen, and which I immediately planned to break in a melodramatic moment the first chance I got. The room itself was otherwise sparsely decorated, bar for a small brown bouncy castle in the corner. That should have rung alarm bells, but I stupidly presumed it was some weird sex thing. Or great sex thing, who am I to judge, and I planned to create one of my own when we arrived home to find out. Bar that there was a single couch facing the mirror, and a bookshelf on the side of the room, and using x-ray vision I tracked down a small safe behind a painting of a unicorn fucking a centaur while a Minotaur looked on in a disinterested manner. That was another sign that Fisher wasn't the most normal of individuals that I should have paid more attention to, but I was distracted by what I hoped would be incredibly exciting things inside the safe. Yet it was a bit disappointing to be honest, I'd hoped for something a bit more from a major criminal, so we could have one of those "Whoa, look at all of that gold, and the mountains of heroin. I mean, should we? Just a tiny sample?" moments, but it wasn't to be, just a small amount of money and a few wraps of cocaine, plus a collection of papers which were written in legalese and so meant nothing to me, but Karoline believed suggested ownership of a large amount of properties across the country, along with a lot of different bank accounts. I had no idea if burning them would change anything, but I figured it couldn't be a bad idea, fire is always fun, so I closed the safe and then made it internally combust.

Then we sat about for a bit. Ages actually, which was quite the annoyance, to the extent that I was starting to wonder if we were going to have to return another night, but thankfully Andrew Fisher finally turned up. But then you probably guessed that would happen, as I try not to tell dull anecdotes about times I went somewhere and nothing happened too often.

As it happens we were making out on the couch at the time when upon hearing voices I grabbed Karoline's hand and turned us invisible, before slamming us against the ceiling. Fisher entered, gossiping blandly on his phone, the kind of thing that's not even worth reporting as it was so dull. He was wearing a smart, expensive suit and had slicked back black hair, and looked quite the young professional, I'd hoped for a traditional gangster look with at least two or three cigars on the go, but his appearance reminded me of a city banker and he certainly didn't look threatening in the slightest. Once he finally finished his phone call I waited for him to take a seat, and then after floating down to the floor and walking over to the door so that he couldn't make a speedy exit, I made us visible.

"I'm here to take you down," I said, woefully attempting a menacing voice once again.

"Oh. Hello. I'm Andrew Fisher," he said, standing up and extending his hand. "And you might be?"

"I'm your worst dream come true," I replied.

"And I'm your worst dream come true's girlfriend," Karoline interjected.

"You certainly are something," Andrew replied, "It has been a far too long a time since my day's been brightened up like this."

He was a little too overconfident for my liking, and charming, too, I was supposed to be hauling him out of there as a bruised bundle, but instead he was making casual small talk.

"So do you do this often?" he asked.

"Occasional Saturda- I mean, shut up. And listen. We know who you are. How you make your money. We're here to end that."

He laughed. Which was sign number four that I'd messed up once more.

"Ah. No. I hate to break it to you, but that's not how this is going to pan out. I've seen your clips on the news and it did make me smile, but you really have no idea what you're facing now. But because I like you I'm going to give you an option to live. Walk away. Now. Go. Your costumes mean I've no idea who you really are, and apart from the odd fancy dress party I'll be happy to never see you again. But if you stay, all I can say is that there is no possible outcome other than a negative one for you."

Now Karoline looked a tad nervous, but I had to hope he was bluffing.

"No, I think you have no idea what you're dealing with," I responded, sounding less threatening by the second, and even slightly petty.

"I can only think of two scenarios," Andrew replied, "One, you're costumed vigilantes who have found out about the kind of man I am, and want to put me in prison, which would truly be the best one, personally I'm hoping for that outcome. Or two, you're magicians and here to kill me. There's one very easy way to find out, too." With that, electricity sparked from his hands, and shot across the room towards me, I'd already cast a protection spell earlier that night, but it still hurt like a bastard.

"Fuck," was my ever predictable response.

"Ah, boo, I was hoping this wouldn't be the case, between you and me I took a pill a couple of hours ago, and I'm really not in a murderous mood. Ah, it is what it is I suppose, and it always was only a matter of time. You're the first since I've set up in London, too, but over the years, ha, so many corpses, it gets a bit embarrassing after a while."

Karoline pressed her hand against my back and whispered into my ear "I think we might've screwed up just a tiny bit."

Which didn't help with my already dwindling confidence.

"I'm surprised you didn't notice something was up as well," Andrew said, "I mean how many normal criminals have their own bouncy castle? And one made out of chocolate at that?" This made me feel even stupider. I mean I really should have been curious about the bite marks at the very least.

"I guessed it was an unusual sex fetish," I mumbled.

"Nah, not my sort of thing," Fisher said, "I have more of a roller skating kink. Ever since Boogie Nights. I'm not alone either, one club I'm a member of is shockingly busy."

"I'll have to have a search for it," I commented, to which Karoline muttered things I shan't repeat.

"Right, enough of this small talk, let's see what you can do then," Andrew shouted, seemingly having swapped places with us as he was now the one speaking in an overdramatic manner and clearly rather enjoying it.

Out of nowhere five upsettingly muscular men appeared, all looking rather like Hulk Hogan in his prime, albeit thankfully without the terrible mullet, and armed with machetes so huge they could easily slice a statue in half. A big statue at that, maybe even the one of all those pretty horses at Piccadilly Circus. Fortunately, finally, my brain clicked into comic book mode, and I knew I had to do the utterly unpredictable to get out of this situation alive. Luckily my wasted youth included reading everything from *The Fantastic Four* to the adventures of *Arm Fall-Off Boy*, so I had a lot to draw on, not that I could see the latter's skills coming in handy any time soon but the former definitely would. So as all five of the muscular men ran at me I became elasticised, albeit with fists of gold and dagger like fingers attached to my stretchy wrists that moved at an impressive rate. I decapitated two of them before they'd even begun to understand what was happening, and then threw two more at the wall. Bones broke, organs failed, and now I only had one to deal with. Unfortunately he'd had plenty of time to get into a position where he could slice through my arm, and didn't hesitate to do so. I howled in pain, shocked that my force field had failed me while cursing my stupidity at not turning off my pain receptors once again just in case, which was starting to become a rather irritating habit as blood splattered everywhere, including over Karoline, who was rather understandably panicking at this point. But I grabbed my lost limb and stuck it back on before transforming into a gigantic crab, using my pincers to cut the final Hogan impersonator in half, and though I'd lost a fair amount of blood another spell soon sorted that out.

"Well done, well done, that was some impressive work," Andrew said, "And I hope you do believe me when I say that I would love to do this all night long, I haven't flexed the old magical muscles that much in a fair while, but sadly, and I do really regret this, but I've got things to do. There's a slight issue with an old colleague and a missing shipment of cocaine, it's very frustrating to have to deal with such nonsense, but if I don't my reputation would suffer. Not that you need to know all of this of course, but I simply want you to know that I have enjoyed meeting you, and in other circumstances I could happily have made your deaths last for hours. But now's the time to call it a day."

The next twenty seconds Karoline would later refer to as a weird psychedelic and psychotic blur, as we were transforming constantly, ever trying to outwit the other. He became a gigantic sword with a demonic head and tiny little legs and flung himself at my all too fleshy body, but I transformed into a diamond which fortunately saved my life, and then into a burning fireball, as I'd hoped that melting his flesh might finish him off. But alas it was not to be as he then turned into the coldest of ocean waters and filled the whole room with himself, well, bar a small meaty bag of organs in the corner that was presumably keeping him alive and also contained a mouth so that he could still cast spells. To prevent the two of us from drowning I became Big Fuck Off Salt Man, a superhero who I don't think existed previously, in the hope I'd absorb Fisher's watery state, it kind of began working but then I think he became bored and so turned into a Hoover. That was a weird sensation, I can tell you, I was almost fully inside of him when I changed into a ball of gherkin flavoured snot - hey, I was panicking, okay - which he thankfully all but choked on before spitting me across the room. One moment I was bouncing off the ceiling, the next I was hitting the giant glass mirror and smashing through it, and I was briefly pissed off as my plan had been to dramatically throw him through it and not the other way round.

It was only a fleeting thought however, before I resumed being terrified that I was about to die, as he was making it more than apparent that he was more than capable of doing that as I landed on the stage and heard bones crack. I could hear him laughing, which was quite surprising given the amount of shouting and screaming coming from the male strippers and their customers as they ran out of the building, and as he stood by the mostly shattered window I really wasn't sure what I could or should do, until Karoline snuck up and shoved him as hard as she could, causing him to fall through the remains of the window to the stage, and for a second I had a fleeting moment of hope that he might not get up. Sadly the spoilsport did.

"Ow, that bloody hurt," he muttered, touching the back of his head and noticing it was bleeding. "I'm impressed. Have to say, never had anyone last this long before." He then stood up, and walked to the centre of the stage. Grabbed the pole. Slithered up and down it a bit.

"Now you know, we could kill each other, or we could have a dance off!" Which I know is the kind of nonsense that normally comes out of my mouth, but it genuinely emerged from Andrew's, and I started to think that if he wasn't a murdering bastard who profited from the misery of thousands that we could have been friends. Until he giggled again.

"Sorry, just fucking with you. I am going to have to kill you. Unless. Hmmm. You're really quite skilful on the magic front, aren't you? Full of ideas. Bit bizarre, but then I like that. I don't suppose you'd be interested in working with me? The businesses I run, they're a mere annoyance, a way to generate an awful amount of material I can blackmail people with. I have plans, you see. Oh, it will be somewhat astonishing."

"It's tempting," I lied, "But no. Call me crazy, but you make your money through human misery, through drugs and sex trafficking and I've always thought that people who do that aren't something to aspire to."

"Those morals will kill you one day. Probably today, as it goes," Fisher said with a grin, "I'll give you one last chance though, are you definitely sure you want me to murder you today?"

It was a good question, I'd not been murdered before but I'd seen it happen on tv and it never looked fun. Of course there was the possibility that I could be responsible for his death, but that felt doubtful, I was way over my head here, and the sight of Karoline running out of the door of Fisher's office only seemed to back that up.

"Sorry. I probably should lie to you, say I was on board. But I can't."

"That's okay, I'd have been able to tell anyway, I came up with the perfect lie detecting spell ages ago."

"Sounds cool," I said, hoping to buy Karoline the time to get out of the building, to escape with her life at least, "I don't suppose you'd share it with me?"

"It'd be a bit pointless, wouldn't it?" Fisher asked, "Knowing it for a few seconds, then dying?"

"You've got a good point," I replied, "But it was worth a shot."

"Not really. Anyway, enough wasting time, your girlfriend will get away soon if I don't kill you and then chase after her."

I was starting to really dislike how smart a man he was, and that sensation grew as his body lit up like a burning sun. I was blinded within seconds but quickly regrew my eyes, and then I replicated his spell. Launched myself at him, and we became two fiery forms desperately trying to decimate each other. Soon the building burst into flames, and for a second it felt like time had stopped, and everything looked so beautiful. Pure fire tearing the world apart. Then I felt myself changing back, he'd somehow made me utterly human again, and I felt his hands around my neck, choking me, and I couldn't speak, which meant there were no spells I could cast to save my life. This was the end, and such a bloody stupid one at that, one which could have been avoidable if it wasn't for the dumb ideas I insisted on carrying out. Turning back into his human form as I started to black out, I heard him mutter "Well that was easy, I'm almost a little disappointed," as his hand transformed into a blade, but just as he thrust it towards my poor, lovely brain his head exploded, leaving behind the kind of mess you really don't want to see on a full stomach.

I didn't have time to be confused as George stepped over his body, picked me up, and carried me out of the burning building. Repaired me. Told me I owed Karoline a great deal of thanks as she had called him, hence him saving the day with seconds to spare. But he didn't look happy about it, and as he flew us home he didn't respond to anything I said, and only spoke four further words just prior to his leaving. "I'll be summoning you." It was as ominous as it sounds.

Before he did that, Karoline and I had a number of uncomfortable conversations. She partially blamed herself for what had happened, was aware that she'd gotten carried away as well, that she'd encouraged me to involve her with this magical mayhem. Yet at the same time she was understandably slightly traumatised.

"We nearly died Ben," she said, "You nearly died. Were seconds away from death, from what George told me"

"I know," I said, as she wasn't wrong and there was no claiming otherwise.

"And from what you told me, one day, out of the blue, George is going to call you again and ask for your help and chances are you might not survive it." She was close to tears now. Reality had hit home, and hit hard, leaving a sod load of psychological bruising.

"I'm sorry," was all I could think of saying. "I should never have involved you in all of this. I didn't think it through."

"No," Karoline responded, "I mean, no, it's not that, I'm glad I know you and what you've shown me and what I've discovered about reality and everything, it has been amazing. But Jesus, this is also really fucked up Ben. I need time to think. Work out how to cope. Work out if I can cope. Is that okay?"

How could I say no? Because it was, of course it was, but at the same time, Christ did the dark thoughts kick back in, dark ideas I thought I'd no longer suffer from. And no manner of magic could make up for what I thought I might be losing. Turns out I valued love over magic, that I wasn't the shallow shit I'd suspected myself of being, and even though she hadn't made any decisions I still fell into the deepest pit of despair, the kind of size which would tear through the planet and emerge on the other side. The following hours and days saw me only lie in bed, with enough tears shed to fill, well, an ocean would be an exaggeration but I have a suspicion that a decent size paddling pool would have been filled to the brim, which might not sound like a lot but I've done the maths and it's still a bucket load of crying. It was a pity party of the kind that even Sylvia Plath might have found excessive and despite everything suicidal thoughts began flirting through my mind again. Fortunately I was able to dismiss them reasonably easily, persuade myself that things could be fixed between us, but Jesus was my mind doing its best to push me over the edge. Just like the good / bad old days. I'd presumed that magic was the cure to my mental health issues but it was clearly only a plaster, one that fell off and let my emotions bleed all over the frickin' place all too easily. I should have done something about that. Sought out help, and I thought about calling my doctor, but what could I say? Okay, I could mainly talk about my relationship problems and how I hated the unpredictable mood swings, but the fact that I might only have a year left to live and that could be the cause of my relationship ending wasn't exactly something I could easily explain. So I did nothing. Stupid, stupid nothing.

Four days later she called, told me that this was something that was going to take a long time to adjust to, and it really wasn't the way she wanted to live her life and she was terrified as to what might happen to me in the future, and yet, yet, yet at the same time she'd fallen in love with me. Couldn't imagine a life without me. I told her I felt the same way, and so we both did our best to live in the moment. Love in the moment. And try not to think about what might happen. Because all of the best relationships are built on denial, right? Right?

During this time I couldn't help but worry about what George's response was going to be as well, and a few days later after Karoline and I had resolved our issues I got the call. I'd spent those days in a strange place, relieved to be back with Karoline but also fairly panicky as to what George's response was going to be, Karoline had done her best to calm me down but I knew I'd made a huge mistake. Quite possibly of the "This is going to haunt me for the rest of my life, which might be a very short time indeed" variety.

When he contacted me George said very little but gave me an address in Chinatown, and instructions on how to find his actual location. So on a wet, shitty Thursday evening I found myself entering a small Chinese restaurant that thrived on all you can eat buffets, walking through the kitchen without anyone seeming to care, and reaching a door at the back. Opening it, I discovered that long, oddly disturbing and dark corridor once more, and after I knocked twice upon the door George opened it and I walked into exactly the same drinking establishment. The only change was that the original barman was absent, replaced by a nervous looking forty year old woman, who as soon as I entered walked away into a back room, and George and I were alone.

"Look, George, I'm so sorry," I said, "I didn't know he was a magician, I didn't know-"

"Please be quiet and let me speak," George replied, "Now let me tell you, in any other situation, you wouldn't be here. I'd have wiped your memory, removed your abilities, returned you to the life you used to live. This hasn't been easy either, a lot of cleaning up has taken place, a lot of conversations have been had, a lot of lies have been told."

"George-" I attempted to say.

"It's okay. It hasn't been a complete waste of my time. in Andrew Fisher you could not have chosen a worse person to pick on, yet you were actually incredibly lucky. This is a once in a lifetime kind of luck too, so never, ever do anything this stupid again or they'll be nothing that I can do to protect you. But fortune has smiled on you. Laughed like hell, if anything. You see, Fisher was on a lot of radars, and he'd made a lot of enemies, but he'd also been pretty meticulous in obtaining evidence against anyone who might want to dispose of him. But for a while many people have wished he was no longer around anymore, and that has now occurred, and everything he had on anyone went up in flames. So not too many questions are being asked. Some, oh yes, some were asked, but not as many as there could have been, and while no one has any idea who the hell did this, hardly anyone really wants to know either. And those that do have been persuaded to look the other way."

"I had no idea, I swear, I just got carried away."

" Yes, I warned you that would happen, and I knew you wouldn't listen, but even then I could never have guessed you'd screw up this badly. Kid, you've got to be more careful. I get it, I did some stupidly silly things the first few years, but the world was a different place then. Undeniably still rather insane, but a hell of a lot safer. And it's not going to be like that again anytime soon, so you must now be really goddamn cautious. And don't do anything like this ever again."

"Of course I won't. And I truly am sorry. I just wanted to make a difference. But it seems like that's not really possible. At least not without risking everything."

"Sadly not," George replied, "And don't think you're the first to try. Back in sixty six, even I donned a cowl and cape one night, but, ah, it's a long story, and I've not the time for it. Now, I need your help with a little something, and perhaps those skills you've recently picked up might come in handy."

"Okay," I replied, "What can I do?"

"Another magician, a feisty bastard of a man if ever there was one. I need his help, yet it's possible that he's gone over to the other side. We need to track him down, see what's what."

"I've got to admit, after everything I'm surprised you really want my assistance," I replied.

"Ah, there's the rub, he knows every magician by sight, he's made it in his interest to do so. If he saw me or any of my associates, one of us would end up dead. At least if the rumours are true. But you, you're an unknown quantity. No one knows you exist apart from me."

I don't think he meant it to sound as unsettling as it did. Or maybe that was exactly his intention.

"So what do you need me to do?" I asked.

"We need to go to Birmingham," he said, "And find out whether or not Orson Welles is evil."

CHAPTER 5 - BIRMINGHAM

"Oh fuck off."

"No, no, really," George replied.

"You're telling me that Orson Welles is a magician? And an alive one, too?" I asked.

"Yup."

"Christ."

After the last few months, I thought I couldn't be surprised by anything anymore. Apparently not.

Explanations then took place, which went something like this: Back in Nineteen Seventy-Nine the well-known filmmaker, actor and charlatan Orson Welles became a magician, albeit slightly by force. Over the decades he'd collected a number of historical artefacts which were of the kind that magicians didn't want to enter the public domain, objects which had been imbued with magic over a period of time and which in the right hands were ridiculously powerful. Welles had supposedly hidden them all over the world, along with enormously complicated arrangements so that if anything were to ever happen to him, or if he didn't behave in a very specific manner, they would be released into public hands and the whole world would be made aware of magic. It was a long, long game which paid off eventually, and after blackmailing his way into becoming rather powerful. Six years later it was announced that he had died, but of course he'd faked it all, made a bloated corpse for the authorities to bury and afterwards via the use of several of artefacts he'd created he rejuvenated his entire body and became a much younger version of himself. Since then the relationship between George and Orson had been capricious, at times passionately friendly, at others passionately passionate, but what happened upon their last meeting was only hinted at, and for the last decade Welles had seemingly disappeared. Indeed it wasn't until the previous week that he'd turned up back on the scene, which George was concerned by, presuming something was amiss.

My response was a horrendous fan boy moment which may have involved clapping. I'll save us both the embarrassment of describing it, yet afterwards George looked at me like I was a twit, and I couldn't argue with him. But you see, I'd always loved Orson Welles. For his films, sure, his version of *The Trial* is deeply disturbing, with Anthony Perkins turning in a performance that's even better than the one in *Psycho*, and Welles' *Macbeth* burns so brightly you can almost forgive the dodgy accents found in the film, and hey, maybe Orson had only met some Scottish folk with speech impediments before directing it. Plus *Citizen Kane* is, um, well really good. Incredibly important, not as fun as *Return of the Killer Tomatoes* but it's one of those films you can't help but admire, and note how much it changed cinema. Yet while I enjoyed his work enormously, the man himself, that's what truly astounded me. The life he'd led, the lies, the mischief and the myth making, he created a character that no one will ever forget. There's an amazing book, *This Is Orson Welles* by Welles and fellow filmmaker Peter Bogdanovich which are transcripts of conversations the men had over the years, but what I love about it the most is that after each chat Bogdanovich would type them up, deliver them to Welles, who the next day would post them back, often altered outrageously or now completely fictitious. Reading the book you could never quite know what was true and what wasn't, but all of them were delightfully funny or point blank bizarre stories from the kind of inventive mind that never failed to impress. So to say that I wanted to meet him, man, it was crazy. You just don't get to meet your dead heroes often enough, after all.

I told Karoline about George's request and she was a little sceptical about it, and who could blame her after the recent vigilante disaster. Plus she really wasn't impressed with the way Welles had blacked up in *Othello* and I wasn't going to suggest that she was in any way wrong on the front, though I feel it's a case of a man with a wayward ego rather than any racist intentions. Karoline also surprised me by insisting that she came along with us, the idea being that I was less likely to end up dead if she was by my side, that at the first sign of trouble she'd whisk me away. Persuading George to let her join us took a little while longer than I'd hoped as he had concerns for her well-being, but after pointing out that I would be a feast for worms right now if she hadn't been present the night that Fisher almost decimated me, he slowly backed down and agreed to her coming along.

George wanted to track down Welles as soon as we could, but first off we had to dress for the occasion, and the one thing magicians rarely are is well attired. The idea being that it's always best to hide in plain sight, wear casual clothes like jeans and a t-shirt, and not to bring attention to yourself by wearing a designer suit worth thousands of pounds, or an enormous cape that changed colour upon a whim. On this occasion George however felt the need for us to look respectable, thinking Welles might respond better that way, and as neither of us were particularly adept at designing clothing it led to a quick trip to Savile Row. In the past when I'd visited the area I'd noticed stern security guards who simply shook their heads very slowly if I approached the door, but this time they begrudgingly opened it. Half an hour or so later while trying on yet another suit, I found myself looking rather dapper for the first time in my life.

"I feel like James Bond in this one," I said.

"You really shouldn't want to," Karoline replied.

"Well you look like a Bond girl in that," I said, as I wasn't great at compliments and needed to practice more.

"One of the ones he tries to rape?" She asked.

"God no. And that only happens in the original books," I said.

"So that makes it alright then?"

"No, of course not. And okay, I feel like Keanu Reeves in *John Wick* in this suit, is that better?"

"Isn't he a man who commits a massacre because someone shot his dog?" A clearly quite exasperated Karoline queried.

"Yes. Hell, if I had a dog again I'd do it if someone deliberately ran over his tail."

"Huh. I suppose that is fair enough."

"Christ on several motorbikes, the absolute nonsense you two talk about sometimes," George intervened, "Now what you're wearing is absolutely fine, and we've got things we need to do. Plans to make. Welles is paranoid in the extreme and is likely expecting us, or someone like us at the very least, so the difficult part will be getting into the same room as him. According to my source he's currently staying at the Hyatt Regency Hotel, and I've booked you both the honeymoon suite to stay in, thus if you pretend to be a newly married couple and dress appropriately he may not suspect you're magicians."

"You're not going to accompany us there?" I asked.

"I'll be close by, don't you worry dear boy, but Welles knows me by sight and even if I transformed my appearance I'm not sure he wouldn't be able to recognise me by smell."

"Surely some deodorant would solve that problem. Which I've been meaning to mention, it's not tha-" I replied.

"Why you cheeky sod," George cut in, "I bathe daily I will have you know. And the point was that he has artefacts which would detect a man of my age, a magician of my power, whereas you're a newcomer and hopefully won't set off any of his devices. Now all you need to initially do is stay in the suite, I've had my source plant cameras outside of Welles' room, and the moment he leaves I'll contact you, and you should follow him until he's in a public space. Then speak to him, keep him occupied until I can get to you, and as we'll be in the public eye he won't be able to do anything impossible."

Some painfully expensive purchases and a long car journey later and we arrived at the Regency, and once we'd occupied the honeymoon suite we sat around watching television, though as the hours passed by we grew increasingly bored. George had made it clear that we could be called upon at any time, that we were to be ready to burst out of the room and dash to wherever Orson was headed at a moment's notice, but with little to do it became tedious and given we were in such opulent surroundings it was hard not to become distracted. Which is why rather inevitably, and rather annoyingly, I was only wearing socks and Karoline had even less on than that when the phone rang, and as

I picked it up George shouted for us to dash to Orson's room that very second.

I tried a spell that would see us clothed immediately but something went wrong along the way that led to my boxers attempting to cover my head and my socks were on my balls, so we had to get dressed the traditional way. I was panicking that we might have already missed the man, but thankfully that wasn't the case as the moment I opened the door he was running past shouting "Fuuccccccccccccck offfffffffffffff!" at the top of his voice, and two men in black suits ran past just seconds later. As the two men sprinted around a corner I heard Welles' voice shout out a spell of the variety that I didn't recognise, and I have to confess to being filled with dread as to what we might see next. Instead it was adorable, as the two men were shrinking in size until on the floor were two babies, about six months old at best, but still dressed in now tiny versions of their suits. One gurgled away happily, while the other decided to take a nap.

"Good lord, I really wish you hadn't seen that," Orson exclaimed.

"Oh I don't know," Karoline replied, "Considering the things I've witnessed lately that was rather sweet. Especially the matching pacifiers, that's a really nice touch."

That took Orson by surprise, albeit not for long.

"Ah, I see, you're magicians as well then. Bloody hell, it seems like this hotel is full of the bastards. I really hope I won't have to transform you two as well. I just wasted an artefact that was over four hundred years old and I've only a couple of others left on me."

I waved my hands frantically at this.

"No, no, we're the good guys," I said, "Unless you're the bad guys, then we're the bad guys too."

"I'll have you know that I'm morally irreprehensible," Orson replied, and I smiled and pretended to know what that last word meant, "Unlike the two individuals from your depressingly unpleasant government there who it appears have decided they no longer want me around. I have to say that my feelings are a tad hurt as it happens. Now, given that you are magicians and an unknown quantity to me, I hope you don't mind my asking, but who the hell are you? And what do you want with me?"

I was about to answer, but Karoline got their first.

"I think it's best we be honest with you. I mean, we're not supposed to be, but the lies he was about to tell you weren't going to be convincing in the slightest. So, he's a magician, I'm not, and we were asked by a man called George to interact with you, keep you in a public space until he could get here. Then he was planning on finding out if you're evil or not."

"Well I appreciate your candour dear girl," Welles replied, "Would that be George Hartman by any chance?"

Both of us were suddenly lost for words.

"That's a good question," I replied, "He's never actually told me his surname. But he's a man who looks like he's in his seventies, despite being a couple of hundred years older than that, and bears a very vague resemblance to Donald Sutherland"

"That does indeed sound like the Mr Hartman I know and tolerate, and I was planning on visiting him in the near future so we might as well meet today. It's probably best to get out of this hotel before someone spots the babies and tries to make me parent them though. I know of a delightful little public house a short while away, shall we repair there and then ask George to join us?"

It was as pleasant as Orson had suggested, spacious and decorated with care, with real bookshelves instead of the fake ones bizarrely found in too many public houses. While we waited for George I asked Orson a few questions as to whether he'd made any more films since his supposed death, but he brushed them away and flirted with Karoline instead, who really did not seem to mind. When George eventually arrived he was wary, to the extent that he was quite possibly the wariest person I'd ever seen, with his left eyebrow almost permanently arched, and there was something in his eyes that suggested he wouldn't be surprised if his brain exploded at any moment.

"Orson," he said, nodding to the great man before taking a seat.

"George, it's good to see you after all this time," Welles replied.

"Is it Orson? I struggle to believe that."

The tension was palpable. And slightly annoying. I wished they'd cut to the chase and stopped being so oblique, but they took the long way round.

"I understand your scepticism, I do, but I had reasons for everything I did that day. And you left me unharmed, unlike... Let me put it this way, everything I did that day was for the best. Some of your associates truly couldn't be trusted," Orson said.

"I wish you had let me be the judge of that," George replied.

"It was a complicated time."

And so it went on, as George and Orson discussed the past for twenty or so minutes. It took a while but I slowly got the gist, that at one point in the eighties there'd been some murky infighting within the magic community and certain individuals had disappeared from sight ever since. I had no idea who any of these people were, nor who was in the right or wrong, but after all too long a while the conversation became less hostile, probably due to George remembering why we were there in the first place.

"Look Orson, I'm prepared to discard our differences for the time being. Forget what happened with Agatha," he said, without ever explaining exactly who Agatha was. "Rather distressingly I'm in need of your help, as someone who thought I had died a long time ago is now aware that I am alive and well. It's something I managed to avoid for decades, but now I'm in a lot of trouble. To be honest with you I'm a little scared. I've made a mistake and I need to make amends, and I need an artefact from you. The Yuasa artefact "

"I know of it," Orson replied, "But I don't have it George. Not anymore."

"Oh come now, everyone knows you stole it from Niven back in eighty-one, the day of that idiot's marriage, it's common knowledge."

"I know, that was always part of the plan. If everyone thought I had it, then they'd never be able to guess who actually did."

"Please Orson. I'm begging you, I need this. If it is the case that you are telling me the truth then surely you could return it to whoever has it afterwards, and I'll never know their identity."

I'd never seen George like this before, and it was perturbing to say the least. Sure, my entire world had been changed and was ridiculously messed up if you thought about it too much, which is why I chose not to as much as plausibly possible, but George had always been the one, I don't know, rock of sanity? Nah, that sounds rubbish, but you know what I mean. To see him scared, this really wasn't good, and neither was the fact that Orson wasn't moved by such a thing.

"I'm sorry George, I truly am, but I simply can't. You see, I let them use it on me afterwards. It's ironic, all I know is that they're the one person I absolutely trusted in the world, and I've no idea who they are. That they ever existed."

"But why?" I asked, trying to make sense of proceedings.

"It's too powerful an object, Ben. No one should possess it, yet due to the amount of magic that's been cast upon it, it's also indestructible. So something needed to be done."

George put his head in his hands, and sighed, deeply.

"Crowley's artefact, then."

"No," Orson responded, "That will never happen either."

"Orson, please."

"Sorry, but no."

"Then I'm as good as dead."

"George, that artefact can essentially remove a person from history. Every single human being they've interacted with will have no memory of their ever existing. Used on the wrong person reality could be damaged in ways we can't comprehend. You know what happened in ninety eighty, the shockwaves that it caused."

"I can't take no for an answer Orson," George all but shouted, causing a wary barman to stare at him, "I'm sorry. Trust me, using it the way I intend to, there will be no repercussions. Except that I will survive."

"I'm afraid you'll have to find another way, and if I think of one I promise I will tell you. But right now I cannot help, and I also feel that it really isn't a good idea for three magical individuals to be in one place at the same time," Orson replied, before standing up. "Goodbye George, I really hope this works out for you, and I hope this does not damage our relationship further. I would help if I could, if there was any other way. I hope you know that."

Then he mouthed a silent goodbye to Karoline, and walked away. George turned from disorientated and distressed to determined within a blink of an eye, and with sudden clarity ordered us follow Welles.

Orson had already made it outside and was climbing into his car when he saw us, and in a move which I truly hoped had first involved disabling any CCTV cameras, and perhaps even the eyes of anyone passing by, he turned himself and the car invisible and we soon heard a screeching sound as he pulled away.

"Get in," George shouted, motioning towards his old Austin Allegro, which looked like it had seen better days, though admittedly that tended to be the case with Allegros when they were brand new. As we clambered inside of the car George pressed a small button on the dashboard, causing it to flip over, revealing ten larger buttons, all marked with letters of an alphabet I was unfamiliar with.

"I take it this is no ordinary car," I said, as George pulled out on to the road and then up into the air and the car and everyone inside of it became invisible.

"No, not quite, I've made certain modifications," George replied.

"So what can it do?" I asked.

"It can fly, as you can see, but also travel underwater, shoot missiles, eat motorbikes, etc. I've had this beauty for forty years, and have cast a sod load of spells upon it. But don't push any of the buttons, only I know what they all do. And which ones not to touch unless we're really in trouble."

He then pushed one of the buttons and the windscreen instantly became a thermal imaging camera, and we were once again able to see Welles' car, and which suggested this was far from the first time George had been involved in a magic based car chase, I was about to ask but Welles then pulled away at an enormous speed and was almost out of sight. One of those new-fangled turbo booster spells helped us catch up, though the shockwaves caused minor hat related confusion below us.

"Why don't you just fly over him, cause him to land somehow?" Karoline asked.

"His car is almost as unusual as this one," George said, "Before I joined you in the hotel bar I checked it out, there were so many spells cast upon it that its abilities were obscured, but knowing Welles we need to be very, very careful, and if we're to do battle we really need to get out of the city and into the countryside where there will be a lesser risk of accidental murder."

"Okay. Good answer," Karoline replied, looking at me a little nervously. I would have felt the same way too if I hadn't been feeling queasy, I'd never been a great passenger but at the speeds we were doing I was close to vomiting. George noticed, and cast a spell.

"Hey, ask permission first, please!" I shouted, but he just shook his head and responded that he didn't want vomit obscuring his vision and I suppose it was a good point, especially given what I'd consumed earlier that day.

After what then turned out to be a rather bland chase with Welles darting across the sky but failing to shake us, we eventually arrived in Surrey, that most hateful of English places. Which might sound harsh to anyone who's only briefly visited the picturesque towns and cities that it consists of, but I'd grown up here in one the smaller villages where not only did everyone know your name but also every sin you'd ever committed, and the populace had nothing to do each day than to use that knowledge to try to make existence grimmer, at least when they weren't enjoying being casually racist, sexist, or homophobic. The local pub had at least one fight a week, with the locals laying bets over who would kick off next and why, and the only hints of culture were misjudged school plays of things like To Kill A Mockingbird, despite their being no black actors in the cast, and Christ I wish I was joking but I'm not, it's up on YouTube if you want to see something really misguided and wrong.

Now I'd left the place a while back, and maybe there are delightful parts of Surrey, and maybe I'm being unfair, but given what I'd experienced I felt it more than fair that I still held a grudge, and dreaded returning to it even in circumstances like these. One thing which did come in handy though was that I knew the area well, knew the local woods and countryside and where we would be able to confront Orson without any potential witnesses. So when we reached such a place I told George that here was as good as any, he pushed another of the buttons on his dashboard and the Allegro shot forward at an alarming rate, finally smashing into Welles' car, sending it spinning into some nearby woods and bouncing from one tree to the next until it finally came to a rest on its side next to a particularly large oak tree. George landed nearby, and with the engine still running he leapt out and ran over to Welles' vehicle, shouting loudly and telling him not to move. Except that he wasn't there. Having now made himself visible he was sitting on a branch above us, brushing a leaf off of his shoulder with one hand and dropping a large anvil with the other, and as I stupidly decided against moving it smashed down upon my foot and caused much squealing.

"That's just a warning shot," Orson shouted, "Now leave. Please don't make me break your spines and tear out your vocal cords, needlessly bloody and graphically over the top bloodshed like that really does turn my stomach."

George of course ignored such a threat and flew up into the sky, but I didn't know what to do and so just sat down, until Karoline spoilt my ingenious scheme.

"Go to him," Karoline said, "I honestly don't know if you should help or hinder him, but make sure they don't kill each other."

Thus I flew straight up, through the clouds, where I saw them facing off against each other.

"You owe me Orson," George shouted, "You're the reason Natasha left me, and you know it, and you're the reason Berlin in ninety-two was such a bloody mess."

That last one seemed to faze Welles for a second, and he almost stuttered his reply.

"We've both got a lot of blood on our hands George. At least mine isn't fresh," Orson retorted.

"I'm dead if you don't do this," George said, "You can help me."

"I'm afraid I can't."

"Then I'll have to take what I need," he shrieked as he launched himself at Orson at quite the speed. Rather than running, Welles transformed into an enormous platinum dragon, which George bounced off of.

"I've been watching quite a lot of Japanese manga recently, never had the time for it back in the day but I've got to say it's culturally fascinating. Plus it taught me that I could do things like this," Orson said, drawing in an enormous breath and then spitting fire at George. He would have been engulfed in flames had he not transformed into a concrete knight from the fifteenth century, and as the flames dissipated he changed into a gigantic bear, clamping hold of Orson's dragon-y mouth and preventing him from becoming fiery again. I thought the way I'd battled Fisher had been fairly smart, but these two were clearly masters of the art of transformation, and so rarely stayed in any form for more than a second or two. Keeping about thirty foot away from the mad bastards, I hovered in the air, without a clue what to do. It was a feeling I was getting rather used to, and though part of me wanted to get involved I worried that they might accidentally destroy me if I got in the way, a thought all but confirmed as Orson metamorphosised into a two hundred ton elephant and wrapped a diamond encrusted trunk around George's neck, which slowly began to crack. This led to George turning into a mouse and dropping through the sky, before turning back into himself. Orson did the same. Bar the mouse bit, that would have been pointless and weird.

"George, this isn't going to get us anywhere. You're going to have to kill me before I hand over the artefact, and trust me, that's an outcome neither of us want. Preparations have been made if I suddenly die, there will be repercussions."

"I'm not going to kill you Orson," George replied, "But I'm more than capable of subduing you and taking what I need. I'm sorry. This life thing, as fond of you as I am, I'm much more attached to it."

"You're fond of me?" Orson asked, and George shook his head.

"No. Just a misused figure of speech. But I once was. Maybe one day I will be again, after enough time has passed. I haven't forgotten everything after all, like that night at Oliver Reed's and the fireplace wrestling."

"You were indeed mighty that evening," Orson said, "But that changes nothing"

Hence they squared off against each other once more, and now traded blows, brawling like drunken boxers, it was both messy and alarming at the same time, and deep cuts and much blood were soon involved, as it slowly became clear they were running out of steam, and the need to really hurt the other increased.

"For God's sake George, this is all rather ungentlemanly. Has it really come down to slowly trying to beat me unconscious? We're supposed to be better than this," Orson spluttered, before he spat quite the quantity of blood from his mouth. As both of them regained their breath, George stared at him for a long time before sighing.

"No, not today. Sorry, but as Nelson Mandela once said to me, fuck you, you unhelpful turd." I'd expected him to thrust himself at Orson yet again, but instead he shot towards me instead.

"Sorry about this, er, again" George said, as he stole another hour of my life, and before I knew it Orson was also apologising for the same bloody thing. So much for being an innocent bystander.

"For fuck's sake, now I'm going to die three hours before I was originally supposed to, this really isn't on," I shouted, though both ignored me, somewhat rudely. George then exploded into fire and leapt at Welles, but he did the turning into a giant

swimming pool filled with water trick and so George was quickly extinguished. And on and on it went, with Welles turning into a giraffe with machine guns for legs being my personal high point, as he presumably was trying to psychologically confuse George and make him do something stupid, but it failed on each and every occasion. I wondered how long this could possibly continue for, and warily considered buggering off just so the bastards didn't steal any more of my life, when Orson grasped a small pendant from his neck, whispered an incantation, flew towards George and punched him so hard that he was nothing but a blur in the sky for a millisecond, and then could no longer be seen. After this Welles flew up to me in a rather alarmed manner. "Don't worry, he's alive, I just needed a few seconds with you. I don't have many of these artefacts left you see and I'm loath to use them, so please recognise this as being important. Now I've known George for a long time and despite everything I think he's a good man, Ben, but you cannot trust anyone at any time, especially with artefacts as powerful as the ones he's requesting from me. Which is why I need a favour," he said, handing me a small dagger, "It's the Yuasa artefact. I know I told George I no longer had it, and there are many reasons why, it would take too long to get into here, but I simply cannot give it to him. So I'm asking you to keep it safe. Hide it. I'll return for it when I can."
"But what does it do exactly?"
"It gives you complete control of a person's mind. Complete access to all of their memories and their thoughts. Slice open their skull with it, and you can discover their true motivations, their hidden secrets, and, if need be, you can manipulate their reality. Change everything they believe about the world, about

themselves. Which is why it's such a dangerous tool in the wrong hands."

"Why trust me?" I asked.

"I used it on you and your lady friend when we met in the hotel. I needed to ascertain whether or not you could be trusted, if you were who you said you were, but then removed the memories of my doing so. Now, George is due to return in about ten seconds, so I must be off. But please Ben, don't give him the artefact. Never let him know that you have it."

Upon George's return somewhat unsurprisingly he wasn't in the best moods. Crashing through the roof of a small Russian bar hadn't endeared him to the locals, and he looked exhausted. Orson didn't care at all of course, and perhaps because he'd relieved himself of the artefact he felt able to enjoy himself, as he shaped his body into his most famous film character, one Charles Foster Kane, the young, passionate version in his mid-twenties but quadruple the size.

"Kane smash!" Welles shouted, before thumping George's arm so hard that it detached it from the rest of his body and dropped into the trees below us. Stemming the bleeding George flew back, and it looked like he was going to fly straight into Orson until he transformed into an enormous vagina and swallowed Welles whole.

"This Rosebud's got teeth motherfucker!" he screamed, and taking a closer look I noticed it was unpleasantly the case. Orson grabbed hold of one of the bloody fangs and tried to climb out, but George was able to suck him inwards, and soon all I could see was the ginormous genitals being punched relentlessly from the inside, for several minutes, until thankfully, finally, it stopped.

George transformed back into himself, with an unconscious and far too damp Welles beside him.

"Don't worry my lad, I know that looked grotesque but he's still alive. And will remain so, I promise."

"Grotesque isn't the word George. I mean Christ, that's going to be a part of my nightmares for the rest of my natural life."

"I did warn you that might happen, more than once, but if it helps I am sorry you had to be around to see it."

"But, I mean, well, you think you know someone," I muttered.

"Stop it Ben. For once, please, just be quiet. I'm bloody knackered after that."

"Fine. Whatever. One last thing, just promise me that you're not going to kill him. I'm still hoping for a Citizen Kane sequel where he finally finds that arse of a sled for one thing."

"Of course, of course, I promise you, I'm not going to harm him. Or at least not permanently."

I'd never seen George look so determined, or demented, and given that I was in possession of what he wanted, I thought it unwise to keep him with me for any longer than was needed.

"Okay, well, I guess I should get back to Karoline. Oh yeah, and you really owe me for the life stealing shite okay? Will you please stop doing that without permission?"

"I promise you Ben, and I will return the favour. In fact I've an idea that I'll set in motion as soon as I can that I promise you'll love."

With that he flew away, dragging Welles along with him, and I returned to his car, and all but collapsed into the back seat, suddenly aware of how tired I was as well. Karoline asked only a few questions, most of them relating to whose arm it was that had almost landed on her head, and soon I was passed out, reportedly sleeping for hours. Though even in my unconscious state I almost caused her to crash, as at one point I screamed out "George, no, please, no, don't come anywhere near me with that toothy vulva."

CHAPTER 6 - A TRIP TO THE MOON

After that Karoline and I took more than a few days off, ignoring the outside world and, well, it's something I'll keep between us if you don't mind. Which is something I've never said before. All of my friends know me as being ridiculously too open, a typical conversation might go like this: Steve: Hey, Ben, it is good to see you, it's been a while, how the devil are you? Me: Pretty fucking awful to be honest. Sarah had an abortion without telling me and then broke up with me a couple of weeks later, and I've spent the time since drinking too much wine, listening to Tindersticks and The Fall and crying. Steve: Oh. I'm sorry to hear that. Me: Ah, these things happen. How are you, anyway?

But this time around, I didn't want to share everything with the world. Not the intimate details at least, though I could go on and on about how crazily I was in love with her for decades. I'll spare you though, as I remember how much I hated hearing such things when I wasn't in that place.

About a week after the Orson experience Karoline told me that she reluctantly needed to visit her family back in Norway as a greatly loved Uncle, Marius, the only family member that she actually cared for, was in a very bad way and only had a few more days to live. I offered to accompany her, offered to cure him, but apparently the cancer had spread so viciously throughout his body that it would be deemed a miracle if he were to suddenly survive, the kind that would make every newspaper in the world. I still wanted to go with her, to be there for her, but she said this was something she needed to do alone, and also that as she loved me she didn't want to inflict the rest of her family upon on me, especially in these bleak times when they really weren't going to be at their best. I tried to insist that I really didn't mind despite everything that she'd told me about them, but she said that it could wait a little while, maybe a week or two, perhaps at the sadly inevitable funeral.

Once she was gone boredom soon kicked in again, but this time around I decided not to be a dick and do something stupid and / or dangerous that would possibly get me killed. But with a lot of spare time on my hands I didn't want to sit around doing sod all either, and so I decided I should head out and see a bit more of the world. Or a completely different one, as it goes. See there's this movie that was made in the nineteen sixties based on H. G. Wells' novel *First Men In The Moon* that I've loved since I was a child, a gloriously innocent, beautifully daft British romp where a mad scientist builds a rocket and lands on the moon, only to discover a bunch of angry giant alien ants are living beneath the surface. It's a film that's a huge amount of fun, one where everyone involved looks like they're having the greatest time making it, and every few years I watch it again and only love it more. With Karoline gone I watched it once again, and suddenly had the realisation that I was an absolute idiot. Now you may have worked that out a long time ago, but it made me realise that I could do something that very, very few people had ever done, and visit that possibly made out of cheese place that floats above us.

The last thing I ever expected was for it to turn out that H.G. Wells had been their first. That or he was remarkably prophetic as those ant bastards, Christ, who would have thought they'd be such evil monsters and... Fine, fine, I'm making it up. There were no giant alien ants. No disturbing adventures where I almost died. Going to the moon was one of the dullest things I've ever done and it was enormously disappointing. I flew around it time and again, investigated every nook and every cranny, and as much as I wanted to get excited about it, it's just all grey and lumpy and rocky and dangerous to consume, like nineteen eighties school desserts or the music of Marc Cohn.

There was one highlight, I'll give you that. Looking at the Earth from the surface of the moon, okay that's something you should do if you ever get the chance. Looking back at our delicate piece of rock floating in space and seeing the entire human race, it gives you a certain perspective on existence. But after a while it too becomes a bit mundane. For one thing I've seen it on tv loads of times before, but also I've always bought into the "Earth is just a tiny speck of dust in an enormous universe, and there's billions of other galaxies and everything is meaningless and will one day come to an end and nothing I can do will ever change anything" idea. And along with my "Humanity's proven itself to be on too many an occasion horrendous and petty and scared and angry, and due to this it looks like thanks to climate change most of us are going to be dead soon anyway" theory, it was only a very brief period of time where I was excited about seeing the Earth from an unusual perspective. I don't think I'm being overly pessimistic as well, maybe in a few thousand years we'll get to the *Star Trek The Next Generation* kind of existence where Earth is a war free and peaceful world, where you don't have to work unless you want to, there's replicators for free food and holodecks for free sex. But not in my lifetime, or any potential great-great-great-

great-great grandson's either.

Anyway, I know I'm rambling, but all of the above is why I didn't stay on the moon all that long. Yet before leaving the moon I, and okay, look, the next part is something I'm not particularly proud of, but I wanted to make a little history, be the first person to do something there, perhaps the only person ever to do such a thing, which lead me to digging a small hole and inserting my penis into it. Afterwards, full of shame, I buggered off quickly.

CHAPTER 7 - A TRIP TO MARS

A few days after my return to the planet I finally received a call from Orson.

"I presume this is about this Yuasa artefact of yours?" I asked, and it was.

"Yes, I can't thank you enough for that. In the end I had to give George the Crowley artefact, but it's a million times better than him ending up with the one I gave you."

"I'll have to take your word on that," I replied.

"Yes, well, when I have the time I'll explain it to you," he responded.

"I have to say that you seem very calm about the whole thing," I said, "Given that we had to chase you across the country and your fight with George was an alarmingly strange thing to witness, I'd have thought you would be more upset. Especially given the suffocation aspect."

"Oh, I was furious initially," Orson said, "But fortunately for George there won't be any form of retribution. I've seen the outcome of why he needed the artefact and it appears I may even benefit from it, which I wasn't expecting to be the case at all."

Again I asked for details, and again he promised a longer explanation when he was able to.

"Now, as for the Yuasa artefact, I'll be back for it soon, I promise you, but I'm a little tied up right now with a complicated matter in Paraguay, so can you hold on to it until then?" I asked him if I had any real choice in the matter, and he admitted that I didn't.

"I really do appreciate this Benjamin," Orson said, "And I will make up for it. Now I'm afraid as much as I wish I could chat for longer, I really do have to go."

"Okay," I said, "But one thing very quickly, it's just that I went to the moon the other day and it was quite frankly rubbish. Yet I was considering a trip to Mars, and was wondering if you'd ever been? And if so, was it worth it?"

Orson chuckled at this.

"Ah, yes, I've been to the moon myself. Absolute balderdash, nothing to do there at all. I'm afraid due to that I haven't been to Mars either, and didn't see the point as I presumed it'd be another tiresome experience."

Stupidly undeterred I still wanted to see the red planet for myself, and travelling at speeds that had previously been thought impossible it only took me a couple of days to arrive. Yet I only stayed for an hour, that's how pointless it was. There was hardly anything of interest to see, no aliens or signs of life, it was mainly a large red dust bowl with some fairly tall mountains and a rocky terrain, indeed it was so irritatingly bland I didn't even bother trying to fuck it.

CHAPTER 8 - A TRIP TO THE SUN

I'll never learn it seems, but the very short version is that afterwards I needed new eyes. Zero stars out of five, I will not be returning, and may hold a small grudge against that fiery gas giant for the rest of my life.

CHAPTER 9 - A TRIP TO SOMEWHERE ELSE, I'LL TELL YOU IN A MINUTE

It was a Saturday morning when George called around again. Karoline had returned a few days prior, slightly despondent as her Uncle had passed away during her time back home, but a couple of nights where I turned us into puppies and we rolled around in toilet paper seemed to have picked up her mood, she wasn't quite herself but she was slowly getting there. When George arrived she'd just left to return to her flat to feed her fish, not allowing me to turn them into incredibly smart animals who could hunt for themselves, and I had transformed my living room into a Parisian bar from the nineteen twenties where I was hanging out with robotic versions of Ernest Hemingway and Dorothy Parker as they tried to outwit each other.

"Hello Ben. Good lord, I see you've spruced the place up a bit," George said.

"Just briefly. It's amazing really, being able to do things like this, it's just like having a holodeck."

"A holo-what?" George asked.

"You know, from *Star Trek*?" I replied.

"I'm afraid I don't know what you're talking about. Sorry Ben"

"You've never watched *Star Trek*?" I exclaimed, genuinely surprised.

"I'm aware of its existence and may have caught an episode or two, but when you've lived as long as I have your memory tends to forget a great deal which isn't of importance. So what exactly is a holodeck?"

"Oh, well in that fictional future they had the technology to make hard matter holograms of anything they wanted, that you could touch and feel and it would seem completely realistic. So they could essentially recreate any environment and any person they wanted to."

"Ah, so it's like magic then."

"Yes, but most of the time it went terribly wrong and something bizarre would happen, like the holograms gaining sentience."

"Ah, so it's absolutely like magic then," George said once again, a smile flitting across his face.

"I suppose so."

"And the *Spiderman* pyjamas, is that something to do with *Star Trek* too?" he asked.

"Ah, ha, no, they were a sarcastic present from Karoline, but hey, they fit, and when no one's around I can't resist swinging around the house like a demented idiot."

"Please tell me it isn't some weird sexual thing," George muttered.

"No, no, that's not the case I swear," I lied.

"I'm still picturing it though. Perhaps you might put on some proper clothes before answering the door in the future," he said.

"Fine, fine. So how are things? I haven't seen much of you lately," I said.

"Everything is much better thank you. I'm sorry I haven't visited but I've been rather busy, once I'd resolved everything with Orson I realised it was time to up my game a little. There's only so long before I'll need your assistance with political matters, and it can't be only the two of us, so recently I've made three more magicians. Lisa, Vanessa and Michael. They're rather decent sorts. And a little less daft than you."

"Oh. Right. So I'm not good enough for you am I?" I responded, slightly more sulkily than I'd intended.

"You should be thankful if anything Ben, if events are as I've predicted them then we'll need all the help we can get," George claimed.

"I guess that does make sense. When can I meet them?"

"You can't. Or not until you absolutely have to," George replied.

"Aw, why not?" I whined.

"You'd be a bad influence. A very, very bad influence."

I was going to argue with him, until I realised he was probably right.

"Okay, fine, be like that. Now how are things with you and Orson?" I asked, hoping that it might suggest I hadn't had any contact with him myself.

"As you might imagine he wasn't best pleased when he awoke back at his abode, but tied up and unable to escape."

"How do you do that to a magician?" I asked.

"You take away their mouth," George replied, leaving me with an image that wasn't the most appealing, and one I truly hoped would never happen to me.

"Oh," was all I managed to say.

"I know," George replied, "It wasn't something I did lightly either, and I am very aware that it sounds unhinged, but it was the only way. And once I had what I required I did of course give it back. Though it was on a timer, I thought it best I was several hundred miles away when he regained the ability to slaughter me."

"Yeah, that makes sense," I said.

"Look, Ben, I know I come out of this whole thing looking like something of a shit, and that's not too far off the mark, but I did what I had to do to ensure I continued breathing."

"And the end result?"

"I persuaded him to write down the location of the Crowley artefact. Now someone no longer exists, and certain individuals have no memory of his existence either, which has resulted in my life no longer being in danger. Which means your life is no longer in danger too."

The low moan I emitted made it clear that I hadn't put two and two together and realised that if George had feared for his life then I should have been fearing for mine as well.

"Now, I have another favour to ask you Ben," George said, and a sinking feeling descended upon me, one he clearly noticed as it led to a brief chuckle.

"There's no need to worry, I just thought your presence might be helpful, but there will be no risk of death. All I'm suggesting is a day out by the coast, you see I've heard of another artefact, one in Brighton, that a friend has made me aware of. Lovely chap too, we go back centuries. In fact I used to own him."

"What?" I exclaimed, somewhat alarmed.

"I know it sounds horrendous, but everyone owned slaves back then."

"Fucking hell," I responded, shaking my head and feeling genuinely shocked, "And he still speaks to you?"

"I was the one who made him a magician. After a year I knew he was a suitable candidate."

"And what about the other slaves you owned?"

"Look, as I said, it was a different time. And I was a good slave owner. Gave them steak, potatoes and sumptuous desserts every night. Which thinking about it now probably explains the high heart attack rate."

Once again I wasn't sure if George was joking or not, and even if he was, it still made me question the kind of man he was.

"Christ George," I said, "How can you be so flippant about this?"

"It was decades ago," he replied, "A short time period in a very long life. Am I to apologise to you for all of the mistakes I've made? Is that what you want Ben?"

"Not to me, no. But I imagine you really should make amends to an awful lot of people"

"I have, I promise you. Now please, let's not spoil the day, it sounds like the artefact should be simple to acquire, and then afterwards we can go down to the pier and fuck about on the arcades."

An hour later and we were in one of the most run down pubs I've ever seen, the juke box only had mostly scratched vinyl from the eighties, and the rest of the furnishings didn't look like they'd been updated since then, yet despite all of this it was packed and without a single unoccupied table. The moment we walked in we were approached by a grinning hulk of a man who was at least six foot six, and who came with a massive shock of white hair, I guessed that he was in his fifties but I'd have bet on him winning any professional boxing match, even against Mike Tyson in his bitey ear period.

"George Hartman. You oldest of the old devils. It is good to see you," the man said, before hugging him. He seemed genuinely happy to meet George again, which made for a refreshing change after the Orson ordeal, and the other magician we met who's dead famous, but where an embarrassing incident involving accidental testicular nudity took place, and I swore I'd never breathe a word of it to anyone. Least of all you.

"Larry James Wilson," George replied, "What's it been? Twenty years? Thirty?"

"At least," Larry replied, "Thought you were dead for a long time to be fair, but even after I heard about your apparent resurrection I never could track you down. Seems you move about a fair bit."

"Always pays to be careful in this game. But I do apologise, I should have called in a long time back. How have you been?"

"Oh, good, bad and everything in between. And a fox for two weeks in Wales, when I was on the run from some of those bastard CF1 agents," Larry replied, "You?"

"Pretty much the same, Larry, except for the fox bit. I always used to pretend to be a goose if I needed to hide from any authoritarian figures."

"And the boy, who's this then?" Larry asked.

"Mr Benjamin Holland," George replied, "He's one of us. Albeit only recently."

"It's a pleasure to meet you then Mr Holland. So how many hours of your life has this old bastard stolen from you so far?"

"Only a few," I replied, "Though I'm sure it'll be weeks before the end of the year."

"Ha, seems like he already knows you well George," Larry said, laughing as he did so, "Now, as much as I might wish you'd popped by to catch up for old time's sakes and swap tormented memories, I'm guessing you wish to hear about the artefact?"

George explained that this was sadly the case, along with why he was creating a number of new magicians as often as he could, and all but whispering that the inevitable clash against authority would soon be occurring.

"You're not the first person to suggest that George," Larry said, "Orson was only here a week ago as it happens. He told me about your little encounter."

"Henry Thomson discovered my existence. I couldn't let that last."

"Thomson? There's a name I hoped to never hear again, and wish I never had in the first place. I'm not surprised you were so panicked then. And I take it he's now at least six feet under the ground?"

"Thirty two, to be precise, I didn't want anyone to accidentally discover his body, or what I'd had to do to it."

"I won't ask, and I won't imagine either. And you're certain the end times are upon us?" Larry asked, showing he too had a flair for melodrama.

"It seems so," George replied, "I listen to the chatter on the street, hear the rumours and the mutterings and they're getting louder. Impossible to ignore. Sooner or later, with sooner being worryingly far more likely, The CF1 agency will attempt to take us all out. Or at least take us on. You know how much every political party in power loves a good war, and we should provide a spectacular epic."

"How very true. So this artefact I mentioned, I have to say I can only point you in the right direction, I haven't seen it myself, but while out for my evening constitutional on Friday I sensed a sudden change in the area. Not one I thought was worth risking further investigation in case it was a trap, but it made me a little uneasy that an object of such power was so close by."

"How close by?"

"It's near the pier, that part of the coastline," Larry said, "I couldn't tell you exactly where but you'll sense it the moment you get there."

I presumed that we'd head off straight away after that, but George decided there was no dire rush and a brief catch up and a small tipple couldn't cause any harm, and predictably it soon became a large tipple and the exchange of outlandish tales, with Larry more than his equal when it came to the latter. Hence I got to hear about why he'd turned the bar into a giant fish tank the other day, everyone could still breathe and drink without problem, but sharks and dolphins swam among them, as an aquatic version of Marillion played on the stage at the back as Larry was seemingly also fond of a daft gag. Of course no one went home completely sure of what had just happened, and what drugs they must have been slipped, but they did know they'd had a great night out.

Naturally George had to try and outdo his friend and so told a story where he claimed he was responsible for accidentally starting the Falklands War when he'd got drunk with some Argentinian scrap metal workers, and the two carried on in such fashion all afternoon, each tale becoming so increasingly preposterous that I wasn't completely convinced that they weren't making them up to tease me a little. I was especially dubious of the one involving George and a one legged celebrity who George claimed he briefly gifted eight limbs to, along with the ability to cartwheel while giving a world famous musician the finger.

Eventually they wished each other the best, and we went our

separate ways, with George casting a spell to sober us both up.
We headed towards the shore as George's theory was that if he
had needed to hide an artefact he'd bury it underwater, yet not
too far from the shore so it wouldn't be difficult to locate. Like all
sane people I'd always hated the beach at Brighton due to the
millions of pebbles that desperately try to make you slip over
with each and every step you take, and that I swear look actively
annoyed if you don't, but George bounded down it with glee while
I nervously stuttered my way to the coastline.

"Get some invisible hover shoes lad," George said, "Makes such
situations much easier, and they're also good if you ever need to
parkour to impress a lady. Oh, and you can walk on water with
them, but don't do that. Really, don't ever fucking do that, the
last person who did was burnt to death by a bunch of villagers
who presumed he was a witch."

"A magician invented hover shoes in the 17th century?" I all but
gasped.

"No, no, this was last year in Crawley."

"Bloody hell. So what about Jesus?" I asked, "Was he a magician,
and did he really walk on water?"

"I'm not that old," George said in a slightly pissy way, "And I told
you, the first magician wasn't created until the sixth century
according to what I was told, so it seems like he was a con man. I
mean anything's possible, perhaps the creator did a test run a fair
few centuries prior, but it seems unlikely. I mean, if Jesus was
able to do magic you'd think he'd have at the very least given
himself giant legs to stop the crucifixion being so painful."

"It's a good point, well made," I replied.

Having reached the shore George was just about to step into the water when out of nowhere a booming voice shrieked the word "No!"

I looked all around us but could not see anything, yet George looked very concerned all of a sudden.

"Er, you might want to turn your eyes into infra-red cameras my lad," he advised me, to which I did, only to see a whale facing us from about twenty feet away, kind of like the one from Free Willy, but angrier and with the ability to talk. So, er, maybe that comparison isn't all that accurate.

"Hartman, you are not welcome in the oceans," the whale said in perfect English. George tried to explain how he thought that should no longer apply, and how his offence had taken place years ago.

"Mr Hartman, we do not forgive and we do not forget, especially in matters involving regicide," the whale replied. I looked around us and no one was paying any attention to us, so I presumed that we were the only ones able to hear the beast.

"I see. If you insist. But I shall attempt to broker a peace deal in the near future, please tell that to your current Monarch," George replied, looking downcast, before turning away and walking up the beach and towards the pier. I followed him, quietly, in possession of about seventy two questions but with the feeling that if I asked even one I wouldn't get anything near to a reasonable answer, which proved to be the case.

"Another time Ben, another time, it's too beautiful a day to tell such a murky story, and as I couldn't sense the artefact it is not an issue. Also, they cannot at least prevent us walking on to the pier, which is rather handy given that is near to where Larry first sensed the artefact.

I hadn't been on Brighton pier for twelve years but the front of it was exactly the same as the last time I'd visited it, and the rest hadn't changed that much either. Yeah, the arcade machines were newer, though not that new, and the slot machines had higher prizes, but it was hard to get excited about. Bar *House of the Dead III*, the shooting game with the enormous shotguns, that was still ace and due to an unlimited amount of money I finally got about halfway through it before getting frustrated and annoyed at how often I was dying. And also because I got the idea that creating a massive underground complex and filling it with zombies and killing them with a real life shot gun would be more fun. Which it was, as I found out a couple of weeks later as I dashed about endless corridors whilst cackling like the kind of lunatic you'd run several miles from if given the chance, murdering everything in sight. After a few days I even let myself get bitten once and played the game in reverse where I was a zombie who had to try and kill a heroic clone of myself, one with a wisecrack for every occasion, but I inevitably got shot in the head each time rather quickly. That lacked pleasure, you'll no doubt be unsurprised to know, and even though I'd protected my brain with a force field so only a few bits of blood, scalp and hair flew across the room it's still not something I'd recommend.

"Hmmm," hmmm'd George, waiting for me to ask what he was hmmm-ing about.

"I definitely sense something, but I couldn't quite tell you where. We should investigate without any doubt though."

Once we'd reached the arcade George motioned towards a game called *Dance Dance Revolution*, where you have to attempt to replicate the movements the machine suggested, and whoever did so for the longest period of time won. I'd always had disdain for such machines as they highlighted what a clumsy man I could be, but George seemed intrigued by it.

"You think the artefact might be inside it?" I suggested.

"Oh no, no, but I've got moves boy," George said, "And I challenge you to a dance off."

"Christ, what is it about magicians and dance offs? First Andrew Fisher, now you," I whined.

"I imagine in a life or death situation it's about misdirection. Right now, it's about having fun. You remember having fun don't you?" George gently teased, "Now come on, get on the bloody machine and try to defeat someone several centuries older than your good self."

It was a challenge I was always doomed to fail, once when I was dancing at a nightclub a friend shouted over the all but deafening music that 'I looked like I was on fire tonight', and I took it as a compliment until he dragged me aside and explained that I literally appeared to be burning in agony, and desperately trying to extinguish flames with my hands. Despite a lack of confidence I tried my best against George though, but the sound of the children laughing and chanting "Twat Dance Man, Twat Dance Man" will haunt me for possibly ever more. The little shits.

"Okay, that was humiliating," I said, "Can we please track down the artefact now?"

"Fine, fine, if we must," George moaned.

Alas the further away from the shoreline the weaker George's sense of the artefact became, and as we stood by Horatio's, the small pub at the end of the pier, he could no longer sense it at all.

"We're definitely heading in the wrong direction," he said, "But as we're here, do you fancy a swift pint?"

Without waiting for my reply he opened the door, and grinned as he discovered that karaoke was occurring.

"You know Ben, I used to do a kick arse take on *'Cromwell's Panegyrick'* back in the day, I'd belt it out around the camp fire. I've forgotten half the words now, but I think it began 'Shall Presbyterian bells ring Cromwels praise, while we stand still and do no Trophyes raise unto his lasting name?'. Something like that anyhow, and what a tune, they really knew how to write a song back then."

I smiled and nodded and let him ramble on, before he ordered two pints of lager and I fumbled my way through the song book, noticing that there were very few numbers in it that came from the last decade and most were nightmarish eighties pap. George joked about us doing a duet of the only song in the book that he'd heard of, *Paradise By The Dashboard Light*, but that definitely did not happen and definitely did not lead to loud booing whenever I opened my mouth, and if anyone suggests otherwise I'll see you in motherfucking court.

Once we'd swiftly downed our pints we left the pier and walked along the promenade, and George claimed he was sure that we were now walking in the right direction. After a while even I slowly began to sense it, the sun was attempting to set but it felt like there was another source of heat in the sky, and so it proved to be as the closer we got to Brighton's once beloved Ferris wheel, the hotter it became.

"Ah, of course, the Ferris wheel. Hidden in plain sight," George said.

"How can something invisible be in plain sight?" I asked, but he just ignored me, though I had a fair few other questions, the most important being, "How do we know it's not a trap?"

George nodded, admitting it was something he should consider. "I'll cast some spells, see if anything untoward is taking place," he said, and after doing so, he claimed that everything seemed okay, and that the artefact simply needed to be retrieved from its position at the very centre of the wheel.

"What's the plan then?" I asked, and George explained how we'd get on the Wheel, he'd grow an extra set of very invisible and very long arms, and it would come into his possession that way. It was a simple scheme, and one that seemed to work as we paid to ride in one of the capsules, waited until we were adjacent with the centre, and before I knew it he'd obtained the artefact, with a very minor spell making it visible. A small piece of coal, visually it was unappealing, but I was reliably informed that it was more powerful than I could imagine, but before George was able to elaborate, I suddenly found myself asking yet another irritating question.

"Is it just me, or is this Ferris wheel getting faster and faster?"

"I was rather hoping I was hallucinating," George replied.

"Oh. Dear. It seems th-" but I couldn't finish the rest of the sentence as I was drowned out by a small explosion, and the shrieking that followed as the next thing I knew we were hurtling towards the sea. I braced myself for a very damp impact and took a huge gulp of air, only to find that we'd somehow bounced off of the water and into the sky, and far into the sky at that. George had projected a massive force field around us apparently, and all were safe. Unhappy, but unharmed.

"I really didn't want to do that but I saw no other choice. Now transform into someone else, it's vital no one sees us here," George said.

Fortunately there was no close up footage of the event, and I'd turned the glass opaque so that no one close to us could see, but if we had been caught on camera then the world might have been confused to witness a present day version of Jack Nicholson sitting next to someone the spit of Diana Rigg as she looked in 1968, just after she'd finished making *The Avengers*. Stranger still was that I suddenly became attracted to my mentor even despite the forthcoming potential doom, it seems my penis really has no sense of danger at all. Meanwhile as we flew into the sky miscellaneous bowels were being evacuated, and oh how I wish that aspects of the capsules weren't made of glass.

"Ah Jesus, I didn't need to see that," I shouted, "So what happens now?"

"Now we bounce back," he said, and made the wind blow so hard that it changed the direction the wheel was spinning in. We hit the water again without the tiniest of drops touching us, before bouncing up, right over the beach and on to the road. I felt like I should be panicking for about thirty different reasons, but I was strangely calm, as I presumed George knew how to save the day. Naturally, that didn't last long.

"Bugger. Meant to land where we'd started, must have got the maths wrong," George cried out, and this time I joined in with the screaming as we burst through the sky once again, and were now heading straight towards Brighton's sea life centre.

"Oh God, this is going to turn into a shark related massacre," I shouted, though thankfully that was avoided when George made a huge gust of wind take us in a different direction once more.

"You've got to help Ben, I'm pretty much out of magic after all of today's shenanigans, so it'd be rather appreciated if you take control of this bugger."

"Great. Thanks for that," I replied, before managing to make the Ferris wheel land on the main high street leading up to the station without falling over, and um, yeah, a few cars were a bit mangled and one guy lost his leg which I truly regret, but I was unprepared for such events, I'd not received any training for flying Ferris wheels at school, which was clearly now a major flaw of the British education system.

The next time it hit the surface of this now quite annoying city I made it bounce even higher, and we cavorted through the sky, over the railway station, and after another ten seconds landed on a thankfully unoccupied piece of track, which was by luck more than anything else but at least it meant I wasn't responsible for the deaths of hundreds of innocent commuters. We bounced along for a mile more until finally grinding to a halt in an empty field, implausibly upright once again and with everyone alive. George and I hopped down the few carriages below us with the aid of his hover shoes, and then on to the ground. Before dashing off rather swiftly, it has to be said.

Naturally the story went viral within seconds of us landing, and was being reported across the world only a couple of minutes later. Within the hour the most respected of scientists were wheeled out on all of the major networks to try and explain how such a freak occurrence could take place, with the gist ultimately being "God only knows, as according to everything I've ever been taught, what we just saw was impossible."

The cause of the explosion was easily explained at least, a bomb detonated by someone who could only have activated it at close range, and it was declared an act of terrorism before the smoke had cleared, but no one took credit for it sadly for us. Which meant it was definitely an "Ah Jesus, that might be us on the radar now" situation.

After we'd fled into an adjacent field and collapsed by a fence I turned us invisible, and once we'd shared a brief moment to get our wits about us I flew us to George's home. Downing a very large glass of whisky George told me that we both needed to go into hiding, handing me a mobile phone and telling me not to use it, and that I should only return home once I'd heard from him. Quickly calling Karoline on my own mobile to explain what had happened, before destroying the phone, I flew out of the window, and headed to where I'd prepared for, well, not anything like the events of that day, but for an emergency situation nonetheless, and was soon located in the Lake District where I'd previously constructed an underground bunker. I know I shouldn't complain too much either as it was a fortification with a lovely swimming pool, and library, and an unlimited supply of food, alcohol and all that kind of shit, but it was still an underground dwelling I was using to avoid all detection, which also meant no further contact whatsoever with Karoline.

A very long week followed, one in which I seriously considered emerging from the bunker to break into a pharmacy and take some much needed anti-depressants as my moods became bleaker yet again, but I somehow managed to find enough distractions to stop my brain from torturing me at least some of the time. After what felt like an ice age, or a severely nippy winter at the very least, George sent a message informing me that we were safe, that no one had connected us with the incident, yes, certain figures in the Government knew magicians were involved, but thankfully weren't aware that it was us.

CHAPTER 10 - KAROLINE PARK

When I returned home Karoline wasn't upset or pissy with me at all, which surprised considering how much concern I'd caused the rest of the world. But she explained how when I first told her I'd been involved in what the media were calling "The Brighton Ferris Wheel Miracle" she'd gone into panic mode, but that surprisingly it hadn't lasted that long, that she was now getting used to the insanity of my life. Which she should probably have been worried about too, but oddly wasn't. More than that, after the death of her Uncle Marius, of the last family member that she'd loved, she said felt she appeared to have taken on a devil may care attitude. That apart from me and a few of her friends she didn't have anyone to live for, which was both depressing and distressing to hear, and though she made it clear she was in no way suicidal, she was oddly prepared for everything to go horribly wrong now and didn't even care that much. That bar initial distress she was easily and quickly settling into the realisation that this was just the way things were now. I had a feeling this wasn't going to end well for her or for me, and I only hoped I was wrong.

Concerning her Uncle, she had to return to Norway for what she described as the final time, for his funeral, and once again I offered to go with her, but once again she said she didn't want me to have to meet her family, mainly as after this she would have nothing to do with them. Before saying that she did have a request that would most likely take up my time while she was away, anyhow.

"Do you still have that island in the middle of nowhere?" she asked, "The one filled with magical strangeness and a couple of things you should never tell a single soul about?"

I didn't, but I told her it could easily be rebuilt.

"Okay, good, now how about this time it's Karoline Park? Can I get you to do a whole load of magical nonsense, and then maybe Orson or George could delete your memory of it so that it comes as a surprise?"

"Um, yeah, that would be complex. But do-able," I replied.

"Good. We deserve a break after all. So, I want you to do the following..."

Five days later we arrived on the island for a second time. From the beach it looked the same, apart from the logo displayed on the ominous doors was of Karoline's smiling face, but once we ventured inside the park it was evident that everything else was very different. For one thing she'd created her fantasy of a large grassy field containing hundreds of clones of me, who were doing their oh so very best to eat us, and she took great pleasure mowing them down with a nearby shotgun, one of those you'd normally find in a movie as it never ran out of bullets.

"Er, have I upset you lately?" I asked, before realising what a stupid question that was. But she laughed, and said no, not really, bar the fact that I really needed to make the bed more often, and to stop leaving so many crumbs in it. I couldn't argue with that, so I grabbed a gun and joined in. Killing yourself is kind of fun in such scenarios, especially when it comes to hand to hand combat, but when I shouted "This is for the time you failed to notice that Sarah Hathaway was desperate to have sex with you, you blind idiot" before caving one of my clones' heads in I realised I'd gotten a bit too into it.

"Okay then, probably best to call this part of it a day now, plus I'm a tad bored of killing you. Never thought that would happen, but it has," She teased, and took me by the hand, leading me to a nearby tent.

A Victorian freak show, it was, well, it was the sort of thing I loved. Which delighted and concerned at the same time, and I suggested I wasn't a good influence on Karoline, but she mocked the idea, explaining that she'd had a twisted sense of humour long before she met me.

"Um, the freak show thing though, isn't it a bit politically incorrect, having people laugh or express shock at anyone who isn't normal?" I asked.

"I get where you're coming from, but I hope not. Especially as we're the only two who will ever see them. And I've plans for them all after the initial viewing, trust me, don't think you're the only one who has been looked at by psychiatrists and then heard the words 'That's a very disturbing mind you have'."

The first booth contained the once famous but now mostly forgotten British strong man Geoff Capes, except instead of lifting weights he had picked up two grand pianos and then using his long tongue he tickled the ivories, and his tongue had clearly trained for years as it was very, very good. Accompanying him on vocals was a bearded woman, except that wasn't quite true as it wasn't she who was singing, but five mice who had taken up lodgings in her beard and who were belting out squeaky renditions of fifties rock and roll classics. The next member of the group was located in a large water tank and of course he should have been drowning, but instead he sat in a tuxedo and gently played the cello, with its watery setting making it sound more beautiful than ever, while finally on percussion was the lead singer of Maroon Five, except that he was a zombie and using his head and a wall instead of drum sticks and a drum.

I gave Karoline a look that she often gives me, but she just laughed and suggested that they might just be the greatest band ever created, it was an argument she would definitely have lost, but I loved her so said nothing.

Leaving Capes And Co behind the next booth contained an individual who was easily the most bizarre yet, as it was a woman with breasts for a head and heads for breasts, which would have been strange enough as it was but she also had the ability to blow a variety of bubbles that eventually floated up into the air and created a 3D model of the much loved fictional dog *The Littlest Hobo.*

Naturally this was harrowing, as I was unable to pet it without it exploding, and the same applied to a clone of me Karoline had made which was absolutely identical except with an enormous penis. Like, metres long.

"Haha, very funny," I said, "But we've talked about this. If you want me to use magic during sex-"

"No, no," Karoline interrupted, "That could take us down roads we might never recover from. I just wanted to see what it'd look like."

"I'm going for the word majestic," I said, knowing this image would haunt me for years to come but pretending otherwise.

Finally the last booth featured the Elephant Man, except that he had eight legs, and was incredibly quick on his feet.

"Before you say anything," Karoline said, "As I said before, there is a reason for all of this."

Despite enjoying the madness I was glad that she said that, and once we exited the tent she led me on to a football pitch, albeit a quarter of the size of a normal one.

"Now's the fun bit," she said, before whistling, and all of the people we'd just met came out and joined us.

"Right, there are nine of us in total, so we'll have two teams of four, and one referee. Anyone fancy that job?" Karoline asked.

"I'll take it," said the previously underwater Cello player, "Still got a bit too much water in my lungs and I'm not feeling my best to be honest."

"Uh, yeah, sorry about that," Karoline replied, "Right then, well this is basically your standard game of football, except as you might have noticed there are eighteen balls, and you're allowed to use your hands and any other limbs you might have. Everyone's got force fields on, so fouling is allowed, if not encouraged, but no ear eating, okay? Never understood why that fella enjoyed doing that."

What followed was chaos. Beautiful, beautiful chaos. The moment the underwater cello player blew his whistle the pitch became a blur of madness as these strange creations desperately tried to score a goal. Geoff Capes was the first to do so, which wasn't a surprise as he'd thundered down the pitch knocking away everyone in sight, with Zombie Maroon Five bloke taking the worst of it as his force field failed to prevent the loss of a leg, zombies being tragically fragile. He did still score later on in the game, but to be honest we kind of gave him that one as he was clearly not enjoying hopping everywhere. The Elephant Man scored after that, and punched the air while shouting "In your face, mofos!" at the opposing team, I'd always heard that he was a polite gentleman but this clearly wasn't the case and what he said after his second goal was so abhorrent that I cannot in good conscience repeat it.

Soon the goals came even thicker and faster, as the woman with breasts for a head and heads for breasts proved adept at scoring with both her relocated heads and her relocated breasts, while Karoline also scored a few, as it turned out she'd gotten George to give her Ronaldo's feet. I mean, not his actual feet, he'd have noticed if they suddenly went missing, and would probably have written an angry letter of complaint to the local paper, but replicas of them at least. Also adept at the game was the clone of me who was far better at football than I was due to him using his mighty penis to whack the ball past the goalkeeper, and when Zombie Maroon Five bloke got his goal it meant I was the only player left not to have scored. Which might explain why I sulkily turned Geoff Capes feet into jam, he claimed that was a foul, but everyone else was on my side because cheating is fun.

We called it a day after forty five minutes as even with magical abilities such exercise had exhausted me, and we all sat down on the pitch as I made some sandwiches with Capes' jammy feet.

"Okay," I said, "That was a ten out of ten start. So much better than what I'd managed at this point."

"That's because I'm better than you," Karoline said, and I wasn't going to disagree.

Once I'd suitably recovered we left our fellow players behind to finish eating Geoff Capes, and Karoline led me towards a small patch of woods. As we walked I considered myself to be luckier than ninety nine point nine percent of the population as I loved her so much, and maybe I was luckier than everyone, but I didn't want to risk being that unbearably smug.

"So what else have you planned?" I asked, "A basketball game with all of Henry the Eighth's wives, including the ones he viciously beheaded?"

She laughed at that.

"Oddly not, I thought one bit of exercise was enough for one day. But next up is a roller coaster ride, and it's one that even you'll like."

This I doubted, as I sadly hated them, if only because they made me feel nauseous. And it's weird, people nearly always took offence when I said I didn't like riding them, acting as if there was something mentally wrong with anyone who didn't enjoy being flung through the air, that you were a shit example of a human being for not wanting do something that might make you need to hurl unpleasant pieces of half-digested food for about twenty minutes afterwards. But no, despite that I should enjoy them apparently, and was a twat if I didn't. Which had always been a source of confusion and annoyance.

"Um, but, you know that I despise roller coasters, yeah?" I said.

"Of course, you go on about it enough after all. But can't you cast a spell so you won't throw up on me or suffer any other unpleasant reaction?"

"Ah, um, yeah, I hadn't thought of that, I guess I could give it a go then."

The roller coaster was purposefully hidden by a small but dense forest, so I could only see that it went up high into the sky but had no idea what would happen next. Once we'd sat down in the car at the front and the safety bar had lowered, the coaster slowly moved up the track, but Karoline noticed that I was still looking extremely nervous. I thought I had good reason though, asking her "Is this made out of cardboard?" and her reply being in the affirmative. In a non-magical environment I might have started crying, but she gave me a look to suggest my doing so might end our sex life forever.

The roller coaster continued to crawl up the track at a ridiculously steep incline until it finally reached the top, and I swore quite a lot as I noticed that the rest of the track had rusted away and now resided on the ground. As would we, or bits of us at least, in about ten seconds. Plummeting towards the earth had never been less fun, though just before we hit it the car flew back up into the air and landed on the remaining track. Thank god for the nausea curing spell is all I can say, as I'm certain I'd have vomited up everything I'd ever eaten at that point, and that undoubtedly would have been the case once again only a few seconds later due to the five loop the loops all inches away from each other, where it looked like my beautiful face was going to be cruelly crushed every two seconds or so. Shortly after that we dived underwater before emerging into the mouth of an enormous gorilla, and proceeded to shoot through his bloody intestines before emerging out of his thankfully clean anus, and then straight up into the air once again, once more without any track underneath us.

"Ah, I remember now, I never did get around to finishing this off, simply ran out of time," Karoline unconvincingly claimed, as we carried on a now invisible track for thirty seconds while being thrown all over the place in scientifically impossible ways, before a large boom caused us to fly ever faster, leaving the Earth behind as we crashed through the atmosphere and into space, and then on to the moon.

"Have to admit that I was a bit fucked off with you for not taking me here," Karoline said.

I apologised, and assured her she wasn't missing much.

"I never thought I'd say it, but you've no imagination sometimes," she replied, before the roller coaster car flew deep inside one of the moon's caves where we were propelled from side to side as we fell down a tunnel, initially it was made out of only rock but after several miles it became hot and muddy and I noticed there was something, or indeed some things, pulsating on the walls. I tried to take a closer look and I'd like to describe it in more detail, but it chose at that point to leap on to my face and so all I saw was darkness. You could hear my shrieking really well though, where I learnt that when I'm really scared I sound like a three year old child having a tantrum. Fortunately Karoline punched me in the face and it made whatever the bastard thing that was trying to remove my face bugger off and sulk off into the darkness, which felt unfair as that's what I wanted to do as well.

But once I'd regained my eyesight, and briefly swore at Karoline, I stopped complaining as we flew into an enormous cavern, lit by a miniature sun that should have blinded us but thankfully didn't, where surprisingly enormous mice were making cheese.

"Haha, very funny," I said, until the mice noticed us, and started to growl as if they had Rottweilers trapped in their throats.

"Here have a disintegrator," Karoline said, taking two guns from the floor of the car, and we spent about two or three minutes killing an ever increasing amount of twelve foot tall and rather rabid rodents, all who appeared from twenty or so giant tunnels, it was kind of like a real life *Whac-A-Mole* except infinitely more exhilarating.

Once they were all deceased, or had headed off to live somewhere else in the moon as they thought we were tossers, the roller coaster took off again, through another tunnel in the roof of the cave, travelling at exceptional speeds as we sped out of the moon and were thankfully back on the earth before we knew it, landing right where we began.

"What do you reckon then?" Karoline asked, "Are you a roller coaster fan now?"

I had to confess I wasn't, as even without the nausea factor I'd not enjoyed fearing for my life, and when we finally stopped I kissed the ground. Over and over again.

"Spoil sport," Karoline said, but I thought it was best to be honest, and I did tell her that I liked aspects of it, though I feared the genocide of the alien mice bit would haunt my nightmares.

"I know right," she replied "When I thought of it, I knew it was perfect for you. See, I'm sweet like that."

Due to all the ground kissing I hadn't initially noticed that we'd parked up next to a fifties style diner, but once I did we partook in a worryingly large amount of burgers and fries, what with my ability to transport food out of our stomachs and into a bin. When we'd decided we'd been revolting enough we headed off to the motel behind the diner, where a lot of cute couple-y nonsense that I'm sure most sane people would find equally disgusting occurred, but once again I'll spare you the lurid details.

The next morning we were up early, with Karoline in a very excitable mood.

"Right, it's time for us to take part in my movie parody," she said, "Though there's no wolves or mysterious wells in this one I'm afraid, it's a more innocent and fun paranormal action flick, and just so you know I'm not the beautiful damsel in distress, I'm more of the kick-ass able to survive without anyone's help sort."

"And I'm the dashing hero who in the end gets the girl?" I suggested.

"Nah, I've cast Chris Pine in that role, you're just his nerdy best friend. This is my fantasy come true after all."

"Do I at least get to make out with him in one scene?" I asked, to which the answer was once again no. I mean I'm not really bi-sexual, only about five men in the entire world turn me on, but Chris Pine, you just would, wouldn't you?

As we walked away from the motel and diner I discovered that our surroundings had changed overnight and opposite us was a very large office building. One quick hop, skip and a jump (and a fair amount of walking) later we emerged from the other side, and onto the streets of New York.

"Man I'm getting good at magic," I said, for which I was suitably chastised and told that George had been responsible for most of the best bits. I was tempted to moan, but was interrupted by an Ed 209 from the much loved eighties movie *Robocop*, who stomped down the middle of the street. Given his previously psychotic tendencies the urge to run was unusually strong, even despite the lazy legs I'd cultivated over the years, but Karoline assured me he was a friendly fella these days, he'd been to anger management classes and worked out all of his issues. He wondered off down the street whistling a happy tune, which turned out to be a shame as shortly afterwards he really would have come in handy, as a ghost started floating down the main street.

One ghost on its own wouldn't have normally bothered me, and chances are I'd have annoyed it to a second death by asking what it's like to be ectoplasmic, and whether or not every time it slimes someone it gets a little bit smaller, but this was a fifty foot tall ghost, and one who came in the guise of the actor Peter O'Toole. I'd always read that he was a lovely man in real life but for some reason today he was angry, angry and extraordinarily drunk, and stumbling into buildings, causing brickwork and glass to fall and shatter on the ground nearby. I was bemused initially, and so stupidly didn't move away in time, as before I knew it he'd stumbled on to me.

"Yeesh, this stuff is horrible," I said, grabbing handfuls of the mucky ectoplasm he'd covered me in, "It's like old, cold stodgy lube that smells of rotting corpses."

"Jeffrey Bernard really is unwell," Karoline quipped, and I was on the verge of complimenting her on her knowledge of obscure theatre when Chris Pine ran up to us.

"Finally, where the hell have you guys been?" Chris asked, "I was calling your mobiles for ages, we've got major paranormal disturbances all over town. And only us Ghoststampers can save the world."

"Ghoststampers?" I said in a slightly mocking way, "Do we get enormous feet instead of proton packs?"

"Nah, I just couldn't be arsed to come up with a better name. Anyway, before Peter O'Toole drowns the city in slime we really should fuck him up a bit," Karoline said.

"What's your weapon of choice?" I asked her.

"There's a vacuum cleaner in my car, the green Volvo on the right there, in the boot." Having a rough inkling of what she'd planned, I opened the boot and took out the small, round twat of a vacuum cleaner and waved his nozzle about. "Um, and this will suck up fifty feet of O'Toole?" I asked.

"Nah, but an army of them would. Now, Vacuum Cleaner, summon your comrades," Karoline shouted. The hoover let out a piercing squeal, and there was a loud rumble as hundreds of the cleaners poured out of the office buildings and retail outlets, all roaring forward to their possible doom. Suction began, and O'Toole started screaming as his foot disappeared into the machines.

"I'll see you in Hell you paratrophic bastards," the ghost version of Peter O'Toole shrieked, and it was only due to my magicking up a dictionary that I understood what he was going on about. Yet when I told him I had hoped for something funnier he wasn't overjoyed.

"You try to be witty when you've been dead for two years, you twunt," he responded, "Now please would you mind silently screaming for a very short while until you're deceased?"

I was very briefly confused by his words until he turned and hurled a big enough lump of ectoplasm to take down a jumbo jet at me. I couldn't breathe in it, no matter how much I struggled, and that also meant I couldn't cast spells. The vacuum cleaners were decreasing him in size, but it was a slow process, and I feared I wasn't going to be around to see his eventual destruction. Fortunately I'd underestimated Karoline once more, as she'd created a version of Chris Pine who not only rushed over to help me, but who could gulp down large quantities of ectoplasm each and every second, saving my life as he devoured the stuff impressively quickly. Soon I was able to breathe once more, which I'd definitely missed doing.

"Can we eat the stuff too?" I asked Karoline.

"Nah, I mean you could try a bit but it's not easily digestible. Luckily Chris is half human and half Hoover," she replied.

"I give the best oral sex in the world," he laughed, before clarifying that this only applied to his current fictional state and not his real life counterpart, who was in fact rubbish at giving blow jobs.

Once we were free of the ectoplasm Pine reached for his phone. "My contact at city hall just texted me," he said, "So that we don't have to do the long boring finding out where the evil villain lives bit. Apparently it's, er, oh yeah, that big massive skyscraper over there which has an enormous black and fiery cloud hovering above it. Yup, that's your standard dimensional tear where some kind of demon or Hell beast is trying to enter our universe with the plan of ruling over us all, I can't believe I didn't spot it before."

"We should probably pop over and politely ask him to leave before he kills and eats everyone on Earth," Karoline said, "Or at least the fit and healthy folks, rumour has it that he's a fat phobic bastard."

Hearing this meant that for the first time in my life I was pleased that I'd never visited a gym, that seemingly greed could be great. Who knew?

By the time we reached the building I was out of breath, but Chris bounded in and bounced up the steps, ignoring the lift completely, which at least gave Karoline and I a chance to make small talk on the way up, mostly about the joys of Chris's taught buttocks, but whenever I tried to get Karoline to hint at what might greet us when we opened the lift doors, she simply said "Spoilers!"

"Aw that got annoying in *Doctor Who* so quickly, please don't do that," I begged. She just laughed slightly maniacally and replied "Maybe. But only maybe."

Once we reached the top the lift bell rang and the doors slowly opened, to reveal a large staircase leading up into a rather apocalyptic storm that was in full flight above us. I wish I'd taken a picture, it was very pretty. Pine was already present, but pleasingly out of breath.

"Okay, definitely getting the lift up next time too," he said, "Even if there's the risk the world might end as it's so slow."

"That's always been my philosophy," I replied, "My terrible life endangering philosophy."

The storm that had formed above the building became thunderous and a bolt of pure white lightning struck the top of the steps. As the smoke slowly cleared we could now see that stood at the top of them was a shadowy male figure whose features I couldn't quite make out, but next to him were his two demonic pets which resembled lions if they'd been turned mostly into living stone and had serrated scalpels for claws. Impressive teeth, too, no fillings or anything like that, their dentist bills must have been miniscule. I didn't have as much time as I'd like to have admired them however, as they noticed we were standing at the bottom of the stairs and decided to leap down, yet rather than devouring myself and Mr Pine they vomited out a dark muddy substance that immediately hardened around us. Encased in a now rocky skin I was unable to move in the slightest, I could see everything but that was all, which was just not how I'd wished to spend my summer holiday. Meanwhile the beasts dashed about, trying to kill the woman I loved, until from her backpack she whipped out the kind of gun that would give Arnold Schwarzenegger a hard on, and that doesn't happen very often these days, not with all the guns he's seen, some say the last time was in two thousand and five.

"You bastards," Karoline shouted, "I can't believe you killed my beloved, even though I kind of told you to last week and I know he's not really dead and ah, sometimes attempting a memorable speech is harder than you'd think. Eh, anyway, I'm gonna have to kill you now. Soz."

Which she did, as Karoline's enormous weapon emitted a foot wide white laser beam that decapitated the beasts, and upon hitting Chris and I it freed us instantaneously, albeit leaving our barely conscious bodies lying on the floor and feeling rather rubbish.

The man at the top of the stairs slowly tap danced down them, chuckling as he went.

"It's going to be nice to kill you, to kill you nice."

I would have gasped if I wasn't so exhausted, but instead just made do with a mind gasp, which wasn't as dramatic.

Nonetheless I was still quietly traumatised, for it now became clear that the monster responsible for all this madness, the despicable villain of the piece, the abject bastard that Karoline had created, was the television personality and entertainer Bruce Forsyth.

For those not in the know, Forsyth had been a star in England since the nineteen-fifties and during that time he'd been an old style comedian, a song, dance and accordion act, a strong man, a film actor, a presenter, a game show host, a dancer and a bit of an annoying twat. Now he was in his late eighties, still sprightly and apparently wanting to take over the world. I guess that's what happens when you sort of get fired from presenting *Strictly Come Dancing*.

"I'm the leader of the pack, which makes me such a lucky jack," Forsyth shrieked, "And here they are, they're so appealing, okay dollies do your dealing."

At which point two women with quite frankly appalling haircuts emerged from behind him, armed with playing cards, silver plated at that and as sharp as a knife that's just returned from a five day knife sharpening convention. Karoline had to dive left, right and centre to avoid them, it was quite the balletic affair, especially when she cart wheeled up the steps, grabbed one of the women with her thighs and broke her neck. The remaining female screamed "My Sister! You dirty cow!" and somersaulted towards Karoline, who calmly took one of the playing cards she'd caught and slashed the creature's neck open, before leaping back down the stairs again.

"Good game, good game!" Bruce laughed, "Now you're through to the final. Where things get serious. There's a lot at stake here, if you win, you'll have saved the world. Prevented mass misery and destruction on a global scale. But if you don't defeat me, and you won't, then I'm going to destroy you all. I've come from another dimension to team up with my counterpart from this universe, and we will rule you with fists of blood and steel. We will tear your planet a new anus and make everyone live in it. Right inside. I don't think I need to describe it any further, but I will if you ask nicely."

"Fuck you Forsyth," Karoline shouted, before taking out two enormous machine guns and shooting at him.

"You get nothing for a pair, not in this game," Forsyth cried out as he managed to avoid the bullets, and then he grabbed a laser gun he'd strapped to his leg and shot both of the weapons Karoline was holding, turning them into mouldering lumps of metal.

"Now I'm afraid you've lost, my commiserations my dear, but don't worry, you won't go away empty handed. Because we're going to send you on an all-expenses paid holiday... In Hell!" With that he pointed the gun at Karoline. "Any last words for the people at home, my darling?" Forsyth asked.

"Yes, just a few," Karoline replied. "You see you made one big mistake Bruce. One fatal mistake."

"And what might that be, my love?" he said.

"Everyone knows how to kill Bruce Forsythe for god's sake," she replied.

"Oh?"

"Yes, you're eighty seven. All that needs to happen is that you fall down some stairs, break your hip, end up in an NHS hospital where you'll die painfully due to neglectful care."

"But what if I have no plans on falling down any stairs?" He asked, once again laughing.

"No choice I'm afraid. You see when I was up there a minute ago I planted a small explosive device in one of your female friends.

Which is timed to go off right... Now!"

With that the headless woman exploded, splattering the stairs with blood and guts and causing Forsyth to slip and fall, tumbling down the stairs, with various bones snapping time and again. When he eventually landed at the bottom, Karoline clicked her fingers, the lift door opened, and two paramedics rushed out with a stretcher on wheels. They lifted him on to it, and carried him away as he begged them not to, ignoring his every word.

With our enemy defeated, Karoline sashayed over to me.

"Hello, you," she said.

"Gah, I didn't get to do anything at the end there," I said.

"Sorry baby, but like I said, it was my turn to have a fantasy come true, and so it was only fair that I'd get to save the day."

"You're my hero," I said, and kissed her, before we both helped Chris to his feet and stepped into the lift, travelling back down to street level. Upon leaving the building Karoline said "Now, I've one last suggestion. We've saved the universe, me, you and Chris. Billions and billions of lives. We really should get our reward."

"Are you suggesting a threesome?" I said.

"You did mention fancying him earlier. And it wouldn't be like a real threesome."

Suddenly I felt a bit insecure. "But, I mean, what if after him, I'm inferior. It's pretty likely to be the case to be honest."

"Oh don't be silly. I love you. This would just be sex. And, look, if we do this, afterwards you can have a threesome with me and a robot-"

Alas I never found out who she would suggest we'd involve in carnal congress, as we were rather rudely interrupted by a tall, raven haired nun, who landed on the ground in front of us.

"Um, Ben," Karoline said, "This isn't anything to do with me."

The nun was wearing sunglasses and smoking a cigarette, and it was at this exact point in my life that I discovered I had a fetish. It came as quite the shock, I'd always been quite tediously vanilla when it came to sexual fantasies, but I'd finally found a slight kink. Which inevitably meant that she wanted to kill me.

"I've seen a lot of things in my life," The nun said, staring at the bizarre mess that we'd created, "But nothing like this. Now, are you both magicians? Or just one of you? Actually, I don't really care and should execute you both just to make sure."

"Wait!" I squawked, though it was meant to be a shout, "Why? Why do you want to kill us?"

"I'm CF1. You're clearly not."

"How can you be sure of that?" Karoline asked.

"You've created a magic island in the middle of the ocean and we're currently in a facsimile of a New York street which has been partially destroyed and covered in slime, while Chris Pine is barely conscious in the corner. Which breaks about twelve of the rules my employers say I must abide by."

"It's not actually him, just a robotic copy," I replied, "Which might seem like a pointless thing to point out but I wanted to stress that we'd never kidnap someone famous and then use him for nefarious means. Or try to seduce him. That would be plain wrong after all." Now you know I like to ramble away but for once I was doing this on purpose, as I had a horrible feeling that the CF1 agent was going to find it rather easy to kill us, it'd been a long day and I was low on magic and had no plan at all. But I figured if I kept on talking shite it might give me time to formulate one. Or Karoline might, which would definitely be the better of the two options.

"You're right though," I continued, "I'm not CF1. I'm CF2. And boy, if you were to terminate our lives while I was in the middle of training the latest addition to our side, good lord, I imagine our superiors would not be happy. At the very least you'd be given a verbal warning, and quite possibl-"

Unfortunately at this point she tired of me, as so often happens after about two minutes of conversation.

"Enough of this, there is no CF2, and we both know this. I've no idea what you are other than a rogue magician, and sadly for you it's my role to eliminate anyone who fits that description."

It happened in slow motion. Before I could even move she'd flown across the street, picked up Karoline by the throat and thrust her into the side of a building. I had time to put a force field in place for both of us, but seeing the woman I loved being treated in such a way was rather upsetting. Distressing, even.

"Now you," the CF1 agent said.

She slammed me into the wall of one of the buildings, and I endured an all new level of pain. Bones broke and my skin screamed and I had a horrible feeling I was, as you might say in polite company, absolutely fucked. At least like most magicians she enjoyed making misery into a spectacle, and so after creating a crossbow, arrows were now flying towards me. I constructed what I'd hoped would be a sturdy brick wall but they smashed through it, and I was lucky that only one of the arrows somewhat callously impaled me. Whatever force field I had left was clearly now pathetically weak, and thank god I've never been bothered by the sight of blood as there was rather a lot of it.

The nun smiled with glee.

"I truly did not expect it to be this easy," she said, as she magicked up a missile launcher, and I think the end would have come right there and then if Chris Pine hadn't run up to her, naked, begging for sex. While I'd been preoccupied Karoline had beckoned him over and persuaded him to attempt to distract the CF1 Agent with his penis, and it briefly worked as well, or she at least seemed to be considering the idea as Karoline crept over towards me.

"Take an hour of my life."

"I can't."

"If you don't we'll both die, and do you really want that?" She managed to utter.

"No, but, it's you. Your life. I can't do that."

"I want you to. I also don't want to fucking die. So please shut the fuck up and do it right now, okay?"

So I grabbed her hand. Absorbed an hour of her life. I wish it wasn't an orgasmic feeling, but I'd be lying if I claimed it wasn't. Which also made me briefly very confused about the times George had taken an hour from me, but thankfully my thought patterns were disturbed by the threat of oncoming death once more. At least this time I was able to magic up some rather powerful force fields for myself and Karoline, and now fully energised, fear turned to anger.

"I don't care that you tried to kill me, but your attempt on the love of my frickin' life is not acceptable."

The CFI Agent laughed.

"You're a walking cliché" she said, and again aimed the missile launcher at me. A small hamster emerged from the weapon, causing the CF1 agent a moment of confusion, though it was only a very minor and miniscule measurement of time before she'd dropped it and created two rather large machine guns. I didn't give her the chance to use them however, as I turned myself into a one hundred ton weight and slammed myself down on her. It caused her to fall to the ground, but crushing sadly did not ensue. "Damn. I was hoping you'd be as flat as a pancake. As crushed as, er, a crushed grape," I said, causing a brief memory of an annoying children's tv presenter from the nineteen eighties to flash into my mind.

"Do you ever stop talking?" the CF1 agent asked.

"No, and you're not the first to be agitated by it," I retorted.

"It only makes me want to maim you more."

"When you say things like that you really do remind me of my mum," I said, though my being a dick was once again a deliberate decision, as I hoped I could irritate her to such an extent that it might cause her to make a mistake.

"Just shut up!" she screamed, and propelled seven fireballs towards me. I caught them in a cauldron and lobbed them back at her, and for the first time she looked briefly dazed. During which time I flew over to Karoline.

"I've got no idea what I'm doing," I said, because I'm quite skilful at reassuring people.

"I think I've got something," Karoline thankfully responded, making me want to kiss her even more than I usually did.

"What about making use of the hoovers?" she suggested.

"What?" I replied, because yes I am that dumb sometimes.

"The hoovers, get them to cover her in ectoplasm," Karoline explained, "Encase her in it, somehow, stop her being able to cast any magic."

"But her force field will repel it."

"Is there no way you can turn it off?" She asked.

"Yeah, but it'd be pointless, the moment I'd cast the spell she'd realise and just put up a new one."

"Well, squirt first, remove the force field second."

"Ah, that old trick," I replied, but then for once stopped talking as I realised that Karoline's idea was a bloody good one. That and because at this point the CF1 agent was walking over towards me looking quite, quite furious. And then a little confused, as I cast a spell which caused all of the vacuum cleaners to join together to create a freaky if overtly low budget *Transformers* rip off, and before she knew it she was covered in the gooey substance that had once been Peter O'Toole. One quick force field removing spell later and Karoline's plan was successful, and every time the CF1 agent attempted to cast a spell she found herself only swallowing more of that ugly foul smelling gloop. We watched her choke and panic and flail, and bloody hell did it take a long time, as we discovered that films and tv had lied to us so much when it comes to how long it takes a person to asphyxiate, but after far, far too long she passed out, unconscious.

While she was in that state I removed her arms and sealed her mouth but quickly took away all of the slime via her nose, and then woke her up. Her eyes burnt with hatred and she kicked out and attempted to claw out my eyes with some impressively long and sharp toenails, but without magic there was nothing she could do to harm me other than minor scratching. I bound her legs as it was irritating nonetheless, and flew us both into the air, far out of Karoline's sight, before turning us both invisible. One quick bit of mucking around with the Yuasa artefact and all of her memories of meeting us were wiped, and she flew away without a care in the world. Which made her the luckiest out of all of us.

By the time I returned Karoline was sitting next to Chris Pine and both were looking pretty devastated. I explained the problem was dealt with, hinted that she was still alive but wouldn't be able to inform anyone of our existence, but Karoline didn't look any happier.

"I thought we were going to die Ben. Got to say, I'm not getting used to that experience. The Andrew Fisher situation was one thing but this, well, we didn't exactly go looking for trouble but it sure did find us. And I'm scared. I wish I wasn't, but I am," she said.

"Likewise," was all I could think to say, as for once I wasn't making any attempts at humour, any attempts at hiding my own true feelings.

"That was horrible and scary and I'm sorry. I never wanted you to be in any danger."

"It's okay, I mean, I know her discovering us was accidental, and I knew a day like this might one day come given everything you've told me about George. But I didn't expect it so soon. Now... Now reality's kicked in and it's wearing boots with steel toecaps."

"I know, " I replied, not knowing what else to say.

"How much time do you think we have left?" Karoline asked, "How much time until you get that phone call from George saying that he needs you to fight with him. Possibly die with him."

"I don't know," I replied, "I've got to admit that I was always hoping that it might never happen. That there was always a glimmer of hope that the war wouldn't take place."

Which was naïve of me in the extreme, as Karoline went on to suggest.

"Because that happens a lot, I'm guessing?" she said, in a downbeat manner.

"I know. I'm just an optimist I guess. Or stupid. I've never been quite sure."

"You're not stupid. And one of the things I love about you is your positive outlook. It's just occasionally misplaced. As was mine. But I think I now need to know when a potential end will take place. To somehow try to prepare myself for it."

"I understand," I said, "I'll talk to George. I'll find out one way or another."

After that we thought it best to dissolve the island on the off chance that my memory wiping of the CF1 agent might not have been perfect, that even if she didn't remember us she might have known something was wrong, something had changed. Once our work was complete I flew us back to my home in London, where we talked late into the night, and slowly and vaguely recovered, often counting our blessings, of which there were thousands, and talked further about everything and anything and something and nothing. Until:

"I know it's something we've spoken about before," I said, "But are you sure you don't want to become a magician? I, er, don't know how to do it myself, but I'm sure George would help out if we asked. I know he's created others recently."

She didn't respond at first, and I could see a mix of emotions flutter across her face.

"I don't know Ben. It's something I've thought about too, thought about an incredible amount. I mean, what you can do, it's astonishing. But there's the two worlds, aren't there? There's the world where we mess about and do silly things, and weird things, and things we probably shouldn't ever discuss ever again, but that's just the two of us. Then there's the world where people try to kill us. And George, and his quite frankly baffling relationship with Orson Welles, and, and I don't know. It all freaks me out if I think about it too much. That a day is going to come where someone decides to try to murder you all, and I know this isn't a popular opinion to have in this day and age, and not exactly common, but I really do quite like life, and want to carry on living it. As today truly confirmed. So I don't know. Or I do, and at least the answer right now is no. And I'm not saying no for forever. Just today. Tomorrow. The time being."

The following day I contacted George and asked him all of the questions we wanted to know the answers to. Yet George didn't have a clue, he was apologetic and said he wished that he did, that he thought it was likely to be soon, but he just didn't know. Unfortunately he was in Spain at the time as well, involved with a couple of magicians on a project he hoped would give us a tiny advantage if and when the war did break out, so would be unable to help any further. Which is why I ended up calling Orson. "Hello old chap," Welles said, "What can I do to help you?" "It's a complicated matter," I explained, "And I'm not quite sure how to go about it. But the long and the short of it is, I really need to know my future. Know when the government might decide to attempt to decimate us all. Any chance you can help with that?" "It has been weighing on my mind too," Orson admitted, "Give me a day or two, and I'll get back to you."

Three days later and Orson woke me up at six in the morning with a phone call, explaining how he'd been up to no good and as a result was now able to help me out, before giving me an address and asking me to fly on over, bringing the Yuasa artefact with me. A couple of hours later and I was in a small unloved and rather dingy cottage in Wales, where two CF1 agents were tied up using the only furniture in the building, and as was the popular trend of the time they were missing any hint of a mouth.

"Ah, you weren't lying when you said you'd been busy then," I said.

"You truly do not know the half of it my lad," Orson replied, "These two people have not been the politest of houseguests."

"So what's the plan?" I asked, somewhat intrigued, somewhat worried.

"We're going to impersonate these two, infiltrate the CF1 base, find out what the hell is happening with those bastards, and hopefully discover when they're going to make all of our lives something of a misery," he responded.

"They won't tell you, then?" I asked, nodding at the two clearly miserable agents.

"No, and I truly don't think they know yet either."

"How come you need the Yuasa artefact?" I asked.

"Somewhat rudely they won't tell me where their base is. And I did ask in an awfully friendly manner." Noticing their badly bruised faces, I started to doubt that.

"Well, here you go," I said, handing the artefact to him. One bit of forehead slicing later and we had the coordinates, and once

Welles put the agents into a coma for the foreseeable future we transformed into their doppelgangers.

"What if it goes tits up though?" I asked Orson, "Do we have a back-up plan?"

"Several," Orson claimed, "But most of them involve butchery, so let's really hope that it doesn't come to that."

On the flight over to the base Orson was in a chatty mood, to the extent that I found myself wondering if he was interrogating me in what he presumed was a subtle way, just on the off chance that he needed to destroy my life in the future.

"I'm sorry I haven't been in touch until now," he said, "How have things been? George tried to kill you yet? Or consume you within a gigantic sexual organ?"

"Ha, no, not yet," I replied, "And it has been a mixture of the horrendous and the amazing, if I'm to be honest."

"That sounds about right. How are you finding not telling anyone about your shiny new if unhinged life, though? I know many a magician who's found himself in boiling hot water, and sometimes boiling hot acid, after letting it slip one alcohol fuelled night."

"It's been okay, I mean I've got Karoline, and to be honest I've been a bit shit keeping up with my friends. We've chatted online, exchanged messages, but I've barely seen them. I'm not too sure if that's because of the magic side of things or due to Karoline either. Probably a bit of both. But whenever they ask what I'm up to I kind of blame her and say we're just really busy, and I will see them soon. The actions of a true gentleman, I'm sure you'll agree"

"Indeed. What about your parents though? Isn't it hard keeping the truth from them?"

"Not really," I replied, "I'm down to just one anyhow, my Mum, both of my Dads are dead."

"Two dead Dads? That seems careless," Orson said, before winking in a manner which suggested I was supposed to find that funny instead of annoying.

"I didn't kill either of them for the record. Indeed my biological father died before I was born."

"Ah, I am sorry to hear that," Welles had the decency to say.

"Thank you. It's odd, for the longest time I thought I didn't care, I hadn't met him, so what did it matter that he wasn't around, especially as my Mum remarried. But then over the years I've found myself feeling a little resentful that I didn't have the childhood I could have, didn't have the kind of father who-" and I would have carried on complaining away except that we arrived near to the CF1 base at that point, setting down about a quarter of a mile away from it.

"Right, from now on you should respond to the name Agent Clive McNulty, and call me Agent Juliette Pierce."

"You do look very pretty, and that's a smashing blouse," I said.

"Yes, yes I do. And the fact that these two agents were having an affair is what made them so easy to apprehend, so remember we're a couple if anyone asks. On the flip side, do try and say as little as possible, that way hopefully no one will question if we are the real deal."

Once we reached the checkpoint we flashed our identity cards and the gate opened, and we wandered into a large, blandly constructed government building as it appeared that those in authority hated any architects who had even the slightest hint of creativity.

"Late again, I see," the receptionist moaned.

"Where is everyone?" Orson asked, ignoring her.

"Meeting room B, as per usual," the receptionist responded, as if saying the words was making her lose the will to live. With the aid of some x-ray vision I led Orson over to the meeting room, which at the time contained about twenty agents, one of whom was standing by a whiteboard at the front of the room.

"Pierce, McNulty, this is truly unacceptable," the agent said, a woman in her forties with grey hair and the kind of demeanour that reminded me of all of the teachers I'd known who had hated their pupils.

"I'll speak to you after this," she went on to say, "Now please sit down and attempt to catch up as I'm not starting again from the beginning."

We muttered apologies quietly and sat down, suitably chastised, and I couldn't help but notice that even though these were the equivalent of magic secret agents they still had to put up with irksome government bureaucracy, which almost made me feel sorry for them. The lead agent, whose name turned out to be Weaver, spoke in depth for another thirty minutes, most of which was humdrum in the extreme, involving discussions of paperwork that needed to be filed and examples of magic which had been declared off limits as the British public might find it objectionable. Finally towards the end Weaver declared she had been given the news that that we should all be prepared for October 21st 2015, as that was the new date for when the general public would be made aware of the existence of magic and the war against rogue magicians would begin. Hearing it out loud like that sent shivers down my spine, the kind of shivers you think may be close to making your skin contort like crazy. But I eventually managed to pretend that such news wasn't terrifying, as we were forced to sit through another ten minutes of drab nonsense from Weaver who gave an all but insufferable rant about how certain forms of training needed to be completed by then. When the meeting eventually ended Orson whispered in my ear that we should leave, hopefully without making any contact with anyone else, but just as we were about to do so Weaver called out to us.

"Pierce, McNulty, a word please."

A sinking feeling kicked in.

"Now, I know the two of you are a thing," Weaver said, spitting out that last word as if it was repellent to her, "But repeatedly arriving late is not something which will be condoned, if I have to take it upstairs I certainly will. And I think you both know what that means."

Naturally we didn't, but another apology was made, and once again we tried to depart, but she prevented us.

"I need you to join Agents Menke, Berger and Hodges in my office. There's another matter we need to discuss," Weaver said, before sternly walking away and leaving us with no alternative but to follow her. When we reached her office the three aforementioned CF1 Agents were standing outside of it, and Weaver motioned for them to enter the room. Once we were all seated in what was a surprisingly roomy office, she opened a drawer from a nearby filing cabinet and took out several files.

"Thank you for joining me," Weaver said, "Now I was looking at your files and it appears that the five of you have yet to complete training activity 3-GAPT, is that correct?"

Not having a clue what she was talking about, I could only nod and murmur that she was indeed right, and the others did so as well.

"This really isn't good enough, as everyone else finished it by the 31st of last month, as ordered. I'm aware it's unpleasant, but nonetheless it needs to be done. So I've spoken with your team managers and organised it so that we can do it now," Weaver continued, "So please meet me out in Building 4C in five minutes. And wear appropriate clothing, this will be rather filthy work after all."

I glanced at Orson and all he was able to do was weakly smile, a smile that suggested we should go along with this, and so we sheepishly followed Menke, Berge and Hodges to the staff changing room, where they cast spells to generate beige jumpsuits and we followed suit, pun vaguely intended.

A few minutes later we were in Building 4C, an all but empty warehouse with an awaiting Weaver looking rather annoyed that we'd taken so long. Also present was a man in his late forties, scruffily dressed and tied to a chair, with his mouth gagged and his wrists in handcuffs.

"As ever our friends at ATOS have provided us with a guinea pig to practice upon, and don't worry, he doesn't have a family or a job so I'm sure he won't be missed," Weaver said, grinning for the first time in a very unnerving manner.

"I never do understand why we don't just use clones," Agent Menke muttered, looking a little sickened, which suggested that not all CF1 agents were abject shits. Ignoring this, and proving that she was indeed such a thing, Weaver continued explaining our task.

"Now the following methods of torture are something we will only use unless we have no other options, and of course always use the non-magical ways taught in training activity 21RB4 first." The sinking feeling I'd had ever since Weaver had pulled us aside was now accelerating in an alarmingly brisk manner. I looked at Orson once again, but he chose to ignore me, presumably not wishing to break our cover and give up what we'd learnt today.

"Alas sometimes you will need to extract information with speed, hence why you are learning the following," Weaver said, "We'll start with something simple, now Agent Hodges, please cast a spell causing the gentleman's hand to explode."

Hodges attempted to do so, but it was a shoddy effort, a couple of fingers splattered against the wall but the majority of his appendage was intact. Not that the victim wasn't crying out in agony of course, and his muffled sobs were more than a little unsettling to us all, bar Weaver who was proving herself to be quite the sociopath. Maybe even a psychopath, but I'm not an expert so can't precisely label evil people.

"Not bad Hodges," Weaver exclaimed, "Though more practice is needed. McNulty, you're normally adept at such things, please show Hodges what he did wrong."

No one moved, until Orson kicked my foot, and I realised it was my turn to hurt the poor bastard. For what seemed like a particularly long ice age I didn't know what to do, I didn't want to hurt him but felt like I had no choice in the matter. I thought about making the wall behind him shatter instead, or causing the four CF1 agents present to disintegrate, but before I could make a decision Orson softly shoved me again and I cast a spell causing the man's hand to take leave from the rest of his body and fall to the floor. Immense guilt followed, so I quickly healed him, with the way his hand regrew seemingly appalling him more than the original explosion.

"I didn't request you do that," Weaver complained.

"I, er, I thought I should, just in case the pain was too severe and he had a heart attack," I replied.

"Hmm, I suppose your thinking is understandable," Weaver said, "Though I issued him with a new heart prior to our training today so you have no such need to do so again. Now, however painful a hand exploding is, it may of course not be enough, a resilient rogue magician may be able to withstand such pain, which is why you need to be able to cause other body parts to no longer exist. So, Agent Pierce, please cause his testicles to burst."

Even Orson looked briefly taken aback by this, but unlike me he didn't hesitate for long, and soon the man's trousers were turning dark red, and his wailing was harsh and haunting.

Similar acts of horror ensued over the proceeding thirty minutes, with each being more disturbing than the last. I quietly had to cast a spell to stop myself from being violently sick, but there was no spell that would ever help me recover mentally. Or one which would lead to my forgiving Orson for placing me in this position in the first place. By the end the man was bleeding from every orifice, and I'm not certain how he was still alive. Not that it soon mattered.

"Fine work today Gentleman, Ladies," Weaver said, "Now, Berger, will you do the honours and vaporise him?"

I'll never know why I didn't stop him. I could have freed the poor man. Saved him. I could have killed the CF1 agents within a blink of an eye and created clones that would have survived for a day or two at least. But I didn't, the piss poor excuse for a human being that I now was. I attempted to explain my behaviour to myself, tried to persuade myself that we'd already gone this far, we'd already crossed far too many lines, and what was the point if we didn't gain important information from the day? But none of it rang true as I sat back and did nothing and Berger caused the man to decay until only a thin pile of dust remained.

"Good job Agent Berger. Fast, efficient, I'm impressed," Weaver said, "Now, we have another training session this afternoon but until then please return to your office, and carry out the paperwork concerning everything you've achieved today."

Finally free to leave, we did exactly that.

Upon returning to the cottage in Wales Orson used the Yuasa artefact on the real McNulty and Pierce once again, firstly to remove their memories of us, and then to replace them with the ones of torture and dismay we'd engaged in, and finally let them go with their believing they'd flown over to Wales for lunch as there was a really great Toby Carvery in the area.

"I feel... Broken," I said.

"I'm sorry, Ben, I truly am, and trust me, I wanted no part of that, and it's not like we had much choice either."

"Yeah, yeah, yeah, I was just following orders. Now where have I heard that before?" I replied, bitterly.

"Come now, it's not like that Ben. What we've learnt today may not only save many, many lives, but possibly change the outcome of the war. We know now when they'll strike, and that knowledge is invaluable."

"I hope you're right," I replied, "Not that it changes anything."

"I don't think you're seeing the big picture here Ben. This isn't only about self-preservation, if the Government wins this war then we may well be in a world far worse than anything Hitler ever dreamt of. We're not the ones who are Nazis here I promise you."

"I caused someone's hand and kneecaps and ears to explode today Orson. And I'm one of the fucking good guys?" I said, the anger pouring out of me now.

"Yes. It may not seem like it, and what you did of course was painful and terrible and something I wish had not occurred, but ultimately what we learnt might stop the world from being irredeemable," Orson replied.

"I'm not sure it's not that already that," I replied.

"And that's maybe a good thing," Orson said, "I'd be disturbed if you didn't feel like this, if you weren't traumatised by what we had to do."

"That doesn't help."

"I could use the Yuasa artefact on you, if you like. Remove your memory of today completely?" Orson suggested.

It was an offer I would have been stupid to refuse given my current mental state. Yet stupid I was.

"No," I said, after a very, very long time, "I appreciate the offer, I do, but no. I did something today that I should be forced to remember. That should become a part of me. Should be a reminder of exactly what this life is."

"It's not normally like this, if it helps," Orson said.

"But it's going to be from now on, isn't it?" I responded, "What with the war taking place everything's going to become..." And I couldn't think of the word. Until I did.

"Deranged. Everything's going to become deranged isn't it?" I muttered, "I'm going to have to fight. And most likely kill. Slaughter."

"Yes, yes, you most likely are, but Christ Ben, I really don't think you understand the scale of events. Again, this isn't only about us fighting back, it's about what will happen afterwards. If they win Ben, do you think everything will return to normal? Go on as it did before? Because that's not going to happen, the world will know about the existence of magic, and everything will change. And do you think every other country will be perfectly happy with the knowledge that Britain has an agency full of magicians who can essentially alter reality and then just do nothing about it?" Orson said, with a hint of frustration towards the end, and I had to admit that I hadn't really thought about it, being something of a selfish, self-obsessed shit.

"And who knows what other countries have been up to. I very much doubt that the United Kingdom is the only one which has recruited magicians. It's simply that you're the first to decide to act, to make it public knowledge. But at best you'll be looking at a magical cold war, at worst a magical world war. And can you even begin to imagine the devastation caused by a magical world war, Ben? If we're lucky the body count would only be in the hundreds of millions."

"Oh," was all I was able to say to that.

"Which is why we need to do the things we did today. We have to destroy the CF1 Agency. And after that, most likely any other magician attached to any government, if that's at all possible. The end game needs to be that we have to take magic underground again."

"And how do we do that?" I asked.

"We know when your government wants the war to begin, now we need to plan a way to prevent it from ever occurring. And as much as I wish it wasn't the case, I'll need to sit down with George. Discuss our options."

"And in the meantime what am I supposed to do? Sit around and wait for death?" I asked.

"No. I'd do the opposite," Orson replied, "Live. Live while you still can."

CHAPTER 11 - AMERICA

"Would you mind ever so much if I knock you unconscious?"
It was a week later and George had once again visited me at my
home. As threats of violence go it was exceedingly polite, only
one person had been more gracious, and given that she'd found
me urinating in Ten Downing Street she'd had every right to be
rude.
"Well George," I replied, "It's a wonderful offer that I'm sure
would tempt millions, but I'm not sure if I'm in the mood today."
"There's a good reason, and you won't regret it," he replied, and it
goes to show how easily led and idiotic I am as the next thing I
knew I awoke in a large, dusty library, the kind of which that
wouldn't look out of place in a period drama. The shelves must
have contained tens of thousands of books, going up so high that
I swear I saw a bit of cloud floating past, while in one corner he
also had a small area for vintage pornography that was peculiarly
dull, all un-risqué shots of Victorian ankles that did nothing for
me at all.
"Sorry about the subterfuge," George said, "But I wanted to show
you my latest base without you knowing exactly where it is. And
it's not that I don't trust you my boy, but there are experts in
torture out there who distress even me, and would have you
squealing the address within seconds."
"But if I can't tell them won't that end up with them torturing me
for ages?" I asked.
"Yes, that is quite true. Sorry about that."
"It's fine. I guess. I mean it's not like I have any say in the matter
anymore."

"That indeed is often life's way," George replied, "Now I need to have a serious chat with you. As you know, after your little adventure with Orson the war is definitely coming. And coming soon."

"Yeah, yeah, the trailers are in the cinema already, release date's only a couple of weeks away," I said in an oddly slapdash manner, and I've really no idea why I was being so flippant. Bar fear. Actually, that sounds like exactly the reason why.

"And Karoline? Does she know what's happening?" George asked. I sighed.

"Yes. I've told her about October 21st. In fact she was kind of hoping that I might be able to talk you out of my involvement. Remove the magic, be no part of what happens."

"And I presume you told her that I'd never agree to such a thing? That too much is at stake for you to walk away now after all of the time I've spent preparing you for this moment?"

"No, because I was, in the tiniest of ways, hoping that perhaps you might," I said, enlarging my eyes to look like a puppy who was pleading for love and affection and who surely couldn't be resisted.

"I can understand that. But the answer is still a negative one. The future of this planet is at stake Ben, a world without magic, or at least a world where the only magicians are those controlled by the governments of this planet, trust me, that is not an existence you'd wish to be part of. And I need you. I need you and all of the others I've created, or we haven't a chance in hell. And it's not like I didn't tell you the full terms and conditions before you signed up for the job, as it were."

He was right. There was no arguing with any of it. Still, I had to give it a try.

"It's just that the one thing I never expected was to fall in love. For the first few months I thought that you'd given me the greatest gift of all. Until I met Karoline. Now I'd give everything up in exchange for more time with her."

"I do hear you. But no. Afterwards, of course, if we're successful, if we live, then I'll take it away if you still wish. But not now. You have to be a part of this. If you're not, magic could be controlled by the worst of hands. I very much doubt humanity as we know it would survive."

The way he glared at me suggested there was no point in my attempting to persuade him otherwise.

"So what happens now?" I asked.

"On September twenty fourth we'll launch our attack at the CF1 base. Attempt to destroy it, and destroy all of the agents within it."

"So I've three weeks left before I'll probably die?"

"I think we have a fifty-fifty chance, Ben. Try to be a bit more optimistic. And if we do win, things will change. Change indefinitely."

"That sounds vaguely disturbing to be honest."

He magicked up a very large armchair, sat down on it, and then smiled at me. It wasn't reassuring, despite that being his intention.

"It's why I wanted you to come here today," George said, "Because I should have told you this before, I do feel a little guilty about not doing so. You see, Ben, my friend, I have to admit that I have not been completely honest about my future plans. I wouldn't say that I in any way outright lied. I simply withheld certain aspects of the truth from you."

"Oh God," I sighed, and felt something wilting inside my skull, something that felt like the death of a sense of hope.

"It's nothing that bad, dear boy. It just happens to be the case that once the war is over, if we're successful, I've decided I need to become king of the world."

I really wasn't sure how to react to that.

"Sorry," George continued, "I was being a bit melodramatic there. But I think it's time for a change. There's too much misery, too much corruption, too much all round shittiness in the world, if that's a word and I really should check one day since I use it so much."

"So you're going to take over the world? Is that, like, even possible? I mean how will you do it? I'd imagine quite a few people would object, and even though we're powerful, there's only so much we can do."

And lots of questions like that.

"I've been preparing for this day for a very long time, Ben. I hoped it wouldn't come, I hoped we could live on in the shadows without anyone caring about our existence, but that time has passed. A long time ago I started creating artefacts, devising a scheme, and I've had decades to spot flaws in it, and there were plenty of them initially. But not now," George said.

"So come on then, spill the beans," I responded.

And he did. And I'd really, really like to say it wasn't the deeply upsetting ramblings of a mad man. But you can't win them all.

"We're so fucked."

Karoline had known something was wrong even before I said

that, mainly as my face was the colour of the cruellest of winters.

"I take it you found out what George's plans for you are?" She asked, slowly becoming that same colour as I told her.

"Yeah, and you know all of those times you suggested that I shouldn't trust him completely? That he might not be all he seems? Well hey, looks like you were right. Won the lottery, not the normal one either but the EuroMillions draw, the highest ever prize."

Karoline sat down on a nearby sofa, a glassy look in her eyes.

"I saw this coming, I want that on the record, okay? So what's he done?"

"It's not what he's done that's of concern, it's what he plans to do afterwards. At least if there is an afterwards. He's created fifty of us you see. Fifty new magicians, all of whom will serve him, in a manner of speaking, as he plans to go up against the government. All governments. Take control of the world."

"Christ. That's quite the opposite of what I hoped you'd say," she said.

"Yep," I replied.

"We're so fucking stupid as well. Me and you. Us," Karoline said.

"Yeah," I said, "That can't be denied. Though you're less stupid by far, I mean I was the one who got us caught up in all this."

"For once I don't agree Ben. I mean, you were honest to me from nearly the get go, and told me all about the magic side of things pretty early on. Well before I'd fallen in love with you, that's for certain, it was back when I could easily have walked away. That said, at the time I was just, I don't know, I guess looking back I was in a bit of a weird shitty place when we met. A bit lost. And I'm in no way suggesting you took advantage of me, but then you changed my world. And I let you, with glee. I mean I wanted this just as much as you did. It's just a shame we spent so much of it in denial. That we didn't prepare for it all going horribly wrong, it's not like he hadn't sort of warned us, even if we didn't get the full version of events."

"I know," I replied, "But before I met him I was in a really messy place too, leading up to my meeting George I was only a few steps away from suicide if I'm to be horribly honest. And then my reality changed and I just didn't think about how everything might end."

Silence fell over us. We both sat back on the sofa and looked terrified. After far too long a time I was the first to speak.

"I've been thinking about this, and trust me, my soul is screaming at me right now not to say it, but you can walk away from this Karoline. I can take you away, hide you somewhere, until this is all over with. Because I have to help George. I truly have no choice in the matter, as I've just learnt that when he made me a magician he planted a tiny but powerful explosive somewhere in my body, in case I ever crossed him. It'll only take one word apparently, one word and my body will start to spontaneously combust and within only a few seconds the breeze would scatter my ashes far and wide."

"Oh Ben," she said, tears flowing now.

"But you don't have to be part of this. Witness this. So let me fly you to a location where there's no chance of your being hurt."

"No," she replied, about as firmly as any human being had ever said that word.

"Karoline."

"I'm not going anywhere Ben. I've got these pesky emotions for you, and they just won't let me. It's bloody annoying, but it's the truth."

"So what do we do?" I asked her, despite knowing there was no answer that could make things in any way better.

"Pray that you're victorious I suppose. Pray that the world George builds afterwards isn't as traumatic as the one we're currently in?" Karoline suggested, "So, how's the end of the world as we know it going to take place?"

I filled her in on the full story, and to be honest was surprised she wasn't more appalled.

"I've got to admit, that's not quite as bad as I thought it might be. In this version of events you might not even die."

"You're more optimistic than me."

"Maybe," she replied, "But George's vision of the future, at least it's vaguely peaceful. At least it's an attempt to change things. And as we have sod all choice in the matter it's not like we can do anything."

"I know."

"So how long have we got?"

"He says we're to attack on September the twenty fourth. About a month before the Government had planned to take us out."

"Three weeks left then. What are we going to do until then, Ben?"

"I've no idea," I muttered, dejected, "Other than spending every second of it with you."

"That's what I want too," she replied. "But perhaps not here? Maybe we could have one last adventure. See some of the world we've yet to see. Just in case we don't have that opportunity even if you do survive?"

"I'm so good with that," I replied, "Anything you want is what I want. I mean it's either that or panic and be abjectly miserable, and I've spent too much time in that place in my life as it is."

Discussions on what we could do continued long into the night, and though conclusions weren't made the next morning Karoline seemed ever so slightly happier.

"Given that we might have three weeks left to live I should at the very least quit my job then," she said, "And can you give me ten million pounds so I don't have to worry about money ever again? And then maybe we could go to the United States? Have a crazy ass ridiculously idiotic American adventure as far, far away from all of this as possible for two weeks?"

I was packing our bags halfway through the suggestion.

We did all the things you'd expect first, from making out on top of Lady Liberty's torch to watching Broadway shows floating invisibly above the front of the stage. We narrowly avoided a hundred baseballs at a Knicks game and we bought back long dead rock stars to get drunk with in the Chelsea Hotel, though I wish I hadn't gotten Sid Vicious involved, he's not a happy soul and he left the bed in a terrible mess. Not as awful as the last time he'd stayed there, admittedly, but I'll never trust him with a Marathon bar again. During a trip to Vegas we gambled away five million pounds, while on Hollywood Boulevard I was the spit of Alfred Hitchcock, going up to couples and saying things like "You're a beautiful woman, but good lord your husband is a majestic beast. I'd like to cast him in my next film, about a man who fights dinosaurs in space." Most didn't know who I was, and those who did looked aghast, but hey, everyone has off days I suppose.

A trip to Yellowstone National Park saw the Geysers spurt out absinthe, hence why neither of us could really remember the rest of that day, though I know at one point there were a whole load of kids running about and throwing up, and shortly afterwards I realised I probably should turn it back into water, especially when a few of their parents attempted to make more offspring. I awoke the next morning as a Grand Piano with Karoline lying across my lid, and initially all but shit myself as I panicked that I might have been so drunk as to not give myself a mouth, but thankfully loud screaming revealed some lips, a tongue and vocal cords hidden underneath one of the pedals.

Washington came next, where we snuck into the White House in the middle of the night, leaving post it notes in Obama's bedroom saying things like "Why didn't you close Guantanamo Bay, you promised to after all?" and "Look, I know you tried to do some good, it's a crime Obamacare wasn't supported in the way it should have been, and I imagine there were some scenarios where you made choices that you desperately didn't want to, but Jesus, did you have to fuck about with civil liberties so much? And all the crap with the NSA? Oh yeah, and could you have not killed so many innocent people? I mean, the drone warfare man, the drone fucking warfare..."

The day after that came the news Karoline had been waiting for since our arrival, as a skyscraper sized tornado was about to hit Oklahoma. On the Enhanced Fujita scale it was an EF4, which in layman's terms meant an "Oh Jesus, was that was that a McDonalds that just flew by us? Aw man, we're all going to die" scenario, if you were unfortunate or stupid enough to be anywhere near one. We were in the latter category of course, as we met up with it a little outside of Grady County. Due to my hatred of roller coasters I was a little wary of being sucked into such a force of nature and thrown all over the bloody place, but Karoline insisted we did so, and at least now I had that spell that would stop me throwing up everywhere. Initially it was quite awe inspiring too, at a guess it was about three hundred yards wide and in the worst of moods, like someone had insulted its mother with the ugliest swear words from about twelve different languages. I could only gasp as we watched the world around us be torn apart, with hopefully abandoned buildings evaporating in front of our eyes. Afterwards I planned to down vote all of those Hollywood twister movies on IMDB, they hadn't come close to capturing the horrifying beauty of it at all.

It was at this juncture that Karoline grabbed my hand and we dove in, which became number two hundred and forty one in our long list of bad, bad ideas. Maybe at first it was slightly fun as we were shot into the sky at quite the speed, but I was expecting a Wizard of Oz experience where we spun through the air hand in hand, dancing through the storm with gay abandon. But oh no, seconds later the enjoyable element came to a close as I was unable to see more than a few inches in front of my face, and even with a force field around us it felt like I was repeatedly being smashed into by an out of control locomotive, one of those Japanese trains which goes stupidly fast, leading me to crash into and mostly destroy a house in the not that nearby town of Bridge Creek. At least the tornado had already passed through the area so I was able to blame the damage upon it, the bastard had treated me cruelly so it felt only fair, plus I presumed the owners of the property had storm insurance whereas idiot magician insurance probably isn't a thing. But once I'd dusted myself off I slipped into panic mode as I had no idea where Karoline was, only to find her stuck on top of a tree a mile away. She didn't seem that bothered to be honest, yet I thought it'd be the gentlemanly thing to fly up and rescue her.

"Okay, tornadoes aren't the child friendly fun fair ride I'd thought they'd be," she said, "Sorry about that."

"It's okay, but let us never do that again," I replied, "And at least now I know not to trust moving air ever again."

After that night we decided to go on a mini-road trip, bar the fact that it was in an invisible car travelling a good forty feet above any traffic, if only so that we didn't waste time at stop signs or crashing into large trucks and dying. Our plan was to visit as many of those small towns which boast about having the world's biggest item that we could, hence their being photographs of us standing next to the world's biggest metal horse, and one with the world's biggest inflatable Jesus, and because we're predictably infantile we took many a photo of road signs that were slightly rude sounding. That was why we visited Alaska and the small town of Ballplay, with suitably x-rated pictures soon on Karoline's phone, but it was bloody cold so we didn't stick around for long.

A while later as we were flying across the Midwest I started to run low on magic, and so suggested to Karoline that we found somewhere to eat and then crash for the night.

"Cuh, Superman never got exhausted by just flying about for a bit you know," she teased.

"Yeah, well Superman was an alien whose strength was boosted by the frickin' sun, which is always up in the sky above some bloody part of the planet," I sulkily responded, "I'm just a twatty magician who runs out of magic the more he uses it, and I did spend a fair bit of it making the inflatable Jesus turn water into wine, I mean even you have to admit that was a pretty big lake."

"I stopped listening three words in, but Ben, I was just joking honeybear," Karoline said, "Whatever you need, you need."

Thus we set down in Emmitsburg in Maryland, the kind of town that had all but fallen apart a long time ago and was only kept alive by those who refused to live in the modern age, or those who couldn't afford to escape it. It had a population of around three thousand and I only hoped that they didn't all look as depressed as the couple who ran one of the local motels.

"What'd you like?" Kathy, the younger of the two asked.

"Just a double room, tv, that'll do us," I replied.

"Not a problem. Now what are you guys doing in a shitty place like this? Car broke down? It's normally when a car breaks down. Or a suicide pact. If you're going to do that, can you do it in the bath so there's not much cleaning up to do afterwards?" She said, with a smile.

"Hah, um, no, we're just on a road trip. It got late, we needed somewhere to crash for the night."

"That's an interesting accent," Kathy said, "I'm guessing English?"

I confirmed that it was.

"Your not being local explains why you made the mistake of stopping here then. But you sure you can't drive for another hour or so? There's nothing to do here, trust me."

"Nah, it's okay, all we need is somewhere to eat and a bed to pass out in," I replied, though we were out of luck on the food front as the local diner closed at 9PM. Fortunately Kathy was happy to throw together a few sandwiches, and soon we were knocking back beers with her and her husband Paul as they told us all about their un-beloved hometown. It sounded exactly like the small town I'd grown up in, a place you'd want to escape from at the age of four, with Kathy possibly joking about how they'd had to put a big fence around parts of the town to stop toddlers from trying to do exactly that. Hours later, when we finally declined yet another bottle and drunkenly stumbled into the room we'd hired and collapsed on to the bed, Karoline said "We should do something here."

"Um, this is a bit embarrassing, but, well, I'm a little bit too drunk right now for those kinds of frisky adventures," I shamefully confessed.

"No, not that you idiot, I mean something fun, something for the town that'll brighten it up for a bit. Even if it's only for one night."

"What kind of thing?"

"I'm not sure. Maybe a weird-ass music festival or something?" Karoline said.

"I don't know, that might draw a bit too much attention. And getting the bands to play in a town this tiny might be a bit of a problem."

"Just use clones. Or robot copies. Or flying bears with amazing voices?" Because yes, Karoline was very drunk indeed.

"I have a feeling the bears might get me into trouble, and the clones thing might be all kinds of complicated, I mean, what if real versions are playing live somewhere else that night? Or seen by someone, somewhere else?"

"Gah, you're no fun," Karoline said. And it's true, I wasn't.

"Look, I'm not against the idea," I responded, "We just need to tone it down a bit."

"Okay. So?"

"Er, how about mini-golf?"

"Ben, if we were married I'd be very tempted to divorce you right now. I suggest an enormous, mad, music fuelled party in a park, and you come back with well, how about we get them to hit some tiny balls about pointlessly?"

"No, hear me out," I replied, "What if it was the biggest, craziest crazy golf course ever made? Kind of almost impossibly crazy?"

"You really love crazy golf, huh?"

"Yeah, a little bit. And trust me, it'll be memorable I promise."

The following day we set up in a field about five miles away from Emmitsberg, and created the course within a couple of hours. If I described all of the different holes it'd take an age but the least bizarre was covered in flowers in the middle of which was the man eating plant Audrey II from *Little Shop Of Horrors*, who happily sang away when anyone took a shot. Another featured a *Scalextric* track that could be played on while others attempted to not hit any of the cars going around, something we tried to make all but impossible as the cars exploded dramatically into flames when a ball even gently touched them. Other holes also featured a variety of slightly unusual things, with one including a small tear in the space time continuum that you needed to hit your ball through, and another saw a new species of animal called Spiderbats who did their best to eat any balls that went near them. Meanwhile the final hole served as a homage to horror films, as hands plunged out of the grass at random points, grabbing the balls and dragging them into the ground, while a miniature knife wielding maniac occasionally ran across the course stabbing any balls that he saw to death. The screaming of the balls was perhaps a little too haunting, and we did get a couple of complaints, but as per usual I regretted nothing.

After we'd finished making the course we laid back in the cool grass and observed our creation. I had a feeling people would either love it or have me arrested for crimes against sanity / humanity, but I thought it worth the risk. We put up adverts all across the town the next day, with a big "One night only, free crazy golf, and hey, we're also giving away free booze" campaign, and I'm pretty certain every single occupant of the town attended. And sure, a few looked distressed and appalled, but mostly everyone got pleasantly drunk, played the game all night, and then went home without anything interesting happening at all. So you're probably wondering why I'm even bothering telling this tale, and what can I say other that a) I really bloody love crazy golf and it's lucky I didn't create another nine holes which were even more bizarre, and b) I wanted to mention one story where I didn't screw things up, and where terrible things didn't happen, if I'm to be completely honest.

The next morning it was as if we'd never been there, and we left simply hoping that we'd pass into urban legend, with it perhaps becoming more and more exaggerated over the years. And hey, if not, well I eventually got a hole in one on the Spiderbats course which impressed two passing young kids who shouted "You're the Spiderbats king, dude!" before running off. And what more can you want from life than that?

CHAPTER 12 - UNDER ATTACK

"Get in formation, right now, Ben, behind me, John to the right side, Stephen to the other, and just smash the shit out of them!" Karoline screamed. We were trapped, with thirty of them coming towards us from all sides.

"There's so many of them, all over the place," I cried, "Oh Jesus, they're going to fuck us all to death."

"Except me," Karoline said.

"That's not helping you know," I replied.

"There's no time for this," Karoline said, "Now draw your swords, and decapitate as many of these naked women as you can."

Three days earlier we'd been having the holiday of a lifetime. And shhh, I know I said right at the beginning that I hated it when people did the whole flashforward / flashback thing, but hey, you'll just have to live with it one final time. Sorry. Anyhow, following Emmitsburg we'd carried on travelling around the country, taking the time out to meet a few of our idols and gush like exasperating fan boys / girls, in stories which are so embarrassing that if you wanted to hear them you'd have to pay me several billion pounds. A couple of days were also spent careering around as many famous museums and monuments as we could visit, mostly at night as it's far easier to draw moustaches on famous paintings when the general public aren't around to complain. But then George had to go and spoil it all, as appears to be his wont.

"Ben, hi, it's George," George said after I'd stupidly answered my phone.

"Hi George, it's good to hear from you," I replied, in what was the most sarcastic sentence I'd ever uttered. He chose to ignore my derision.

"Look," he said, "I need a favour. You're still in America, right?"
I confirmed that I was.

"Good, good. You see, there's a magician I know, Theodore Goldman, who I've been unable to contact, I've tried phoning him but he hasn't answered, which is unusual for him. Normally I'd fly over and see what was going on, but I'm a little tied up right now."

Presuming he was talking about something unpleasantly sexual, I didn't ask for further details.

"So do you think you could head over to Pennsylvania? It's a small town, name of Lancaster, I'll text you the exact address. Shouldn't take you long either, and if you do find him, just tell him, well, tell him everything I've told you about my forthcoming plans. That I'm calling in that favour from Eighteen Ninety Three. He'll know the one I mean."

That's why only a few hours later we were flying over the rather picturesque and beautiful state of Pennsylvania, enjoying the scenery and the pleasant late summer's day, at least until I heard screaming coming from a small barn in the middle of nowhere, the kind of building that you'd expect serial killers to spend their summer holidays in. As we flew closer the screaming grew louder and I could hear someone shouting "No, no, no, no, no, no, no, no!" over and over again. Casting a couple of spells on Karoline to protect her from whatever monstrosity might be responsible for such a sound, we burst through the door.

Only to find a man having sexual intercourse with a woman. It didn't really make sense, she looked like she was having the time of her life, squealing with delight, but he was shrieking in such a way that it looked like he was about to shuffle off this mortal coil. And then he did.

With one final drawn out cry of derision his body stopped moving and his eyes glazed over, which was alarming enough, but suddenly he started to decompose and within twenty seconds he had crumbled into dust. Both Karoline and I were silent for about ten seconds, as the naked woman lay on the floor looking rather pleased with herself. Then she began convulsing, and opened her legs to expose every millimetre of her genitals, as a child slowly crawled out of her.

"What the living fuck?" Karoline said.

"Now that's not normal," I muttered, as I always try to be a master of the understatement. What was even less normal was the rate the child was growing, and within a minute she was a fully grown adult, of around the age of twenty five, and identical to her mother.

"Make love to us," they said, "Make love to us now."

Karoline politely turned down their request on my behalf, but whatever these creatures were they had clearly not been educated concerning the nature of consent as they ignored her and lunged at me. I cast a spell that was supposed to cause their legs to stop working, but it had no effect, and then another, different spell, and another and another but nothing seemed to stop them, and the next thing I knew one of the two had pushed me down to the ground and was desperately trying to unbutton my trousers. Deeply unimpressed, Karoline grabbed a rusty spade from the side of the barn, and swung it at my assailant, saving the day.

What neither of us had expected was for the woman's head to come clean off, and bounce across the floor. Though weirdly there was no blood, and only death.

The newly born adult woman hissed in rage, and leapt at Karoline, who defensively swung the spade once more. Cue a second bouncing head.

"Oh Jesus," Karoline cried out, "Oh Christ. I, I murdered them." After I'd taken a few seconds to recover I examined the bodies. They appeared to be normal, despite their flimsiness.

"What should we do?" Karoline asked, "Ben, this is insane, I don't want to go to prison. I didn't mean to kill them, I thought it'd knock them unconscious at best. But, but, oh Jesus. I'm fucked. I'm so, so fucked." I could understand why she was so distressed, if I'd been responsible for the decapitations I'd probably have felt the same way, but I knew that all wasn't as it seemed, and not only because two beautiful women had wanted to have sex with me.

"Look, something strange is clearly going on here," I replied, "I mean, that one screwed a guy to death, his corpse then decayed and crumbled in front of our eyes, and she gave birth to a baby that became an adult within about sixty seconds. Unless I missed a really important biology class, I'm pretty sure humans don't do that."

"You think she might not actually be real?" Karoline asked, hope emerging in her voice for the first time.

"Absolutely. I'm pretty certain of it as it goes, this reeks of magic, and dark, despicable magic at that."

Relieved, Karoline was at least partially able to smile.

"I really miss the days where my life wasn't incredibly traumatic," she said, and I nodded in agreement.

"What should we do now? I mean, should we bury the bodies in an unmarked grave, just to be safe?"

"Given how close we are to Theodore Goldman I can only presume he's somehow involved," I replied, "But yeah, you're right, we should hide them away somewhere as I've a feeling bringing the police into this wouldn't be a good idea."

Two very shallow graves later and we were in the air again, but only for about ten seconds as I quickly spotted Goldman's home, a seemingly deserted farm with it not just being absent of people but animals as well, while the crops were overgrown and starting to die.

We flew right up to the farmhouse, landed, became visible and knocked on the door. There was no answer, so I kicked it in due to the dramatic mood I was in. Inside the farmhouse was empty though it looked lived in, there were plates by the sink, food in the fridge, all of that kind of thing, but a distinct lack of life in each and every room, and we were almost about to leave when I decided to give myself x-ray vision just to check that there were no hidden areas, no secret rooms. Which was a rare smart idea of mine, as I found an enormous bunker right under the house. An enormous bunker where twenty people were all shagging each other senseless, but where hundreds of others were huddled together, bound and gagged and shaking and shivering. One quick description to Karoline later and:

"Great, so it turns out George's friend is even more insane than he is."

I had to nod in agreement.

"Part of me wants to walk away, but given how it appears that in this town sex equals instant degeneration we probably shouldn't," I said, and this time it was Karoline's turn to reluctantly nod.

With that I made us invisible, found the entrance to the bunker under a badly flea bitten rug, and entered a large, concrete structure where absolutely no expense had been spent making it look nice, the walls were covered in mould and what looked like rust, but it might easily have been blood, I never did get round to checking. Along one side were a group of desperate, crying men, though it was so dank and dark in the structure that I couldn't guess how many.

Then there was the fucking. The men were barely able to move as their arms and legs had been chained to the ground, and it wasn't taking long for them to die, either. You'd have to have a pretty worrisome fetish to get a kick out of this, so I was not looking forward to meeting Theodore Goldman, I was certain of that. Because more births were all but constantly occurring there were over thirty women now, as we hovered by the ceiling taking it all in, and after each death and birth, one of the newly born women would chain another prisoner to the floor and the whole nightmarish horror show would begin again. Staring down at them aghast I'd failed to notice that on the wall furthest away from us was a naked man, with large nails in his hands and feet ensuring that he wasn't going anywhere, but Karoline soon brought him to my attention. He'd been gagged so I couldn't make out what he was shouting at us, but that was also due to the mixture of noises coming from below which were what you might imagine hearing if the Marquis de Sade had travelled through time and somehow forced David Lynch to make a porn film with him, a sound so foul that no one should ever be subjected to it, bar maybe those involved in the creation of Noel's House Party. "I've got a feeling he might have something to do with this you know," Karoline whispered, pointing at the crucified naked man, and so saving him became our priority. I gave us both an extra strong force field, and for my own safety a very large metallic pair of pants which came complete with a big old bastard of a padlock. Then we very slowly flew over to the man and removed the nails implanted in his limbs, and took the gag from his mouth.

"Save them too, save the men before they're killed," he hoarsely whispered, which was rather patronising if you ask me, it was a rare day I left a big bunch of blokes to be murdered after all.

"Soon, soon, I promise," I replied, "First off all we need to get you out of here."

I grew an extra arm so that I could carry him, also made him invisible, and glided across the room before shooting out of the bunker, right through the roof of the house and half a mile into the sky. Then I flew another ten miles just to be safe, before landing in a field and mending his wounds.

"So that's sex ruined for good," I said, and Karoline nodded in agreement once more.

"Thank you, thank you so much for saving me," the man said.

"You're Theodore Goldman, I take it?" I asked, to which he shook his head.

"No, no, I'm John. John Taylor."

"Any relation to the Duran Duran bloke?" I asked, but sadly he wasn't. "Okay, well John, I don't suppose you care to explain what was going on there?"

"It's a long story," John replied.

"Is it though? I mean, didn't you just create a shed load of sex slaves and then it all got out of hand?" Karoline asked.

"What?" John said, seemingly perplexed, "Oh lord, if only it were that. But it was far more appalling, I wasn't responsible for anything that you just saw, I can tell you that."

"So what did happen?" I asked.

"I was with my friend. Stephen. Stephen Caldwell. Who, Christ, might still be alive. God, please, please, can you go back there to check?"

"Soon," I replied, "But I really need to know what I'm dealing with first."

"Okay. I guess. So it all began about three days ago, we've been on a gap year, Stephen and I, backpacking around the country, checking out the smallest of towns, the ones that have somehow remained outside of the twenty first century and maintained an element of charm. We ended up here a couple of nights ago and it was late and there was nowhere else around other than the farm, and so we thought we'd take a risk and ask if we could crash there. This old guy, Ted something, he said sure, that wouldn't be a problem, invited us to eat with him, share a few drinks, and as he got drunker he started babbling, and then out of the blue he claimed he was a magician, that he could do things that no other human could, how he could change the world if he wanted to. That was when we started to try and come up with a polite excuse to leave, but he carried on, one long monologue about his escapades, mostly sexual too, how he experienced orgies of the type that even the ancient Greeks would have blushed at. I tried to insist that I was ready to drop, and had to call it a night, but the old man insisted he show us a party trick."

"Which involved creating naked women, I take it?" Karoline asked.

"No, no, it started off as a handkerchief trick, you know the one where they pull it out of their pocket and it just keeps coming and coming and coming until there's about half a mile of the thing. But then he started to change it, and the handkerchief became snakes and squids and boiled rabbits and octopuses and finally a wet giant tongue. He was cackling away the whole time, until I accidentally upset him by suggesting that though this was impressive, we really needed to sleep, that I was exhausted, and could barely keep my eyes open. I mean, it was fucking freaky and I just wanted to get out of there. But at that point he became enraged, said something in some language I've never heard before and I was suddenly knocked out. When I woke up I was crucified in that dungeon, and I've no clue where Stephen is. But given what those women were doing to the other men, I really don't have a good feeling about it."

"Jesus, that's messed up," I said, before turning to Karoline, "Um, any ideas on how to deal with this? I mean, you know what happened in the barn, and if they were to tear this padlock off I might be dust within seconds."

"Well, I guess the only sensible thing would be to turn yourself into a woman?" Karoline suggested, which made perfect sense, hence I cast the spells to ensure my safety. But even missing a penis and with slightly larger breasts I still wasn't quite sure how to defeat some insane lunatic who'd decided to create an army of sex obsessed women with murderous vaginas who might just end up destroying humanity. Or at least kill all men, and without men who would create war and misery? The world wasn't ready for that kind of change.

I also had no idea what artefacts the old man might have too, if he was a friend of George's, and had been around since Eighteen Ninety Three, I suspected he'd probably created a fair few. I was certainly ill prepared for that level of magical abuse, guessing that the best case scenario was him turning me into an ever sentient pile of manure.

"Okay, we need to get into that bunker, hopefully rescue John's friend, destroy all the women even though they're seemingly impervious to magic, defeat the dangerously demented magician, and then have a nice BBQ and some drinks afterwards, yeah? Kind of sounds easy? Apart from everything before the BBQ bit?" I said.

"Maybe you could reprogram the women? Cast a spell to stop them having killer genitalia?" Karoline said.

"I don't know, I mean, magic doesn't seem to work on them. At least not anything I've tried this far, so I don't quite know what to do." But the moment I said it the solution suddenly popped into my mind. I still hadn't told Karoline about the Yuasa artefact and I still didn't quite know why, though it had crossed my mind that Orson had tweaked my brain when he'd taken a look inside, but either way I guessed I could use it if worst came to the worst. Which I'm pretty sure was happening as we spoke.

"We need to take out the old man first then," Karoline replied, "See what we can do afterwards. Which means getting him out of the bunker and somewhere far away as soon as we can. If your magic works down there at all."

"The old man," John said, "He was casting spells like there was no tomorrow, I hadn't a clue what he was doing or saying, but he spent hours and hours doing it, I never saw him sleep."

"Either way, we need to end this now. I mean, they could plausibly take over the world. Plus once they've fucked all of the men to death, what might they do afterwards? It could only be a matter of time before they turn on the animals, and surely camels don't deserve a fate like that," I uttered, though both John and Karoline didn't seem to be that bothered about the camels, if I'm to be completely truthful.

"Fuck the camels, we need to save those men first," John said.

"Okay, okay," I said, "How about I make us all invisible, and give you the ability to fly along with extra strength and force fields? Then I'll turn our fists into steel and we can all try to knock the old man unconscious? Hopefully. Or, er, we might have to smash his brains to pieces?"

"It truly is going to be a lovely day," Karoline sarcastically uttered.

"Yeah, yeah, but I can't think of anything better, and time's not exactly on our side," I replied, before casting the required spells and flying back to the bunker.

It was the same set up as before except the number of naked women had already doubled, so near on a hundred men were in the process of being screwed / murdered. I couldn't see the old man anywhere, so quietly suggested that we free the men still trapped down there, and go on from there. Flying over to the wall where the majority were gathered I grabbed as many of them in my now giant hands as I could, which was seven as it turns out, and flew them to safety, with Karoline and John doing the same.

A second trip followed, but I noticed that Karoline and John weren't with me this time, and upon heading outside I discovered why, as somewhat annoyingly John was holding a knife millimetres away from Karoline's throat.

"Sorry about this," John said, "Especially as you've been such a great help, as everything got out of hand there. Oh, and before you try to make me implode or something, I've removed your protection spells, and could slice her to pieces in a millisecond. If you make even the slightest of sounds I will presume you're casting a spell and will kill her."

Before I had the chance to try and work out what the hell was going on, one of the naked men I'd rescued approached me, his large penis swaying in the gentle breeze, which might be an odd thing to notice when your girlfriend is in danger, but Jesus it was an impressive cock.

"Hi, I'm Stephen," the owner of the mighty penis said, "Could you give me your jeans please? It's a bit cold to be naked right now and I don't know a jeans making spell sadly."

John moved the knife closer to Karoline's arteries to make sure I didn't do anything stupid as I slowly took them off, wishing that I'd remembered to wear underwear that day. Especially as doing so led to both John and Stephen laughing at my own sexual organ.

"Dude, you're a magician and yet that's what you've given yourself?" John said, before commenting, "No, no, don't say a word, but haha, you poor fucker. Ah man, wait until we tell Seth about this, he'll piss himself. Right, haha, sorry, back to business. Now, as you might have realised, I didn't give you the full story earlier, other than that the backpacking around the country part was true. But what really happened was that we met the old guy a month ago, and his strange wife who rarely said more than a couple of words an hour, and it played out mostly as I told you, except that once we saw what he could do we waited until he'd drunk himself into a stupor, and in the middle of the night we bound and gagged him and his wife before he could react. It took three and a half weeks to torture him into making us magicians. Had to keep him separate from his wife too, and do... Do things which I regret. They were not the best of times. But once he'd made us magicians we did the understandable thing and started setting about making the best orgy ever."

"Ugh, I knew it," Karoline spat out, "This was all about you being dirty bloody perverts."

"That's us!" John said in an annoyingly arrogant manner, "It went all a bit wrong though, I thought I'd killed the old man but it turned out he'd managed to partially fool me. In the final few seconds of his life he cast spells that crucified me, bound and gagged Stephen, gave the women killer vaginas and made them invulnerable to magic. So we definitely owe you a favour for saving us. Was very kind of you."

"But where the hell did all of those men come from then?" I asked.

"Oh, they're made of magic too. Stephen's bisexual you see, the plan was to have a giant fuck fest featuring both sexes."

The whole time he'd been chatting away I'd been trying to work out a plan, failed, and then realised something. John and Stephen might have been psychopathic bastards, but magic wise they were a league two side compared to my premiership team.

"Now listen Ben," John said, "I can imagine that you're quite the powerful magician. Given that you've got this honey as a girlfriend and a tiny penis, it's surely the only reason why she's with you. Just doesn't make any sense at all otherwise. I mean, look at her, and sorry, but you're the luckiest man alive. And I really don't want to have to kill her. So walk away. Then fly or whatever, fast. Don't come back. And in two weeks' time, once we're very long and very gone I promise you I'll set her free, alive and well. So what do you say?"

I nodded. Several times. Looked suitably distressed. Turned my head away. Uttered a spell which turned the knife to jelly. As soon as I'd started to speak he'd begun cutting, but fortunately had drawn only a little blood and Karoline was otherwise unharmed. Then I transformed his and Stephen's heads into space hoppers with no mouths and only very small noses. They shook their giant heads angrily and bounced them against the floor, falling all over the place for thirty seconds or so, before realising there was nothing they could do.

"That was quite the risk you just took," Karoline angrily said.

"Not really. Which I know makes me sound over confident, but they gave themselves away by talking so much," I said, "Letting me know they were pretty new to the whole magic game. No proper training, didn't even know spells about how to make your own clothing, and once I realised that I knew defeating them both was going to be really easy once I'd disposed of the knife. And it's not like I could leave you with them like they suggested. Not after what we've seen them just do."

"I suppose. Not that I'm any happier about it, but we'll talk about that later. But what now? What should we do with two sex crazed murderous magic arseholes, oh, and a mini-army of killer women?" Karoline asked.

"It's a good question. I guess, there is one thing I could do, there is an artefact that I could possibly use to solve everything. Though I'm guaranteeing nothing, and I need to dash back to England to get it first."

"And what about the women in the bunker in the meantime?" Karoline asked, "At least one of those women escaped beforehand, who's to say the others won't follow suit?"

"How about I make you a machine gun or twenty?" I asked

"For Christ's sake Ben, I don't want to kill any more of them. Couldn't you just seal all of the women in the bunker?" Karoline said, because she's far smarter than me. Just to be safe I did both, creating the kind of arsenal of weapons that could win a large war, like that nineteen forties one historians keep blathering on about, before tying up Stephen and John and gluing them to the top of a tree so that they couldn't do anything annoying.

Dashing over to England and then back to America only took fifteen minutes, but when I met Karoline outside of the farm house she wasn't happy with what I was dragging behind me.

"What the hell are they doing here?" Karoline asked as I landed beside her, with Stephen and John by my side.

"Don't worry, they've agreed to help me out. They really don't have any choice in the matter as it goes, and if they try to hurt you in any way there's a device which will blow their heads off. And then there legs and arms, I'm nothing but thorough. Plus, you know, they have space hoppers for heads and we need as many distractions as possible. It's probably best you stay out here though, I don't want to risk your being hurt."

Karoline was not impressed by my patronising behaviour.

"But they don't give a toss about me," she said, "It's only men who they find attractive, isn't it?"

"Ah, but what if they suddenly become lesbians?" I said

"Ben, why are you doing this? Look, tell me, what's really happening here?" She asked.

"Okay, I'm sorry," I replied, "The long and the short of it is that some of the magic I'm going to have to do down there is likely to be all kinds of distressing. Especially if my initial idea doesn't pay off, and I don't want you to see that."

"Alright. I get it, and I suppose you can probably handle this, but the first time I hear that girlish scream of yours, I'm coming running," Karoline responded.

"Okay, that's fair enough. Right, Stephen, John, do what I suggested earlier and I might, just might, one day return you to human form."

I cast a spell to unseal the bunker at this point, took a deep breath and prepared myself for the atrocity I was about to commit. Before not getting the chance, as a whole host of naked women burst through the farm house door, shrieking and running at us.

So here we are pretty much back at the start then, surrounded by naked beautiful women who wished to kill mankind. My energy levels were flagging as well, and though I could use the Yuasa artefact that was a process which would take way too much time for the majority not to escape.

"Ben, I think we need to skip Plan A and move on to Plan B," Karoline shouted.

"Which is?" I asked.

"I think we might need to just chop them up. And fast, before we lose sight of any of them and they make it into town and start duplicating all over the bloody place."

I created the kind of swords that Jamie Lannister would be impressed by, and handed them out to everyone. Naturally John and Stephen tediously tried to kill us, but unfortunately for them Karoline and I were protected by fresh force fields, and so they reluctantly turned their attentions to the women.

"Get in formation, right now, Ben, behind me, John to the right side, Stephen to the other, and just smash the shit out of them!" Karoline screamed. After a bit more of my idiotic banter that you've already been privy to, the slicing and the cutting and the murdering began, okay, they might not have been born in a conventional manner but they still looked human and I was feeling sickened, and I could see that Karoline was too. Until I suddenly realised I was being an idiot once again. We'd learnt that magic didn't affect them, but the spades and the swords had proven there were ways of defeating them. Which meant there must be other ways of disposing of them in what would hopefully be a far more efficient manner. One spell later and we were in the sky and the ground they were walking on turned into lava, with the plan being a little too effective, largely as despite being thirty feet from the ground I could still smell their burning flesh, which I really wish hadn't made me as hungry as it did.

"Jesus, Ben," Karoline shouted.

"I'm sorry," I replied, "I panicked. There were just so many of them."

"It's okay, I know they had to be dispatched. I just didn't expect it to be so sudden and brutal. Do you think that's all of them though? Or could more be inside?"

It was a question I'd considered myself, having just killed thirty of them I was feeling nauseated and would have been happy to put it off for an age, but I knew this needed to be finished once and for all. There was only one slight problem, in that I was absolutely and categorically shattered.

"I wouldn't normally suggest such a thing, but could you steal an hour of John's life?" Karoline said after I told her of my predicament.

"You think?" I replied.

"I mean it's a shitty thing to do, there's no doubting that, but then he did create this situation. And tried to kill us, um, so thinking about it you should nick two days from the little shit."

I settled for just the one hour in the end, and soon after I grabbed both Stephen and John and demolished the farm's walls and pulverised everything in sight until I was down into the bunker again. The women briefly stopped having sex and turned and hissed at us, and in the hope that they'd be even more distracted I created fireworks which shot off in all directions, bursting into quite dazzling displays, even if I do say it myself. Wishing to perplex them further I caused rain to pour from the ceiling, drenching everyone, and Stephen and John ran around head butting walls and bouncing off of them, with the ensuing confusion giving me the time to quickly create and drop fifty or so metallic cells upon the remaining magical creatures. Unfortunately my aim was occasionally a bit off and a few limbs were chopped off, but once imprisoned I took a breath, sighed loudly at the lunacy surrounding me, and began one by one to cut open their skulls.

You'd think you'd get used to doing such a thing after the tenth or fifteenth time, and maybe a slightly less irritating man than me would have, but every incision still made me wince, and it's not one of my happiest memories, with not a single picture taken for our holiday photo album.

Eventually my work came to an end and oh did I thank the lord, even though I knew that he never listened to our prayers, the lazy turd. Oh, and I gave them all clothes too, as I knew Karoline would probably never speak to me again if I didn't. An hour after it all began I sealed the bunker, leaving all inside.

"That's not exactly a great permanent solution, Ben," Karoline said, "Magic or not they're still sort of alive. Some kind of life form at least."

"I know, I know, I'm going to contact George. I need to tell them that his friend was murdered by those two bastards for one thing," I said, pointing at John and Stephen who I'd still not yet returned to normal, and was still very tempted to leave them with space hoppers for heads.

"You think that's a good idea?" Karoline asked, "Gotta say, I'm really not happy about the whole them trying to kill me thing, but if you leave it up to George he'll either murder them or recruit them, and I'm not sure either's a good idea."

"I'm with you on that one, and there is something I could do. Except I can't tell you what."

"Why?" Karoline asked, "I truly don't care if it's something horrendous, not after what they've done."

"No, I mean, I genuinely can't. Something's been done to me to prevent me from doing so."

"Oh," Karoline said, "I'm guessing George is behind that then."

I shook my head. "No, for once he isn't to blame. It's someone else. I... I keep on trying to tell you, but the words won't come."
"So it's Orson then. And don't worry about trying to say whether it is or not, I know he's the only other magician you know."
She was right of course, but even when I tried to nod my head it wouldn't move.
"Whoever it is," I replied, "I'm going to try to confront them. Gah, this is so frustrating. Hopefully at one point in the future I'll be able to tell you everything. As soon as I can I promise I will. In the meantime, I need to deal with these two. Privately."
Which I did, by flying them over to the barn we'd visited earlier, slicing open their skulls, and removing their memories from the past month, before replacing them with new ones. Ones which suggested they'd been in a serious car crash, and spent a month in hospital, but were now almost back to normal. I broke their legs and mostly mended them too, just in case they ever had x-rays in the future, and then punched them in the face several times each. There was no reason for that of course, I was just fucked off no end with the suffering they'd created.
After reverting back to my male self a few hours later I phoned George, told him a mostly true version of what had happened, albeit claiming that Stephen and John had been screwed to death by the women, and he promised to come over to the bunker when he could and resolve the issue. I asked him what he was going to do with these magical beings and for once he was honest and said he didn't know. Said he'd try to think of something. A brief moment of dread ensued, but I did my best to be selfish once again and not think about it for a second more.

Shortly afterwards I flew back to Karoline, and we headed to the nearest motel, and collapsed into a deep sleep. Hours later, despite being exhausted, Karoline couldn't sleep.

"Are you awake?" She asked, causing me to stir.

"Almost. Are you okay?"

"I can't stop thinking about what happened today. I mean, I killed someone. More than one. Whether it was intentional, whether they were magical and turned out not to be really human, or whatever it is we consider to be human anyhow, I still took a life. Lives."

"They were magical constructs, and had only existed a very short while."

"You're not listening," she said, a gentle sob escaping from her throat.

"I'm sorry. And you're right."

"I keep picturing it in my head. The decapitation. I want it to go away but it won't."

"It'll pass," I said, "In time."

"That doesn't change what happened Ben."

"I know. I wish I knew what to say," I said, "I wish this hadn't occurred. I did things in there which will haunt me for a long time, but the only way I can cope with this life is by burying the more harrowing moments deep inside."

"It's just that every time I feel like I can cope with the magical madness that is your life, something else happens and I'm no longer certain at all. And I know it feels like we keep having this conversation and I know you care and I know I've said I'm okay or I will be, but now, now I'm not sure. It's such a crazy whirlwind, life with you. One minute we're messing about with magic in ludicrous ways and it's so much fun and I'm caught up in the craziness and I love it, I truly do. But then something like this happens. Something like Andrew Fisher happens. Something like that CF1 agent happens. And I don't think I can carry on doing it. I keep on trying to persuade myself I can, that I love you so much that I can't imagine life without you. Except right now I'm beginning to. And I can't imagine coping with more death, more abhorrent people, and any more horror."

"Please," I started to beg.

"I don't want to leave you," Karoline said, "I swear I don't."

"Then don't. "

"It's not that simple Ben. You know it isn't," She insisted, "It's something that I thought I could cope with, and now I don't think I can. I think after my Uncle died I was in such a messy place and I stopped caring a little, I thought life was pointless and so what did it matter if it came to a premature end? I had no one to live for apart from you, and I thought that what we were doing, well, it wasn't really going to hurt anyone else. But that was me living in denial, and today, today's been a huge wake up call. Which is why things need to change. Have to change."

"Then they will do, because I don't want to lose you. I can't lose you. I couldn't live without you," I said, not regretting that last part even though I should have given that it was essentially emotional blackmail.

"Ben," was all she said, it being the most miserable way my name had ever been uttered.

"I'm sorry. And I could live without you. I don't know how, but I would. And I'll do anything for us to stay together. And I do feel the same way I hate the madness aspect too. Especially..."

"Especially what?" She asked, sitting up in bed, and I followed suit.

"Something happened with Orson and I, at the CF1 base. Something that I'm so ashamed of."

"What was it Ben?" she asked.

I told her, even though I knew what her reaction would be. What anyone's reaction would be.

"But how? How could you do that?" She asked, utterly stunned.

"I had no choice. Orson made that clear. The information we'd learnt, it was too important, we had to go along with it all."

"Ben, that's so wrong. So unbelievably wrong."

"Don't you think I know that?" I said, angrily, "Don't you think I hate myself for what I did? I've tried to forget, I've tried to persuade myself that it happened and I couldn't do anything about it, but I know that's not really true. I could have broken cover. I could have just flown off and left him to pick up the pieces. But at that point in time, I guess I just panicked. Did what he told me to do."

She stared at me. Then the sobbing began. I went to put my arm around her but she shrugged it off. Both of us sat there in silence. Occasionally I uttered her name, but she didn't respond until the final time.

"I thought I knew you, Ben. I truly did. And I knew you were capable of violence, but... Christ, the signs were there all along, and I can't believe I didn't notice them."

Tears were streaking down my face now, as I could see the inevitable coming, and knew that whatever I said wouldn't be able to slow it down for even a second.

"I never hurt someone purposefully. It was always self-defence," I tried to explain.

"Apart from at the CF1 base," she managed to utter.

"But that was the only time," I responded, knowing how weak an argument it was.

"That doesn't change anything, "Karoline said, getting up from the bed and walking towards the door.

"I need time away. From you. I need a break. I'm not saying it's over between us, but I'm not saying it isn't either. Fuck. I don't have the words to explain how I feel. But you need to take me home. And after that I need to be on my own and see... See if there's any way I can get past this."

I wish that what followed wasn't so abjectly miserable, but essentially a whole lot of crying and a whole lot of begging didn't change her mind one iota.

CHAPTER 13 - PRIME MINISTER'S QUESTIONS

So how about we have a nice gentle night in playing the blame game? Not that I'm in denial, I was accountable for my actions, but if I say that then my brain has to take a certain quantity of the blame, as it had been responsible for some very, very poor ideas in the past. I also knew it wasn't going to enjoy this latest trauma one single jot, and due to that the moment Karoline and I went our separate ways I broke into a pharmacy and stole a sod load of Paroxetine, the anti-depressant that had helped me the most in the past, as there was no question I needed it right away as I was really struggling when it came to suicidal ideation. I knew I wouldn't end my life, not while there was even the slightest chance Karoline might one day want to get back with me, but my brain didn't want to stick around, he was fed up to the back teeth with all of the choices I'd made and had simply had enough.

I kept on trying to force myself to acknowledge that someone very wise had once said that suicide isn't about wanting to kill yourself, but to kill a feeling, kill the emotions that you're being overwhelmed by, and that's what I clutched on to, repeating it to myself whenever I woke up and had the urge to jump from a very tall building and land on the floor without any functioning organs. But it was an argument that was quite tiring, and there were occasions that even when I was screaming at my brain "Why are you making me feel like this? We don't know if it's over with her for good? You know you're predicting the worst possible outcome and it might not be like that?" it wouldn't listen, it wouldn't do me the kindness of shutting the hell up.

Now at this point you may be wondering if I was suffering from some form of schizophrenia, but that's definitely not the case, several doctors have checked to make sure. I just have one of those minds that isn't always helpful, that doesn't always have my best intentions at heart. A lot of therapy in the past had helped me spot the warning signs when it was going to be an arse, when it was going to suggest things that not only weren't true but were actively cruel, the cheeky little thing that it was, but it was going in to overdrive now, pulling out all the stops, suggesting ideas which really weren't for the best.

Unfortunately despite now being on anti-depressants there's the slight issue that they don't immediately work, and can sometimes make you feel worse than you did originally, or suddenly make you feel anxious, or over-confident and a little hyper, a combination that can make those first few difficult days or weeks absurdly challenging, and it's very hard to know when they do start working until you look back and go "Oh, yeah, I was not myself during those weeks", or as I like to phrase it, "Jesus I was cray cray last month. Sorry everyone".

It might sound like I'm being a little flippant about mental health issues as well, but I guess I'm just trying to bring some humour into a time which floored me, which almost killed me, which made me re-evaluate what depression could be once a fucking-gain. The irony being that I had no idea how bad things could get. Would get. But let's not get ahead of ourselves. Right now the general gist was that I was abhorrently low one hour, but hyper and manic by the evening, all of which brings us back to the blame game. And why I chose to do the things that I did, which began with George turning up a few days after my return to the UK.

Pushing past me as I opened the front door he walked into the living room, which due to my mood now looked like a grungy, student affair with half eaten takeaways and bottles of spirits propping up tables, and the accompanying smell was just as unpleasant. Not that George was fazed.

"I've bad news Ben. It's Larry, he's dead, and that messes things up in ways that scares me."

Seeing George this nervous on top of everything else was galling.

"What happened?" I asked.

"The nun. The nun killed him."

"Who?"

"A CF1 agent. Though she used to be someone else altogether, there was even a time when we were close. But six years ago, for reasons I shall never understand, she swapped sides."

"I think I've met her."

"What?" George exclaimed.

"I know I should have told you about this at the time, but I thought I'd dealt with the matter in a way that meant it wasn't important."

"Go on."

"When we created that island for Karoline and I to go on another magical filled date, on the final day the Nun discovered it, completely by chance, as she accidentally flew into the force field. We fought, and it got all kinds of grubby and obnoxious, but with Karoline's help I managed to defeat her."

"So why isn't she dead?" George asked, his voice trembling with anger.

"I couldn't kill her. I couldn't take a human life."

"Then how did you escape?"

"I just did."

"Tell me."

"I... I... It was..." I spluttered as I tried but failed to tell him. Fortunately he was smarter than me.

"Oh, I think I see. You can't tell me can you? Which must mean... Oh, dear lord, I cannot believe I didn't realise this earlier. Orson used the Yuasa artefact upon you. So he's had it all this time," he said.

I couldn't reply. I just sat down. He cast a spell on me and the artefact began glowing.

"What?" George said, "You've still got it? Blood hell. That sly little bastard."

He crossed the room and took it out of my jeans pocket. Stared at it. Chucked it up in the air and then caught it in his right hand. Before giving it back to me.

"I see it's been used a fair few times."

"There have been a fair few complicated occurrences."

"Well if it has kept you out of harm's way and stopped you dying, then I suppose it's for the best that you had it. Plus I have my own now, my new recruits have been rather helpful on that front."

"You're not angry with me for lying?"

"Not you, no," George said, "It's not like you had any choice in the matter. If anything I'm disappointed in myself for not realising that Orson might have done this. But he is the least of our problems. Like I said before, Larry has been murdered. We can't afford to lose any more of our own kind. So I've brought forward the day of the attack. We strike on Thursday. You have three days to attend to your affairs and tie up any loose ends."

The first thing I did after he left was call Orson. Now I wouldn't call it PTSD exactly but on top of everything else I was having a lot of horribly vivid dreams which involved either naked women drowning in lava and slowly burning to death, or homeless people having parts of their bodies burst, and that's not the hilariously laugh out loud experience you might imagine it to be. The fact that Orson had sliced open my skull and screwed around with my mind frustrated as well, and so when Welles finally answered his phone you could say I was in quite the pissy mood. He didn't seem impressed.

"You lied to me, Orson. You begged me not to say anything about the Yuasa artefact and for the longest of times I didn't. Until I realised I had no choice."

"I couldn't trust you, you idiot," he snapped back, "When I gave it to you I'd only met you an hour before and Yuasa artefact or not I wasn't able to tell what you might do in the future. You've got to remember that I didn't exactly have a lot of time to think things over, I knew I'd either have to kill George or succumb to him, and so had to have a back-up plan in place in case it was the latter. I mean you've used the artefact and know what it can do, and what it could do if it ever fell into the wrong hands?"

"Yes. Not by choice, either. But that's not the point. You fucked with my brain, Orson."

"Jesus, just get over it Ben. These things happen, and be honest with me, was my doing so in any way truly detrimental to your life?"

It's possible he had a point, but I really wasn't in the mood to admit that. But when I tried arguing it turned out he wasn't in the mood to listen.

"Oh just quit your whining Ben, we've got more serious things to worry about after all. I take it you've heard about Larry."

I confirmed that I had. And though I'm still not quite sure why, I explained to him what George had planned.

"So what is the score between you and George?" I asked.

"George is, Christ, I don't know what he is right now. Or what he has been in the past to be honest. Rather skilled at revising history, that one. Or making you see it in a new light. Either way it's a complex and irritating relationship that we have, and as I said before, he's not exactly someone I trust. Plus power can easily corrupt even with the best of gentlemen, which he really is not. So his planning on taking over the world is something of a concern. And I'm truly not sure how to deal with it, considering the little army he's built up around himself. Either way, I really should get the Yuasa artefact back off you soon. I'm in Iran tonight and my appointment book is unpleasantly full, but I should be able to see you on Wednesday evening if you have no plans?"

"No, no, Wednesday's fine" I replied, "Especially as I'm probably going to die on Thursday."

With yet another deadline imposed on me, and with it being more than possible that he might arrive earlier than threatened, I left the house immediately before I could talk myself out of it, before my mind insisted that this was a bad, bad idea. When it didn't I should have been even more wary, but ever since returning from America when I hadn't been berating myself over potentially losing Karoline I hadn't stopped thinking about how my time in the world of magic was going to be coming to an end one way or another. I'd either die during the war or survive and make George take my abilities away, with my theory now being that it was more likely to be the former than the latter. And it played on my mind that I hadn't really made any kind of a difference during all of this time, made any real change to the world. George had warned me not to do anything stupid on an almost daily basis, even if only by text message if he couldn't speak to me personally, such was his lack of trust, but I found myself thinking sod it, why should I go along with anything he's said anymore? I mean Christ, he was planning on taking over the world if we survived, what I'd been thinking of doing, it was extremely minor in that regard. It wasn't flimsy stupidity like in the past either, it was something I'd powerfully believed in long before I'd become entangled in this preposterous absurdity with George, as I felt that the world didn't make sense when someone was never made to pay for the war crimes they'd committed, and on the nights I couldn't sleep I'd found myself carefully constructing a plan where justice would be done. Now I'd reached boiling point, with maybe only a few days left I didn't want to die knowing I could have made the smallest of differences but had been too much of a coward to do so.

It didn't take long to arrive at one of the many properties he owned, and knowing that he had been in the city earlier that day suggested this particular disgustingly luxurious establishment would be the home he returned to, and only an hour later I was proven right. Yet I initially bided my time, waiting for hours until I was sure he was finally alone in his house. Once he was, I transformed into a fly, nipped in through an open window and into his bedroom, as the former Prime Minister was taking his trousers off and preparing for bed, and one quick spell later and I was God. A glowing caricature of the good lord, at least, complete with enormous white beard and burning eyes.

"Good evening Mr Briar," I uttered, ominously as possible.

"What? Jesus. What- Who-" he stuttered, looking panicked.

"No, I am not Jesus. I am the God of your father, the God of Abraham, the God of Isaac and the God of Jacob," I replied, having read up on the Bible a couple of days ago, though only on the internet so blame that rather than me if I get any of the quotations wrong, and as you're about to see half the time I tried to get away with speaking normally and only chucking in the occasional "thou" or "hadst", or some other words that sounded biblical but probably didn't actually exist.

Toby fell back onto the sofa. The blood drained from his skin, and for a second I was briefly concerned that he might have a heart attack. Before realising I didn't mind either way.

"You can't be," he uttered, but I simply smiled, and he began to sweat.

"Do not worry my son, for there is no madness in your heart, thou art sane," I said, "I hadst been considering when I should introduce myself into thou life, there were many times I chose a path before deciding upon another, for I hath always avoided directly interfering with my creations if possible."

"I've always believed in you," he said, "Always."

"Even if that is the case, you truly thought you could commit the sins that you hath and not be held responsible?"

"Sins? What sins?" he replied, and I know I shouldn't have, not wanting to break character and all, but I burst out laughing.

"Toby, Toby, Toby, you of all people should know, there are seven things that the Lord hates, that are an abomination to him. For I despise haughty eyes, a lying tongue, hands that shed innocent blood, a heart that devises wicked plans, feet that make haste to run to evil, a false witness who breathes out lies, and one who sows discord among brothers, and you are guilty of each and every single one of them on multiple occasions."

"I don't know what you mean. I've," Toby tried to say, but I interrupted as I was getting irritated with him now.

"The war crimes, Toby," I replied, my voice booming, "The war crimes fill me with righteous indignation as you felt it was tolerable to take the lives of so many, to cause such distress and calamity."

"There were reasons," he squeaked, "I swear, you don't know the pressure I was under."

"I care-eth not," I replied, pretty certain that care-eth was a word that I'd just made up, "After everything that you did, the urge to bring the flood of water upon the earth, to destroy all flesh in which is the breath of life a second time was enormous. But I have decided instead that rather than the entire human race suffering, it should be only you."

"I'm sorry. I always tried to do what I thought was best for this country," this now very wretched mess of a man responded.

"In my son's name, stop speaking in falsehoods," I replied.

"What?"

"The eyes of the Lord are in every place, keeping watch on the evil and the good. Now be honest. For once in your life tell all of the truth."

"What do you mean?" he asked.

"Confess!" I howled, in what was now becoming an embarrassingly over the top performance even by amateur dramatics standards. Yet it appeared to do the job as finally he did so. Finally the truth began to spill from his lips, all of the lies, all of the tragedies, all of the massacres he'd been involved in, it went on for so long that I started to become even angrier, my rage towards him burning ever hotter as I learnt of excruciatingly awful incidents that had been covered up. Finally he began to beg me to absolve him of his guilt. I laughed once more.

"The opposite applies, for you deserve no form of abatement from thou disgraces, and I shalt destroy your life. Except thou will do it for me."

He didn't seem to understand, but he also didn't move as I walked over to him, placed my hand on his head, cut open his skull and used the artefact. After that the world was my oyster. His world at least.

The Former Prime Minister awoke in his bed, sweating, on edge, and not sure why, with no memory of the past few hours, of returning home, or why he was lying naked under the covers. Then he noticed the body next to him. Completely covered by the duvet, and breathing shallowly, he truly didn't know who it was. Laura was the obvious suspect, but there were others that it could quite easily have been. He pulled the sheet down, and screamed. And screamed. And screamed. Which you would if you'd just discovered a demon in your bed. An old style fifteenth century edition complete with red scales and horns and hoofs, leering at you, drool pouring from its mouth, with bits of what Toby prayed was animal meat in between its teeth.

"I ate her, Toby! I ate the publisher of lies, the queen of the perjurers, the redheaded whore!" the creature screeched with delight.

And so Toby ran.

And ran and ran and ran. Not even taking the time to put on clothes but oddly grabbing his mobile, he emerged into a world where there were no other human beings, into a world that when he desperately attempted to phone someone, when the call connected on the other end was only ever demonic laughter, with that applying when he punched in numbers randomly into the keypad. He was sobbing now, and gasping, as every time he turned around to see if he had escaped the demon he saw that it'd grown larger, bloodier, angrier, roaring that soon Toby would be his. Briar pounded against car windows but none would smash, no matter what he used to try and break them.

To amp things up even further the demon threw a car in front of him, which exploded, the shrapnel tearing into his skin. Not enough to kill him. Just hurt. Then in the distance, emerging from out of the smoke, he slowly began to see his wife.

"Oh, God, Laura, oh darling. Please. Please help me," he cried, before noticing that something was wrong, something was missing and as the smoke cleared completely he saw that where her heart once was, there was now a gaping wound.

"Sorry it's such a literal metaphor for what you've done to her, but I couldn't resist," the Demon cried.

"Why are you doing this to me?" He begged.

"You really have to ask?" it replied.

He looked at the creature and pleaded for his life. Instead the demon reached out and tore an arm off and Briar roared in agony.

"Run Toby. Run for what's left of your life."

Leaving a trail of blood that appeared to last for miles, unable to comprehend how he was still alive, he sprinted, only knowing that he must get away from the creature, he must reach safety, he must live. He was for a time even faster than the devil, though I made sure it was never completely out of sight, and eventually Briar reached an underground station and all but fell down the stairs, before jumping over the ticket barrier and diving down the escalators at such a speed that if he had tripped there is no doubt he would have broken his neck. If any of this were actually happening, at least.

He tore around the corner, praying for an awaiting train, only to find the demon standing in front of him.

"Hello again Toby. What kept you?"

There was no response. Unless you call guttural yet pathetic blubbering a response. Which you probably do, thinking about it. As he wiped the tears from his eyes he became aware that behind the demon on the train platform, and some of the track, were thousands of children. Children missing limbs, children bleeding from every orifice you could imagine. Children screaming. Children dying.

This wasn't my creation. This was his.

"All your beloved bombs and bullets, Toby. The ones that came from jets, from drones, from soldiers. Aren't you proud of your work?"

He didn't respond. He just continued to weep. At this point it appeared he wasn't capable of rational thought.

"Now it really is time for you to confess Toby. Tell everyone in the world exactly how much misery you've caused. You may choose how to do so, be it a newspaper, video, or even an appearance on the BBC, I care not, but you only have twenty four hours or I'll return. And next time, I'll take the gloves off. This will seem like a walk in a park in comparison."

I didn't give him the chance to respond, and his world went black, and would remain that way for several hours, until he awoke at home, horrified. Terrified. And hopefully ready to admit that he was responsible for so many atrocities. That the war had been illegal, and that he'd always known, right from the beginning.

I waited a day but nothing happened. I had hoped he'd appear on television, break down, beg for mercy, or at least try to make some kind of an apology, however pointless it might be. That or turn himself into the police in a misguided attempt to cleanse his soul, but no, it seemed there was no news about him at all.

I'd wanted him to confess off his own back, to know what he'd done was unforgivable, to need to tell the world how much he regretted his decisions, but now I was considering returning and forcing a confession, using the Yuasa artefact once again and making him tell all. But then there was a pounding on my front door, and the moment I opened it Orson Welles stormed in.

"What the fuck were you thinking?" he screamed, "Oh dear god. I mean, I'm all but speechless. How could you do that? How could you kill him?"

"What? I don't understand," I managed to reply in a panicked voice, even though I knew I hadn't physically harmed anyone .

"Briar," Welles responded, "Why did you murder him?"

"No," I managed to spit out, "I didn't, dear god no. I used the Yuasa artefact on him, to torment him, to get him to confess, to tell the truth, but I didn't hurt or kill him."

"And on the eve of the beginning of the war, you didn't think that might backfire?" Orson asked, "That they might use your stupidity for their own advantage?"

"But how?" I asked, and he just glared at me.

"Go on the BBC's website."

I grabbed my laptop, opened up Google chrome and did so. On the front page was a headline reading "Prime Minister Makes Historic Announcement" with a link to a video which I instantly clicked. On the screen a visibly upset David Cameron began speaking in front of 10 Downing Street, barely withholding fury.

"People of Britain, today I have learnt information which has shocked me to my very core. I have news that will change the way we see the world, knowledge that many will question and doubt at first until they see evidence of the terrible truth. For we are now at war with a new variety of terrorist, a type of monster I did not know was possible, and for which every single person in this country will be required to help fight against. To help you understand the way the world has changed I am about to show you a video, what you will see might seem unbelievable, but I can promise you that the footage was recorded at eleven o'clock this morning and witnessed by Professor Brian Cox and Stephen Fry among others, as you'll now witness."

At this point the picture cut away from Cameron to a large warehouse, which was empty except for a man in a glass box that looked to be about eight foot high and the same amount wide, and a small number of people who were sitting outside of it. The man in the glass container seemed frantic and kept pounding against it, with it soon becoming apparent that he was running out of oxygen. When it came to the moment that he was desperately gasping for air and seemed about to pass out, he gently placed his hand on the glass, could be seen to mouth several words, and the glass disappeared. Audible gasps and expressions of disbelief could be heard, and they grew louder as he flew up to the ceiling and began to burn a hole into the concrete ceiling, but he failed to complete it as he was shot repeatedly by previously unseen figures, and his body hit the floor with a thump so sickening that Cox vomited on to Fry. The video then cut back to Cameron.

"What you have just seen is evidence that magic exists. At this point I'm aware that many will not believe me, that they will think this is a hoax, but much more evidence will be presented within the following few days. I have already spoken to President Obama, and he is on his way to England this very second to see it for himself."

A thousand thoughts raced across my mind as I silently sat there watching the Prime Minister reveal our supposedly secret ways, though the main one was why Orson thought I was to blame for any of this. But then it became apparent that the worst was still to come.

"Unfortunately there is also another reason I showed that video footage," Cameron continued, "As it is my very sad duty to inform the world of the passing of former Prime Minister Toby Briar, who was tragically executed in a terrorist attack last night by one of the magicians we now know to exist." For a few seconds I couldn't understand how it was possible, that they had such an image, as on the screen a photograph of my face from a couple of years ago appeared, while Cameron went on to explain that the following footage should not be viewed by those of a nervous disposition as it was enormously distressing. The very worst then arrived, as a grainy CCTV video was shown of my slicing open Briar's skull. I felt sick to my stomach, and a sinking feeling that I'd never felt before, a feeling where my brain whispered "Oh come on, you've surely got to kill yourself now?"

Yet before I had time to think further the screen cut back to Cameron, who initially remained silent, as if he himself had been traumatised by the imagery, yet it was not long until he spoke again.

"We have learnt from certain sources that a collective of magicians wish to cause the downfall of our civilization, and from the intelligence so far gathered we know there are hundreds of them already in the United Kingdom. As I am sure you are no doubt aware they are extremely dangerous and should not be approached or apprehended in any manner by members of the public. But if you believe you know someone who might be a magician, please contact the emergency number shown at the bottom of your screens. This is the greatest threat our nation has ever had to respond to, these individuals have powers which can warp reality, they are able to control others against their will, and they can kill with a single touch. They can sub-"

At this point Orson closed my laptop, and glared at me.

"I didn't kill him," I said, "I swear on it."

"So you say. And not that it matters, but I suppose I do believe you, every time I've tinkered with your brain there's been nothing there to suggest you are capable of that level of immoral conduct. Not that it matters, as you gave them the chance to frame you with ease. To begin... The End probably. Quite fucking probably. Dead soon, I believe is the phrase the kids use these days."

"I fucked up. Ah Jesus. I really fucked up. But I'm sorry. I'm so sorry. I never meant for this to happen."

"I should probably kill you myself," Orson said, "But I don't want any more blood on my hands. So I'm just going to walk away. Everyone else? All bets are off. You're fair game for anyone on either side."

And with that he left. And that's when the terror really began.

Luckily for you I'll spare you the majority of the details of my following behaviour, other than to inform you that I went into hiding in a new underground bunker in a very different location to the first, and a distressingly long period was spent largely rocking backwards and forwards, sobbing or screaming, and I no longer knew how to exist without my brain angrily assaulting me. During this time I expected to hear from George, expected him to find me, expected to see him on the news waging war, but there was no sign of him at all, and I could only presume that what I'd done had forced him to revise his plans, to go to ground and hide as the government attempted to track our kind down. Perhaps I should have cared more too, perhaps I should have gone to him, begged forgiveness, tried to explain, but if I'm being completely honest, I didn't give a fuck about him. All I cared about was Karoline.

Weeks passed, and each day the only thing that kept me going was the hope that I could see her, explain to her that what she had seen wasn't the truth, and each day I briefly left the bunker and tried to call her, but she always refused to answer. Text and social media messages were sent on my brief expeditions, but all were read and then ignored, and as miserable as that made me, I could understand why.

Until what I thought initially to be a miracle occurred, as she sent a message saying she would see me one final time if I agreed not to contact her again afterwards, at least if she so wished it after listening to what I had to say. My bastard face had been plastered all over the media so she suggested I transform into her favourite character from the sixties movie that she loved the most, and that we meet in public so that if I was somehow tracked down I hopefully wouldn't be murdered in cold blood. All of which made sense to me, and which is why on the day itself I invisibly flew to London, dived through the open doors of a well-known fast food outlet and used one of their disabled toilets, and emerged looking like Bud Court from the film *Harold and Maude*. Even with a disguise like that, and an enormous amount of protection spells which I'd cast on myself and planned to use on Karoline, as I walked towards the pub in Soho where we'd agreed to meet I was filled with fear. I knew how risky this was, but I had to see her, every single atom of my body longed to be with her, needed to be with her, couldn't not be with her.

Initially I didn't quite know how to greet her as we ventured into a small pub where hardly anyone lurked, and when I hugged her I sensed a definite reluctance, one which didn't bode well, but I hoped if I could explain everything she'd understand. She'd forgive. She'd want me back. We talked for over an hour, and I did everything that I could in the hope that she would take my hand in hers and say that it was okay, it would all be okay, we'd somehow get through this. But she didn't.

And I suddenly saw them. And I was shot. And I was bloody, and missing a limb, the majority of my left arm as it goes. Karoline screamed, but before she knew what was happening I'd grabbed her hand and was tearing down the street at a speed that made everyone double take, I wasn't technically breaking the laws of physics but I would have won a gold medal at most Olympics. Following me were five men in suits, looking like a cliché right out of a Bond movie if ever I saw one, but maybe that was the point, as they shouted at me to stop but I chose to ignore them. More ducking and diving took place down minor alleyways until suddenly we burst on to Leicester Square, and the men in suits could no longer be seen. People gathered around us though, looking at my bleeding body, and some were shrieking and others were on their mobiles calling for help, and a couple simply filmed me possibly dying, and I knew I had about ten seconds to do something before I passed out from blood loss.

"Why aren't you healing yourself?" Karoline shouted, and I explained how I'd tried. That'd I'd been lower on magic than I realised, that the protection spells I'd cast, that had turned out to be so bloody useless, had all but drained me.

"Take an hour of my life," She said. Firmly. And I knew I had no choice.

And I was hit by such a powerful bolt of energy that I no longer knew anything. I was just existing in a state of pure bliss, pure white bliss where all I could do was feel joy, where other thoughts no longer existed. Until darkness descended. Then I opened my eyes, and I was greeted by silence. Ten long seconds of silence where I tried to understand but I couldn't, I couldn't, I just couldn't fucking understand because how could you? Until I heard screaming from far away. I began to hear weeping and wailing and sirens and I looked all around me, I looked at the whole of Leicester Square and all I saw was a hundred, a hundred and fifty burning corpses.

I was holding the hand of one of them.

I was holding her hand.

A guttural roar emerged out of me, a sound I hadn't been aware I was capable of making.

I gradually became aware of the five black suited men slowly and carefully approaching me, and I shot into the air. I don't know why but they didn't follow me. And before I knew it I was crossing the ocean, flying over Europe, and all too suddenly was back in the underground bunker. And my head was exploding. Unfortunately not literally, though Christ how I wish it had been as I couldn't cope I couldn't do anything, other than scream and scream and scream and yet no one would ever hear me, no one would ever know the agony I was in. As far as I was concerned no one existed outside of these four walls and I didn't want them to, and all I wanted was for everything to end, everything to stop, everything to no longer exist for ever more. A life without memories or any kind of rational thinking, but that did not happen, would never happen, as all I could think was "I killed her, I killed her, I killed her" over and over again.

I spent hours and hours and then days and days drowning in hysteria, only stopping to tear at my flesh, desperate for some kind of pain to override what I was feeling, but it didn't help, everything I did to myself was like the tiniest pin prick compared to the realisation that I was responsible for her death. Eventually I passed out, but what followed was one long deranged nightmare. Something terrible. Something impossible.

As every day was identical, every day was a relentless shower of self-hate and misery, and the image of my holding her charred hand is one I couldn't escape from, but no matter how much I hurt myself, whatever physical damage I caused myself, it wasn't permanent. I ripped my flesh apart and yet inexplicably healed. It didn't matter what I did, what I created to cause self-harm, whatever I did in the hope of ceasing to exist, it never worked, and I could only presume that whatever had caused Karoline and so many others to die had led to my immortality. That what I wanted the most in the world I could not have, and this existence would never end. More days of endless torment passed, but then one morning, quite unpredictably, a new kind of ordeal began. Initially I'd no idea what was happening. All I knew was that suddenly I couldn't breathe. It couldn't be seen or touched, but there was a force that was slowly strangling me. My heart felt like it was going to explode, and I heard my throat make ugly cracking noises meaning I could no longer cast magic. I was lifted into the air, and then thrown against the wall, held there, my feet half a metre from the ground, and I prayed that this time I would die. That this was finally the end, and for a brief second even felt a glimmer of joy, as the world slowly began to fade to black. But no, at the very last second I fell to the floor. Gasped for air. One minute later my throat repaired itself. The pain subsided.

I presumed George was responsible, or another magician, but oddly no one appeared. Something odd was occurring without any doubt though, as when I tried to leave the bunker I discovered I couldn't. That I was somehow trapped.

Days of periodic torture followed. At first I wasn't sure what or who was doing this to me, other than that they appeared to enjoy causing me the kind of pain I didn't think a human body could tolerate. It wasn't until the words "You killed us" were daubed in my blood on the wall that I began to realise what was happening. And despite everything I tried, nothing could prevent them from doing this to me. Though don't think for a second that I didn't believe that this wasn't exactly what I deserved.

Sometimes nothing happened for hours, days on one occasion, but somehow that was worse as I awaited the next act of suffering. But then it arrived. One moment I was lying on the bed, quietly weeping, then I was smashed on to the floor and I heard the sounds of the bones in my legs breaking once more, before I was forced to stand, forced to walk in circles for hours. Another incident saw my stomach ripped open and my intestines slipped and slithered to the ground, before they slowly crawled up my legs and around my stomach, chest and neck, where they twisted around me getting tighter and tighter until I could no longer breathe. I was on the point of falling unconscious, yet once again it ended before that occurred. Further days passed, with all manner of torment raining down upon my pathetic body, but I was now almost grateful, it meant that at times, however briefly, that I was able to think about something, anything, other than Karoline.

All good things must come to an end and that's apparently also the case with all abjectly horrendous things too. I'm not sure quite how long I'd been tortured for, though looking back I think it was six or seven weeks, when out of the blue George smashed through the ceiling and was standing there, and I was saved and oh god oh thank fucking god this was over. You've probably guessed I was wrong however, as he was joined by a female CF1 agent, Weaver, the one who had made Orson and I torture that poor homeless man.

"Hello!" George said in an oddly perky manner.

"What the fuck?" I managed to utter, "What's she doing here with you?"

His sighing undercut my babbling.

"Ah, Ben," George said, "Poor stupid, dumb Ben. First off, don't worry, we are here to kill you. We've no use for you anymore, as much fun as it has been to torture you these past few weeks it's time to call it a night."

They were both smiling. It was all kinds of not right.

"Wait, what?" I somehow uttered.

"You think you're in your hilariously un-secret bunker, right? I mean you were, for a few hours, but once you passed out on that first night I transported you to a security area deep within the CF1 base, and recreated your surroundings," George said, still grinning in an unnerving manner.

"I don't understand. I mean, what's been happening to me over the last few weeks then?"

"The last few weeks you've given my agents the perfect opportunity to hone their skills," Weaver said, "We should probably be thanking you really for everything you've done." Once again I prattled away, a small number of words to show I had no idea what was taking place.

"Ah, you poor sod," George said, "You really haven't worked it all out yet, have you? It was me. All me. From the get go."

I said that "What" word again. A fair few times as it happens.

"Ah fuck it. Might as well fill you in before I kill you, it's irritating when the villain doesn't do that. But ultimately, you're a, well, you're not a good kid, that's for certain, not after what you did to poor Mr Briar. But you didn't deserve this I suppose."

"Deserve what?" I asked.

"Jesus Ben, get with the programme. It was a set up from the word go," he replied, "Basically put, I'm a CF1 agent. Have been for about six years now, I changed sides at the same time as the nun, we are married after all. See, the war was always going to be declared and I had to decide which side to take. I worked out the odds, saw who would survive, chose to spend my time with them. Then over time I helped form the CF1 Agency. Created the agents. Devised a long and complicated plan with those in power. Then you were chosen to become a magician in the knowledge that you could be controlled easily, and used however we saw fit. Sure, we let you mess about for a bit, have some fun, get over confident, but a day where you were responsible for beginning the Government's war on magic was planned long before I ever met you."

"You fucker. You complete and utter c-"

"You're not responsible for the Trafalgar Square massacre or

Karoline's death either," George continued to confess, "If that helps. We just made it look that way. Or to be precise, I did. Needed to up our game you see, needed to make you out to be a credible threat. So I visited Karoline. Sliced open her skull, made her want to see you at least once more, and after planting a tracking device on her I sat back and waited for you to leave your hiding place and emerge in public."

My mother had tried to kill herself when I was twenty. I came home from work one day to find my Uncle sitting in the living room, waiting for my arrival, waiting to tell me what had happened. That she was hopefully going to be okay, though it was still a little touch and go. Said he'd drive me to the hospital, that we'd wait, be there for when she hopefully came round. Which she did, after the longest of hours. The reason I'm mentioning this now is because I thought I understood shock. Or had witnessed enough of it to cope. Apparently not. I tried to speak, create coherent sentences, but only random words fell from my mouth. Then George spoke again.

"Afterwards we decided to keep you here, allowed some of the newer agents to practice magic upon you, hone their torturing skills. But there's no time left for such fun hijinks, and you're still a minor threat, so it seemed like it was time you ceased to exist. Sorry. Still, I thought you should know the truth before I killed you. Go to your grave without guilt, and all of that sort of malarkey. For this is the end now, I'm afraid."

Everything clicked back into place.

"Oh God. Karoline, I... I thought I'd killed her. But you. You murdered her."

"Yeah. These things happen."

I'd never believed in the idea of a soul, but I swear, in that moment, I'm certain I felt mine break. Crack. I couldn't move, though I slowly became aware that I was creating a high pitched wailing sound.

"Perhaps telling you all of this was a step too far. Maybe you didn't need to know after all. It's of no matter, I've no more time for this."

George cast a spell and his hand became covered in flames, and for a second I thought he might actually kill me. But no, there was no such luck, as to his side Weaver began to change. Transform. As I struggled to understand what was happening it became apparent that Orson was now standing next to George. George hadn't noticed however, and he never did, as he was more concerned by the fact that his hand was in the process of exploding. Bits of blood and meat and bone sprayed against me. He looked at me, perplexed, before the rest of his body followed suit and was soon spread across the room, his head landing next to me on the floor looking more than alarmed.

"This is quite the coincidence," Orson said, "I have to admit I had no idea you were here Ben. Indeed it was only yesterday that I'd discovered who George really was, and so thought I'd pop by and assassinate the little bastard, though I spent a little time in disguise to discover what his plans for everyone were."

I think he expected me to be impressed. Or even grateful. The opposite was true.

"He was just about to kill me," I said.

"Yes, yes, I heard his little speech. Heard that he was responsible for Karoline's death. And I am sorry about that Ben. But now's really not the time to talk, we need to leave before the rest of the agency discovers what I've done and attempts to kill me. Us."

But I just shook my head.

"No, I'm not leaving," I said. He stared at me, then nodded, and walked away. For a short time I sat there. Trying to take it all in. Trying to understand. Then I created a hefty, sharp knife and gently slit my throat open.

CHAPTER 14 - GLASTONBURY

Hell is the worst festival you could ever imagine, and then about a million times more hideous. It's all of the misery of the worst mud soaked Glastonbury's, but one where it has been raining non-stop since nineteen seventy four, creating the largest sludge and vomit infested swamp ever seen by man, and every one trudges around it in a zombie-esque fashion, unable to walk more than one mile a day as they're so caked in mud and other substances it's best not thought about. The rain is relentless, bitterly cold and you would think eventually you'd get used to it, but no, no, that never happens.

The weather conditions are alas only a small part of the shittiness, as you also can't escape the worst music the world has ever been subjected to, at a volume that causes permanent tinnitus but sadly never deafens. On the main stage Rolf Harris is duetting with Gary Glitter and someone else who I can't mention, sorry, my lawyer says I shouldn't ever say his name, while singing a medley of their greatest hits. Rolf looks like he's lost his mind but Glitter and the other one are enjoying every second of it.

If you try and find anything which might be even slightly more bearable you'll fail, as over on the Pyramid Stage The Libertines are playing, but it's the fucked up drugged up Pete Doherty era where he's barely able to recognise what a guitar is, let alone remember the lyrics and he slurs every line, god knows if he's even aware he's on stage. Sometimes he slips out of consciousness, falling to the ground as if he's died, which would be for the best in such a situation, trust me, but the band play on until he eventually wakes up. Occasionally, hours after it began, a song might finally end. There was no way I could cope with that for long, but the John Peel Stage was a far bleaker alternative, where a distressed singer who I really used to love back when she was alive is screaming abuse at the audience, but who from time to time looks up, wide eyed, with the realisation that this is her life now. Death now. And that it will be like this forever. Then she drinks to forget, but she can never drink enough.

And you can't escape. When you eventually leave one stage or area you'll suddenly find yourself assaulted by even more distressing musical atrocities, while it takes so long to walk even the shortest amount of distance that whatever choice you make means you are subjected to it for days on end. The second worst thing I ever did was check out the comedy tent, it's like they knew my passion for comedy, my absolute love for all it's capable of, so Matt Forde was on stage doing a routine about mortgages that lasted for fifty one hours. Everyone around me roared with laughter as I desperately tried to escape, to run away from my greatest nightmare. But running's not possible here.

The food was another form of torture. Now that wouldn't be a shock for any seasoned festival goer, but all I consumed caused an example of dysentery that would destroy any sane mind, and any sane arse, it's the kind that explodes from your bowels in lava hot streams for what seems like forever. But if you don't eat the hunger pains become insufferable, so you try a new stall, a new cuisine, hoping it won't poison you. Yet of course it does and you end up back in the toilets for hours at a time, which are, well, actually they're exactly the same as at a normal festival. But if you've been to Glastonbury and used one on a Sunday afternoon then you know how even spending a minute enclosed with such a stench makes you wish you could cut off your nose, even if it's with a blunt pair of scissors and takes half an hour to do so. Perhaps if only it was all this alone I might not have lost my mind, but nah, there were a couple more kicks to the soul, one being my normally beloved festival goers, who here were a mixture of the most terrifying of Millwall and Chelsea hooligans from the seventies and eighties combined with groups of inebriated Blackpool style stag and hen do participants. Then to make it somehow more abhorrent they'd thrown in some teenagers who'd never been to a festival before, and who had gone quite, quite mental within about thirteen minutes. Some were ferocious, and did whatever it took to survive, even if that included eating human flesh rather than anything pre-prepared, plus they got especially riled up if they lost their mobile phones and would search a hundred bodies for them, not caring that it didn't make sense for anyone to have swallowed a phone or hidden it inside their foreskin. To top things off there were a dash of random murderers, the type who had once died of old age in prison even if they'd been sentenced as a teen, and the violence was never ending. As was the howling, the agonised begging for death from those who had been all but ripped apart but were defying medical science and still breathing, creating a cacophony of sorrow that never stopped at any time of the day or the night. So I could never sleep, and it wasn't only due to their bawling either, as with every festival in the nineties, bunches of seventeen year old boys ran around the festival screaming "Wanker!" at the top of their voices and then finding it hysterically funny for several hours, which of course it wasn't then and it wasn't now. Inevitably boredom would set in and they'd pour lighter fluid on to a random tent or random human being and watch them burn, I'm still not sure which was the more annoying, and after only a few days of this lunacy there weren't many times I wasn't extraordinarily mad. This was a post sanity existence. An all new state of mental illness where I was patient zero, as all of this appeared to have been constructed to destroy every single one of the eighty six billion neurons and eighty five billion non-neuronal cells that made up my shitty, shitty brain.

On the twelfth day I saw her. Alive. Or at least, not the scorched corpse I'd last seen. There aren't words to explain the mixture of horror and delight. She shouldn't have been here, but she was, and she still existed and we were together and-
"Karoline!" I screamed. She looked at me. Confused.
"Sorry, do I know you?" she replied.
"Karoline, it's me. Ben. Me."
"I'm sorry, but I don't know who you are," Karoline replied.
"What? I, I don't understand. It's me."
"Look, you're frightening me, will you leave me alone, yeah?" And with that she walked away. Only to be stabbed in the stomach by one of the Millwall fans. I leapt at him, he beat me unconscious, and when I awoke her body was gone.
I saw her eight times after that. Each time I tried to talk to her. Each time my heart broke further. Each time I tried to persuade myself that it wasn't her, that it was a doppelganger, a duplicate created to make my existence even more dismal. But I couldn't be sure, and the doubt, oh Jesus, that was an exquisite form of torment in itself.
At this point you might think the situation couldn't get any

worse, but this was Hell so of course it could, because as my heart broke my erection throbbed like a tasered stallion. I'm not boasting here either, ever since I'd arrived I'd had a hard on which wouldn't go away. Even more annoying was that my penis had relocated itself to the middle of my back, the bit you can't really reach however much you try. The only satisfaction I ever got was via the involvement of an inflatable armchair, but that was followed by uncontrollable crying as I realised that this was the day that my dignity had finally died. Then there was vehement laughing. It was a confusing time.

I found out on the thirteenth day that I couldn't die. At least not for good. I'd been considering a second suicide for a fair old while, but the main concern was whether my existence would be over and done with for good, like I hoped, or whether I'd descend to some other lower level of Hell in the manner that Dante had described in his famous poem. A location far worse than this, involving, I don't know, being stuck in bed with Bono from U2, with him drunkenly caressing you for what seems like forever until eventually he reaches down and slowly begins stroking your cock, and to your horror it hardens, and you lose your mind and never stop weeping, until the scene resets and begins again. But this time you're aware that you slightly fancy Bono, and have to live with that knowledge for ever more.

I hadn't originally planned to kill myself that particular day either, but I had idiotically decided to take any illegal substance I could find. Bar a stereotypical dalliance with weed in my university days, and maybe four or five years afterwards, I'd never trusted drugs due to my mind always being a tad on the fragile side of things, and I didn't want to risk breaking it permanently. Life had tried to do that enough as it was, and giving it any extra help had never seemed a brilliant idea. Not that I'm anti harder drugs, over the years I've had a lot of friends who have taken them and had a gosh darnit good old fashioned time, they just weren't for me. Being in Hell though, I didn't care if they damaged me in a permanent way, as I presumed my mind couldn't be further shattered. It's times like this that I wish time travel existed if only so I had the ability to go back and repeatedly punch myself in my face. The horrendous twelve hour trip which ensued is forever marked in my mind as if it were an eternity. Well, maybe not that long, but a good five years of my life. Once the tab I'd taken kicked in, everything slowed down to the point that it took an hour to blink. The music became louder, my ears felt like they might explode, and then my heart decided to follow suit, beating a thousand times a minute. I'd have been relatively happy if that was all that happened, but hallucinations soon arrived on the scene, and that meant that it wasn't long before thirty foot tall versions of Glitter and Harris tried to suckle on my nipples, and a tiny Michael Eavis attempted to crawl into my nostril and host a barbecue for family and friends that I wasn't invited to.

When I finally sobered up, presuming weeks had passed, I quickly discovered it had only been about ten hours. I'd had enough though and no longer cared what happened to me, and dashed up onto the main stage, picked up a guitar and killed Glitter, Rolf and the other guy with it, and then electrocuted myself.

Unfortunately it was at this point that I discovered that death around these parts wasn't permanent, and the second after I stopped breathing I woke up, in my tent, right back at the beginning of the festival. Weirdly it wasn't such a bad thing however, I wasn't pleased to still be there of course, but I no longer felt exhausted, no longer felt like I hadn't slept for many a millennium.

The next few weeks were predictably messy, and yeah, I definitely completely lost it at this point, my sanity not just flying out of the window but leaping past clouds and swiftly leaving the Earth behind, only pausing to briefly wave goodbye as it abandoned the solar system. I was no longer queuing for the toilets and just shitting wherever I walked, endlessly trudging around the festival hoping that somewhere some tiny sliver of lucidity could be found, but the non-stop rain, eye watering violence and ear damaging songs from the very worst examples of humanity couldn't be escaped from.

At one point I found a medical tent at the top of a field but it was like stepping into a world war one triage with limbless, rasping creatures desperately pleading for the agony to end, while Doctors tried to operate without anaesthetic, and that wasn't exactly improving anyone's mood. Such brutality was enough to push me over the edge once again, so I headed to the main stage, shoved my way through security and began climbing up the outer frame of the stage. The crowd cheered, and when I reached the top, created a large space for me to smash onto were I to jump. They were sweet like that.

Once again I instantly awoke in my tent, and noticed with disgust that death had briefly restored my sanity, which didn't seem fair as I was clearly going to lose it again bloody shortly. Still, it at least made my days a little more interesting, and I spent a fair few weeks finding increasingly difficult and complicated ways to die, just to keep myself busy, and I mixed things up by occasionally by viciously slaughtering various performers and then singing karaoke versions of songs I loved. They never lasted for long, at best I might get one or two verses in before the crowd sensed I was enjoying myself and so rushed the stage and murdered me, but eh, it meant that sometimes I was back to laughing as well as crying.

Unfortunately such hijinks only lifted my spirits for a short while and soon I was back to being absolutely full on batshit crazy. To be honest I'm surprised I'd regained my sanity for more than a couple of minutes given that I was surrounded by the shittiest members of humanity, and the lack of any genuine and caring human contact, along with the knowledge that I'd never experience it again, was repeatedly breaking me. I'd dug my heels in for a bit, tried to grasp at a hint of rationality and the idea I wouldn't devolve into a monstrous mess, but it soon became clear that wasn't really possible. Most of the time there was only a lot of weeping, screaming, laughing and a modicum of violence. Rinse, repeat, despair.

How much time was spent in such a state I have no idea as I completely lost track of time and weeks and then months passed while I was in this raging state. Until out of the blue just when I was about to kill myself for what felt like at least the hundredth time, a tear in my dimension appeared. I mean, given how crazed I was I didn't know what it was initially, but simply stared at this weird electrical silvery wormhole thing, and then someone walked through it. George walked through it.

I tried to kill him for days.

And he let me. He let me do it, over and over again. In those moments I had absolute certainty. Clarity. The only thing I wanted to do was make him suffer, to induce agony, for as long as I could. I ripped into him, I tore off every limb and organ and artery countless times. And he howled in pain. But not once did he beg me to stop.

I don't know what I was back then. I was something I never realised existed within me. It was a terrible purity of anger and anguish which felt like it could never be sated, that I knew I must cause this man woe, and it was the only thing I wanted. Every time he died, I wanted to kill him again. Every time he was resurrected, it began again.

Yet eventually I became exhausted by the pointlessness of it all. Like me he couldn't die in Hell. And physical pain wasn't enough. I needed to hurt him in ways he didn't even know were possible. So I stopped slicing his skin and organs open. Regretfully.

"I'm going to kill you, George, end your existence for good. I don't know how, but I want you to know that, one day, hopefully soon, I am going to permanently fucking kill you for what you did to me. To Karoline."

"I know," George replied, "It's why I came here. I want you to do it."

"What?" I asked, exasperated.

"I want you to kill me. Cease my existence. The things I've done, I have to live with them here. They never used to bother me on Earth, but in Hell I feel all of the pain I've caused. I feel the sorrow I've brought to thousands of people. And I'll be here forever. Feeling this sickening perception of the agony I'm responsible for."

"I hope that's true. I don't believe or trust you, but I really hope you're suffering as much as you claim. Now I need to know something, back there, I saw Karoline, but she didn't recognise me. Was it really her?"

"I don't know Ben, I really don't know. If it helps, I doubt what you saw was her, especially if she didn't respond to you. But this is Hell, there are no hard and fast rules as far as I can tell."

Which didn't help at all.

"On that front," George continued, "Her death, beyond all of the others, is the one I regret the most as she was a true innocent in all of this."

Hearing him say that led to the murderous rage returning, but I tried to resist its siren call.

"I know you will never believe me," George continued, "But I am beyond sorry. Yet I know there are no words that will ever persuade you, so I'll just prove it to you with my actions. And I wish it was simpler than this, I wish you could just kill me instantly, but I can't die here. We can't. At least, not by each other's hands. You've seen that. But if you help me, you will get to see my death. That is the truth."

The audacity of the man was astonishing. Almost impressive. At least it would have been if he wasn't the human being I despised most in the history of the planet. And yet what choice did I have but to listen to him? To find out if there was any alternative to spending an aeon in the insanity that was Glastonbury?

"Okay," I said, "While I want to fucking remind you a-fucking-gain that I'm not buying into any of this, tell me, what in Christ's name do you want with me?"

"If you haven't worked it out yet, this is your own personal Hell," George explained, "Most of us have them, especially when you first arrive. But there is another section of Hell, akin to a traditional Christian description, though with the odd tweak here and there. And in that place is a being named Lucifer who is the administrator of this dimension, and the only way anyone can cease to exist is by his hand. He alone has the power, and can only be challenged to a duel by a council of five beings. We've no idea why. The rules of this reality rarely make sense, which I suppose adds to the chaotic nature of it all."

"So you need four other people to help you?" I asked him.

"Yes. All magicians, and I do know where the other three that might help us can be found."

"And then?" I asked, warily.

"Then we travel to Lucifer's house."

"Lucifer's house?"

"I suppose it's more of a mansion, but yes, basically. We then challenge him to a duel, and either we win, or he kills us, destroying our souls forever. But we're not going to win, I should stress. We're nothing to him, an irritating ant or moth at best."

I didn't want to trust him for a second. Yet ceasing to exist, no longer being, no longer thinking, it was more than I could ever have hoped for.

"This is too good to be true," I responded.

"You don't have to join me, Ben," George said, "You're free to leave your own personal Hell, explore other aspects of the afterlife. Your powers will work once we leave here as well, it's not actually all that bad. At least once you get used to the weather."

"And if I follow you to Lucifer, is it really a true death? No more existence, full stop, ever?"

"Yes. I swear it's all true. You will see my soul be destroyed. If you wish to join me, well, that's optional. It truly is. It's completely up to you."

Every single atom of my body was telling me not to have any faith in what he was saying, not to go with him, but something pushed me forward. A sense that anything had to be better than the Hell I was currently in.

"I don't know how, but your death will be by my hand," I spat at him.

"Good. I hope so."

I stabbed him in the heart one more time. Watched as his face contorted in excruciating pain. Watched him die. Watched him return to life.

"I can't promise I'm not going to keep doing that pretty often as well you know."

"I understand," he replied, gravely, "It's the least I deserve."

So I agreed to go with him. With that he grabbed my hand and guided me through the tear in reality.

On the other side was a burning apocalypse where the screams of the undead all but deafened, and the stench of their burning souls made you want to retch constantly, a world where the ongoing agony would drive a lesser man insane once more, but hey, compared to what I'd just been through? Okay, actually, it was just as bad.

At least there was one difference, in that I was a magical twat again. Yet at first it took a while to understand what was happening, and understand where I was, as in this dimension the flames of Hell instantly caused blistering pain as my flesh bubbled and boiled, I thought I'd experienced every variety of distress but this was a unique kind I'd never known existed. But from my literally flaming lips I managed to utter a protection spell, and slowly healed myself as I took in my surroundings.

A new Hell then. Or rather, the older one. As George had mentioned they'd got the fiery bit right in those crazy old religious books, or had inspired the creator to invent such a place. Either way every physical object here appeared to be burning, from the hard stone ground to the forests in the distance, while all of the mountains I could make out were of the volcanic kind. I never thought I'd miss the grim, grey clouds of England, but an ever burning reality shouldn't be anyone's cup of tea. Especially considering the amount of human beings who were desperately gasping for air, struggling to crawl along the ground as they eternally burned. I did try to help, dousing one in water, but within five seconds he'd dried up and started burning again. And in that five seconds he didn't even thank me once, the ungrateful shit, so I didn't bother doing that again. Plus, you know, there were millions of them littered across the dimension, there was no way I could help them all.

They were the nicer inhabitants of Hell as well, as a number of other creatures existed here, and did so quite happily. Too happily. More on that later though, as I desperately needed to sit down, to take a brief breather, and recover and recuperate from everything I'd been through, and so I built a large stone dwelling and dragged George inside of it. I had so many questions that I wanted to ask him, that I needed to ask him, but I didn't know where to start. Until I realised it was often best to begin at the beginning.

"So why me, eh George? Why did you choose me? Why did you decide my life was worth destroying?"

He was silent at first. Perplexed as to what to say.

"I'll be honest with you, and state that it wasn't personal. But back in 2014 when I devised the plan with Weaver, I realised I needed a patsy. To track down some poor fucked up sod, one who was potentially suicidal, and then give them the world. Albeit subtly controlling them at the same time so that they did everything I wanted. You just happened to be one of the first people I came across who was a suitable candidate. Which in London is terribly bad luck, I mean there's potentially millions of them."

"And if I hadn't met you in Soho, which I... Ah, I'm so fucking stupid. Because that was all staged too, wasn't it?"

"I'm afraid so," he replied, "We had you watched for a couple of weeks prior to that, along with a few others, to see who would make for the most suitable scapegoat. Once we'd made our choice, Weaver transformed into someone you would find attractive, with the idea being to get you drunker and more morose, and once she succeeded in doing so she left, we waited for you to leave, and hey presto, one dazzling if slightly grotesque magical fight to capture your attention."

"I'm such a fucking idiot. For trusting you. Believing in you."

"No. I mean, maybe, a bit," George replied, but with sincerity and an attempt at kindness for once, "But as I keep on telling you this was all planned in advance. The Government wanted to begin the war against magicians, to make it out that you were a dangerous terrorist, and one of hundreds at that, and it was a case of being in the wrong place at the wrong time when we initially noticed you and thought you'd be easily duped.Originally we were going to expose you in Brighton, when the explosion on the Ferris wheel took place there were two CCTV cameras set up to record our every move, including our transformations into Nicholson and Rigg. Bloody things malfunctioned though, so your inevitable fate was delayed, especially as there was a problem involving the leaders of other countries which needed to be dealt with before we could reveal the existence of magic to the public. On that front we did have another plan that we were about to set in motion, I was to persuade you that Jeremy Corbyn was a rogue magician who needed dealing with, and there was going to be an obscenely diabolical fight between the two of you on the South Bank just by the London Eye that would have been captured by the BBC and shown live. But then you were kind enough to help us out by torturing Mr Briar, and gave us an in that way, and saved a lot of time and money. Either way, you never stood a chance, and it wasn't just me but many, many others who orchestrated your manipulation over the past year."

"And then you murdered Karoline."

To this he did not have any retort. He simply nodded, blinking away tears.

"I truly re-" he began to say, but I didn't let him finish.

"Stop. Now. Don't say anything about that. About her. I don't want to hear that shite. Trust me, I'm really struggling with my urge not to slice you open with a blunt blade right now. But I'm aware that repeatedly spilling your blood is ultimately pointless, so from now on please only give me the answers to my questions, and nothing else. No more apologies, because I truly don't believe them, or care about how you feel."

He nodded, looking vaguely chastised.

"Now this entire plan, what was the point of it? I'm guessing it was just so that the Government could eliminate all rogue magicians?"

"Yes. I mean, it was far more complicated than that, but ultimately that's what it boils down to. They wanted control of magic. Had plans to take over all of the other countries in the world by killing their leaders and replacing them with highly skilled shape shifters."

"Why did you side with the government? Align yourself with those utter, and obviously evil shits? Is any amount of money worth that?" I asked.

"It essentially came down to common sense," George responded, "Rogue magicians are a surly bunch at best, absolutely useless at working together the majority of the time, and I had no doubts that the government would win in the end. Wipe us all out. Basically I wanted to live. Though I'd be lying if I hadn't considered betraying them as well, to double cross the government and take over the country. For starters."

"And all that King of the World stuff, where you told me that you had plans to rule the world," I said, "Why did you tell me that?"

"A mixture of reasons. Partially so you'd never even think that I might be connected to the government, but also to unnerve and upset you. Make you perhaps do something rather stupid that would see you falling right into our hands."

Ignoring the fact that his idea had been painfully successful, I continued to quiz him.

"And Orson? Was he in on it all along too?"

George looked surprised. "Christ no, Ben. He did kill me after all. The one mistake I made was letting him live after Birmingham, but I thought if I took him out of the game too early on it might have caught the attention of certain magicians who it was always best to avoid."

I looked at him. For a painfully extensive period of time.

"You know, thinking about all of this George, you really truly are the most horrendous bastard I've ever met. And quite possibly who has ever lived. Or who I thought could exist."

"I deserved that."

"Yep. And so much more."

We talked further, and he clued me in on all of the small details, all of the answers I now regret hearing, as they proved how naive and stupid I'd been. Looking back, once again I wasn't sure what I was during this time. Bar broken. Broken and fractured and exhausted. So bloody exhausted by everything. And then we had to run like crap, as a loud crashing noise and worryingly furious snarls announced the entrance of several beasts who thought living in Hell was just swell, especially when they got the chance to hunt sentient humans, and were doing a worryingly good job of destroying my hastily constructed domicile.

"Shit, should have told you about them," George shouted, "Er, we need to get the hell out of here. No pun intended. But now. Fly. As high as you can go."

We demolished the roof and flew away from the creatures that I looked at once, and decided against ever looking at again if I had any choice in the matter. Which of course I didn't. As we flew through the burning sky George briefly warned me about other pesky varmints we might encounter, beings from planets we'd yet to discover that had not only existed for billions of years but had also evolved while in Hell, those who had not only survived but also thrived. Creatures who had built armies, who had fought for control of Hell for millennia. All pointlessly, of course, but then that's life for you. Or death for you, at least.

As for the fuckers that were still chasing us below, they'd evolved from your standard normal rather stroppy wolves into something that flourished here, and so now their outer shells were metallic and jagged and could tear through skin as if it were made of semolina, the creatures claws were almost diamond-esque given how sharp and hard they were, and they decimated many a burning dead human as they thrashed through the throngs of those who also suffered here. Oh, and they also had enormous anuses, which was the first thing in Hell to make a glimmer of a smile appear on my face, until I discovered it was so big it could shit out a child's skeleton, and as one did so I felt repulsed once more.

Despite being high above them they didn't give up the chase, presumably hoping at some point we'd exhaust ourselves and need to land. George screamed something at me but I couldn't hear his words due to the growling of those irksome beasts, so before I knew it he'd caused the ground to tear apart, and dragged me into a hole that he'd created. He instantly sealed it with platinum once we were safely inside, meaning that for a short while those ever vicious turds couldn't reach us.

"I'm guessing they were never going to give up?" I asked.

"Quite. They're relentless and would have chased us until we ran out of magic. The same rules apply down here after all and so we couldn't have flown for ever, and the only safe bet was to do this, I found out the hard way too many times, trust me."

"But they'll bugger off now?" I asked.

"They'll circle us for a while, but soon enough someone or something new will arrive, and they'll leave to kill them."

"Oh," I replied, "Good?"

"Yes, on this occasion. Now we need to create a living space here that we can survive in for a few days. I need to recover from what you did to me in your personal hell, and it looks like you could also benefit from forty winks. Sorry, but you are looking bloody awful right now."

Ever the charmer, eh? But with no real choice I went along with his plans, as we created a small bunker with beds, food, water and a PlayStation 4 in case we got bored. It didn't take long for me to pass out, though I cast protection spells around me beforehand as I still did not trust George an iota.

When I finally awoke I walked into the kitchen to find George preparing breakfast. Fried eggs, sausages, bacon, a slice of Hell beast, fried bread and baked beans. Gotta say, it was delicious, despite the desire to smash it into his face and claw out his eyes with bits of hardened sausage. While I ate he cautiously tried to win me over yet again. Persuade me that he truly regretted everything. I ignored it all, but decided to get the answers to a few more things which had been bothering me about our time in the afterlife.

"How come you were able to save me then?" I asked, "How come you weren't trapped in your own personal Hell?"

"The moment had been prepared for," George responded.

"I recognise that line from somewhere," I replied, "But anyhow, go on?"

"I suspected that I would end up in Hell when I died, and so a while back I managed to contact someone who was already down here, someone who had already escaped his own Hell, and who owed me a quite large favour."

"And who was that?" I asked.

"You won't believe me, but it was Gandhi."

For once George was right, and I really didn't believe him.

"You're seriously telling me that Gandhi is in Hell?"

"He is, and the only reason you're surprised is because of the favours I did for him. The secrets I managed to keep hidden about him."

"And those secrets were?"

"You can ask him yourself as you'll meet him soon enough, he's one of the three I believe will help us."

"How come you didn't return to your personal Hell each time I killed you though?" I asked.

"It no longer exists. That was partially why it took me such a long time to rescue you, as even with a magician as skilled as Gandhi it still took the two of us combined a painful amount of time to destroy it, especially given the size of the bastard. But I couldn't risk returning there, especially as I knew there was a good chance no one would be coming to save me a second time, and I was all but certain that when I met you that you would be of a murderous persuasion. Not that I blame you, I should stress."

"What was your personal Hell?" I asked.

To that he shuddered.

"It's complicated. And involved someone I once loved very dearly being subjected to terrible misery."

"Something a little similar to what you put me through when I was alive then?" I said, hopefully.

"No, much, much worse," he replied, but I decided against hearing another tale of woe from the man.

"Is this how Heaven works as well then?" I asked, "Personal Heavens and then a main central area type thing?"

"No one knows," George replied, "No one's ever chosen to leave Heaven, which hopefully is a good sign. I'd like to think it was something similar to what you suggest but it might be just one giant orgy. I'll never know, that's for sure, I have tried to contact people as well, but no one was prepared to take my call."

"I don't blame them," I muttered, and before he had the chance to respond, "And just so I can prepare myself a little, what's the deal with Lucifer?"

"He's a life form who was created for the singular role of orchestrating as much pain and misery as is possible, to continue generating negative energy even after we've died. Haven't yet met anyone who's had a good word to say about him."

I started laughing. Almost hysterically. It took about two minutes before I stopped, despite George slapping me twice, and shaking me repeatedly.

"Oh God," I said, "I'm so going to end up being utterly screwed to pieces by all of this. Like, my existence is going to be so horrendous no one could accurately describe it without going crazy. I truly have absolutely no doubt about this. Yet I'm still going to go ahead with it. Still going to follow you."

"Ben, trust me-" he began saying, until I punched him yet again in the face. You'd think he'd be used to it by now, but it wasn't the case. Then I walked away from him. Sat down. Clutched my head for a while. A long old while.

"I hate you so much, you know. I didn't realise it was possible to hate a human being in the way that I do. I mean it's pure, white, terrifying hatred. And no, don't say anything. I've just got to live with it for the time being. Die with it, or whatever. But I can't return to Glastonbury. And I don't want to live any more that's for sure. So if there's even the slightest chance of the end of my existence, I have to go with you. Despite every fibre of my being telling me not to, I will. But we'll have no more discussion of anything involving the past. You. Karoline. That's all off topic now. All I want is death. And as quickly as possible, please."

"I... I...," He stuttered, before looking me in the eyes and realising that there was no point arguing.

"Okay. I do want to say so much more to you Ben, but okay," he said.

"So what's next?" I asked.

"We need to find three more magicians," he said, before going on to explain how two of the other magicians he thought would help us were trapped in their own personal Hells, so we should start with the one who wasn't. The one who'd saved him. And by happy chance it didn't take us long to find Gandhi, who was holed up in his own bunker underneath the ground only a couple of hours away, and which due to their previous encounter George knew exactly where to find.

"You can fuck right off," the once popular religious fella said,

"I've already helped you out once and I really didn't want to do that, but as you well know I didn't exactly have a choice in the matter."

"Gandhi, look, I know we've had our disagreements in the past," George replied, but Gandhi's laughter drowned him out. Before he sternly looked him in the eye and said "Fuck you George Hartman, fuck you. I want nothing to do with you. Now leave, or your personal Hell will seem like a bloody utopia compared to what I'll do to you. All without a flicker of guilt."

That was enough to persuade George to make a very hasty exit.

"Hmmmm," he mumbled, "I hadn't expected that."

"So even Ghandi hates you," I said, "At least I'm in good company. Well, sort of. Some of the time."

The next person George suggested we approach needed to be plucked from her own personal Hell. Christina Lawton, an ex-flame of George's from the nineteenth century, she'd survived their relationship and lived until nineteen fifty six when she'd died in a car crash. Such mundane ends to a magician's life were rare but this was one of those occasions where it had simply been a tragic accident, she'd been knocked unconscious and then bled to death in the wreckage of her car before anyone with magical abilities reached her.

Her personal Hell was being repeatedly murdered by Albert Fish, which was considerably different from the actual events that had taken place, as after splitting up with George, Christina had spent the next seventy or so years as the world's first serial killer profiler. Devoting her life to tracking down as many of the criminally insane as she could, and saving countless lives, I felt a bit guilty I'd never thought about doing the same thing, though it was a minor regret considering the thousands of others. Thanks to the press it normally wasn't long before she heard about another array of death, and she'd found herself in the big apple in nineteen thirty four, where it took her under a week to find Albert, and as she had possession of the Yuasa artefact at the time she'd operated upon him and forced him to confess by letter, leading to his capture shortly afterwards. I was surprised by her compassion given what I'd read about him, that she didn't chop him into tiny Rubik's cube sized pieces, or leave him limbless in a dustbin or something, she later told me that she had her reasons, but then refused to expand upon them. I think that's why we never became close friends, as I've never been fond of the annoyingly enigmatic.

Despite this, her personal Hell, lordy, I wouldn't even have wished it upon my new worst enemy, aka George. On the first day of her death she had stood inside the hallway of Fish's apartment but instead of him quietly introducing himself as he had the day they actually met, and allowing her to cut open his skull, he launched at her with alarming speed, a blur of limbs and switchblades. She was suddenly powerless. Incapable of magic, and in that hallway she'd tried to cast a thousand spells but not one would work. She'd tried to escape, to fight back, even seduce him a few times, and once it turned into a game of Hide and Seek that lasted three hours, but every incident ended with him gleefully gorging upon various body parts. Never to the point of death though. Or at least, it should have been, but somehow she would survive, and in the middle of the night as he slept she'd crawl along the floor, leaving an impossibly bloody trail behind her, until she was out on the streets and someone would eventually find her. Then she'd awake. Back in her home. Heavily scarred, her recovery took weeks and every fragment of her ruptured skin felt like it might split open at the merest touch. But, because this is Hell we're talking about, when finally healthy enough to stand, to walk, if little else, she found herself unable to control her body, she was unable to stop it returning to Fish's residence. And the nightmare began again.

When George tore into her reality she was mid-fight, her abdomen leaking blood on to the floor. He pulled her from her Hell into ours, cast protection spells and healed her instantly. She looked into his eyes, and then slapped him in the face.

"Not that I am displeased to see you Mr Hartman," Christina said, "But you took a very long time to arrive. I have to say my afterlife was unpleasant in the extreme, and I was not enjoying it at all."

"I'm sorry, Christina, I wish I could have been here sooner, but not being dead made it all a tad tricky," George replied, "I came as quickly as I could though."

"I'd like to believe that," Christina said, "Except for the boy standing next to you suggests that your words are not entirely true."

"It's a long story," George replied, only for Christina to suggest that it always was.

"What was happening to you there by the way?" George asked, "And who was that surprisingly well dressed entity trying to cut you to pieces?"

She explained the entire Fish situation to us. Wincing took place many times.

"I've been murdered over a thousand times, and I'm not quite sure why I'm not some kind of animalistic lunatic. I've without doubt been fairly savage many times, but in the last year I've managed some level of resilience to this. Or I've utterly lost my mind and am not the person I believe myself to be. Who knows, given what I have been through of late. Now, I am not ungrateful for your untimely rescue, but I can only presume there is a reason for your arriving now?"

"I need your help," George said.

"I shouldn't be surprised," Christina responded, shaking her head, "There was always going to be a bloody price to pay with you."

"It's optional, I swear. But I think once you hear it, you'll want in," George said.

"So what is this plan, then?" she asked, "Or are you just winging it as usual?"

George explained everything.

She sighed. "Winging it then. You never change, do you?"

Helen Archer had been dead for precisely two years and forty five days, and on each and every one of them she awoke out of a deep sleep, feeling refreshed, relaxed, which when alive had been a rare occasion. Her husband Paul had already left for work for the day and she looked forward to the following ten or so hours as she had all but nothing to do other than care for their three year old son Michael, as she'd made sure the major chores had been taken care of the day before. Michael had not always been the easiest of children to deal with but in the past two months he had slowly become much calmer and far less erratic and unpredictable. She was a little surprised he hadn't woken her, but he was at the age now where he was content to play with his *Doctor Who* toys or put on a dvd, to the extent that she sometimes felt alarmed at how adept he already was with technology, and she dreaded introducing him to the internet. But that was a minor concern, and one a couple of years down the line, and nothing when compared to everything else she had been through over the course of her lifetime. Nothing compared to the way she had successfully faked her own death, moved to a different country, and settled in a small town they all loved and which was so quiet that the local newspaper had closed down six months ago as they had so little to report. One kid down, one on the way, and now she hardly ever performed any magic, sure, she dabbled occasionally, but only minor spells, like making birds shit on any builder who wolf whistled at her, or letting a small monkey do all the washing up before bed if she and Paul were truly shattered. She smiled, and dozed for a while, and it was an hour before she got out of bed. By this point she knew she couldn't put off making breakfast for Michael any longer, and so knocked gently on his door, calling out his name. With no reply she felt a flicker of panic, but it still did not prepare her for what she saw when she opened the door. That led to delirium as she tried to understand the horror. Her son's blood had soaked through his mattress and dripped from the edges of the bed on to the floor, and as she moved towards his body, and clearly saw what had happened to him, she collapsed. Lay on the floor, her body shaking, distraught raucous noises emerging. She lay there submerged in grief for hours. Unable to move. Somehow, some way, she eventually managed to find the strength to crawl to her room, to grab her phone, to call the authorities. Soon she was surrounded by strangers, many of them trying to talk to her, to force her to engage with existence, but all she could do was lie there, the only sign that she was alive being the slightest hint of breathing. After another hour she was sedated and taken to the hospital. There a man tried to interrogate her, slipped in the smallest of hints that she was the individual responsible for her child's death. Rage erupted from her previously frail body as she launched herself at the man, beating his face, his chest, until two nurses arrived, held her down, sedated her further, and she finally fell unconscious.

And time flew backwards, and she found herself waking up once again, yet with no memory of forthcoming events, no memory of the trauma she was about to experience again. Over and over again.

Unfortunately that didn't last. When George opened up a tear in her reality and pulled her into ours, every single day that she'd experienced while in Hell hit her all at once. Suddenly she had memories of discovering her dead son hundreds and hundreds of times. As with me, it took a long time until she was something close to becoming a sentient human being again, even though we all did our best to help her understand what was happening to her.

Eventually explanations were made, stories were told, and plans explained. She seemed unfazed by everything that was being suggested. Her response was immediate.

"Yes. I'm with you. I hope he destroys every aspect of my soul."

She was only thirty two, but looked like the oldest and most fractured of humans that I'd ever seen, and normally I'd have made a joke about having once met The Rolling Stones, or something like that, but she looked so distraught that any vague attempt at humour was the furthest thing from my mind. She was also undoubtedly attractive, with the whole blonde hair, large chest and legs that make you weep thing going on, but one glance from her and you felt appalled for ever having had carnal thoughts. Like me, she only sought death, and cared for nothing else.

George then cleared his throat. "Now, we have to convince one more person to help us. We need to find Hitler."

"Ah fuck off George," we responded in unison.

That caused George to laugh for a little too long. It was a sound I hadn't heard him make in Hell, and one I could have happily gone without hearing for the rest of my death.

"Sorry, I couldn't resist," he said, "Of course it's not that one, it's Jonathan Hitler, a completely different chap, no moustache or violent haircut."

"And what's his personal Hell? Hanging out with his namesake?" I asked.

"No, no, he escaped his Hell a long time back, and has been residing in Lucifer's since, Gandhi occasionally visits him and he's doing rather well for himself as it goes, created a home in a large mountain range which is fairly luxurious. The only problem is that it's millions of miles away, and a journey that isn't going to be exactly relaxing. To be honest he's something of a last resort, I had hoped that I wouldn't have to call on him for help, that Gandhi would have been on board, but it was sadly not to be."

As George predicted, the expedition to Hitler's wasn't fun in the slightest. There were no hijinks or exciting adventures either, only yet more witnessing others in the worst squalor that appeared possible in this loathsome dimension, of humanity at its very worse, torturing themselves or others in ways that made my mind break time and again. Even more distressing were encounters with aliens and demonic creatures that were so repulsive that the mere sight of them would normally have made me crap myself, at least if I hadn't already cast a spell to prevent that from happening a second time.

On two occasions George had to save my soul from being eaten by random flying creatures, though I suspected it was just so he didn't have to waste time saving me from Glastonbury again. We spoke sparingly, yet frustratingly as much as I didn't want to trust him, I was starting to believe that he really didn't want to exist anymore. The tales of his life, the true tales that Helen and Christina often took turns telling, rather than the crap he'd told me when he was alive, convinced me further and he did his best to persuade me that he hadn't always been the man I'd known. And I wasn't sure what to believe.

Weeks passed in a humdrum fashion, our days spent flying towards Hitler, the nights in hastily constructed bunkers, and I slowly got to know Christina and Helen a little, though the former tended to spend most of her time talking to George if she could as she had little interest in my ramblings, and the latter only spoke about how much she desired obliteration. Even though we bonded over that it soon became a little one note and dreary, and yes, I wanted to no longer exist but I slowly started to think that while waiting for it to happen I shouldn't be in a state of despair every single second of every day.

Eventually we arrived at The Red Plains where Hitler was supposed to reside, and which were quite frankly the most disgusting of all of the areas in Hell. The majority of the time we were able to fly over it, but when we needed to land and build somewhere to rest, the moment I stepped on the ground there were so many bloody organs, intestines and other unidentified chunks of flesh lying around that I found myself slipping and sliding all over the place, leading to my jeans becoming covered in all round foulness and an aroma that made me want to slice my nose off. Such a response seemed a popular idea among the creatures that chose to live here as well and so there was also a lot of nostrils and a lot of snot to deal with on top of everything else. I was initially surprised that anyone would want to spend any time in a region like this by choice, but soon released it was because such awfulness was a source of food for those who could be psychologically described as "really fucking bananas."

Due to that where there wasn't flesh or organs there were broken and crushed bones and skulls, while it occasionally rained blood, and though in the scheme of things that might seem a minor annoyance it still really got to me after a while, especially as it ruined my favourite *Over The Garden Wall* t-shirt.

On the third day we approached a mountain range which served as an ending for this aspect of Hell, and a beginning to another I imagined wouldn't be a whole barrel of fun either, I'm cynical like that. Pointing at what looked like a rather old castle among the mountains, George told us we'd arrived, but that Jonathan wouldn't be exactly overjoyed to see him.

"I probably should have mentioned this, but the last time we spoke I'd hoped he might have forgiven me, that a friendship might be forged," he said, "It wasn't to be, so it's probably best if you don't mention my part in this until you absolutely have to."

"I can't say I'm in shock right now," I replied.

"There's also a bit of a catch as it goes," George said, "As he's been in Hell for a long time now, attained rather a lot of power, so why he can't technically kill us he could strip you of your magic and leave you a normal soul, burning and shrieking day in day out. It's probably a fate best not thought about too much."

Much swearing at George took place, and I decided to go with a slightly different plan to the one he had suggested. Sauntering up to his castle with Christina and Helen, I knocked loudly on the rather large door. Initially there was silence. And then: "Leave. Now. Please."

I knocked again.

"Hi, look, I'm really sorry to bother you," I said, "But I'm here with George Hartman and I'll be more than happy to let you kill him if you like."

This time the reaction was all but immediate, as the door opened and a fairly short, blonde man of about thirty appeared. He sighed, hard and for quite the time, the longest sigh I could recall ever hearing as it goes, and it felt a real shame that the *Guinness Book of Records* people weren't around as I'm certain it would have led to him appearing in their publication. At long last he muttered "You best come in then."

Jonathan Hitler turned out to be a mostly lovely man, albeit one with an unfortunate surname. Born in America in Eighteen Forty-Five, Jonathan was the son of a Germanic couple who'd travelled to Ohio a decade earlier, he'd met George in his late twenties and the two had instantly struck up a friendship, and after one drunken night where George couldn't resist showing off Jonathan discovered the existence of this messed up magical world. Alas he only lasted two years as a magician before miscasting a spell that was supposed to build him an impressive house but which accidentally turned him into a horse, and an old horse with damaged vocal cords at that, with him dying before anyone realised what had happened. After his demise he'd spent seventy years in his own personal Hell, stuck once again as an old horse, being mercilessly irritated by other younger, prettier horses. He was absolutely insane by the time a magician by the name of Arthur Hoult had pulled him out of his Hell and into this one and requested his help, with Hitler the only one who had escaped with his life. Since then he'd spent his life living within the mountain range, creating artefacts and experimenting with magic, finally managing to make a connection with the corporeal world forty years ago, he couldn't leave Hell but he could at least witness our reality, which explained how he'd an extensive knowledge of pretty much every tv show and film ever made, and how much happier he'd become when Netflix went online.

We spoke for about an hour in total, as he had so many questions about the history of the Earth. He knew the version of events that the various news networks had fed him, but none of the actual truth. And we discussed George of course, as his hatred almost matched mine as he was quietly convinced that George had taught him the house/horse spell on purpose, and then ignored an awful lot of whinnying. Finally much discourse took place about the plan that had been devised, how it was essentially a suicide attempt, and despite his opulent surroundings Jonathan immediately agreed to take part.

"Like you Mr Holland, I do not trust Mr Hartman, but I do not want to exist any longer either, the loneliness is distressing in the extreme and while I have attempted to construct friendships with the smattering of humans found here, I have failed each time."

As he gathered a few belongings I stood by his side, making stale conversation that neither of us was enjoying. Then I made things more uncomfortable, as is my tendency.

"You seem like a really decent chap Jonathan, so how come you're in Hell?" I asked. He looked crest-fallen, as if this was a question he'd hoped he'd never have to answer.

"It is a tale I wish had not taken place Benjamin," he replied, "And one that I'm deeply ashamed of. I swear to you that I was a good man for most of my life, I truly was. Which may sound somewhat arrogant, but it's because I forced myself to be. Yet I made one mistake, before I became a magician, when I was very young and only in my late teenage years. For there was a woman, a woman I loved deeply, who did not reciprocate my feelings. She loved another, and I was consumed with jealousy. I knew I could not force her to love me, but I thought that if he was no longer present in her life she may begin to think differently of me. So I kidnapped him. I paid for him to be taken to the continent of Africa, and left naked and penniless as soon as the boat docked. After a year I came to realise that she would never feel towards me the way I had hoped she might, and I visited the dark continent to try to bring him home to her, but it was too late, as he had died in an alcohol soaked brawl."

"Blimey," I replied, "That must have been hard to live with."

"Almost impossible," Jonathan said, "Which is why I dedicated my life to carrying out acts of kindness afterwards. Though clearly they weren't enough to save my petulant soul."

CHAPTER 15 - A LONG JOURNEY TOLD AS BRIEFLY AS I CAN, I SWEAR

The end seemed in sight now and how I welcomed it, until George stepped into frustrate us all once again. This was due to the fact that the trip to see Lucifer was apparently going to be disagreeably long and arduous, and I found myself missing the days when he was a lying bastard as it was indeed the case and then some, it took frickin' months and months. We left the Mountain Range where Hitler had lived in late April and didn't arrive at our final destination until November, it was a right bloody arse. And mostly bleakly boring I'm afraid to say, if I wrote it in full it'd be three times the length of the Lord of the Rings novels but so mundane that J.R.R. Tolkien would have come back from beyond the grave and beaten the shit out of me for dragging out such a story. With Hitler's artefacts we were stronger now at least, so able to fly over the terrain at speed while avoiding most of the more psychotic creatures who were out and about looking to eat some limbs, but Christ did it take forever and a day, and was mostly the dictionary definition of banality. Even the really disturbing moments had lost their edge, it was just like, oh, yeah, there's someone else being deformed in traumatic ways, oh well, these things happen, hope all that screaming doesn't mean it hurts too much.

In some ways I wish it had all been like that, but two events are worth speaking of, if only so that you get an idea as to my state of mind when we did finally reach Lucifer, along with just how bizarre Hell could be.

The first took place three months into the journey, and as per usual we were flying over the squealing, decaying bodies of thousands when out of the blue we suddenly heard singing. A demon singing. Twenty foot tall, covered in black scales, and wearing a tuxedo, sparkly trousers and tap shoes, he looked like he was having a whale of a time.

"Ah, bollocks," George said, "I'd forgotten about him."

We'd come across a fair few demonic pricks along the way, creations of Lucifer's partially invented to keep himself entertained but also to ensure misery flowed and there wasn't a single part of Hell where the sound of frenzied suffering couldn't be heard. Several of these demons had been pretty disconcerting, the beast who was half a giant happy cow and half a surly scorpion especially, but combined we'd been able to dispatch most of them with ease. The Rogarth, an eight headed ninety foot wide brick shithouse, and I mean that quite literally, had proven the most troublesome, but eventually we combined our powers to create an enormous drill to blind him. Though as he had thirty six eyes it took a fair time and became weirdly dull, in another lifetime if I was offered a job drilling out people's eyeballs I'm all but certain I'd turn it down.

This singing weirdo was the first time in a good while that I'd seen George worried however, I'd had a feeling that dispatching the rest of them was something he'd taken some pleasure in, but now all of the colour had drained from his face. It looked as if, as the old cliché goes, a ghost had crossed over his path, which might've been the case as that was supposedly possible down here, but due to their invisible state you'd never know for sure unless they stopped off for a brief chat / possession.

"Pcarasus, the Singing Demon," George whispered, "I've heard tales about him, but never really believed it, I presumed nothing so evil, so malevolent could exist."

"What does it do?" I asked, "Is it some kind of siren that will draw us to our deaths? Will he transform into a sexy lady with enormous breasts?" I said, before deciding to stop, mainly as I had become aware that I'd briefly found myself sexually frisky again. I thought I knew my penis, but it seems it still had the ability to depress me at the drop of a hat.

"Er, anyhow, ignore that, what the hell is a Picarus Demon?" I asked.

"Pcarasus, and it forces you to sing," George replied.

"Christ no," I said, fainting dead away like a Victorian lady. Except that I didn't, because I really couldn't see what the fuss was all about.

"Um, that doesn't really kind of sound like the worst thing in the world, George, why are you so freaked out by him?" I asked.

"It's not that simple, you have to... Sigh, dear lord, it's all very undignified. You have to become involved in a singing competition with him, you see, and if you amuse and entertain him he'll let you leave, let you escape. If not he captures your soul and traps it in inescapable cages of misery where all day, and every day, you have to sing along to a karaoke version of that fucking Fast Food Song by the Fast Food Rockers."

Christina stared at him, somewhat confused.

"George, what are you talking about? What is this Fast Food Song you speak of?" she asked.

"Several years ago some of the most psychotic individuals the planet has ever known came together to devise a piece of music that would destroy the minds of even the sanest individuals in the world, at least if they were forced to listen to it over and over again for hours at a time. It was meant to be used as a way to torture someone if there was no other way to get them to speak."

"Christina, he's once again taking the piss," Helen said, "Yes, it's bad, but it's not that bad."

"Have you ever listened to it more than once?" George asked, and she admitted she hadn't.

"Its power is in its repetition. Once it merely annoys, one hundred times it destroys. Trust me, I've seen it happen."

"And if we fail to win this singing competition, would that be our fate?" Christina asked.

"Yes. Though it would only be the beginning, given that he'd keep us here until this universe finally came to an end," George replied.

"Why would he do such a thing though?" Helen asked.

"He's a chaos demon, and a rabid one at that. He exists only to annoy."

"What are we going to do then?" Christina asked, "As singing is not one of my many talents I'm afraid."

"I'll try to bargain with him," George responded, "Suggest that just one of us compete against him, we can't all attempt to face him individually, it's too risky, if even one of us were to fail it would mean having to find another magician who would join us on our quest to battle Lucifer, and I've no idea how to do that. Hence we need someone to represent us all, someone who can think quickly, deflect any barb and smash something back which will make this monstrous aberration laugh."

I began to open my mouth when George spluttered "No, Ben, no, I appreciate the offer, but I also know your sense of humour so don't even suggest it. The best thing to do is to use our magic on Helen. There are a few spells which can help. Confidence, vocabulary, and others along those lines."

"Can't we just run away?" Jonathan asked.

"Alas not, he's a speedy bugger, this one."

It took a while but George eventually convinced Helen to go along with his idea, and then he slowly and casually approached the beast. Much devious wordplay took place and I wasn't certain that George would be successful, the deranged demon appeared to initially refuse to entertain logical discourse, but eventually George managed to bargain for our potential freedom and it was agreed that if we bored or angered Pcarasus we would be his personal slaves for all of eternity, yet if we pleased him he'd let us leave, kind of like a reverse X-Factor except that I'd much rather hang out with Pcarasus than I would Simon Cowell.

Once they had finished conversing Pcarasus led us to a large stage, and sauntered on to it, and I have to confess that I thought he might have looked quite handsome if it wasn't for the horns and the many weeping wounds his face contained.

Launching into a tap dance he shrieked out the words "Hit it boys" and a small eight piece orchestra I hadn't noticed before began playing a tune I vaguely recognised but couldn't put my finger on. And then the strange old monster burst into song.

"Ohhhhhhhhhh, when the sun hits the sky like a big piece of pie, that's Amore,

When you devour vagina off your grandmother's best china, that's Amore,

When you eat live horses for your second courses, that's Amore,

When you rain down shitting arses upon our armed forces, that's

Amore!"

The creature took a breath, gave me a saucy wink, and then continued.

"When you're murdered in a dream, with no mouth to scream, that's Amore,

When you eat your brother's liver and it gives you an erotic shiver, that's Amore

When you weep as you clean your lover's brain from your foreskin, that's Amore

When you burn here for ever more watched by laughing friends you adore, that's Amore! That's Amore! That's Amore!"

Helen stared at us, gobsmacked. And then noticed we had the same look on our faces.

"What the fuck?" she said, "How am I supposed to follow that? I mean, it doesn't make any sense, I've no idea what he's going on about."

"It's a parody of an old Dean Martin song," George replied, "Pcarasus is worryingly even more unstable than I'd heard. Whatever we reply with has to please him, but Christ knows what that might be."

"I'm guessing something even more insane?" I interjected, "And I know we thought Helen might be the best person for the job, but I think I know what to do to beat him."

"Are you sure?" George asked.

"Yeah, for once I am. Because a few years ago, during a low patch when I briefly got heavily into smoking a lot of marijuana, I wrote a musical. It was never performed, I didn't even show it to anyone, but I think one of the songs might be the sort of thing that a diseased mind like Pcarasus would like."

"I think we should let him try," Helen said, "Because I sure as hell do not have a clue how to respond to that." The others agreed as they had no idea either, but George wasn't so convinced.

"This is our lives at stake here Mr Holland, so I truly hope that you're right."

"Well, we're about to find out," I said, before belting out the following song, a ballad which wouldn't have sounded out of place in a Disney flick, one which possibly rhymes with Joanna, and I know the rhyme scheme's all over the place but hey, that's the joy of mild drug abuse for you.

"Without my family I'm the loneliest shark in my locale,
Lonelier than Jaws, whose only friend was his Japanese pen pal,
I've been lost in the sea for so long without them,
As they were taken by ninja sharks that I condemn.
They weren't kind, they didn't care, they weren't good,
Those dirty shits destroyed my beloved shark brotherhood.
Dressed in black they swam through the sea so silently,
So violently,
One minute the water was so beautifully pure and blue,
The next it was red and uglier than the views
of Gerard Depardieu.
Ninja Sharks took away those I loved from me,
Until I seek revenge I'll never truly be happy.
Ninja Sharks destroyed my hopes and my dreams,
Now I can't rest until I hear their anguished screams.
Ninja Sharks are the bane of my life it's true,
But there'll be a Ninja Shark graveyard when I'm through.
Those little turds will regret the day they messed with me,
I'm the shark equivalent of a rather angry bee."

I stopped, and silence fell. George, Christina, Jonathan and Helen didn't know where to look. If what I'd sung was truly weird enough. And then, after what felt like hours of him mulling it over, Pcarasus spoke.

"Yeah, I liked that."

Relief flooded through me.

"So it is your lucky day, I won't imprison you in the cages of misery, as you do intrigue, and your presence in Hell may be of interest again," the demon concluded.

"Okay. Thanks!" was my brief reply, and with that we ran. As quickly and as far away from that barmy old bastard as we could.

For once the next couple of millions of miles were pleasingly bland again, and I didn't mind at all after that madness. Though I hadn't said anything at the time I had been terrified and it was only due to a particularly handy spell that my voice hadn't trembled throughout the song, while another stopped accidental urination. Yet the whole time we flew towards Lucifer I knew it was only a matter of time before something new would torment my mangled mind again, and yeah, that's not a nice feeling to carry with you. But to my surprise, after about five days something actually happened which made me happy. Not for long, but at least it was a brief period where something wasn't emotionally scarring me for the rest of my hopefully short life.

"Is that... Is that a Tyrannosaurus Rex?" I spluttered.

"Yeah," Hitler replied, somewhat blasé.

"What the heck?" I responded.

"Seriously? Dinosaurs surprise you considering what we've been through of late?" Hitler responded, a little patronisingly to be honest.

"Hell's been around since the beginning of time as a place where evil souls pass on to," he went on to say, "And just like humans, or any other animal or life form, some dinosaurs had an innate goodness within them. Or learnt how to get through life without being too much of a twat, at least. But some, well, some dinosaurs were simply absolute motherfuckers."

"Huh. There was me thinking that the Jurassic Park movies were all a bit xenophobic," I responded.

"Nope," Hitler replied.

"And this applies to all animals then? Are there bits of Hell where all the evil dolphins live? Because if so, I want to go there."

"There is, and you do, but there isn't time," George interjected, "Which is a shame. I'd really like to take you to cat Hell as well, especially the killer kittens. So fetching, but so, so deadly."

During this admittedly pointless conversation I slowly began to notice that more and more dinosaurs were careering towards us as we'd entered the expanse of Hell they felt most comfortable in. There was no end to the roaring and growling and a minor bit of screeching, a stampede of death that in other circumstances I'd have been mortified by but here my only reaction was vague concern. It was one of those "Ugh, I bet this is going to be a bit of a pain in my sexy old posterior, but I can't deny being quietly delighted" moments, as seeing dinosaurs for the first time in my life thrilled me to pieces.

Yet the negative aspects soon outweighed the positive, especially as the sky began to darken as a bunch of flying dickheads arrived, though not literally I should stress, that would have chilled not only my spine but every other bone in the my body.

"Ah. Bollocks. Pterosaurs and Pterodactyls, and what appears to be the mutant offspring of both" George said.

"Retreat?" Christina suggested, which we all quickly agreed was a rather good plan, and that's why we flew to a nearby mountain and created a small construction where we could take a breath and witness the beasts congregate. First thousands, and then hundreds of thousands, before it became a case of millions, and other long numbers with way too many zeros. Seventy two billion five hundred and twenty six million and two hundred thousand and ninety two, to be precise, Helen announced, having created some kind of a scientific gizmo to count them all.

"Isn't that also the amount of women who have made it adamantly clear they wouldn't have sex with you Ben?" George joked and my murderous rage returned, though for the time being I pushed it down and tried to ignore his attempt at banter, as the dinosaurs sadly did need to be dealt with. Oh, and yeah, for the record lots of them have feathers, but it doesn't make them any less scary. More so, thinking about it, it's like they've dressed up for a bizarre fancy dress party but then decided to go on a psychotic rampage instead.

"They're all arriving at the same time. Without trying to devour each other. It's most strange, normally they attempt to eat each other whenever they're given an opportunity," Hitler commented, "I've seen my fair share of dinosaurs in Hell, be it dinosaur dinner parties, dinosaur orgies or dinosaur sleepovers, but they always end in bloodshed as they turn on each other."

I presumed he was attempting to make a joke, but when I raised an eyebrow he ignored it.

"That leads me to believe in only one possibility. That this is no accident, that we're their prey. We're all powerful beings, perhaps they're now able to detect us. They've been here for billions of years, who knows how they might have evolved," Hitler continued.

"Surely we could just fight our way through though?" Helen suggested, "There's five of us, with our abilities, we must be able to do so."

"I wish I shared your confidence," Christina responded, "They're coming from all directions, and there's so many different species. Also, what if we only get half way through and run out of energy? And we don't know what we're dealing with. How strong they are."

"A test run, then," Helen suggested, "We don't attempt to get too far, we stay together, work consistently as a team, and see how far we get?"

"That sounds good to me, and we've got to try something," I cut in.

"Okay, okay," George replied, "But the moment things look even slightly perilous and anyone starts to flag we should plunge into the ground and build a bunker to stay in while we regroup and perhaps consider another plan."

We chose our weapons, and devised a basic strategy of attack, but all too quickly it was apparent that there were too many of them. Initially Hitler had attempted to see how far he could get by flying above them but was immediately grabbed out of the air by several stroppy pterodactyls and smashed into the ground. A force field prevented him from being hurt, and he fired off an alarming amount of missiles which caused the creatures to explode in a fiery mess shortly after impact, but it only gave him a few seconds to escape and join up with the rest of us again. Meanwhile I'd come up with a different tactic and turned all of the dinosaurs nearest to us into the size of hamsters, before stamping on them. It felt oh so wrong to treat such a majestic beast like that but it was a them or us scenario, and I'd no urge to explore the stomach of an Allosaurus while taking my final gasps of air. Unfortunately once again the flying dinosaurs were the most difficult to deal with, partially as they attacked before we'd had the chance to shrink them, and that meant a whole bunch of Pterodactyls and Aurornis Xui's had swooped down upon us, the former able to swat us to the ground, the latter pecking annoyingly, the evil bastard proto chickens that they were. I'd never even heard of the things until that day but despite their size, man, they're on my nemesis list now. As were the Pterosaurs, who were doing their best to pester us, and given that they're shaped like a giraffe that can fly was quite a lot. Force fields prevented bleeding but heavy bruising took place, and I wasn't exactly enjoying myself any longer.

Along with his feet George was using the good old fashioned ridiculously massive machine gun with a never ending supply of bullets method, which was pretty effective though I got the feeling he was mostly using it because he knew he looked damn cool at the same time. I noticed at one point he was chuckling away as he shot the crap, and brains, out of a triceratops, and then winked at Christina after doing so, which depressingly suggested that committing mass murder didn't dampen his libido and if anything encouraged it. Given his track record I shouldn't have been surprised, yet somehow he always managed to do so. Meanwhile Helen was dispatching them by something which absolutely definitely wasn't a light sabre, even if it looked a bit like one which no, actually, thinking about it, it in no way did. She proved herself to be far more athletic than the rest of us as well, leaping onto the back of one Carcharodontosaurus and plunging her weapon into the creature's brains and then jumping on to a passing T-Rex and removing his eyes with the device. Finally there was Christina who had tripled her size and was throwing large bombs hundreds of feet away in every direction in the hope that doing so might give us the odd breather, which also explained why a lot of the dinosaurs were arriving covered in blood or with severe burns, yet still in a huffy mood.

At this point I wish I could say we were making an impact, but it became obvious that wasn't the case at all, and the problem now was that we were trapped in a circle, firing in all directions, and while the body count was rising quickly, the onslaught was ever oncoming and it didn't look like it would let up for several days yet. Over the hullabaloo of death George screamed "Throw everything at them, now!" and his machine gun quadrupled in size, spitting out missiles at a speed where they could barely be seen, Christina's bombs became atomic, Helen made her ligh- her fire sword the size of a pine tree, and Hitler created three napalm filled guns, growing an extra arm so that he could shoot all of them at the same time. I was also responsible for my fair share of bloodshed as I continued to make many of them tiny, and after magicking up a large lawnmower there was soon a carpet of blood and flesh behind wherever I walked.

Yet though it briefly felt like we were making a difference, that we were getting somewhere as I guessed that we must have taken out a million or so, as we edged our way forwards and moved slowly towards our destination, it wasn't to last. We'd dealt with an arse load of T-Rexes and raptors and the odd diplodocus, but then the Giganotosauruses and the Spinosauri arrived on the scene and we were quite simply screwed. They looked upon us with glee, I'd never seen a dinosaur smile before, but it caused dread to sweep through my body. The Spinosauri swiftly leapt across the ground, keeping eye contact throughout so that there was absolutely no question over whether or not they'd chosen us to dine upon this evening. I shrunk and mowed seven or so, but then they were all around us, and just as I was about to miniaturise another a Pterosaur slammed into my head, flooring me, and the moment I hit the ground I became aware that I couldn't feel anything below my neck. Panic rippled through my body as I cast a healing spell, looked up, and instantly wished that I hadn't for a Spinosaurus lurching towards me had a jaw that was exactly six foot long, which I know for certain as that's exactly how tall I am. I yelped as his teeth cut through my fading force field and into my stomach, and his enormous jaw was about to slam down upon me again when he burst into flames. As did I. I attempted a spell which would extinguish the fire, only to discover that I'd exhausted my supply of magic, and my skin burnt, my eyes melted and the agony, oh god, the agony, as it felt like my entire body had been plunged into the sun.

I awoke in a bunker, shrieking, as Christina and Helen held me and spoke soothing words, and I slowly began to realise that the suffering had ended, though considering that I thought I'd died once more it took a while to understand what had happened. The short version being that Hitler had stepped in at the last moment and saved me from a return visit to Glastonbury, and then they'd all fled and created the underground bunker I now found myself within. A luxurious affair with oak panelling and a roaring fire, with five separate bedrooms, I've got to say that if I hadn't been a gibbering wreck at the time I would have been impressed.

After an annoyingly slow recovery I returned to something which vaguely looked like normality, and the five of us spoke for a short time, ascertained that our plan to defeat the dinosaurs had been a weak one, and that there were billions of the shitters still out there. But no one had prepared an alternative scheme, and that was put on the agenda for the next day as all were somewhat exhausted, and wished to retire to their individual rooms. I went into mine and climbed on to the rather comfy four poster bed someone had made for me, but I couldn't sleep. The spells they'd cast to heal me had the unfortunate side effect of making me actually feel good, and my body felt new, full of energy, and I had nothing to do but sit there and think.

And that was a problem.

Whenever such occurrences had recently taken place I'd concentrated on the anger I'd felt towards George, and then on his plan that promised an end to our lives, but there was only so much time I could do that and incredibly depressingly I found myself thinking about Karoline, and Jesus, that led to sorrow, guilt and regret and what felt like a million and one variations upon them. But always with the same end response, that it hadn't mattered how much I'd loved her, I'd fucked up, she'd left me, and now she was gone forever. I'd never see her again. And as much as I wanted to blame George, I knew I was responsible for her ending the relationship. Yeesh, the self-pity that followed was not pretty.

I'm nothing if not slightly bi-polar though, so soon enough I was back to hating George, which was definitely the more preferable hobby. Over the last few days he'd seemed to be enjoying his death as well, which didn't make a huge amount of sense given that he was supposed to be enduring all of the suffering of his victims, especially when he'd shouted "Get back to the arse end of the' Jurassic age you dirty fuckmuffin" while shooting a Velociraptor in the head. Plus everyone knows that they weren't around in that era and were from the Cretaceous Period, if you're going to try and spit out snarky one-liners at least get the bloody science right. Still, it had one positive aspect, as if I'd ever had any doubt that he was going to betray me to Lucifer that was gone now. But the problem was that I couldn't think of a way out. I couldn't help but think that George held all the cards, he knew what the devil really was and how to manipulate him, and it wasn't going to end well. Or worst of all, not at all. I'd still exist here, or in another personal Hell, maybe in everyone's personal Hells, a different Hell a day. Which might not have made much sense, but I wasn't exactly at my sanest here. Thus more crying, until Helen came into my room and sat beside me.

"I do have to say that I'm not too impressed with this afterlife either," she said, gently caressing my arm.

"Oh god. It's all such a nightmare," I said, "And I keep on pinching myself, I've made so many holes in my flesh, but however many times I do it I never wake up."

"You're not alone there," she said, which did nothing to soothe my soul.

"I know it's only going to get worse too," I replied, "That's

George's trademark move. I have no doubt that he's going to screw me over and life will only become more desolate."

"I'm sure he can't be trusted at all, you're right," Helen said, "But given that we both know this, why are you here? Why did you agree to help him?"

I looked up at her, a tad surprised.

"For the same reasons as you, I imagine. I've no real choice. My own personal Hell wasn't my cup of tea in the slightest."

Helen let out a sharp laugh at that.

"No, no, I can imagine. What was it out of interest?" she asked.

So I told her.

"Good lord, you poor, poor boy," was her only response.

"I know. And that's why I can't return there, and it's why we must do something to stop George betraying us. I just don't know what that might be. "

"I wish I knew too. And given that this is Lucifer we're also talking about, I can't imagine it will end well for any of us."

"Then we're screwed?" I moaned.

"Maybe. Maybe not. There's nothing we can do until we arrive. But I'm with you Ben, I thought you should know that, if he tries anything despicable I will do my very best to stop him."

That made me feel slightly better, and she continued to improve my previously desolate mood as we talked into the night, during which she explained why she disliked our mutual enemy so much, the short version being that she'd been burnt at a stake three times in her life, and twice it was due to George's misadventures. She also told me other tales as well, not just those which involved him, and we bonded further over mutual magical misuse. Accidental idiocy. I even made her laugh again, for the second and final time.

Much, much later when we eventually emerged into the main living area Hitler was cooking what turned out to be the remains of a rather burnt Tyrannosaurus Rex, which was curiously pleasant as it goes, not a dish I'd rush to order at a restaurant but something I might go for on the odd occasion if offered at a barbecue. Meanwhile we tried to evaluate the situation, yet it ultimately came down to "We're in a bucket load of trouble without any solution, aren't we?"

"I mean, there's still hundreds of millions of them, aren't there?" Hitler underestimated, "How many did we kill then? Ten million at the very best?"

"Who'd have thought there were so many nefarious dinosaurs?" I commented.

"Ah, but think about how many human beings have lived," George replied, "And take a guess at how many were real shits? Let's take the piss with that statistic, and say it's only one percent, which we all know is definitely not the case. But one percent of everyone who ever lived is one billion and eighty million of the gobshites and we've only been around a relatively short time. Dinosaurs lived for over a hundred and fifty million years."

I shook my head in dismay.

"Christ, it's so unfair we only get to see the shitty angry dinosaurs, I'd love to meet the ones who made it to Heaven. The friendly, cuddly ones, who are fun at parties and who enjoy platonic cuddling."

Which was understandably met by a group of quizzical stares, and made me aware that I was slightly more chipper than usual, that the long talk with Helen had raised my spirits a little.

"This isn't helping us get anywhere. Surely there must be something else we can do?" Christina suggested, sounding less than certain.

"What if we create a giant electrified fence and slowly push them back? At least until we're exhausted, and then we'd build another bunker to restore our strength, and so on and so forth until we reach Lucifer?" Hitler offered up.

"It would work, perhaps, but it would take a ridiculous amount of time. And so far, we've gotten lucky," George replied.

"Lucky?" I pretty much gasped, "Man, we truly have a very different definition of that word."

"Currently we've only had to dealt with the dinosaurs, but if we were to encounter Hell beasts as well, or other beings that can control magic, and mix the three together, well then we'd be in a lot of trouble. I've carefully kept us away from the regions of Hell that contain alien life forms for that reason alone, but that doesn't mean they always remain there," George replied.

Further discussion took place, with all manner of suggestions made before Jonathan eventually piped up with an idea. A ludicrous one, perhaps, but hey, it was better than my plan to give them all erectile dysfunction issues and see if that made them so depressed that they didn't want to eat us anymore.

"What about creating some kind of super dinosaur?" Hitler said, "Or a whole host of them for that matter? Like a Tyrannosaurus Rex but two hundred feet tall, and with three heads, and huge arms and hands made out of swords. And the ability to emit fire, and, I don't know, maybe they'd have missiles shooting out of their knees or something."

The others laughed, mocking him, with Christina saying "That's the kind of stupid thing Ben would come out with," until George responded "Actually, you might be on to something there."

"Seriously?" Christina asked.

"We'd need to manage the project carefully," George continued, ignoring her, "Creating a suitable creature would all but drain us all of magic each day, and we'd need an army of them, but why shouldn't we build one? Nothing is preventing us after all, and then once done we could move at a far faster rate. And an army might be an overestimation as well, as long as we make it so that the creatures can move at immense speeds and we follow in their wake, we might not even have to destroy all of the normal dinosaurs either."

"Which is a good thing too, because I kind of feel a bit guilty about committing genocide, even in this place," I said, my fondness for dinosaurs not quite abated despite how often they'd tried to chew on my skin and bones.

Despite more of Christina's objections we set the plan in motion, beginning with our creating enormous holding cells under the ground to cage them in, and after constructing one creature it was put it into a coma until we had enough to do our bidding. Without Jonathan's artefacts it would have been impossible, and the amount of magic it took meant I felt I'd gone fifteen rounds with one of those men who hit you in the face in a ring for money, a concept that had always confused. Long and arduous days like these inevitably led to frazzled and frayed tempers, and many a sharp word was exchanged. Yet surprisingly Jonathan and George slowly built a fragile friendship over this time, with

Jonathan forgiving George for his past indiscretions, while the latter's friendship with Christina blossomed as well, with flirting irritatingly taking place. Where he had once been sober and serious it became clear that George was happy to be dead, and so my resentment inevitably grew, and as you know that had already been astonishingly enormous in the first place.

Most of the time I tried to avoid him and instead spoke with Jonathan, Helen or Christina, with the latter warming to me as she saw how hard I worked to attempt to complete our goal as quickly as we could. When we spoke when alone she tried to stress that George hadn't always been like the man I knew, how power must have corrupted him and created a preposterously demented ego, someone who thought he knew everything simply because he had lived for so very long, but that didn't reflect her own experiences of their time spent together.

"Has he ever told you about what he did in London in Eighteen Eighty Two?" Christina asked one night towards the end of our time in the bunker. I shook my head.

"It was the second of March, and rumour had it that a rather mad poet, Roderick Maclean, was going to try and kill Queen Victoria once again. The man was sadly very unwell, holding a grudge against her majesty simply because of a rather short reply to some poetry he'd sent her, though as this was his eighth attempt at ending her life I had a feeling she hadn't written the politest response. Either way, upon hearing the news George asked for my help to stop such an event from taking place. Unfortunately Maclean was a slippery bastard, and even with magic we were unable to track him down, as our skills were underdeveloped back then. That led to shadowing her Majesty for what soon became a very mundane and long day as she lived up to her reputation of a woman with little patience, and she was in a particularly crotchety mood that day.

We thought things would start to look up when she took the train from Paddington to Windsor, what with it being a newfangled and rather exciting form of travel, and it seemed the most likely time for a possible attempt on her life. But nothing happened on the journey itself, she just sat there staring out of the window the whole time, failing to converse with a single human being or even amusing herself with a short game of eye-spy, it was most dispiriting. Fortunately things came to a quick resolution shortly afterwards, once we arrived at the station there was a large crowd awaiting her, all desperate to cheer as she passed. Naturally we were on high alert, predicting that Maclean was among the crowd, but we didn't spot him and rather stupidly after a while began to relax, began to think that he was not going to show. Due to that both of us failed to notice the man who opened the gate to let Victoria leave, or that he had a firearm until he raised the weapon and pointed it towards her. George threw what I believe you'd describe as a grenade into a nearby bush to create a distraction, and while Maclean was briefly confused by the explosion it gave us the time to tackle him to the ground. Yet he still managed to pull the trigger, shooting George in the shoulder and leaving a nasty wound that troubled him for many years until scientific research gave him the ability to heal it completely. Maclean then pointed the weapon towards Victoria once more, even though she was being all but carried away by her guards, but thanks to a new American invention I'd learnt about only two months prior, one swift punch while wearing a pair of knuckle dusters knocked him unconscious."

"Wow, that's quite the story," I replied, "And a great advert for knuckle dusters it would seem."

"I never leave home without them, "Christina said in a manner which made me absolutely believe her.

"The whole thing was covered up of course, George and I suggested to one of our friends in the constabulary that a young Eton lad present in the crowd had hit Maclean with an umbrella, causing him to miss, and the young man happily agreed to go along with the ruse. Which I doubt will come as a surprise, it's not as if Eton was known for creating honourable men even back then."

"Great, so you think I should like George now because he once tried to save a member of the bloody Royal Family?" I replied, "Which he probably had some immoral reason for in the first place?"

"That's not the point of the story, Mr Holland, I haven't quite got to that yet," Christina responded, "For George took pity on Maclean, he knew he was mentally unwell, and though there was nothing we could do to prevent Maclean's incarceration, George made sure that he was placed in an asylum instead of a prison, and visited him every week until his death."

"Which I guess was a couple of weeks later?" I queried, still unconvinced that George was capable of any real act of kindness.

"Not at all, Maclean lived until early June in Nineteen Twenty-One. Over those thirty nine years George never missed an appointment either, and managed to find ways to not only help him psychologically but also to stay sane in such terrible circumstances."

"That's not the actions of the man I know," I said.

"And that was why I told you this. I'm aware that everyone here has reasons to be upset with George, but he has been responsible for many great acts of kindness in the past."

I then told her my story. By the end she didn't know how to respond. Yet I couldn't blame her, as I didn't either.

Finally, after far too long, we were finished creating our Super Marvellous Dinosaur Justice Team, though despite my taking out a trademark on the name Christina and the others refused to call them that. It couldn't be denied that they really were gloriously majestic however, a terror of T-Rexes, two hundred foot tall and who came complete with a harder, scalier hide, oh, and four extra heads that were capable of spitting giant blobs of lava on to anything stupid enough to go near them. Upon their universally mocked original arms I'd grafted on razor sharp steel swords and additional joints so they could spin them around wherever they chose, while the boots they wore were covered in napalm that incinerated anything they trod on. One such creature was clearly not enough to solve our issues, but sixty of them? The other dinosaurs never stood a chance.

It was however the most haunting carnage I'd ever witnessed. Our creations were death incarnate, almost nothing survived in their path, with Hell burning even more fiercely than we believed possible thanks to the monstrosities we'd manufactured. After realising just how effective they were we stayed as far away from the front of the pack as possible, clutching on to the back of one of the beasts who was lagging behind but still stomping the remains of so many beautiful creatures further into the ground, and while a few had managed to avoid either being burnt to death, slashed open or stamped upon, they looked traumatised and ran for their lives, no longer interested in us however delightful our flesh might taste.

It took over a week to be free of those once evil asshats, during which we tried to take turns sleeping while at least one of us remained conscious and stood guard, but the sound of continuous annihilation made such occasions fleeting. It was pretty clear that all of us were struggling mentally as well by this point, exhausted and distressed by the oceans of blood we were responsible for. Thankfully when we eventually made it into the White Plains, the frozen lands of Hell, the few remaining dinosaurs declined to follow us, and our days of committing mass murder finally came to an end.

The next morning by the time I awoke George had killed all of the Super Marvellous Dinosaur Justice Team, having placed a small bomb in their brains during their creation. Given how dangerous they were I don't know why I was deeply upset, partially as the carnage was... Ah sod it, I'm exasperated at the amount of preposterous butchery that had taken place down here, and I'm sure you are bored or nauseated after having been subjected to it as well, so let's just move on to the part where I have a bit of a moan relating to my very shaky sense of morality.

"That was decidedly messed up," I said, "I feel guilty when I squash a spider, so right now I'm not exactly a happy boy."

"We had no choice," George responded, "No choice at all. We couldn't risk leaving any of those creatures alive, they may have stayed away from the frozen plains but there are many, many other regions in Hell that we have not visited that they could have feasted upon, and if they copulated time and again it could have led to an afterlife even more terrifying than the one we've witnessed so far."

"I suppose. I just wish I'd thought of that before we began making them."

"We're in Hell, Ben. All of your decisions will be tainted with tragedy whether you like it or not."

"So what now?" I asked.

"Now we travel onwards. It shouldn't be much longer before we arrive, and then we'll do our very best to cease our existence."

"It's the summer holiday of my dreams," I bitterly muttered.

The rest of the journey was thankfully uneventful, at least compared to what we'd been through by this point, and after six more days we finally reached Satan's sanctuary. A rather impressive looking structure, if this was the eighties they'd call it 'swanky', but thank god it isn't. I thought it'd be bigger, and stranger, or maybe constructed with a gothic design meant to intimidate and distress, but no, it was simply a rather pleasant mansion. The only problem was the security. According to Jonathan, Lucifer apparently didn't like to be bothered by unwanted house guests who hadn't made a scheduled appointment, it hadn't always been this way but all of the Jehovah's Witnesses down here had truly done his head in. Which led to my having some sympathy for the devil, a friend of mine had grown up in the religion / cult and told me about their practices, so I understood how even the most despicable of all life forms wouldn't want to spend time with them if they had a choice in the matter. Hence in an attempt to get them to stop knocking on his door every other day Lucifer had created twenty seven flying torture machines, covered with cordless drills, chainsaws and rotating swords and spears, and not only did they fly at an alarming speed but also in random patterns, almost immediately eviscerating anything with a pulse.

"Christ, how do we get past this without losing at least two or three limbs?" I asked.

"Easily," George said, smiling, and I felt like stabbing him again. "No, really. It's one of the reasons why I needed five of us to gather here. We form a five sided star, united by fire, and create an energy beam powerful enough to destroy all of the dark lord's defences."

For the second time in the same week it all worked out as George had promised, which really made a lovely change, indeed I was almost cheerful for a moment. That ended when we flew up towards the great steel door of Satan's home, because as we began to push it open it quickly became clear that no one wanted to enter first. An argument began, though to my surprise it was quickly quashed as we heard a seductive, velvety voice ask "Are you going to come in and say good evening or not? As I do hope I haven't worn my very best outfit for absolutely no reason?"

It turned out that Lucifer had been waiting for us, and was delighted to see us, which I wasn't expecting. As the door opened wider he stood before us, twenty foot high, humanoid-ish yet with red scaly skin, the jaw of a catfish and the cock of a pig, and yeah, I'm not sure why either, but I thought you might like to know. His large black wings flapped gently while his tale swished in the background, a thirty foot long protrusion ending with a spiky silver hedgehog that I would not like to be on the end of. His very best outfit appeared to only consist of a top hat, but it couldn't be denied that it was a bloody smashing one.

"Finally you're here, you truly took your time," the Lord of Darkness said, "There was a shortcut to this location in the mountains where Jonathan has made his home, a small portal that would have transported you here instantly, I really should have mentioned that in this month's newsletter. It's too late now of course, but please, take a seat, make yourselves comfortable." His voice had a gentle and slightly sexy Welsh twang to it, which made it all the more unsettling.

"We're here to bargain with you," George said.

"Please, we may discuss that soon, but first I want to engage in a little discourse for at least a short while. Surely there's no rush, we've an eternity for this to play out. Almost at least, I do have something booked up for 5pm on July the Twenty Third in Two Thousand and Twenty Eight, but I'm free until then."

As despicable beings go he was quite charming, and I was starting to wonder if his reputation was rather unfair. The room he ushered us into was the height of sophistication as well, much loved great works of art adorned the walls while bookcases featured every single novel by Paulo Coelho burning away, and every time one collapsed into a pile of ashes another would take its place. There were a number of Chaise Longues to sit upon, and a number of clones of the band Wet Leg to flirt with if you were feeling coquettish, which unsurprisingly only applied to George. And yeah, you might say, hey, it's what, 2016-ish? How does Lucifer know about Wet Leg? And my reply would be a long and complicated one which would take hours to tell, but ultimately make perfect sense and you'd say "Of course! How could I be so foolish as to ask such a question. But hang on a second, it's a pretty niche reference, and what if you were telling this story in five years' time to someone else and Wet Leg have been forgotten by the music loving public?"

And my reply to that would be a short and uncomplicated one which essentially said, oh for God's sake, I regret even mentioning them now.

Once we'd all sat down and become comfy, Lucifer began with what I can only presume was a speech prepared days if not weeks ago.

"Now to begin with, George, Helen, Benjamin, I just wanted to say that I have enjoyed your ludicrous endeavours over the last few decades. I've this small production team you see, they edit all of the interesting live footage from the Earth into an hour long show each night. It's not as good as it used to be, I really do miss those World Wars you used to have, but recently you three have especially brightened it up. I was particularly fond of the Leicester Square massacre, that was a great episode, loved the ending, it kept me giggling for a long time."

I couldn't help myself. "Is she here?"

"Your beloved Karoline?" Lucifer replied, "No, no, sadly not. She ascended to Heaven, it's most disappointing as I'd loved to have met her, and then forced you to murder her again. Watch you go through all that misery. I have to say when she died, and when you realised what had happened, oh, the look on your face, that never got boring, I almost wore out the tape watching it time and again. Possibly due to the music they used in the final cut though, I've always loved that Polyphonic Spree song."

"Which one?" I asked, as like the devil I was a fan, and inexplicably didn't really care that he was being so bitchy towards me.

"Hold Me Now."

"That makes sense I guess. I gotta say I'm surprised though, even my stoner friend calls them hippy shite and while that's a tad unfair, they are a bit, you know, upbeat. Happy. Optimistic. Traits I didn't think you'd be into?"

"I like to mix it up. There's even one S Club Seven song I like. And it's not Reach For The Stars."

"Fuck off!" I replied, and I imagine this could have gone on all day such was the devil's casual nature, but George interjected.

"Lucifer, as is my divine right, I demand you bargain with me." Which caused the devil to burst out laughing.

"Hahaha, yeah, sorry, but that's an urban myth. One I started, naturally, but there's no rules or laws here. It'd be downright stupid to have them after all, this is a place of utter chaos. I mean, sure, sometimes I've accepted a challenge just to find a new way to pass the time, but I needed some persuading I can tell you."

It was a bizarre sound that followed, a combination of loud sighing, face palming, a hysterical giggle and the words "Oh you c***."

And yeah, I'd never heard anyone spell it out loud using the first letter and then a load of asterisks before either, but even in these circumstances Christina could not bring herself to use extremely foul language.

"So what will happen now?" I asked. "Are you going to kill us? Or toy with us in increasingly violent ways? Or make us play a never ending game of Monopoly? To be honest I'm beyond caring and just want an end to all of this."

Lucifer chuckled again, clearly amused, which hadn't been my intention.

"Do you know, I'm really not sure," he replied, "I had a few ideas, but I like to keep things fresh, do things on the spur of the moment. But I do like that toying with you suggestion. That's a good one."

It was then that I heard that bizarre mixture of sounds again. It was even more upsetting this time around due to my being responsible for it.

"Now, now, there's no need for a reaction like that," Lucifer chided, "I'm lying to you anyway, I've had weeks to come up with a suitable slice of torture as you took so long to reach me, not that I'm complaining as I think I've come up with a masterful plan. Just give me a second and I'll be back with everyone before you know it."

He then sashayed out of the room, and I thought it might give us a moment to plan a new scheme or devise some way of escaping, but before we knew it he was standing in front of us again, except this time three figures stood in the shadows behind him.

"I'd like to introduce you to a few people," Satan said, and clicked his fingers. The three emerged from out of the darkness to be met by at least two gasps.

"Three of you will know one of them, but for the benefit of everyone else, this young slip of a girl is Louise Thompson, the woman Mr Hitler loved so much but who never reciprocated his feelings, while secondly is the all rather dashing Steven Noble, Helen's mentor and one time lover. And Ben, this is your biological father, Samuel Holland."

As you know, I've whined a good few times about how I'd never met my father yet had heard a thousand stories about him. Seen many a photograph, imagined how things might have been if he'd survived or indeed never been ill in the first place. My Step Father had been the opposite of everything my real father supposedly was, I tried to tell myself I was lucky, he wasn't abusive, he wasn't overtly cruel, he wasn't manipulative, he was just cold. Arctic cold at that, of the do not go near unless you're wearing about seventeen layers of clothes variety. Along with being utterly useless with children, I even heard him once say "Children should be seen and not heard", and depressingly no one disagreed with him. No one called him a twat for having such beliefs. All of which added to my bitterness, my anger at having twice been denied a father, at never having had the chance to be brought up by a man who could say that he loved me out loud. Or even in his own mind. And as I grew older I found myself wishing time and again that my biological Dad had survived, that he'd been there to gently guide me through some of the harshest aspects of life. Stopped me from being so bloody stupid on so many different occasions. And now here he was. Every bone in my body wanted to run to him, to hold him, to hug him, to-

"Oh God, oh Jesus, I can't believe we're meeting like this," my father said, before falling to the floor, weeping.

"Oh son, oh God, I'm so sorry. This is wrong. Terribly, terribly wrong," he blubbered, and I barely understood what he was trying to say. In the photographs he'd glowed with life, his smile always beaming, and while I was clearly looking at them with rose tinted glasses, he'd always looked so kind. So honest and genuine. Which is what everyone told me he was.

Now he was pale, disturbingly thin, his skin was drawn and covered in lesions, and only his bewildered eyes showed signs of life.

"What is it? What's going on?" I asked.

"I'm so sorry Ben," he continued to sob, "But I've got to kill you." It was hard to think of any response to that.

"My personal Hell, the one I've been in for the past three decades," he explained, "It was my final two weeks alive. The cancer coursing through my veins, destroying me, the everlasting agony growing and growing until in the final days I was no longer anything resembling my former self. I was desperate to die, yet it felt like a lifetime until I did. And then it would begin all over again, with the knowledge that however bad things were now, soon they'd become far, far worse. Yet the relentless pain wasn't even the worst part. It was seeing your Mother losing me. Losing her mind. Saying goodbye to your sister, who I'd never get the chance to guide through life. Saying goodbye to you. To my son, who I'd never even meet. Hold. Even one single time."

"Jesus," was the understatement I managed to mutter. And I held him. Took him into my arms for the shortest of eternities. Felt absolute peace. Serenity. Then it was gone, never to be recovered.

"I have to do this. I'm sorry. And I know I keep saying that, but I can't go back. I just can't. It has been so many years Ben. So much indescribable suffering. But Lucifer promised me that If I kill you, my sins will be renounced. I'll ascend. Be reunited with your Mother once she dies."

As dreams come true go it wasn't quite what I'd hoped for. I mean sure, the hugging bit had been nice, but the part where he wanted to violently attack me, well, I just didn't predict he'd be that sort of guy. Yet despite this I managed to say "It's okay Dad, it's okay. You can do it, I truly don't mind. I don't want to live anymore. You would be doing us both a favour, trust me."

"It's not that simple," he inevitably replied, "If I kill you, you won't remain dead. You'll be returned to your personal Hell. And Lucifer said he'd make sure there would be no escape from it this time."

Ah.

Fuck.

Lucifer cackled. It was a suitably melodramatic sound, exactly the kind of demented giggle you'd expect from a being of pure evil. "Family reunions, you've got to love them," the demonic twat said, "I don't think I will ever tire of this. I've watched it with others on a fair few occasions, and it just gets funnier every single time!"

I audibly sighed and glared at the lord of this bastard dimension, partially because he had the audacity to misquote *Beetlejuice*, but mainly because of his obscene schemes. It was also at this point that I noticed both Jonathan and Helen were holding their loved ones, lost in confusion and fear, but George and Christina were standing alone, somewhat perplexed.

"Don't think I've forgotten about you guys," Lucifer said to them, "Seeing as you love each other, whether you care to admit it or not, I thought it best if you had to decide who gets an all-expenses paid trip to Heaven, and who returns to their personal Hell, and before you ask, yes George, I have already rebuilt it, and yes, it's even worse this time, and features far angrier dentists."

Neither responded well to that.

"Now just to fill in the blanks for any one not up to speed," the Devil said in a patronising manner, "If you kill the person you've been partnered up with you'll ascend to Heaven, and they'll return to their personal Hell. Which is of course terribly unfair, but then that's always the point, and for the record, I truly don't mind who wins and who dies, just make it spectacularly gory, will you please?"

So here I was. Facing the father I'd never met, the father I'd dreamt of my entire life, the man I'd craved knowing, the man who wanted to kill me.

"This is so messed up Dad," I said.

"I know," he replied, which didn't really help.

"Whatever choice we make, it means suffer in ways I can't even begin to imagine, and for ever more. And I'm your son. A life that you bought into existence."

"I always thought I'd do anything for you. Anything," my father claimed, "But I can't go back there. I can't."

Tears fell from all of our eyes. Until I sighed, to the extent that even I got annoyed by it.

"It's funny, I came here to die, but now it looks like I'll live forever. Except it will be in a place where I'll lose my sanity over and over again in the most gruesome of ways."

"I don't have the words Ben, I'm so sorry. "

"Will you shut up, Dad?" I all bit shouted, "Just do that for me, yeah? Because I've really had my fill of people apologising to me, and that's not exactly your fault but those words right now are enough to make me want to scream, and never stop screaming, and I've a feeling that's soon going to be my existence as it is. But I understand. I don't know what I'd do if I was in your shoes, but I understand. You've something to live for, as it were, and I've nothing. There's no point to my being in Heaven, Karoline will never forgive me for all that I've done, I'm certain of that. So okay. Kill me, Dad. Kill me and be reunited with Mum."

"Thank you," was all he said. Don't you just hate it when that happens? If the roles had been reversed I'd have been a grovelling mess, praising him to the high heavens, I'd have been a brand new member of The Grateful Dead. Sure, I'd told him to stop saying sorry but I thought I'd get more than two very basic words, which didn't exactly endear him to me. Once again Hell really was living up to its reputation of being a thoroughly wretched place,

Irritatingly that was confirmed once again as Lucifer walked over to the side of the room and revealed a display cabinet featuring a collection of weapons to be used for the ensuing murders, and no guns were involved at all, instead present were devices that would cause a great deal of woe, including axes, chainsaws, swords, a strap on vibrator with razor blades attached, flame throwers and pretty much everything and anything that could cause a frightening amount of long-term suffering.

My father headed over to the table, where Lucifer had a quick and quiet word with him, before returning with something utterly confusing.

"Lucifer said I have to use this," my father all but muttered, ashamed perhaps, and yet still more than prepared to follow the devil's instructions.

"Is that sandpaper?" I asked.

"Yes. Well, the, er, Sandpaper of Death is apparently its full title."

"And the difference between that and normal sandpaper is?" I asked.

"This will kill you. Eventually," my father replied, in an outrageously unapologetic manner.

"And how exactly will it do that?" I queried, finding myself genuinely if weirdly wanting to know.

"Lucifer said to start at the top. Sandpaper off your hair. And then through your skin, and afterwards your skull, and then your-"

My Dad at least then had the decency to weep, and to not spit out the word brain.

"Won't that take, Jesus, what, days? Or weeks? It looks pretty worn out as it is. And I'm supposed to simply stand here while you do this?"

"If you wouldn't mind," he managed to say/sob.

The state of my mental health has been something I've mentioned many a time, and as you're no doubt aware I'd lost my mind a good few times in the past year. But this was something new. This wasn't a moment of madness, I was fully aware of what I was doing, conscious that it was perhaps not the right thing to do, but something had instantaneously changed, there was a shift in my reality, and I no longer felt the urge to be considerate or kind. At least not to this man who may have been responsible for my life, but who was also almost certainly attempting to win the "Worst Dad Of The Century" award, and would definitely place in the top three.

"No. That's too much," I said, "Anyone who is prepared to do that to their own child does not deserve a happy ending."

And with that I magicked up a chainsaw and slaughtered my father.

Meanwhile Jonathan and Helen were having complicated conversations with their loved ones, with all involved wishing the other would not suffer. Yet Hitler was the most insistent, lying on the floor while the woman he'd wronged tore his skull apart with a pneumatic drill, and as he took his final breath through what was left of his mouth he dematerialised, leaving not a single drop of blood or shattered bone behind, and a deeply distressed Louisa Thompson slowly faded away, quite uncertain as to what exactly had just taken place.

Helen's discussion with Steven Noble took longer, indeed she seemed to have been enjoying catching up with her possible victim, but after a while I saw her take a flame thrower, as her mentor pleaded with her to murder him and she finally, reluctantly did so. Once his ashes had floated out of the room she vanished herself, not even taking the time out to say goodbye, which felt a little rude to me.

Left standing were George and Christina. Both staring at each other, but unable to speak. For so long that it actually got a little boring.

"Now I'm afraid I will have to move things along a little," Lucifer said, "If you don't make a decision in the next thirty seconds, I'll send you both to your personal Hells. And just to make things a little more interesting, this time if one of you kills the other I will let you either ascend to Heaven, or allow you to completely cease to exist. Whatever you think will make you happiest."

"George," Christina shouted, "Don't you fucking dare."

"You don't understand," George replied, "The things I feel. My specific personal Hell. An eternity of that would be too much. I'm sorry Christina, I truly am, and I do love you, I need you to know that, but I can't stay here forever. I can't live with what I've become."

Covered in my father's blood and with the chainsaw still roaring by my side, once again I was filled with the utter certainty that what I was about to do was the right thing, and I lurched towards George, plunging the weapon into his face and then into his stomach. With what was left of his head he looked amazed, and tried to cast healing spells, but I'd destroyed enough of his mouth that he was incapable of the correct pronunciation.

"No. no, no, not yet, no," was what I presumed George was attempting to then utter, though it sounded more like "Nonnooootyeeeenoo!"

"Oh for once in your life will you shut up and die," I politely requested, and slammed the chainsaw into his spine, enjoying how it all but angrily growled as I pushed it from side to side, slicing up his various organs delightfully, if you've a fetish for making organs and intestines look like a weird swampy meal at least, which at that point in time it appeared I had.

"I wish I could even say I'm sorry George, but I'm not. Indeed the opposite applies, as dear lord this feels good. Now fuck off once and forever," I shouted, before decapitating the man and stamping on his head. Repeatedly.

Christina eventually stopped me, though I noticed she waited until there could be absolutely no doubt that he would not be returning to haunt us any time soon.

"Um, thank you," She said, "I hope I never meet you again, but thank you."

Christina then surprised me by giving me a brief hug, until she too dissolved into the air.

I turned around at this point, expecting Lucifer to be rather furious. But all I got was grumpy.

"Ah, you shitter," the devil responded, "You got your revenge there. Damned the man who destroyed your life to eternal misery and insanity. Have to say, I've mixed feelings when that happens."

"Sorry," I replied, "But really, can we please wrap this up now. You've allowed everyone else to leave and I'd appreciate your completing your side of the deal. Or kill me, return me to my personal Hell, whatever, I don't care anymore. All I know is that I've had enough of your company, that's for bloody sure."

"Boy are you playing the spoilt, petulant brat today," the Devil moaned, "Yeah, yeah, you just had to kill your Dad, shit happens, blah blah blah."

"Oh God. This is going to go on forever," I moaned.

Lucifer laughed yet again, and I thought about attempting to slice him up with the chainsaw, which he must have realised as he took it from my hands, revved it up, and struck the side of his head with it. Sparks flew, but nothing else, and it didn't even create the smallest of scratches.

"You didn't really think there were any weapons that could actually harm me, did you?" he chuckled away, "Far smarter and creative life forms have tried and no one has succeeded. But I do have one surprise for you. Because, and I very rarely say this, but having given it at least three seconds of thought, I kind of like you, Ben Holland. As I said before, I watch you humans, I see and gorge upon the pain and all round wretchedness so many of you cause, and the despair you've generated in such a short life time, damnit, it's been astounding. Genuinely some of the best misery I've ever tasted. So thank you."

"It's not okay?" was all I managed to say.

"It wasn't just during your magic twat period either, but throughout your life. Your heart's such a bloody tender one and every single time it broke it was beautiful to witness. Then throw in all of the deaths and funerals, and oh, the dreams and the desires that would inevitably go horribly wrong, and it was all an absolute delight. And of course because you're a hilarious cliché of a white privileged middle class idiot you'd listen to Radiohead in barely lit rooms while drinking cheap wine, thinking that at least someone understood you and not having a clue that it was making you even more miserable," he said, only briefly stopping to giggle, and clearly enjoying the sound of his voice.

"Always listen to high energy pop when low Ben, otherwise you're just going to be wallowing in self-pity for months on end, if not years. Not that I want you to change, Goodness no, that would take away so much of my pleasure."

"I have to say," I commented, exhausted but still with the urge to be rude, "You really are a bit of a tiresome son of a bitch."

He looked a bit shocked by that.

"Yes. Exactly. Bloody hell, how thick are you? I'm the frickin' devil. It's what I was created for. Nearly all of those stories and depictions of me in religious texts throughout time are completely spot on you know, from when I popped by and mucked around with people to make their lives unpleasant and ugly, and from those alone I'd have thought you'd be aware of what you're dealing with. Not that you're the smartest of cookies I suppose."

"You can visit the earth?" I asked, ignoring his insults for once.

"Yes, it's one of the perks of the job. I can't do anything too serious, it's my role to make sure the balance of energies this world produces is largely fifty fifty, but I like to subtly influence things. I always found that terrifying the writers worked best, and if you can influence the creation of a holy book you can just sit back and relax and watch the atrocities begin."

"You've certainly done a great job on that front," I said.

"Why thank you Ben, you're too kind. Now, what to do with you? Hmmmm. I mean part of me is tempted to send you to Heaven, if only because you'd annoy God so much. And you'd want to at least speak with Karoline and that would no doubt continue to generate an enormous amount of tragedy for all involved."

"You're not going to though, are you?" I replied.

Lucifer laughed.

"Finally you're getting it. Though you should actually thank me, given Karoline's current relationship status."

"What do you mean?" I asked.

"It's better that I show you," the devil said, as he created a screen that flickered for a couple of seconds before showing Karoline. She was lying down in the greenest and most beautiful meadow you could imagine, as doves fluttered around her, expelling what I hoped was hot chocolate into her mouth, from her reaction it certainly seemed to be the case. She was joined by a man who I had a very vague recollection of, but I couldn't quite place, and they began to kiss and frolic, and I turned away as it became apparent that the footage was soon to become X-rated.

"Who is that?" I asked.

"Tom Hardy," the devil responded.

"But it looks nothing like him. Plus he's not dead."

"No, no, you idiot," Satan said, "Not the actor, the Victorian author. You know the one, *Tess of the d'Urbervilles, Far from the Madding Crowd, Jude The Obscure*."

"Him?" I said, "Jesus, I hated reading him when I was at school."

"Everyone did. He's a great author but not for kids. Which is why I had his work put on the curriculum," Lucifer said, laughing hard.

"He's such a miserable bastard though, I can't understand what Karoline's doing with him," I mumbled.

"He's lightened up a lot since he died. It's all down to seventies disco apparently, he bloody loves it."

"Well this is soul crushing," I responded.

"It's what I do," laughed the devil.

"I'm seeing that quite clearly. Though is this really real? Or just something else you've come up with in an attempt to make me demented?"

"No, no, it's quite real. You can speak to her if you like, I have her number?"

I thought about it but declined his offer. Any conversation would only serve to make me realise just how much I'd lost. And also learn how much happier she was without me.

"So, if not Heaven, what next, eh?" the Devil pondered as he switched off the screen, "There is the temptation to keep you here, my wife nags me all the time that I take on far too much of the workload, that I need to delegate some tasks more often. You could perhaps be my personal assistant, or maybe a creative consultant, you've certainly proven that your mind is capable of terrible things."

"Maybe, I mean sure, I guess I could, um, but before I decide, er, you have a wife?" I asked, if only so I could think of a way out of the situation.

"Oh yes, we've been married for what, almost seven centuries now? She's a lovely woman, claims she hears God talking to her all the time and hates it when I get in a huff and burn her on a stake, but apart from that we get on like a house on fire."

"Can I meet her?" I said, for the same reason as before.

"No. And I've a feeling that you don't even want to, and are simply attempting to buy time so that you can try and persuade me that you don't want to be my personal assistant?"

"Yeah," I said, "Sorry, but I just don't think it'd work out. I'm not going to lie to you, killing George wasn't the worst way to spend half an hour, but I feel like I've had my fill of evil for one lifetime."

"I don't believe that."

"It's true, I mean for one thing I know when I wake up tomorrow my arms are going to ache like a bastard, that chainsaw isn't exactly as light as a feather. Plus even if you were able to get me some anti-depressants down here I know what my mood swings are like, some days I'd be like oh yeah, fuck it, let's create a giant combine harvester and go for a drive in Kitten Hell, but the next I'd be all mopey and sad and covered in dead kittens and probably crying a lot. Plus there's the fac-"

"Okay, okay, Jesus, just that small amount of whining proves your point, and I'm pretty sure I'd get sick of your behaviour very quickly."

"Most do," I admitted. "So is there really no chance you can, you know, just kill me off once and for all. Destroy my brain by jumping up and down on it a lot before kicking it into a volcano just to make sure nothing survives?"

"Nah," Lucifer said, "I do that all the time. With you, I want to really fuck you up. Make your life a misery for as long as I can. Ha. Which, yes, yes, I think that's it! Ben, prepare to be overjoyed, because I'm going to send you back to Earth!"

I let out a muffled moan.

"No, anything but that. Please."

"Sorry Mr Holland, I've made my final decision," Lucifer shrieked, before chuckling yet again. I looked at him, my vision blurred by tears, but could not think of a thing to say.

"Try and look on the up side. You'll get to live. Do whatever you want. Your idiocy entertained me in the past and I've no doubt it will do so again in the future. Especially as I plan to upgrade you so you're capable of even more madness. A Magician 2.0 with all the bugs ironed out, none of that running out of energy business and needing artefacts shite."

"I really, really hate you Lucifer. Even more than I hated George."

He laughed again. A long, deep, hearty laugh.

"Good. And I look forward to seeing you back here again in a few decades or centuries time when you eventually kill yourself again. Until then, bye bye Ben. Bye bye."

And with that everything went black. Until it wasn't.

CHAPTER 16 - AN ENDING

Tricking the devil had turned out to be far easier than I'd imagined. A couple of short teary speeches, some mild moaning and the repeated suggestion that I no longer wanted to exist, and bang, I was alive again. You might be confused as to why I'd want that given everything that had taken place, and I can't quite explain what had happened to me after I murdered both my father and George, apart from describing it as an enormous relief. And I know, I know, I know, I know, I know, and please repeat that about twenty more times if you don't mind, but no one should kill another human being and feel good about it. I still believe that. I genuinely do. It's an appalling idea.

Except that Jesus, killing those two human beings felt good.

And I don't want to say that. I don't want anyone to copy my actions. I'd feel horrified and appalled and endlessly distressed if anyone said, hey, Ben Holland killed his father and this weird old man and then felt brilliant, so now I'm going to shoot some people. I don't know how I could live with myself if you did. So please, please, please, don't do that. If you do, I'll track you down and relentlessly torment you, and you really don't want to experience that.

And I should hate my brain for doing this to me. For making me lose faith in everything I've ever believed in. But I don't. I feel a level of peace and serenity that I didn't realise was possible, I'm literally like a new person. No, wait, that's not right, I feel like myself, but a version that didn't suffer from Unwanted Thoughts Syndrome, which isn't technically a medical condition but Maria Bamford summed it perfectly on her album of the same name, and it meant that the inappropriate and stupid things I used to repeatedly think were now gone. I felt clean. All of the madness washed away, my brain was no longer chattering away constantly, suggesting one good or one bad idea after another, with my never knowing which was which. And here I am in territory which is suggesting that murder is a cure for mental illness, and it fucking isn't, I mean look at me, we're at the end and you might think I'd stop whining, I'd stop complaining, especially given that I was the only fucker who survived, that almost every other single person I interacted with in the past couple of years was now dead, but nope, the complaining continues. And I'm complaining now about being happy. You really can't win with me.

Okay, I've had a think about this, and it comes down to extenuating circumstances. If, and it's a bloody big if, but if you have had the last two years of your life manipulated by a magician who was part of an enormous organisation that monitored your every movement and planned to make you a scapegoat where in the best case scenario you would spend the rest of your life in prison, and then they murdered your girlfriend and locked you in a room and spent weeks making you think you were being tortured by ghosts, then, and only then, will you possibly have a case for saying that they deserve some form of punishment. The same applies with my father, if you know someone who was going to be responsible for your being trapped in your own personal Hell, one which would see you psychologically destroyed on a daily basis, and suffering in a way that you didn't think was possible for billions of years, then perhaps a minor bout of retribution is in order. But only in those circumstances. Otherwise don't even think about doing any harm to anyone.

And you know something, I'm still not happy about all of this. I'm unhappy being happy. And would you really want to live with that contradiction in your head every single second of every day? No? Good. Put the gun down. You've seen what Hell is like and you really don't want to end up there. So talk to someone. Reach out. Tell a friend or tell a doctor that your brain is being a right little bastard and trying to make you do things which would lead to incredible suffering for not just you, but all of the people who care about you, and all of the people who cared about the people you hurt. They will listen, and they will help. And if they don't, and worst comes to the worst, come here. Talk to me. We can even spoon if you like, but please remain fully clothed.

Right. Moving on, as mentioned, for the first time in my lifetime I felt calm. You could even argue that I'd not even killed anyone, just sent them back to the prisons they'd spend an eternity in, but eh, I can't see many buying that given just how much time I'd spent running a chainsaw through their flesh. Either way, I no longer blamed anyone or anything other than myself for what had happened to me. My lifelong obsession with the idea that I would have had a better life if my biological father was alive was over with, that's for bloody sure, and I probably should apologise to my deceased step-father. When it came to George, yes, he'd caused me an astonishing amount of misery, but I'd returned the favour, and when I pictured him in his personal Hell it always led to a very broad smile.

I had even come to terms with losing Karoline, as I knew now that she was okay, and more than that, she was in love, she was happy, she was with someone who wouldn't head off and make someone's fingers explode by uttering only a couple of words, well, at least if Thomas Hardy was accurately described in the many biographies about him.

Plus I'd like to think that morally I was still someone who tried to be the very best that he could be, that I believed in kindness and love being the only reason we should continue to exist, and the only thing that had changed was that though I wanted the best for others, it shouldn't be at my own expense, I suppose. But again, don't think for a second that I'm suggesting that what I did was right. I am not a fucking role model, that's for sure. Huh? Everyone wasn't thinking that? Okay. Good.

Ah, I said "moving on" a little while ago and did the opposite of that. Sorry. Let's get back to the narrative then. So there I was, alive again, and feeling good, and once I opened my eyes I took in my surroundings, and it was more than a few seconds before I realised that I was back in the room where I'd died. George's scattered, heavily decaying corpse was covering some of the walls and furniture, but mostly it had rotted away. Seems like the cleaners hadn't been arsed to sort this mess out, and given how odious the remains were and the tiny amount they were no doubt paid I didn't exactly blame them.

As I began to leave the underground prison that I'd been kept in I expected to have to engage in all manner of deceitful behaviour to avoid being seen by any of the CF1 agents, but the building had all but been destroyed, with only a few badly burnt concrete posts still standing in amongst the rubble, which I guessed was due to Orson making a less than quiet escape. It was at this point that I suddenly realised that I had absolutely no idea what the outcome of the war against the government and the magical community had been, so flew to Scotland, chose a mountain at random (Braeriach, as it goes), and deep within it I created a new living space that I hoped would not be detected by anyone. A little magic led to a pleasant and warm new home, and a very complicated spell saw that I could go online.

That was a mistake.

If you've ever lost about eighteen months from your life, perhaps if you were in a coma after a car crash or some other terrible accident, you'd expect to miss out on an awful lot. Coming back to life in February two thousand and seventeen, I found out that I'd missed out on the entirety of two thousand and sixteen. Where it soon became apparent that the magical war was the least of my concerns, and that the war had ended in the way I feared it might. They'd used the day of Karoline's death as the turning point, I'd been portrayed as a suicide bomber, one who had almost been detained but who had managed to escape into a crowded area with the intention of murdering as many people as possible. That was all the Government needed to launch the country into full on panic mode as it was not so gently suggested that because of magic anyone could die, at any minute, and no one could be trusted. Financial rewards were issued for anyone who turned in a live magician, and it was essentially Nazi Germany all over again, along with a rather large dash of the Salem witch hunts. Few cared however, with the majority of the public predictably baying for blood every waking minute. Magic was the new terrorism and the media was ecstatic given the surge in sales and viewing figures, and so only encouraged the pandemonium. There was the odd dissenting voice, some who suggested that as we'd existed for so long and never interfered with the world before that not all magicians might be blood thirsty maniacs, but they were largely ignored.

The Government created a sod load of new CF1 agents only a few weeks after my death, along with a new artefact, an absolute bastard of a thing which could track down any magician in the world, wherever they were. That was the game changer which really screwed things up for the surviving magicians, and one which inevitably led to the final battle. Tired of being picked off one by one, seventy or so surviving magicians grouped together in an attempt to fight back.

It was spectacular by all accounts, I'm really annoyed that I missed it, with the assault taking place at Ten Downing Street which had well over one hundred CF1 agents protecting it. They say it was like watching tornados fighting with tidal waves, witnessing a lightning storm where enormous multi-coloured bolts came from all directions and buildings exploded left right and centre until everything was little more than dust within seconds, apart from Number Ten that is, as it stood unharmed, protected by a glowing force field. In Hollywood blockbuster budget terms we're talking at least a two hundred million dollar set piece, and an eighteen rated one at that as the battle continued and many a head burst, limbs flew at such a ferocity that they killed anyone they struck, and the violence was so extreme that a few weeks later it was discovered that DNA from many of the dead was found in four different counties. About a third of the way through the fight the naked magical women I'd handed over to George arrived on the scene, a distraction which confused and disorientated most, but aroused four, and as they were so difficult to dispatch it was a waste of much needed energy. Subsequently it became even weirder as the magicians transformed time and time again in an attempt to survive, yet sadly there's no footage as all of the CCTV cameras were destroyed and any media owned helicopters that came within a thousand feet had a tendency to explode. Rumours suggest though that the battle was so deranged that hardly any of the survivors have been able to describe it, though one CF1 agent claimed it was as if every hallucinogenic event Hunter S Thompson had ever experienced was taking place in front of him instantaneously. Orson was among it all and reportedly fought valiantly, with a thirst for blood which startled even his allies, but at some point he was slain. His corpse was discovered with a sword piercing his skull while the nun's body lay in his arms, her heart in his outstretched hand.

And in the end the good guys lost. Unsurprisingly most were killed, but a few were captured, tortured and then executed, and once the artefact was used to murder the few who had tried to stay hidden away there were no longer any rogue magicians left.

The new prime minister came on television to declare that the war was not over of course, that magicians may still be out there, in hiding, that we must be ever vigilant and all that rubbish, and in the meantime, don't forget that we still need to be terrified of Islamic extremists of course. And the Russians. And anyone from North Korea. And no doubt a different country next week, because someone had read 1984 a while back and thought "Huh, there are a lot of good ideas in this book you know, and nobody seems to care that we're using them."

Despite it all I couldn't say I was surprised that we'd lost, given George's involvement in building and training an army of CF1 agents I don't think we ever stood a chance. I felt minor sorrow for Orson, but only briefly, it had been so long since I'd last seen him and our interactions were so short that I couldn't claim to have lost a loved one. Everything going to shit seemed par for the course, and so I still felt this strange sense of tranquillity and wasn't really affected by the news.

It didn't last. Or at least, the tranquillity was disturbed, like a giant spoon being plunged into a vat of soup and swirled around at unusual speeds before being poured all over my head, which come on, I like soup, but not that much. The war would have been enough reason to send someone round several bends, but then I discovered everything else that happened during those three hundred and sixty five days, and that's when I fell into a state of shock. I mean, where to start? Gently, I suppose, with the list of celebrity deaths, and the demise of so many men and women whom I'd loved and had been inspired by like David Bowie, Leonard Cohen, Victoria Wood, Garry Shandling, Prince,

Harper Lee, Gene Wilder, Carrie Fisher, Debbie Reynolds and Muhammad Ali, and that's only about 5% of those whose passing led to maudlin thoughts. Yet given the last few years I could get past that, or at least I would get past it, because then I read something which didn't make any sense, something I presumed was a prank, that someone had hacked the BBC news page and placed hundreds of unfunny stories on it. But no, Donald Trump really was now the president of the United States of America. Right, let's get this out of the way as quickly as I can, and yeah, I hear you, after all this daft whimsy and then traumatic horror, now I'm getting into world politics? It's like I'm trying to irritate everyone, I'm well aware of that, but how would you feel if you emerged into the world only to discover that insanity reigned and one of the worst human beings who wasn't a serial killer had been elected as one of the most powerful men on the planet? I'm not ruling out a number of corpses being found underneath his patio in the future either, but once again my lawyers stress this is a joke and he hasn't killed anyone, or at least not with his own two hands. Even despite that, attempting to understand how a man like him had been elected was a gigantic headfuck, and okay, some deeply unpleasant people wanted change after eight years of a black president, the repellent little fuckers that they were, but to vote for a man with a history of fraud, of lying and not caring when everyone knew he was being deceitful, seemed like a level of madness that I'd never be able to explain. I tried however, I tried to think of reasons why some would want a leader who was a racist piece of shit, one who had been publically accused of sexual assault and harassment by a depressingly large number of people, a man who was recorded saying that it was fine to "grab women by the pussy."

But I failed. As I trawled through various news and social media sites I saw people asking the same questions, and the only answer appeared to be "Humanity consists of a surprisingly large amount of incredibly selfish individuals who completely lack consideration for others" and also "Bastards. Lots and lots of bastards."

There was of course one final kick in the teeth, a kick which involved steel capped boots and muscular legs that belonged to a bodybuilder. Brexit.

Now compared to Trump it might not feel so awful, but to me it just confirmed that there were far more xenophobic idiots who lived in what's laughably still called the United Kingdom than I'd ever thought possible. More research followed, and I saw the lies and the manipulation, I saw the abuses of power and the crimes that were committed for which no one was ever held responsible for. I saw people far, far smarter than me write enormous think pieces trying to understand what had happened but failing to offer any real solutions. Yet the more time I spent on the internet, the less sense it made, perhaps some people were tricked into believing the lies, that life would improve enormously if we weren't in Europe, but as for everyone else, well, the more I read the more I was convinced that it was due to the same reasons as Trump's election. Essentially the bastards were everywhere.

The only thing which everyone seemed to agree about was that we needed to accept both Brexit and Trump, that they had happened, it was done, it was time to move on, time to work out a way to survive in this abhorrent new world. But nah, I wasn't in that kind of mood, not after what I'd been through, that and the fact that I now had the power to change the world. So I sat back. Listened to some high energy pop music. I refused to be angry, I declined the suggestion that my mind was making that I should be filled with fury, instead doing the opposite, and I started working on a plan that would force the world to make sense again.

The first problem was that I really didn't want to kill anyone. See, I was telling the truth before, I really don't think murder is the answer to everything. But there were a number of CF1 agents still alive and working for the government and even though I was more powerful than them it was more than possible I could be caught off guard, that I'd make one tiny mistake and find myself hanging out with Lucifer once again, so they clearly had to be dealt with. I mulled over possible fates, and almost went with a plan where I turned them all into hamsters and kept them in a kick ass hamster cage which came with not only your standard wheels and tubes but also a swimming pool and sauna, and tiny robot hamsters that offered free massages. But given that hamsters tend to only live for two to three years I figured that was still a bit too close to homicide, deliberate or not. Until I realised the obvious solution - a far larger kick ass hamster cage which came with not only your standard wheels and tubes but also a swimming pool and sauna, and tiny robot hamsters that offered free massages, but I'd keep all of the CF1 agents human. Admittedly I'd need to remove their mouths and vocal cords so they couldn't cast magic, but inserting a small feeding tube into their necks solved any issues when it came to giving them food and water, and because I didn't want them to go mad with boredom I expanded it so they all had rooms with televisions and game consoles and any streaming service of their choice.

The cage was quickly constructed and I placed it sixty feet underneath Ben Nevis, with a permanent force field around it so it couldn't be accidentally broken into. Capturing the CF1 agents was also a piece of piss thanks to their artefact which tracked down any still breathing magicians, and even though there were over seventy alive it didn't take long to whizz around the country, knock all who I found unconscious, and then quickly alter their bodies so they'd no longer be a threat. I intended to return with the Yuasa artefact and simply remove magic from their minds as well, but that would take ages and I wanted to carry out my scheme before my courage evaporated.

Once the CF1 agents were captured a similar endeavour followed where I tracked down every member of the British government, placing them in a similar environment, except their temporary prison was more akin a giant mouse cage with one toilet in the corner, a water bottle, a refrigerator filled with Iceland All Day Breakfast microwave meals, and one copy of the Daily Mail to either read or wipe their arses with, and I buried them under the Malvern Hills. Robotic copies were quickly placed in Parliament and programmed to be disagreeable, and no one was aware of the changes I'd made.

I'll spare you the details of my doing that to all of the other governments of any importance, but once anyone who might have been likely to commit violent atrocities had been locked away I nipped into the BBC in London. A couple of spells persuaded all involved that my speaking live on television was a bloody great idea, and I sat down behind one of the newscaster's desks and we began broadcasting. Opening with a cheery, "Hi, I'm Ben Holland," I then tried to appear more serious.

"Some of you may be aware of who you think I am, that I'm a terrorist, that I'm a maniac, and a mass murderer. But none of that is true. Apart from possibly the maniac bit, but let's hope not. I jest, I promise, and this probably isn't the time for such attempts at humour. This is all a really long story too, and I'll go into detail at some point, but basically I'm now the only man on this planet who can do magic. Which many will probably be a bit worried by, but please don't be. I'm only here to do good. Now again, I know a lot of you won't like this, but trust me, it's for the best, and to prove it, well, I'm just going to sod off for a bit now, but I'll be back soon."

Within six hours half of the Sahara desert was a luscious green oasis, there were orchards of orange trees in every city, and orchards of chicken and potato trees which grew freshly roasted dinners within a few minutes of the last one being picked. I visited the twenty highest security prisons and made every inmate incapable of violence, spent time in countless hospitals curing what had previously been incurable, made a few lakes in every country consist of free, ever replenishable wine, and then I dashed back to make a second broadcast, showing the world the changes made so far.

"Thanks to the internet you'll no doubt be aware of how I've altered parts of the world," I said, broadly smiling and probably looking a little smug, "And this is only the beginning. I'm going to change the Earth for the better, I swear. Now I know this is going to be a difficult transition period, but look around at the way the world was working. Or not working, as it goes. Look at the terror and the horror and the abject sorrow so many people experience within their lives, and there's no need for such a thing. Not anymore. Of course I can't promise everything will improve for ever more, but I'm going to do my best. And really please don't worry, while technically I'm invulnerable and can change the world at my slightest whim, I swear I'm not going to go all despotic on your arses. For instance, in a couple of months' time I'm going to leave the day to day running of most countries to their current leaders. I'm not going to get involved with all the petty shite, I haven't the time. Bar Trump and a couple who are also batshit mental, but we'll hold elections in those countries with the hope someone less evil gets in. You've got to try to be optimistic after all. After that I'll step away. Spend all of my time trying to make the Earth as nice a place to live on as I can. We've had such a shit time of it for too long, and now that no longer needs to be the case. Thank you for listening, and if anyone has any questions, my email address is benhollandisatwat@gmail.com."

I stopped then, thinking I'd said all I needed to for the time being, that what I had told the world would need time to sink in, but then I remembered one last piece of information I really thought I should share.

"Oh, and one other thing. Religion. Kind of got some bad news on that front. There is a God, and a Heaven and a Hell, but, and this one is a bit of a pisser..." and, well, you know the rest of that particularly mental story.

EPILOGUE

It's seven years later. And ha. Yeah. That didn't work out well.

Was I a better leader than those who came before me? Was I a kinder, considerate, morally correct ruler? Did I actually change the world for the better? I'd kind of claim that I did, hell yeah, but it seems now that it was for the shortest of times. I mean I tried, I really did. But everything eventually became all screwed up and that's why there's now hundreds of thousands of radioactive corpses that need to be destroyed. Oops.

I suppose it could be suggested that I sort of went in a bit heavy handed I guess, I'd tried to create peace, but perhaps hadn't thought it through carefully enough. Yet I'd flown across all of the military bases and turned all of the guns from metal into paper, while tanks and fighter aircrafts were transformed into ice before slowly melting away, I'd changed machetes and swords into plastic toys, and mines became harmless custard bombs, which at worst mildly inconvenienced you and at best provided a delightful addition to a dessert. But despite this violence found a way to survive. Which I feel is quite unfair after everything I'd done. I mean along with the whole weaponry side of things I'd met with scientists and devised machines that ended poverty, that provided enough food for every person on the planet, and nice food at that, which tasted as if it contained thousands of calories but in fact only had three and a half. Along with about a million other things it'd take a lifetime to describe. Yet were people happy? Some. Maybe even most. But not all. Dear lord, no.

Looking back I guess the whole religion thing got to too many. However much I changed the world for the better, some people were unable to change a lifetime of belief. Were unable to cope with a new reality, one where everything they'd ever known had turned out to be absolutely false. Or a bit right, but mostly wrong. And while I spent months transforming any weapons I could detect, bombs rather annoyingly could be made from household goods. When they were detonated I couldn't be everywhere at once, I couldn't save all of the lives that needed to be saved. People were smarter than I'd given them credit for as well, I'd transformed all of the old nuclear weapons into sausage dogs and thought I'd insured that new ones couldn't be created, but it has just become apparent that I failed on that front as two have just exploded, one in London and another in Paris. Lucifer phoned, pissing himself with laughter. I'm not sure why it took me two minutes to hang up, considering.

And now I've got to make a decision. Should I try to stop whoever is behind this mayhem and destruction? Or should I step down, and let them win? Or annoy them further and watch them destroy the earth and let some other species have a go? I mean, you know, humanity, we've done the odd great thing but we're also murderous little gits and I can't see that changing any time soon. You look at the history of atrocities that man has committed and you think, surely even gigantic angry mutant lions couldn't be worse than us, right? Especially given that everything was taking place after I'd spent the last seven years making things so much better. Everyone has a Jacuzzi now for instance. Every single person.

On the flip side, there's the possibility that given everything that's happened to me over the last few years that I might be quite, quite insane and the absolute worst person to be making such a choice. Or that whatever decision I make things will end hilariously badly. It's best never to rule that option out.

And I know this isn't a new question, it's one many have considered before, bar maybe the Jacuzzi bit. Is humanity doomed to repeat its mistakes and murderously slay anything or anyone they fear, including themselves? Or will we one day arrive at some kind of utopia, a bit like how the Earth is in *Star Trek The Next Generation*, with those sexy, sexy holodecks? And am I the man who can take us to such a place, or will I be responsible for us never reaching it? And if we did have holodecks, would we just spend the whole time having gigantic orgies and then start to decay morally and mentally? Or would we simply become happy? Happy, horny sex gods and goddesses.

Sorry, I lost my train of thought for a second there. Oh yeah, the fate of the world thing and all of those recently decimated cities. Ah bollocks, I guess some of this is kind of my fault. So fine, I'll save humanity. But this is a one-time deal, alright?

Acknowledgements

This book only exists because many years ago Kirsty Geddes sent me a short story of hers to read and it made me finally get off my backside and write something of my own, and her feedback on an early draft was invaluable, so I can't thank her enough on both fronts.

I'd also like to thank Simon Coyle for all of his work on the superb cover, which I love to pieces and which is far, far better than my original idea for it. And my gratitude also goes to Fearghus Roulston, Steve Alexander and James Wilkinson for their reading of various drafts of the book prior to its release, and I truly appreciate all of their help and advice.

Finally my Mother and my Sister Mandy, Paul and Jody Monk, Chris and Marianne Denton, Chloe Taylor, Katherine Monk, Ian Lane and Freddie Caron have all been extremely supportive during the time I've been writing this novel, and there aren't words to say how much I value their love, kindness and / or friendship.

About The Author

Alex Finch has been writing online for over twenty years, including for The London Film Festival, Garbled Communications, The Official Big Brother site, The Friday Thing and Comedy To Watch, while he's also worked in television (Big Brother Series 1 and 2, Tomorrow's World: Lab Rats, TxtMe Tv) and in the theatre (Golden Opportunities, Love, Question Mark?). He also spent three years performing stand-up comedy on the open mic scene, which was responsible for some of the best nights of his life, but also some of the very worst. He now teaches both English As A Foreign Language and Creative Writing lessons, and lives in East London.

The website for this novel is:
https://severalmomentsofmadness.com/ - where deleted scenes and additional short stories set both before and after the events of the book will soon be posted online.